PRAISE FOR
The Dutch House

"*The Dutch House* has the richness, allusiveness, and emotional heft of the best fiction." —*Boston Globe*

"As always, the author draws us close to her protagonists swiftly and gracefully." —*Wall Street Journal*

"Patchett's prose is confident, unfussy, and unadorned." —*New York Times*

"Patchett's splendid novel is a thoughtful, compassionate exploration of obsession and forgiveness, what people acquire, keep, lose, or give away, and what they leave behind." —*Publishers Weekly* (starred review)

"This richly furnished novel gives brilliantly clear views into the lives it contains." —*Kirkus Reviews* (starred review)

"You won't want to put down this engrossing, warmhearted book even after you've read the last page." —NPR

"Ann Patchett spins a dark, compelling fairy tale in *The Dutch House*." —*Entertainment Weekly*

"A bighearted, capacious novel." —*Chapter 16*

"*The Dutch House* is unusual, thoughtful, and oddly exciting, as well-told domestic dramas can be." —*Columbus Dispatch*

"Patchett's storytelling abilities shine in this gratifying novel." —Associated Press

"Expect miracles when you read Ann Patchett's fiction." —*New York Times Book Review*

"Patchett is a master storyteller." —*O, The Oprah Magazine*

"A lavishly gifted writer." —*Los Angeles Times*

The
DUTCH
HOUSE

ALSO BY ANN PATCHETT

The
DUTCH
HOUSE

A Novel

ANN
PATCHETT

HARPER ● PERENNIAL

NEW YORK ● LONDON ● TORONTO ● SYDNEY ● NEW DELHI ● AUCKLAND

A hardcover edition of this book was published in 2019 by HarperCollins Publishers.

HarperCollins books may be purchased for educational, business, or sales promotional use. For information, please email the Special Markets Department at SPsales@harpercollins.com.

FIRST HARPER PERENNIAL EDITION PUBLISHED 2021.

Designed by Fritz Metsch

The Library of Congress has catalogued the hardcover edition as follows:

Names: Patchett, Ann, author.
Title: The Dutch house : a novel / Ann Patchett.
Description: First edition. | New York, NY : HarperCollins Publishers, [2019] | Summary: "Ann Patchett, the New York Times bestselling author of Commonwealth and State of Wonder, returns with her most powerful novel to date: a richly moving story that explores the indelible bond between two siblings, the house of their childhood, and a past that will not let them go"— Provided by publisher.
Identifiers: LCCN 2019024072 (print) | LCCN 2019024073 (ebook) | ISBN 9780062963673 (hardcover) | ISBN 9780062963697 (ebook)
Classification: LCC PS3566.A7756 D88 2019 (print) | LCC PS3566. A7756 (ebook) | DDC 813/.54—dc23
LC record available at https://lccn.loc.gov/2019024072
LC ebook record available at https://lccn.loc.gov/2019024073

ISBN 978-0-06-296368-0 (pbk.)
ISBN 978-0-06-307456-9 (Target edition)
ISBN 978-0-06-308054-6 (Hudson News edition)

22 23 24 25   LSC   10 9 8 7

This book is for Patrick Ryan

The
DUTCH
HOUSE

Part
ONE

CHAPTER 1

THE FIRST TIME our father brought Andrea to the Dutch House, Sandy, our housekeeper, came to my sister's room and told us to come downstairs. "Your father has a friend he wants you to meet," she said.

"Is it a work friend?" Maeve asked. She was older and so had a more complex understanding of friendship.

Sandy considered the question. "I'd say not. Where's your brother?"

"Window seat," Maeve said.

Sandy had to pull the draperies back to find me. "Why do you have to close the drapes?"

I was reading. "Privacy," I said, though at eight I had no notion of privacy. I liked the word, and I liked the boxed-in feel the draperies gave when they were closed.

As for the visitor, it was a mystery. Our father didn't have friends, at least not the kind who came to the house late on a Saturday afternoon. I left my secret spot and went to the top of the stairs to lie down on the rug that covered the landing. I knew from experience I could see into the drawing room by looking between the newel post and first baluster if I was on the floor. There was our father in front of the fireplace with a woman, and from what I could tell they were studying the portraits of Mr. and Mrs. VanHoebeek. I got up and went back to my sister's room to make my report.

"It's a woman," I said to Maeve. Sandy would have known this already.

Sandy asked me if I'd brushed my teeth, by which she meant had I brushed them that morning. No one brushed their teeth at four o'clock in the afternoon. Sandy had to do everything herself because Jocelyn had Saturdays off. Sandy would have laid the fire and answered the door and offered drinks and, on top of all of that, was now responsible for my teeth. Sandy was off on Mondays. Sandy and Jocelyn were both off on Sundays because my father didn't think people should be made to work on Sundays.

"I did," I said, because I probably had.

"Do it again," she said. "And brush your hair."

The last part she meant for my sister, whose hair was long and black and as thick as ten horse tails tied together. No amount of brushing ever made it look brushed.

Once we were deemed presentable, Maeve and I went downstairs and stood beneath the wide archway of the foyer, watching our father and Andrea watch the VanHoebeeks. They didn't notice us, or they didn't acknowledge us—hard to say—and so we waited. Maeve and I knew how to be quiet in the house, a habit born of trying not to irritate our father, though it irritated him more when he felt we were sneaking up on him. He was wearing his blue suit. He never wore a suit on Saturdays. For the first time I could see that his hair was starting to gray in the back. Standing next to Andrea, he looked even taller than he was.

"It must be a comfort, having them with you," Andrea said to him, not of his children but of his paintings. Mr. and Mrs. VanHoebeek, who had no first names that I had ever heard, were old in their portraits but not entirely ancient. They both dressed in black and stood with an erect formality that spoke of another time. Even in their separate frames they were so together, so *married*, I always thought it must have been one large painting that someone cut in half. Andrea's head tilted back to study those four cunning eyes that appeared to follow a boy with disapproval no matter which of the sofas he chose to sit on. Maeve, silent, stuck her finger in between my ribs to make me yelp but I held on to myself. We had not yet been introduced to Andrea, who, from the back, looked small and neat in her belted dress, a dark hat no bigger than a saucer pinned over a twist of pale hair. Having been schooled by nuns, I knew better than to embarrass a guest by laughing. Andrea would have had no way of knowing that the people in the paintings had come with the house, that everything in the house had come with the house.

The drawing-room VanHoebeeks were the show-stoppers, life-sized documentation of people worn by time, their stern and unlovely faces rendered with Dutch exactitude and a distinctly Dutch understanding of light, but there were dozens of other lesser portraits on every floor—their children in the hallways, their ancestors in the bedrooms, the unnamed people they'd admired scattered throughout. There was also one portrait of Maeve when she was ten, and while it wasn't nearly as big as the paintings of the VanHoebeeks, it was every bit as good. My father had brought in a famous artist from Chicago on the train. As the story goes, he was supposed to paint our mother, but our mother, who hadn't been told that the painter was coming to stay in our house for two weeks, refused to sit, and so he painted Maeve instead. When the portrait was finished and framed, my father hung it in the drawing room right across from the VanHoebeeks. Maeve liked to say that was where she learned to stare people down.

"Danny," my father said when finally he turned, looking like he expected us to be exactly where we were. "Come say hello to Mrs. Smith."

I will always believe that Andrea's face fell for an instant when she looked at Maeve and me. Even if my father hadn't mentioned his children, she would have known he had them. Everyone in Elkins Park knew what went on in the Dutch House. Maybe she thought we would stay upstairs. She'd come to see the house, after all, not the children. Or maybe the look on Andrea's face was just for Maeve, who, at fifteen and in her tennis shoes, was already a head taller than Andrea in her heels. Maeve had been inclined to slouch when it first became apparent she was going to be taller than all the other girls in her class and most of the boys, and our father was relentless in his correction of her posture. *Head-up-shoulders-back* might as well have been her name. For years he thumped her between the shoulder blades with the flat of his palm whenever he passed her in a room, the unintended consequence of which was that Maeve now stood like a soldier in the queen's court, or like the queen herself. Even I could see how she might have been intimidating: her height, the shining black wall of hair, the way she would lower her eyes to look at a person rather than bend her neck. But at eight I was still comfortably smaller than the woman our father would later marry. I held out my hand to shake her little hand and said my name, then Maeve did the same. Though the story will be remembered that Maeve and Andrea were at odds right from the start, that wasn't true. Maeve was perfectly fair and polite when they met, and she remained fair and polite until doing so was no longer possible.

"How do you do?" Maeve said, and Andrea replied that she was very well.

Andrea was well. Of course she was. It had been Andrea's

goal for years to get inside the house, to loop her arm through our father's arm when going up the wide stone steps and across the red-tiled terrace. She was the first woman our father had brought home since our mother left, though Maeve told me that he had had something going with our nanny for a while, an Irish girl named Fiona.

"You think he was sleeping with Fluffy?" I asked her. Fluffy was what we called Fiona when we were children, partly because I had a hard time with the name Fiona and partly because of the soft waves of red hair that fell down her back in a transfixing cloud. The news of this affair came to me as most information did: many years after the fact, in a car parked outside the Dutch House with my sister.

"Either that or she cleaned his room in the middle of the night," Maeve said.

My father and Fluffy in flagrante delicto. I shook my head. "Can't picture it."

"You shouldn't try to *picture* it. God, Danny, that's disgusting. Anyway, you were practically a baby during the Fluffy administration. I'm surprised you'd even remember her."

But Fluffy had hit me with a wooden spoon when I was four years old. I still have a small scar in the shape of a golf club beside my left eye—the mark of Fluffy, Maeve called it. Fluffy claimed she'd been cooking a pot of applesauce when I startled her by grabbing her skirt. She said she was trying to get me away from the stove and had certainly never meant to hit me, though I'd think it would be hard to accidentally hit a child in the face with a spoon. The story was only interesting insofar as it was my first distinct memory—of another person or the Dutch House or my own life. I didn't have a single memory of our mother, but I remembered Fluffy's spoon cracking into the side of my head. I remembered Maeve, who had been down the hall when I screamed, flying into the kitchen the way the deer would fly across the hedgerow at the back of the property. She threw herself into Fluffy, knocking her into the stove, the blue flames leaping as the boiling pot of applesauce crashed to the floor so that we were all burned in pinpoint splatters. I was sent to the doctor's office for six stitches and Maeve's hand was wrapped and Fluffy was dismissed, even though I could remember her crying and saying how sorry she was, how it was only an accident. She didn't want to go. That was our father's other relationship according to my sister, and she should know, because if I was four when I got that scar then she was already eleven.

As it happened, Fluffy's parents had worked for the Van-Hoebeeks as their driver and cook. Fluffy had spent her childhood in the Dutch House, or in the small apartment over the garage, so I had to wonder, when her name came up again after so many years, where she would have gone when she was told to leave.

Fluffy was the only person in the house who had known the VanHoebeeks. Not even our father had met them, though we sat on their chairs and slept in their beds and ate our meals off their delftware. The VanHoebeeks weren't the story, but in a sense the house was the story, and it was their house. They had made their fortune in the wholesale distribution of cigarettes, a lucky business Mr. VanHoebeek had entered into just before the start of the First World War. Cigarettes were given to soldiers in the field for purposes of morale, and the habit followed them home to celebrate a decade of prosperity. The VanHoebeeks, richer by the hour, commissioned a house to be built on what was then farmland outside of Philadelphia.

The stunning success of the house could be attributed to the architect, though by the time I thought to go looking I could find no other extant examples of his work. It could be that one or both of those dour VanHoebeeks had been some sort of aesthetic visionary, or that the property inspired a marvel beyond what any of them had imagined, or that America after the First World War was teeming with craftsmen who worked to standards long since abandoned. Whatever the explanation, the house they wound up with—the house we later wound up with—was a singular confluence of talent and luck. I can't explain how a house that was three stories high could seem like just the right amount of space, but it did. Or maybe it would be better to say that it was too much of a house for anyone, an immense and ridiculous waste, but that we never wanted it to be different. The Dutch House, as it came to be known in Elkins Park and Jenkintown and Glenside and all the way to Philadelphia, referred not to the house's architecture but to its inhabitants. The Dutch House was the place where those Dutch people with the unpronounceable name lived. Seen from certain vantage points of distance, it appeared to float several inches above the hill it sat on. The panes of glass that surrounded the glass front doors were as big as storefront windows and held in place by wrought-iron vines. The windows both took in the sun and reflected it back across the wide lawn. Maybe it was neoclassical, though with a simplicity in the lines that came closer to Mediterranean or French, and while it was not Dutch, the blue delft mantels in the drawing room, library, and master bedroom were said to have been pried out of a castle in Utrecht and sold to the VanHoebeeks to pay a prince's gambling debts. The house, complete with mantels, had been finished in 1922.

"They had seven good years before the bankers started jumping out of windows," Maeve said, giving our predecessors their place in history.

The first I ever heard of the property that had been sold off was that first day Andrea came to the house. She followed our father to the foyer and was looking out at the front lawn.

"It's so much glass," Andrea said, as if making a calculation to see if the glass could be changed, swapped out for an actual wall. "Don't you worry about people looking in?"

Not only could you see into the Dutch House, you could see straight through it. The house was shortened in the middle, and the deep foyer led directly into what we called the observatory, which had a wall of windows facing the backyard. From the driveway you could let your eye go up the front steps, across the terrace, through the front doors, across the long marble floor of the foyer, through the observatory, and catch sight of the lilacs waving obliviously in the garden behind the house.

Our father glanced towards the ceiling and then to either side of the door, as if he were just now considering this. "We're far enough from the street," he said. On this May afternoon, the wall of linden trees that ran along the property line was thick with leaves, and the slant of green lawn where I rolled like a dog in the summers was both deep and wide.

"But at night," Andrea said, her voice concerned. "I wonder if there wouldn't be some way to hang drapes."

Drapes to block the view struck me not only as impossible but the single stupidest idea I'd ever heard.

"You've seen us at night?" Maeve asked.

"You have to remember the land that was here when they built the place," our father said, speaking over Maeve. "There were more than two hundred acres. The property went all the way to Melrose Park."

"But why would they have sold it?" Suddenly Andrea could see how much more sense the house would have made had there been no other houses. The sight line should have gone far past the slope of the lawn, past the peony beds and the roses. The eye was meant to travel down a wide valley and bank into a forest, so that even if the VanHoebeeks or one of their guests were to look out a window from the ballroom at night, the only light they'd see would be starlight. There wasn't a street back then, there wasn't a neighborhood, though now both the street and the Buchsbaums' house across the street were perfectly visible in the winter when the leaves came off the trees.

"Money," Maeve said.

"Money," our father said, nodding. It wasn't a complicated idea. Even at eight I was able to figure it out.

"But they were wrong," Andrea said. There was a tightness around her mouth. "Think about how beautiful this place must have been. They should have had more respect, if you ask me. The house is a piece of art."

And then I did laugh, because what I understood Andrea to say was that the VanHoebeeks should have asked *her* before they sold the land. My father, irritated, told Maeve to take me upstairs, as if I might have forgotten the way.

Ready-made cigarettes lined up in their cartons were a luxury for the rich, as were acres never walked on by the people who owned them. Bit by bit the land was shaved away from the house. The demise of the estate was a matter of public record, history recorded in property deeds. Parcels were sold to pay debts—ten acres, then fifty, then twenty-eight. Elkins Park came closer and closer to the door. In this way the VanHoebeek family made it through the Depression, only to have Mr. VanHoebeek die of pneumonia in 1940. One VanHoebeek boy died in childhood and the two older sons died in the war. Mrs. Van-Hoebeek died in 1945 when there was nothing left to sell but the side yard. The house and all it contained went back to the bank, dust to dust.

Fluffy stayed behind courtesy of the Pennsylvania Savings

and Loan, and was paid a small stipend to manage the property. Fluffy's parents were dead, or maybe they had found other jobs. At any rate, she lived alone above the garage, checking the house every day to make sure the roof wasn't leaking and the pipes hadn't burst. She cut a straight path from the garage to the front doors with a push mower and let the rest of the lawn grow wild. She picked the fruit from the trees that were left near the back of the house and made apple butter and canned the peaches for winter. By the time our father bought the place in 1946, raccoons had taken over the ballroom and chewed into the wiring. Fluffy went into the house only when the sun was straight overhead, the very hour when all nocturnal animals were piled up together and fast asleep. The miracle was they didn't burn the place down. The raccoons were eventually captured and disposed of, but they left behind their fleas and the fleas sifted into everything. Maeve said her earliest memories of life in the house were of scratching, and of how Fluffy dotted each welt with a Q-tip dipped in calamine lotion. My parents had hired Fluffy to be my sister's nanny.

* * *

THE FIRST TIME Maeve and I ever parked on VanHoebeek Street (*Van Who-bake*, mispronounced as *Van Ho-bik* by everyone in Elkins Park) was the first time I'd come home from Choate for spring break. Spring was something of a misnomer that year since there was a foot of snow on the ground, an April Fool's Day joke to cap a bitter winter. True spring, I knew from my first half-semester at boarding school, was for the boys whose parents took them sailing in Bermuda.

"What are you doing?" I asked her when she stopped in front of the Buchsbaums' house, across the street from the Dutch House.

"I want to see something." Maeve leaned over and pushed in the cigarette lighter.

"Nothing to see here," I said to her. "Move along." I was in a crappy mood because of the weather and what I saw as the inequity between what I had and what I deserved, but still, I was glad to be back in Elkins Park, glad to be in my sister's car, the blue Oldsmobile wagon of our childhood that my father let her have when she got her own apartment. Because I was fifteen and generally an idiot, I thought that the feeling of home I was experiencing had to do with the car and where it was parked, instead of attributing it wholly and gratefully to my sister.

"Are you in a rush to get someplace?" She shook a cigarette out of the pack then put her hand over the lighter. If you weren't right there to catch the lighter, it would eject too forcibly and burn a hole in the seat or the floor mat or your leg, depending on where it landed.

"Do you drive over here when I'm at school?"

Pop. She caught it and lit her cigarette. "I do not."

"But here we are," I said. The snow came steady and soft as the last light of day was folded into the clouds. Maeve was an Icelandic truck driver at heart, no weather stopped her, but I had recently gotten off a train and was tired and cold. I thought it would be nice to make grilled cheese sandwiches and soak in the tub. Baths were the subject of endless ridicule at Choate, I never knew why. Only showers were thought to be manly.

Maeve filled her lungs with smoke, exhaled, then turned off the car. "I thought about coming over here a couple of times but I decided to wait for you." She smiled at me then, cranking the window down just far enough to let in a shelf of arctic air. I had nagged her to give the cigarettes up before I'd left for school, and then neglected to tell her that I'd started. Smoking was what we did at Choate in lieu of taking baths.

I craned my head to look up the drive. "Do you see them?"

Maeve looked out the driver's side window. "I don't know why, but I just keep thinking about that first time she came to the house a million years ago. Do you even remember?"

Of course I remembered. Who could forget Andrea showing up?

"And she said that business about worrying that people were looking in our windows at night?"

No sooner were the words out of her mouth than the foyer was flooded in the warm gold light of the chandelier. Then after a pause the lights above the staircase went on, and a few moments after that the light in the master bedroom on the second floor. The illumination of the Dutch House was timed so exactly to her words it nearly stopped my heart. Of course Maeve *had* been coming to the house without me. She knew that Andrea turned on the lights the very minute the sun went down. Denying it was just a bit of theatrics on my sister's part, and I appreciated her efforts once I realized them later. It made for one hell of a show.

"Look at that," I whispered.

There were no leaves on the linden trees, and the snow was falling but not too heavily. Sure enough, you could see right into the house, through the house, not with any detail of course but memory filled in the picture: there was the round table beneath the chandelier where Sandy had left our father's mail in the evening, and behind it the grandfather clock that had been my job to wind every Sunday after Mass so that the ship beneath the 6 would continue to gently rock between two blue rows of painted waves. I couldn't see the ship or the waves but I knew. There was the half-moon console table against the wall, the cobalt vase with the painting of the girl and the dog, the two French chairs no one ever sat in, the giant mirror whose frame always made me think of the twisted arms of a golden octopus. Andrea crossed through the foyer as if on cue. We were too far away to see her face but I knew her from the way she walked. Norma came down the stairs at full speed and then stopped abruptly because her mother would have told her not to run. Norma was taller now, although I guess it could have been Bright.

"She must have watched us," Maeve said, "before she ever came in that first time."

"Or maybe everybody watched us, everyone who ever drove down this street in winter." I reached into her purse and took out the cigarettes.

"That seems a little self-aggrandizing," Maeve said. "*Every*-one."

"They teach us that at Choate."

She laughed. I could tell she hadn't been expecting to laugh and it pleased me to no end.

"Five whole days with you at home," she said, blowing smoke out the open window. "The best five days of the year."

CHAPTER 2

A FTER HER FIRST appearance at the Dutch House, Andrea
lingered like a virus. As soon as we were sure we'd seen
the last of her and months would go by without a mention of
her name, there she'd be at the dining-room table again, chas-
tened by her absence at first and then slowly warming over
time. Andrea, fully warmed, talked about nothing but the
house. She was forever going on about some detail of the crown
molding or speculating as to the exact height of the ceiling, as
if the ceiling were entirely new to us. "That's called egg and
dart," she'd say to me, pointing up. Just when she'd reach the
point of being truly intolerable, she'd disappear again, and the
relief would wash over Maeve and me (and, we had assumed,
our father) with its glorious silence.

There was the Sunday we came home from Mass and found
her sitting in one of the white iron chairs by the pool, or Maeve
found her. Maeve had been walking through the library and
had seen her through the window just by chance. She didn't call
for our father the way I would have, she just walked around to
the back door off the kitchen and went outside.

"Mrs. Smith?" Maeve said, shading her eyes with her hand.
We called her Mrs. Smith until they were married, having never
been invited to do otherwise. After they were married I'm sure

she would have preferred us to call her Mrs. Conroy, but that would have only intensified the awkwardness, seeing as how Maeve and I were Conroys as well.

Maeve told me Andrea was startled, and who knows, maybe she'd been sleeping. "Where's your father?"

"In the house." Maeve looked over her shoulder. "Was he expecting you?"

"I was expecting *him* an hour ago," Andrea corrected.

Since it was Sunday, Sandy and Jocelyn were both off. I don't think they would have let her in if we weren't home but I don't know that for sure. Sandy was the warmer of the two, Jocelyn more suspicious. They didn't like Andrea, and they probably would have made her wait outside until we got home. It was only a little cold, a nice enough day to sit by the pool, the sunlight glittering across the blue water, the tender lines of moss growing up between the flagstones. Maeve told her we'd been to church.

And then they just stared at each other, neither of them looking away. "I'm half Dutch, you know," Andrea said finally.

"I beg your pardon?"

"On my mother's side. She was full-blood Dutch."

"We're Irish," Maeve said.

Andrea nodded, as if there had been some disagreement that now was settled in her favor. When it became clear there would be no more conversation, Maeve went inside to tell our father that Mrs. Smith was waiting by the pool.

"Where in the hell did she park?" Maeve said to me after our father had gone outside. She almost never swore in those days, especially not right after Mass. "She always parks in front of the house."

And so we went to find the car, looking first on the far side of the house and then back behind the garage. When none of the obvious spots panned out we walked down the driveway, the pea gravel crunching beneath our Sunday shoes, and onto the street. We had no idea where Andrea lived but we knew she wasn't our neighbor, she hadn't just walked over. Finally we found her cream-colored Impala parked a block away, the front left corner crumpled in on itself. Maeve crouched down to inspect the damage and I went so far as to touch the hanging fender, marveling at the headlight which had been spared. Clearly, Andrea had banged into something and she didn't want us to know.

We didn't tell our father about the car. After all, he didn't tell us anything. He never talked about Andrea, not when she was gone or when she was back. He didn't tell us if he had her in mind for some role in our future. When she was there he acted like she'd always been there, and when she was gone we never wanted to remind him for fear he'd ask her back. In truth, I don't think he was particularly interested in Andrea. I just don't think he had the means to deal with her tenacity. His strategy, as far as I could tell, was to ignore her until she went away. "That's never going to work," Maeve said to me.

The only thing our father really cared about in life was his work: the buildings he built and owned and rented out. He rarely sold anything, choosing instead to leverage what he had in order to buy more. When he had an appointment with the bank, the banker came to him, and my father made him wait. Mrs. Kennedy, my father's secretary, would offer the banker a cup of coffee and tell him it shouldn't be much longer, though sometimes it was. There was nothing the banker could do but sit there in the small anteroom of my father's office, holding his hat.

The little attention my father had left at the end of the week he saved for me, and even that he made part of his job. He took

me with him in the Buick on the first Saturday of every month
to collect the rent, and gave me a pencil and a ledger book so I
could write down how much the tenants had paid in the col-
umn next to what they had owed. Very soon I knew who would
never be home, and who would be right there at the door with
an envelope. I knew who would have complaints—a toilet that
ran, a toilet that was stopped, a light switch that was dead.
Certain people came up with something every month and
would not part with their money until the problem was resolved. My father, whose knee had been ruined in the war,
limped slightly as he went to the trunk of his car and pulled out
whatever was needed to make things right. When I was a boy,
I thought of the trunk as a sort of magic chest—pliers, clamps,
hammers, screwdrivers, caulk, nails—everything was there. Now
I know the things people ask you for on a Saturday morning
tend to be easy fixes, and my father liked to do those jobs himself. He was a rich man, but he wanted to show people he still
knew how things worked. Or maybe the show was all for me,
because he didn't need to drive around picking up rent any
more than he needed to drag his bad leg up a ladder to inspect
a patch of loose shingles. He had maintenance men for that.
Maybe it was for my sake that he rolled up his shirt sleeves and
pulled the top off a stove to inspect the heating element while I
stood there marveling at all the things he knew. He would tell
me to pay attention because one day the business was going to
be mine. I would need to know how things were done.

"The only way to really understand what money means is to
have been poor," he said to me when we were eating lunch in
the car. "That's the strike you have against you. A boy grows
up rich like you, never wanting for anything, never being
hungry"—he shook his head, as if it had been a disappointing
choice I'd made—"I don't know how a person overcomes a

thing like that. You can watch these people all you want and see what it's been like for them, but that's not the same as living it yourself." He put down his sandwich and took a drink of coffee from the thermos.

"Yes, sir," I said, because what else was there to say?

"The biggest lie in business is that it takes money to make money. Remember that. You've got to be smart, have a plan, pay attention to what's going on around you. None of that costs a dime." My father wasn't much for imparting advice, and this seemed to have worn him out. When he was finished, he took his handkerchief from his pocket and ran it across his forehead.

When I'm in a charitable mood, I look back on this moment and I tell myself that this was the reason things played out the way they did. My father was trying to give me the benefit of his experience.

My father was always more comfortable with his tenants than he was the people in his office or the people in his house. A tenant would start in on a story, which sometimes was about the Phillies' inability to pitch against Brooklyn and other times was about why there wasn't enough money in the envelope, and I could tell by the way my father was standing, the way he nodded at one part or another, that he was paying attention. The people who were short on the rent never complained about a window that was painted shut. They only wanted the chance to tell him what had happened to them that month, and to assure him that it wouldn't happen again. I never saw my father scold the tenants or make any threats. He only listened, and then he told them to try their best. But after three months of conversation, there would be a different family living in the apartment the next time we came back. I never knew what happened to the people with hard luck, but it happened on some day other than the first Saturday of the month.

My father smoked more as the day went on. I sat beside him on the car's wide bench seat, looking over the numbers in the ledger or staring out the window at the trees as they flicked past. When my father smoked I knew he was thinking, and that I was meant to be quiet. The neighborhoods got worse as we headed into Philadelphia. He saved the very poorest of his tenants for the end of the day, as if to give them the extra hours to get together what they owed. I would rather have waited in the car on those last stops, fiddled with the radio, but I knew enough to skip the part where I would ask him to let me stay behind and he would tell me no. The tenants in Mount Airy and Jenkintown were always nice to me, asking about school and basketball, offering me candy I'd been told never to accept. "Looking more like your daddy every day," they'd say. "Growing up just like him." But in the poorer neighborhoods things were different. It's not that the tenants weren't nice, but they were nervous even when the money was in their hand, maybe thinking how it had been the month before or how it would be a month from now. They were deferential not only to my father but to me, and it was the deference that made me want to crawl out of my skin. Men older than my father called me Mr. Conroy when I was no more than ten, as if the resemblance they saw between the two of us was more than physical. Maybe they saw the situation the way my father did, that someday they'd be paying the rent to me and so had no business calling me Danny. As we climbed the steps of the buildings, I peeled off chips of paint and stepped over the broken slats. Half-open doors flapped on their hinges and there were never any screens. The heat in the hallways either ran to tropical or didn't run at all. It made me think what a luxury it was to rattle on about a faucet in need of a washer, while failing to remind me that this too was a building my father owned, and that it was well within his power to open the trunk of his car and make things better for the people who lived there. One by one, he knocked on the doors and the doors opened and we listened to whatever the people inside had to say: husbands out of work, husbands gone, wives gone, children sick. One time a man was going on about not having the rent because his son had been so sick and he had to stay home himself and watch the boy. The boy and the man were alone in the dark apartment, everyone else had gone I guess. When my father had heard enough he went into the living room and picked up the feverish child from the couch. I had no idea what dead looked like in those days but the boy's arm swung back from his side and his head dropped back in my father's arms. It put the fear of God in me. If it hadn't been for the deep congestion of his breathing I would have thought we'd come too late. The air in the apartment was heavy with the mentholated smell of suffering. Maybe the boy was five or six, he was very small. My father carried him down the stairs and put him in the Buick while the boy's father came behind us saying there was no need to worry. "It'll be nothing," he kept saying. "The boy's gonna be fine." But he climbed into the back seat of our car all the same and rode beside his son to the hospital. I had never sat in the front of a car while an adult was sitting in the back and it made me nervous. I could only imagine what the nuns would have said had they seen us go by. When we got to the hospital, my father made arrangements with the woman at the desk, and then we left them there, driving back to our own house in the dark without saying a single word about what had happened.

"Why would he have done that?" Maeve had asked me that night after dinner when we were in her bedroom. Our father never took Maeve to collect the rent, even though she was seven years older than me and had won the math prize in school every year and would have been so much better with the ledger it was ridiculous. On the first Saturday of every month, after we'd been excused from the table and our father had gone to the library with his drink and the paper, Maeve would pull me into her bedroom and close the door. She wanted a recounting of the entire day, blow by blow: what had happened at every apartment, what the tenants had said, and what our father had said to them in return. She even wanted to know what we'd bought for lunch at Carter's Market where we always stopped for sandwiches.

"The kid was really sick, that's all. He didn't open his eyes once, not even when Dad put him in the car." When we got to the hospital, my father had told me to go to the men's room and wash my hands, to get the water hot and use soap even though I hadn't touched the boy.

Maeve mulled this over.

"What?" I asked.

"Well, think about it. He hates sick people. Has he ever so much as crossed the door of your room when you were sick?" She stretched out on the bed beside me, fluffing the pillow under her head. "If you're going to put your feet on my bed then the least you can do is take off your filthy shoes."

I kicked off my shoes. Did he sit on the edge of my bed and put his hand on my forehead? Did he bring me a ginger ale, ask me if I felt like I was going to throw up again? That's what Maeve did. That's what Sandy and Jocelyn did when Maeve was at school. "He never comes in my room."

"But why would he have done all that if the boy's father was there?"

I almost never got to an answer before Maeve did but in this case it was perfectly obvious. "Because the mother wasn't there." If there had been a woman in the apartment he never would have put himself in the middle of things.

Mothers were the measure of safety, which meant that I was safer than Maeve. After our mother left, Maeve took up the job on my behalf but no one did the same for her. Of course Sandy and Jocelyn mothered us. They made sure we were washed and fed and that our lunches were packed and our scouting dues paid. They loved us, I know they did, but they went home at the end of the day. There was no crawling into bed with Sandy or Jocelyn when I had a bad dream in the middle of the night, and it never once occurred to me to knock on my father's door. I went to Maeve. She taught me the proper way to hold a fork. She attended my basketball games and knew all my friends and oversaw my homework and kissed me every morning before we went our separate ways to school and again at night before I went to bed regardless of whether or not I wanted to be kissed. She told me repeatedly, relentlessly, that I was kind and smart and fast, that I could be as great a man as I made up my mind to be. She was so good at all that, despite the fact that no one had done it for her.

"Mommy did it for me," she said, surprised that I'd even brought it up. "Listen, kiddo, I was the lucky one. I got years with her and you didn't. I can't even think about how much you must miss her."

But how could I miss someone I'd never known? I was only three at the time, and if I knew what was happening I had no memory of it. Sandy was the one who told me the whole story, though parts of it I knew of course from my sister. Maeve had been ten when our mother first started to leave. One morning Maeve got out of bed and opened the drapes over the window seat to see if it had snowed during the night and it had. The

Dutch House was always freezing. There was a fireplace in Maeve's bedroom and Sandy kept dry wood on the grate above a bed of crumpled newspaper so that in the morning all Maeve had to do was strike a match, something she had been allowed to do since her eighth birthday. ("Mommy gave me a box of matches for my eighth birthday," she told me once. "She said her mother had given her a box of matches when she turned eight, and they spent the morning learning how to strike them. She showed me how to light the fire, and then that night she let me light the candles on my cake.") Maeve lit the fire and put on her robe and slippers and came next door to my room to check on me. I was three, still asleep. I had no part in this story.

Then she crossed the hall to our parents' room and found it empty, the bed already made. Maeve went back to her room to get ready for school. She had brushed her teeth and washed her face and was halfway dressed when Fluffy came in to wake her up.

"Every morning you beat me," Fluffy said.

"You should wake me up earlier," Maeve said.

Fluffy told her she didn't need to get up any earlier.

The fact that our father had already left the house wasn't unusual. The fact that our mother wasn't in the house was unusual but not without precedent. Sandy and Jocelyn and Fluffy all seemed to be themselves. If they weren't worried there was no reason to worry. Our mother was the one who took Maeve to school but on this morning Fluffy drove her, letting her out with the lunch that Jocelyn had packed. At the end of the day Fluffy was there to pick her up again. When Maeve asked where our mother was, she shrugged. "With your father, maybe?"

Our mother wasn't there for dinner that night, and when our father appeared, Maeve asked him where she'd gone. He wrapped her up in his arms and kissed her neck. Such things still happened in those days. He told Maeve her mother had gone to Philadelphia to visit old friends.

"Without saying goodbye?"

"She said goodbye to me," our father said. "She got up very early."

"I was up early."

"Well, she was up even before you, and she told me to tell you she'd see you in a day or two. Everybody needs a vacation."

"From what?" Maeve asked, when what she meant was, *From me? From us?*

"From the house." He took her hand and walked her in to dinner. "This place is a big responsibility."

How big of a responsibility could it have been when Jocelyn and Sandy and Fluffy did so much of the work, when the gardeners came to take care of the lawn and rake the leaves and shovel the snow, when Maeve would have done anything in the world to be helpful?

Our mother wasn't there when Maeve woke up the next morning, and again Fluffy drove her to school and picked her up. But when they came back to the house on that second day, our mother was sitting in the kitchen drinking tea with Sandy and Jocelyn. I was playing on the floor, taking the lids off all the pots.

"She looked so tired," Maeve told me. "She looked like she hadn't been to sleep the whole time she'd been gone."

Our mother put down her cup and pulled Maeve into her lap. "There's my darling," she said, and kissed her forehead and kissed the part of her hair. "There's my true love."

Maeve put her arms around our mother's neck and rested her head against our mother's chest and breathed her in while our mother stroked her hair. "Who gets a girl like this?" she asked Sandy and Jocelyn. "Who gets such a beautiful girl who's kind and smart? What did I ever do to deserve a girl like this?"

Some variation of this story happened three more times.

Over the course of the next two months, our mother was gone for two nights, then four nights, and then a week. Maeve started getting up in the middle of the night to check our parents' room and make sure she was still there. Sometimes our mother was awake, and she would see Maeve at the door and lift up the covers and Maeve would float across the room to the bed without making a sound and slip into the warm curve of her body. She would fall asleep without thinking, her mother's arms around her, her mother's heartbeat and breath behind her. No other moment in life could match this.

"Why don't you say goodbye to me before you leave?" Maeve would ask her, and our mother would just shake her head.

"I could never do that. Never in a million years could I say goodbye to you."

Was our mother sick? Was she getting worse?

Maeve nodded. "She was turning into a ghost. One week she was thinner, then she was paler, everything deteriorated so fast. We were all folding up. Mommy would come home and cry for days. I would go and sit with her in her bed after school. Sometimes you'd be in the bed with her, playing. Whenever Dad was home he always looked like he was trying to catch her, like he might as well have been walking around with his hands out. Sandy and Jocelyn and Fluffy, they were all nervous as cats by then, but no one talked about it. When she was gone it was unbearable and when she was home it was unbearable in a different way because we knew that she was going to leave again."

When finally she did leave again, Maeve asked our father

when she was coming back. He looked at her for a very long time. He didn't know what part of the truth he was supposed to tell a ten-year-old, and what he decided on was the whole thing. He told Maeve our mother wasn't coming back. She had gone to India and she wasn't coming back.

Maeve could never make up her mind what part of this story was the worst: that her mother was gone or that India was on the other side of the planet. "No one goes to India!"

"Maeve," he said.

"Maybe she hasn't left yet!" She didn't believe him, not for a minute, but if the story had been started it needed to be stopped.

Our father shook his head but he didn't reach for her. Somehow that might have been the strangest part of all.

This was the story of our mother leaving, and this was the point at which the story stopped. There should have been questions, explanations. If she was in India our father should have gone to find her and bring her back, but none of this happened because Maeve stopped getting up in the morning. She wouldn't go to school. Sandy would bring her Cream of Wheat on a tray and sit on the edge of her bed, trying to talk her into taking a couple of bites, but she said Maeve was rarely persuaded. Everyone saw it as the understandable sickness of a girl longing for her mother. They were all suffering from some related version, and so they let the child sink down into it, never really thinking about the fact that she would still drink her orange juice, and drink her glass of water, and drink the entire pot of chamomile tea. She'd take her cup into the bathroom and fill it over and over again, until finally she stuck her head in the sink and drank from the running tap. Fluffy would bring me into Maeve's room and put me in her bed and Maeve would read me a story before falling back to sleep. Then one afternoon, less than a week after our mother left for good, Maeve didn't wake up. Fluffy shook her and shook her and then scooped Maeve up in her arms and ran down the stairs and out to the car.

Where was everyone then? Where had our father and Sandy and Jocelyn gone? Where was I? Sandy said she couldn't remember. "Such a terrible time," she said, shaking her head. What she knew was that Fluffy drove Maeve to the hospital and carried her into the lobby where some nurses took the sleeping child from her arms. She stayed in the hospital for two weeks. The doctors said the diabetes could have been brought on by trauma, or it could have been a virus. The body had all sorts of means to deal with what it couldn't understand. In the hospital, Maeve swam in and out of consciousness while they worked to stabilize her blood sugar. Everything that happened to her was part of a dream. She told herself her mother wasn't allowed to visit, a punishment meted out to both of them for something she had done and couldn't quite remember. The Sisters of Mercy, all friends of our mother's, came to see her. Two girls from Sacred Heart presented her with a card signed by the entire class, but they weren't allowed to stay. Our father would come in the evenings, though he said very little. He would hold Maeve's foot through the white cotton blanket and tell her that she needed to get better now, no one was up for this. Jocelyn and Sandy and Fluffy took turns staying with her in the room. "One of us for you, one for your brother, and one for your father," Sandy would say. "Everyone's covered." Sandy said that when she needed to cry she would wait until Maeve was asleep, then she would go out to the hall.

After Maeve came home from the hospital things got worse. Logic said our mother's absence had made her sick, and so logic concluded that further talk of our mother could kill her. The Dutch House grew quiet. Sandy and Jocelyn and Fluffy devoted themselves to my sister, the needles, the insulin. They

were terrified of the way every injection changed her. Our father would have nothing to do with it. Fluffy, who in those
weeks slept in the bed with Maeve, ended up taking her back to
the hospital in the middle of the night. Again, they worked to
stabilize her, again they sent her home. Maeve would cry and
cry until my father would come into her room and tell her to
stop. They had all become characters in the worst part of a
fairy tale. He was now a hundred years old. "Stop," he would
say, as if he could barely make the words. "You have to stop."

And finally, she did.

CHAPTER 3

Nearly two years into her irregular tenure, Andrea walked in the house one Saturday afternoon with two small girls. Say what you will for Andrea, she had a knack for making the impossible seem natural. I wasn't clear about whether it was only Maeve and I who were meeting her daughters for the first time, or if the existence of Norma and Bright Smith was news to our father as well. No, he must have known. The very fact that he didn't look at them meant they were already familiar. They were much younger than me. Bright, the smaller of the two, looked like she should have been on a Christmas card, fair like her mother with flushed cheeks and blue eyes, a big smile for everyone. Norma had light-brown hair and green eyes. She was no match for her shining sister, if only because she was so serious. Her lips stayed pressed together in a straight line. Clearly it was Norma's job to look after things.

"Girls," their mother said, "this is Danny, and this is his sister Maeve."

We were shocked, of course, but in our heart of hearts we were happy too, certain that the Smith girls would spell the end of Andrea for good. Our father wasn't about to put up with two more children in the house, especially not two more girls. Who had been taking care of them on all those Saturday nights she'd come to dinner, never once mentioning she needed to get home? This would not be forgiven. When we stood at the door and said goodbye to the three of them after what had been a comparatively brief visit, we thought that we were saying goodbye for good.

"*Sayonara*, Mrs. Smith," Maeve said that night in the bathroom as she put the toothpaste on my toothbrush and then hers. I was perfectly capable of handling a tube of toothpaste but this was our ritual. We brushed our teeth together then said our prayers.

"*Buenas noches*, Bright and Norma," I said. Maeve looked at me for a second, not believing I'd come up with that, then she started laughing so hard she barked like a seal.

Maeve and I were forever under the impression that we were moments away from cracking the code on our life, and that soon we would understand the impenetrable mystery that was our father, but we'd misread the appearance of Andrea's daughters completely. It was not some half-baked introduction. The final disclosure that Andrea came as a package deal was proof that she had fully assimilated, and we, somehow, had missed it. Soon the girls were regulars, sitting with us at the dinner table or taking off their socks to splash their feet in the swimming pool—neither of them knew how to swim. It felt strange to have other children around. Maeve and I both had friends at school but we went to their houses for parties and studying and sleep-overs. No one ever came to the Dutch House. Maybe it was because we didn't want to draw attention to our motherless state, or we feared the house would subject us to ridicule, but really, I think we understood that our father didn't like children, which was why it made no sense that he'd let these two in.

One night the girls showed up with their mother who was

wearing a very fancy blue silk dress. Bright kept running her hands across the full skirt to make it rustle like blowing leaves, while Norma made a game out of trying to step only on the small black squares of marble in the foyer. Andrea announced to the four of us that she and my father were going out for the evening. With no warning at all she planned to leave the girls for Maeve and me to mind.

"What are we supposed to do with them?" Maeve asked, because truly, we didn't know. They weren't our responsibility. We had never been alone with them before.

Andrea waved her question away. She was ebullient in those days, as if everything had been decided. Maybe it had. "You'll do nothing," she said to Maeve, and then gave a great smile to her girls. "You take care of yourselves, don't you girls? Do you have books? Norma, ask Maeve to get you a book."

Maeve had a stack of Henry James novels on her bedside table. *The Turn of the Screw*? Was that what they wanted? Our father came down the wide stairs in his best suit, eyes straight ahead. He was holding onto the banister, which meant his knee was hurting him, which meant he was in a bad mood. Would Andrea know that? "Time to get going," he said to her, but he didn't have a word for the rest of us, not a thank you or goodnight. He went straight for the door. I think he was ashamed of himself.

"You be perfect," Andrea sang over her shoulder and followed our father out. He wasn't waiting for her. The two little girls looked stricken until they could no longer see the top of their mother's hat, and then they started to cry.

"Jesus, Mary, and Joseph," Maeve said, and went off in search of Kleenex. In fairness to the girls, it wasn't as if they were wailing. In fact I think they were making their best effort not to cry, but it overtook them all the same. They sat down together in a single French chair. Bright dropped her head onto her sister's chest and Norma buried her face in her hands like they'd just gotten news of the Apocalypse. I asked them if they really did want a book or if they wanted to watch television or if they wanted ice cream. They wouldn't look at me. But then Maeve came back, handed each of them a tissue, and, speaking as if no one were crying at all, asked if they would like to see the house.

Even in their misery, it was clear that Norma and Bright heard her. They wanted to keep crying, as crying was the direction the evening was headed in, but they snuffled less in order to listen.

"The foyer is not the house," Maeve said. "It's just a little part of it. Please notice that you can see all the way through it. Front yard"—she pointed to the door where they'd come in, then turned in the opposite direction and pointed to the windows in the observatory—"back yard."

Bright sat up to look in both directions, and when Norma had leaked out the last of her tears she gave a tentative glance as well.

"You've seen the dining room and the drawing room." Maeve turned to me. "I think that's it, right? I don't think they've been in the kitchen."

"Why would they have been in the kitchen?" I was trying not to be sullen—the girls were the ones who were sullen—but I could think of about a hundred things I would have rather been doing with my evening than entertaining Andrea's children.

Maeve went off to find a flashlight and then opened the door to the basement. "Don't use the handrail," she said over her shoulder. "You'll get splinters. Just pay attention and look at your feet."

"I don't want to go to the basement," Bright said, peering into the darkness from the top step.

"Then don't," Maeve said. "We won't be long."

"Carry me," Bright suggested. Maeve didn't even answer that one.

Norma stopped two steps down. "Are there spiders?"

"Definitely." Maeve kept going. She was looking for the string that hung from the single lightbulb in the middle of the ceiling. The girls considered their options: up or down, and soon enough they followed her while I brought up the rear of the expedition. The girls were both in dresses, white tights, and patent leather shoes. The basement of the house was from another century. It bore no relationship to the structure that sat on top of it. In certain corners the walls devolved into piles of dirt. I had once found an arrowhead there. I would have dug around for more but the truth was I didn't like the basement myself.

"Why do you come down here?" Norma asked, half in horror, half in wonder.

"I'll show you." Maeve then turned her flashlight to the far corner of the room until the beam bounced off a small metal door in the wall. "That's the fuse box. Say a light burns out in the upstairs hall powder room and you know it's not the lightbulb. Then you have to come down here and check the fuse box. Sometimes if we're out of fuses we'll stick a penny behind it to make the old one work again. And if the heat goes out you have to come down here to check the furnace, and if there's no hot water you have to check the boiler. It could just be that the pilot light's blown out, in which case you've got to be careful lighting a match. There could be a gas leak. Boom," she said flatly.

Honestly, I had no idea.

Maeve went bravely ahead while Norma and Bright and I tried to stay in the general vicinity of her flashlight's beam. She opened a wooden door that creaked so loudly the girls pressed against me for a second, then Maeve pulled another string, illuminating yet another bare lightbulb. "This is the basement pantry where the extra food is kept, just in case you're here and get hungry. Sandy and Jocelyn make pickles and jams and stewed tomatoes. Pretty much anything that goes in a jar." We looked up at the shelves of immaculate jars, every one labeled with a date and organized by color, golden peach halves floating in syrup, raspberry jam. There were crates of sweet potatoes and russets and onions on the cold floor. I had never exactly thought of being rich until then, seeing all that food stored away in the presence of those little girls.

When finally we were ready to go up again, Bright stopped and pointed to the boxes stacked beneath the stairs. "What's in there?"

Maeve turned her flashlight to the musty tower of cardboard. "Christmas ornaments, decorations, that sort of thing."

Bright looked cheerful at the mention of Christmas and asked if she could open the boxes. It stood to reason that where there were ornaments, there would be presents, maybe even a present for her, but Maeve said no. "You can come back at Christmas and open them then."

I didn't say a word to Maeve that night when we brushed our teeth, and when we said our prayers I left her out.

"Come on," she said. "Don't be mad."

But I was mad. I got into bed mad. The tour had occupied the entire evening. She had shown them everything there was to see: the butler's pantry where dishes were kept and the table-cloths were rolled onto wide spools, the closet in the third floor bedroom with the tiny door in the back that led to an attic crawl space. She let them spin around in the ballroom, pretending to waltz. It had never once occurred to us to dance up there. "Who puts the ballroom on the third floor?" Norma had asked.

Maeve explained that when the house was built a third floor ballroom was considered the height of fashion. "A fad, really," she said. "It didn't last. But once you've put a ballroom on the third floor it's pretty much impossible to move it." Maeve showed them every last bedroom in the house. Norma and Bright both agreed that Maeve's room was best, and they sat in her window seat while Maeve closed the draperies over them. The girls squealed with laughter and then called, "No, don't!" when she opened the draperies up again. When the tour was over she brought a stepladder from the kitchen so they could take turns winding the grandfather clock, even though she knew I did that myself first thing Sunday morning.

Maeve sat beside me on my bed. "Think of how overwhelming the house must be to them, how overwhelming we must be, so if we showed them everything instead of just the nice things it would be, I don't know, friendlier?"

"It was very friendly," I said in a voice that was not friendly.

Maeve put her hand on my forehead, the way she did when I was sick. "They're little, Danny. I feel sorry for anyone who's that little."

She had put them in her own bed, and when our father came back with Andrea they each carried one sleeping girl down the stairs and took them out to Andrea's car. Maeve had to run down the stairs after them. They had forgotten the girls' shoes. Maeve told me Andrea was a little bit drunk.

To the long list of things my sister never got credit for, add this: she was good to those girls. If my father or Andrea was in the room, Maeve would politely ignore the children, but leave her alone with Norma and Bright and she was always doing something nice—teaching them to crochet or letting them braid her hair or showing them how to make tapioca. In return they followed her through the house like a pair of worshipful cocker spaniels.

Where we ate dinner on any given night was dictated by a complicated set of household laws put in place by Sandy and Jocelyn. If our father was home from work in time then the three of us ate in the dining room, Sandy serving us our plates while we breathed in the oily scent of the lemon furniture polish that hung in a fog over the massive table. But if our father stayed late or had other plans, Maeve and I ate in the kitchen. On those nights Sandy put a plate of food in the refrigerator under a sheet of waxed paper and our father would eat it in the kitchen when he came home. Or I assumed he did. Maybe he carried his plate to the dining room to sit alone. Of course, when Andrea and the girls were there, we ate in the dining room. If Andrea was there, Sandy not only served our dinner but she cleared the plates as well, whereas if Andrea wasn't there we each picked up our own plate at the end of the meal and took it back to the kitchen. None of this had been explained to us, but we all understood, just as we understood that on Sunday night Maeve and my father and I would gather in the kitchen at six o'clock to eat the cold supper that Sandy had left for us the day before. Andrea and the girls never ate with us on Sunday night. Alone in the house, the three of us would crowd around the little kitchen table and have a sensation of something close to being a family, if only because we were pushed together in a small space. As big as the Dutch House was, the kitchen was oddly small. Sandy told me that was because the only people ever meant to see the kitchen were the servants, and no one in the business of building grand estates ever gave a rat's hind-quarters (that was a very Sandy thing to say, *rat's hindquarters*) if the servants had the room to turn around. There was a little blue Formica table in the corner where Jocelyn sat and shelled peas or rolled out pie dough, the same table where Sandy and Jocelyn took their lunch and dinner. Maeve was always careful to wipe the table down when we were finished and put every-thing back the way we found it because she thought of the kitchen as belonging to Sandy and Jocelyn. What little space there was was mostly taken up by the huge gas range with nine burners, a warming drawer and two ovens, each big enough to roast a turkey. The rest of the house was a polar ice cap in the winter no matter how high Sandy stoked the fires, but the stove kept the little kitchen warm. Summers, of course, were a differ-ent story, but even in the summer I preferred the kitchen. The door out to the pool was always open and there was a fan in the corner that blew around the smell of whatever was baking. I could be floating on my back in the pool in the blinding midday sun and smell the cherry pie Jocelyn had in the oven.

On the Sunday evening after Andrea's daughters had been tossed in our laps, I was watching Maeve carefully, thinking that something about her was definitely off. I could read her blood sugar like the weather. I knew when she wasn't listening to me anymore and was just about to keel over. I was always the first one to notice when she was sweaty or pale. Sandy and Jocelyn could see it too. They knew when she needed juice and when to give the shot themselves, but it took our father by sur-prise every single time. He was always looking at the space just over Maeve's head.

But in this case, it wasn't her sugar at all. While I had my eye on her, Maeve did the most astonishing thing I had ever known her to do: very casually, while spooning out potato salad, she told our father that it wasn't our responsibility to take care of Andrea's daughters.

He sat with this for a moment, chewing the bite of chicken he'd just put in his mouth. "Were you planning on doing something else last night?"

"Homework," Maeve said.

"On a Saturday?"

Maeve was pretty enough and popular enough that she would never have had to stay home on Saturday nights, but for the most part she did, and for the first time I realized it was because of me. She would never have left me alone in the house. "There was a lot of work this week."

"Well," my father said, "looks like you managed. You can still do your homework with the girls in the house."

"I didn't get any homework done on Saturday. I was entertaining the girls."

"But your homework is done now, isn't it? You won't embarrass yourself in school tomorrow."

"That isn't the point."

My father crossed his knife and fork on his plate and looked at her. "Then why don't you tell me the point?"

Maeve was ready for him. She'd thought it all out in advance. Maybe she'd been thinking about it since I objected to the tour. "They're Andrea's children and she should take care of them, not me."

My father tipped his head slightly towards me. "You look after him."

She looked after me morning, noon and night. Was that what she was saying? She didn't need two more children to take care of?

"Danny's my brother. Those girls have nothing to do with us." Everything my father had ever taught her was used against him now: *Maeve, sit up straight. Maeve, look me in the eye if you want to ask me for something. Maeve, get your hands out of your hair. Maeve, speak up, don't expect that anyone will do you the favor of listening if you don't trouble yourself to use your voice.*

"But if the girls were your family, you wouldn't mind?" He lit a cigarette at the table with food still on his plate, an act of aggressive incivility I had never before witnessed.

Maeve just stared at him. I could hardly believe the way she held his gaze. "They're not."

He nodded his head. "When you live under my roof and eat my food I suppose you can trouble yourself to look after our guests when I ask you to."

There was a drip coming from the kitchen faucet. *Drip, drip, drip.* It made an unbelievable racket, echoing off the walls just like the renters said when they complained about their own faucets. I had watched my father change enough washers to think I'd have no problem doing it myself. I wondered, were I to get up from the table and look for a wrench, if either of them would notice I was gone.

"You didn't ask me," Maeve said.

My father was pushing back his chair but she beat him to it. She got up from the table, her napkin still tight in her fist, and left the room without asking to be excused.

My father sat for a while in his customary silence then put out his cigarette on his bread plate. He and I finished our meal, though I don't know how I stood it. When we were done, he went to the library to watch the news and I cleared the table and rinsed and stacked the dishes in the sink for Jocelyn to wash in the morning. It was Maeve's job to clean up after dinner but I did it. My father had forgotten about dessert. There were lemon bars in a shallow dish in the refrigerator and I cut one for myself and got an orange for Maeve and took them both upstairs on a single plate.

She was in her room, sitting on the window seat with her long legs straight out in front of her. She had a book in her lap but she wasn't reading it, she was looking out at the garden. The room was angled to the west while not facing west directly, and the way the last bit of light fell over her, she looked like a painting.

I handed her the orange and she dug in her nails to open it up. She bent her knees so I could sit down in front of her. "This doesn't bode well for us, Danny," she said. "You might as well know that."

CHAPTER 4

S IX WEEKS AFTER she left for her freshman year at Barnard, Maeve was summoned back to Elkins Park for the wedding. Our father married Andrea in the drawing room beneath the watchful eyes of the VanHoebeeks. Bright dropped handfuls of pink rose petals on the Spanish Savonnerie rug while Norma leaned against her mother and held two wedding bands on a pink velvet pillow. Maeve and I stood with the thirty or so guests. That was when we learned that Andrea also had a mother, a sister, a brother-in-law who sold insurance, and a handful of friends who tipped back their heads to gape at the dining-room ceiling while the cake was being served. (The dining room ceiling was painted a shade of blue both deep and intense, and was covered in intricate configurations of carved leaves that had been painted gold, or, more accurately, the leaves had been gilded. The gilt leaves were arranged in flourishes which were surrounded by circles of gilt leaves within squares of gilt leaves. The ceiling was more in keeping with Versailles than Eastern Pennsylvania, and when I was a child I found it mortifying. Maeve and my father and I made a point of keeping our eyes on our plates during dinner.) Sandy and Jocelyn served champagne at the reception, wearing matching black uniforms with white collars and cuffs that Andrea had bought for the occasion. "We look like matrons at a women's penitentiary," Jocelyn said, holding up her wrists. Maeve came back to the kitchen every time another bottle of champagne needed to be opened because she had announced with great bravado that popping corks was pretty much the first thing she'd learned to do in college. Champagne was just a loaded gun as far as Sandy and Jocelyn were concerned.

The wedding was held on a fall day of such brightness that the light seemed to be coming not just from the sun but from the grass and the leaves. All of the windows in the back of the house were triple hung and went to the floor, and for the occasion my father took the trouble of opening every last one of them, something I'd never seen done before. Open, the windows made a dozen doors onto the back terrace leading to the pool, which had been filled with water lilies. Who knew that water lilies could be rented for the day? Everyone was going on about how beautiful it all was: the house and the flowers and the light, even the woman who played the piano in the observatory was beautiful, but Maeve and Sandy and Jocelyn and I knew that all of it was wasted.

Our father couldn't marry Andrea at Immaculate Conception or ask Father Brewer to come to the house to marry them because he was divorced and she wasn't Catholic, which made it seem like they weren't really getting married at all. The ceremony was performed by a judge that none of us knew, a man my father had paid to come to the house to do the job, the way you'd pay an electrician. When it was over, Andrea kept holding up her glass to the light, remarking on how the champagne matched the color of her dress exactly. For the first time I was able to see how pretty she was, how happy and young. My father was forty-nine on the day of his second wedding, and his new wife in her champagne satin was thirty-one. Still, Maeve and I had no idea why he married her. Looking back, I have to say we lacked imagination.

* * *

"DO YOU THINK it's possible to ever see the past as it actually was?" I asked my sister. We were sitting in her car, parked in front of the Dutch House in the broad daylight of early summer. The linden trees kept us from seeing anything except the linden trees. I had thought the trees were enormous when I was young but they'd kept right on growing. Maybe one day they'd grow into the wall of Andrea's dreams. The car windows were rolled down and we each kept an arm out—Maeve's left, my right—while we smoked. I had finished my first year of medical school at Columbia. It would be the summer we would quit smoking, more or less, but on this particular day we were still only thinking about it.

"I see the past as it actually was," Maeve said. She was looking at the trees.

"But we overlay the present onto the past. We look back through the lens of what we know now, so we're not seeing it as the people we were, we're seeing it as the people we are, and that means the past has been radically altered."

Maeve took a drag off her cigarette and smiled. "I *love* this. Is this what they're teaching you in school?"

"Introduction to Psychiatry."

"Tell me you're going to be a shrink. It would be so beneficial."

"Do you ever think about going to see a psychiatrist?" This would have been 1971. Psychiatry was very much the rage.

"I don't need a psychiatrist because I can see the past clearly, but if you need to practice on someone, then by all means, be my guest. My psyche is your psyche."

"Why aren't you at work today?"

Maeve looked completely surprised. "What kind of stupid question is that? You just got here. I'm not going to work."

"Did you call in sick?"

"I told Otterson you were coming home. He doesn't care when I'm there. I get everything done." She tapped her ashes out the window. Maeve had worked as a bookkeeper for Otterson's ever since she'd graduated from college. They packaged and shipped frozen vegetables. My sister had won the math medal at Barnard. She had a higher cumulative GPA than the guy who'd won the math medal at Columbia that year, a sweet fact she learned from the guy's sister who was also Maeve's friend. With all of her knowledge and ability, she not only managed the payroll and calculated the taxes, she improved the delivery system, ensuring that bags of frozen corn would be quickly ferried to the grocers' freezers throughout the Northeast.

"Are you always going to work there? You should go back to school."

"We're talking about the past, doctor, not the future. You need to stay on point."

I tapped at my cigarette. Andrea was the past I wanted to talk about, but Mrs. Buchsbaum came out of her house to check the mail and saw us sitting there. She came straight to my open window and leaned in. "Danny, you're home!" she said. "How's Columbia?"

"It's like it was before, only harder." I had gone to Columbia as an undergraduate also.

"Well, I know this one is happy to see you." She nodded her head to Maeve.

"Hi, Mrs. Buchsbaum," Maeve said.

Mrs. Buchsbaum put her hand on my arm. "You need to find

your sister a boyfriend. There's got to be some nice doctor at the hospital who doesn't have time to look for a wife. A nice tall doctor."

"My criteria go beyond height," Maeve said.

"Don't misunderstand me: I always love to see her back in the neighborhood, but still, it worries me." Mrs. Buchsbaum was speaking only to me, as if she and I were in our own private section of the car. "She shouldn't just be sitting out here by herself. Some people may get the wrong impression. She's welcome, of course, I don't mean that."

"I know," I said. "It worries me, too. I'll talk to her."

"And this one across the street." Mrs. Buchsbaum gestured vaguely towards the linden trees with her forehead. "Nothing. When she drives by she does not wave. She does not acknowledge that anyone else is here. I think she must be a very sad person."

"Or not," Maeve said.

"I see the girls sometimes. Do you see the girls? They have better manners. If you ask me, they're the ones to feel sorry for."

I shook my head. "We don't see them."

Mrs. Buchsbaum squeezed my forearm and then waved goodbye to Maeve. "You can always come in the house," she said, and we thanked her as she walked away.

"Mrs. Buchsbaum corroborates my memory of the past," Maeve said when we were alone again.

*　*　*

AFTER ANDREA AND the girls had moved into the Dutch House and Maeve was back at school, my father and I were closer. My care had always been my sister's responsibility, and now that she was gone he took an unexpected interest in my schoolwork and my basketball games. No one thought that Maeve's role in my life was transferable to Andrea. The real question was to what extent I, at eleven, was old enough to lead an unsupervised life. Sandy and Jocelyn did their part as always, keeping me fed and telling me when I was not allowed to go outside without a hat. They had keen antennae, both of them, for my loneliness. I could be doing homework in my room and Sandy would knock on the door. "Come study downstairs," she would say, then turn around without giving me the chance to answer. I would go, algebra book in hand. In the kitchen, Jocelyn would turn off her little radio and pull out a chair for me.

"Everybody thinks better around food." She sliced off the heel from a loaf of bread she'd made and buttered it for me. I have always been partial to the heel.

"We got a postcard from Maeve," Sandy said, and pointed to a card caught to the refrigerator with a magnet, the Barnard library covered in snow. The fact that the card was displayed was proof that Andrea never went in the kitchen. "She says we should keep feeding you."

Jocelyn nodded. "We hadn't planned to feed you once she left, but if Maeve says we have to then we have to."

Maeve wrote me long letters, telling me about New York and her classes and her roommate, a girl named Leslie who worked the dinner shift in the cafeteria every night as part of her financial aid package and then fell asleep in her clothes while she tried to study in bed. Maeve gave no indication that school was difficult or that she was homesick, though she always said she missed me. Now that she wasn't around to help me with my homework, I wondered for the first time who had ever helped her when she was young. Fluffy? I doubted it. I sat down at the kitchen table and opened my book.

Sandy looked over my shoulder. "Let me see that. I used to be good in math."

"I've got it," I said.

"You only think you want to get rid of your sister," Jocelyn said, clapping her hand on my shoulder in a firm manner so as not to embarrass me. "Then when she's gone it turns out you miss her."

Sandy laughed and swatted Jocelyn with a dish towel.

She was only right about half of it. I had never wanted to get rid of Maeve. "Do you have a sister?" I asked Jocelyn.

Sandy and Jocelyn had both been laughing and then at the same time they stopped. "Are you kidding me?" Jocelyn asked.

"I don't think so," I said, wondering what had been funny and then not funny, but in the second before they could correct me, I saw it: the similarity in these two women I had known before knowing.

Sandy cocked her head. "Danny, seriously? You didn't know we were sisters?"

In that moment I could have told them all the ways they favored each other and all the ways they looked nothing alike, but it wouldn't have mattered. I had never wondered who they were related to or who they went home to. All I knew was that they cared for us. I remembered Sandy being gone for two weeks when her husband was sick and then again for a few days when he died. "I didn't know."

"That's because I'm so much prettier," Jocelyn said. She was trying to be funny, to let me off the hook, but I couldn't see that one was prettier than the other. They were younger than my father and older than Andrea but I couldn't narrow it down any further than that. I knew not to ask. Jocelyn was taller and thinner, her hair an unnatural shade of blond, whereas Sandy, whose thick brown hair was always held back with two barrettes, maybe had the nicer face. Her cheeks were pink and she had very pretty eyebrows, if such a thing were even possible. I didn't know. Jocelyn was married, Sandy a widow. Both of them had children, I knew that because Maeve gave them whatever clothes we'd outgrown. I knew because when one of their children was really sick they didn't come to work. Did I ask them when they came back, who was sick? Is she better now? I did not. I liked them both so much, Sandy and Jocelyn. I felt terrible for failing them.

Sandy shook her head. "Boys," she said, and with that single word excused me from all responsibility.

There was a phone at the front desk of the dorm where Maeve lived. I had the number memorized. If I called her, some girl would be dispatched to the third floor to knock on her door and see if she was in, which she usually wasn't because Maeve liked to study in the library. That whole transaction to find out she wasn't there and then leave a message took at least seven minutes—approximately four minutes longer than my father thought a long-distance call should last. So while I was desperate to talk to my sister and ask her if she knew—and if she did know then ask her how she'd neglected to tell me—I didn't call. I went into the drawing room where I stood in front of her portrait, cursing quietly to myself under her benevolent ten-year-old gaze. I resolved to wait until Saturday and ask my father instead. With every passing day the similarities between Sandy and Jocelyn became glaringly obvious: I saw it every morning as they stood side by side in the kitchen when I left to catch the school bus, I saw it in the way they waved like a couple of synchronized swimmers, and of course they had exactly the same voice. I realized I had never known which one of them was calling for me when I was upstairs. What could have been wrong with me that I'd missed all that?

"What difference does it make?" my father said when finally it was Saturday and we were off to collect the rent.

"But you *knew*."

"Of course I knew. I hired them, or your mother hired them. Your mother was always hiring people. First there was Sandy and then a couple of weeks later Sandy said that her sister needed a job, so we wound up with the pair. You've always been perfectly nice to them. I don't see the problem."

The problem, I wanted to say, was that I was asleep to the world. Even in my own house I had no idea what was going on. My mother hired them because she knew they were sisters, meaning she was a good person. I didn't even know they were sisters, meaning I was a toad. But that's me layering the present onto the past. At the time, I couldn't have begun to say why I was so upset. For weeks I tried to avoid Sandy and Jocelyn whenever I could, but that was impossible. Finally, I resolved to believe that I had always known who they were to each other, and that I had forgotten.

Sandy and Jocelyn had always run the house with complete autonomy. Maybe on occasion we would tell them how nice it would be to have beef stew with dumplings again, or that wonderful apple cake, but even that was rare. They knew what we liked and they gave it to us without our needing to ask. We never ran out of apples or crackers, there were always stamps in the left-hand drawer of the library desk, clean towels in the bathroom. Sandy ironed not only our clothes but our sheets and pillowcases. There was always a bright row of silver-topped insulin bottles that shivered on the refrigerator door whenever Maeve was home. They sterilized syringes, back in the day before they were disposable. We would never tell them the laundry needed doing or a floor needed cleaning because everything was done before we'd had the chance to notice.

All of that changed after Andrea arrived. She made weekly menus for Jocelyn to follow and gave her opinion on every course: there wasn't enough salt in the soup; she had given the girls too many mashed potatoes. How could they be expected to eat so many mashed potatoes? Why was Jocelyn serving cod when Andrea had specifically told her sole? Could she not have troubled herself to check another market? Did Andrea have to do everything? Every day she worked to find something extra for Sandy to do, dusting the shelves in the pantry or washing the curtain sheers. I no longer heard Sandy and Jocelyn talking to each other in the halls. I no longer heard Jocelyn's spectacular whistling when she arrived at the house in the morning. They were no longer allowed to call up the stairs to ask a question, they were to walk up and find us like civilized people. That's what Andrea said. Sandy and Jocelyn made it a point to be less visible, more civilized, to work wherever we were not. Or maybe that was me. I was in my bedroom more after Maeve left.

There were six bedrooms on the second floor of the house: my father's room, mine, Maeve's, a sunny room with twin beds where Bright and Norma slept, a room for the guests we never had, and the last room, which had been made into a household office. There was also a sort of sitting area at the top of the stairs where no one had ever sat until Norma and Bright showed up. They seemed to love to sit at the top of the stairs.

Andrea announced her plans for the reconfiguration one night at dinner. "I'm going to move Norma into the room with the window seat," she said.

My father and I could only look at her while Sandy, who was refilling the water glasses, took a step back from the table.

Andrea noticed nothing. "Norma's the oldest girl now. That's the room for the biggest girl."

Norma's mouth opened a bit. I could see that all of this was news to her. If she had wanted to be in Maeve's room it was because she wanted to be with Maeve.

"Maeve's coming home again," my father said. "She's only gone to New York."

"And when she comes back to visit she'll have a beautiful room on the third floor. Sandy will see to that, won't you, Sandy?"

But Sandy didn't answer. She held the water pitcher to her chest as if to keep herself from throwing it.

"I don't think we need to do this now," my father said. "There's no shortage of places to sleep around here. Norma can have the guest room if she wants it."

"The guest room is for our guests. Norma will sleep in the room with the window seat. It's the nicest bedroom in the house, the nicest view. It's silly to hold it as a shrine for someone who doesn't live here. Honestly, I thought that maybe we should take the room ourselves but the closet isn't very big. Norma has such little dresses. The closet will be fine for you, won't it?"

Norma nodded slowly, both horrified by her mother and mesmerized by the thought of that window seat, those wonderful drapes that could close a person off from everything.

"I want to sleep in Maeve's room," Bright said. Bright hadn't adjusted to living in so much space and she clung to her sister in the way I had clung to mine.

"You'll each have your own room, and Norma will let you visit," her mother said. "Everyone will adjust just fine. It's like your father said, this house is big enough for everyone to have her own room."

And with that the matter was closed. I never said a thing. I looked at my father, who was apparently now the father of Norma and Bright as well, hoping he would give it another shot, but he let it go. Andrea was a very pretty woman. He could give her her way now or he could wait and give her her way later, but either way, she was going to get what she wanted.

All of this happened around the time I'd fallen in love with one of the VanHoebeek daughters, or rather with her portrait, which I called Julia. Julia had narrow shoulders and yellow hair held back by a green ribbon. Her portrait hung in a bedroom on the third floor of the Dutch House above a bed no one ever slept in. With the exception of Sandy, who ran the vacuum and wiped things down with a dust rag on Thursdays, no one but me set foot up there. I believed that Julia and I were true lovers thwarted by the misalignment of our births. I worked myself into such a state over the injustice of it all that I once made the error of calling my sister at Barnard to ask if she had ever wondered about the girl whose painting hung in the third-floor bedroom, the girl with the gray-green eyes who was one of the VanHoebeek daughters.

"A daughter?" Maeve said. I was lucky to have caught her on the phone. "They didn't have any daughters. I think that's Mrs. VanHoebeek when she was a girl. Take the painting downstairs and look at them together. I think they're both her."

My sister was fully capable of teasing me until I could have bled from my ears, but just as often she spoke as if we were equals, giving me an honest answer to any question. I could tell by her voice she wasn't joking, or even particularly paying attention to what I had asked. I ran up the turning staircase to the third floor and stood on the unused bed to lift the carved gilt frame of my beloved off the wall (the frame was grander than what she would have wanted and not as grand as what she deserved). My Julia was *not* Mrs. VanHoebeek. But when I carried the painting downstairs to lean it on the mantelpiece, it was clear that Maeve was right. They were paintings of the same woman seated at either end of her life, old Mrs. VanHoebeek with the black silk buttons marching up to her neck and young Julia caught in a breeze. And really, even if it wasn't the same woman, such a likeness made it clear how one day the daughter would become the mother. Then Jocelyn came around the corner and caught me standing there looking at the two paintings together. She shook her head. "Time flies," she said.

Sandy and Jocelyn moved Maeve's things up to the third floor. At least the room faced the back garden like her old room did. At least the view would be more or less the same and arguably even better: fewer branches, more leaves. But the windows were dormers, of course, and there was no window seat. The new room was also a fraction of the size, and under the eaves so the ceiling sloped. As tall as Maeve was she'd be hitting her head every other minute.

The whole depressing enterprise of turning Maeve's room into Norma's room took longer than anyone could have imagined, since once Maeve's things were out Andrea wanted the place painted, and after it was painted she changed her mind and started bringing home books of wallpaper. She shopped for a new bedspread, a new rug. For a couple of weeks the redecoration was all anyone heard about, but it wasn't until Maeve came home for Thanksgiving that I realized none of us had been brave enough to inform my sister of her exile. Surely that was my father's job, and surely the rest of us would have known that he would never do it. Maeve was in the foyer, swinging me around, kissing Sandy and Jocelyn, kissing the little girls, and suddenly we all understood that she was about to go upstairs and find a raft of dolls spread across what had been her bed. In that moment it was Andrea, always the general, who showed presence of mind.

"Maeve, we've changed some things around since you've been gone. You're on the third floor now. It's very nice."

"The attic?" Maeve asked.

"The third floor," Andrea repeated.

My father picked up her suitcase. He had nothing to say on the subject but at least he was willing to go up there with her. What with his knee that bothered him on stairs, our father never went to the third floor. Maeve still had her red coat on, she was wearing gloves. She laughed. "It's just like *The Little Princess*!" she said. "The girl loses all of her money and so they put her in the attic and make her clean the fireplaces." She turned to Norma. "No big ideas for you, Miss. I will not be cleaning your fireplace."

"That's still my job," Sandy said. I hadn't heard Sandy get in on a joke in months, if there was in fact anything funny about Maeve moving to the third floor.

"Well, let's go then," Maeve said to our father. "It's a long hike. We should get started if we're going to make it back in time for supper. Something smells good." She looked at Bright. "Is it you?"

Bright laughed but then Norma ran out of the room in tears, suddenly understanding what taking Maeve's room might mean to Maeve. Maeve watched her go and I could see on her face she wasn't sure whom she should be comforting: Norma? Sandy? Me? Our father had her bag and was already heading up. After a moment's hesitation she followed him. In truth they were gone for a very long time, and no one went up to the third floor to rush them, to tell them that dinner was on the table and we were waiting.

CHAPTER 5

Maeve came home again for Christmas that year but she stayed only a few days. She'd been invited to a friend's house in New Hampshire to ski and could get a ride up with another Barnard girl who lived in Philadelphia. They were rich girls, all of them. Smart, popular girls who knew how to work a slope and aspired to read *The Red and the Black* in French. When she found out the dorms wouldn't be closed at Easter, Maeve decided to stay at school. Plenty of her friends lived in the city, and there were always invitations to go to dinners. Besides, she had work to do. She could go to Easter Mass at St. Patrick's and walk down Fifth Avenue with girls who did exactly that every year. No one could have blamed her, but I blamed her all the same. How was I supposed to get through Easter without her?

"Take the train into the city," she said on the phone. "I'll pick you up. I'll call Dad at work and get it set. You can manage the train by yourself."

I felt older than my friends at school, the ones with two parents and normal-sized houses. I looked older, too. I was the tallest person in my class now. "Boys with tall sisters wind up being tall boys," Maeve had said, and she was right. Still, I wasn't sure my father would let me go to New York by myself.

Even if I was tall and a good student, even though I largely fended for myself on any given day, I was still only twelve.

But my father surprised me, saying he would drive me to New York himself and let me come home on the train. Barnard was about two and a half hours by car. My father said we would pick Maeve up and the three of us would have lunch, then he would drive back to Elkins Park without me. It sounded so nostalgic when he said it, *the three of us*, as if we had once been a unit instead of just a circumstance.

Andrea caught wind of the plan and announced at dinner that she would ride along. There were plenty of things she needed in the city. But after she thought about it some more she said the girls should come too, and that after they dropped me off at Maeve's, my father could take them sightseeing. "The girls still haven't been to New York, and you're from there!" Andrea said, as if he'd conspired to keep New York from them. "We'll take the boat out to see the Statue of Liberty. Wouldn't that be something?" she asked the girls.

I hadn't been to New York either but I wasn't about to bring that up for fear I'd be seen as asking to tag along. By the time Sandy brought dessert, Andrea was talking about making reservations at a hotel and going to a show. Did my father know anyone who could get tickets to *The Sound of Music*?

"Why do you always wait until the last minute to make plans?" she asked him, then went on to discuss the possibility of lining up some interviews with portrait artists. "We need to have the girls' portraits painted."

I studied the final smear of the rhubarb crisp on my plate. It didn't matter. I was only missing lunch, that ridiculous notion of the three of us. I was still getting my ride to see Maeve, and that was all I really wanted. It didn't matter who was in the car. Disappointment comes from expectation, and in those days I had no expectation that Andrea would get anything less than what she wanted.

But in the morning, my father pushed through the swinging kitchen door while I was still eating my cereal. He tapped two fingers on the table just in front of my bowl. "Time to go," he said. "Right now." Andrea was nowhere in evidence. The girls were still in Maeve's room (they slept there together, as per Bright's prediction), Sandy and Jocelyn had yet to arrive. I didn't ask him what had happened, or remind him that his wife and her daughters were supposed to come along. I didn't go and get the book I planned to read on the train coming home or tell him we were supposed to leave two hours from now. I left my bowl of half-eaten Cheerios on the table for Sandy to find, and followed him out the door. We were ditching Andrea. Easter was late that year, and the morning was flush with the insane sweetness of hyacinth. My father was walking fast and his legs were so long that even with his bad knee I had to run to keep up. We went beneath the long trellis of wisteria that had yet to bloom, and all the way to the garage I thought, *Escape, escape, escape.* We beat the word into the gravel with every step.

I could scarcely imagine the courage it required to tell Andrea she couldn't come with us, and she in turn must have started the kind of argument he found untenable. All that mattered to him was getting out of the house before she came downstairs to make another point in her case, and with that imperative, we fled. We were in the car hours earlier than we had planned.

If I asked my father a question when he was quiet, he would say he was having a conversation with himself and that I shouldn't interrupt. I could tell he was having one of those conversations now, so I looked out the car window at the glorious morning and thought about Manhattan and my sister and all the fun we were going to have. I wouldn't ask Maeve to take me to see the

Statue of Liberty, Maeve got sick on boats, but I wondered if I could talk her into the Empire State Building.

"You know I used to live in New York," my father said once we were on the Pennsylvania Turnpike.

I said I guessed I did. What I didn't say was that Andrea had just brought it up at the dinner table.

Then he put on his turn signal to work his way towards the exit. "We've got plenty of time. I'll show you."

For the most part, what I knew about my father was what I saw: he was tall and thin with weathered skin and hair the color of rust, the color of my hair. All three of us had blue eyes. His left knee was slow to bend, worse in the winter and when it rained. He never said a word about it but it was easy enough to tell when it hurt him. He smoked Pall Malls, put milk in his coffee, worked the crossword puzzle before reading the front page. He loved buildings the way boys loved dogs. When I was eight years old, I asked my father at the dinner table if he was going to vote for Eisenhower or Stevenson. Eisenhower was running for a second term and all the boys in school were for him. My father clicked the point of his knife against his plate and told me I was *never* to ask a question like that, not of him, not of anyone. "It may be fine for boys to speculate on whom they might vote for because boys can't vote," he said. "But to ask an adult such a question is to violate a man's right to privacy." In retrospect, I imagine my father was horrified that I might think there was any chance he'd vote for Stevenson, but I didn't know that at the time. What I knew was that you had to touch a hot stove only once. Here are the things I talked to my father about when I was a boy: baseball—he liked the Phillies. Trees—he knew the name of every one, though he would chastise me for asking about the same kind of tree more than once. Birds—likewise. He kept feeders in the backyard and could easily identify all of his customers. Buildings—be it their structural soundness, architectural details, property value, property tax, you name it—my father liked to talk about buildings. To list the things I didn't ask my father about would be to list the stars in heaven, so let me throw out one: I did not ask my father about women. Not women in general and what you were supposed to do with them, and definitely not women in the particular: my mother, my sister, Andrea.

Why it was that this day should have been different I couldn't have said, though surely the fight with Andrea must have had something to do with it. Maybe that, along with the fact he was going back to New York where he and my mother were from, and he was going to see Maeve in school for the first time, prompted a wave of nostalgia in him. Or maybe it was nothing more than what he told me: we had extra time.

"All of this was different," he said to me as we drove from street to street in Brooklyn. But Brooklyn wasn't so different from neighborhoods I knew in Philadelphia, neighborhoods where we collected rent on Saturdays. There was just more of everything in Brooklyn, a feeling of density that stretched in every direction. He slowed the car to crawl, pointed. "Those apartment buildings? When I lived in the neighborhood those were wood. They took the old ones down, or there was a fire. The whole block. That coffee shop was there—" He pointed out Bob's Cup and Saucer. The people at the window counter were finishing a very late breakfast, some of them reading the paper and others staring out at the street. "They made their own crullers. I've never found anything like them. On Sunday after church there'd be a line down the block. See that shoe shop? Honest Shoe Repair. That's always been there." He pointed again, a shop window barely wider than the door itself. "I went to school with the kid whose father owned it. I bet if we walked in right now he'd be there, banging new soles onto shoes. That would be some sort of life."

"I guess," I said. I sounded like an idiot but I wasn't sure how to take it all in.

He turned the car at the corner and again at the light, and then we were on Fourteenth Avenue. "Right there," he said, and pointed to the third floor of a building that looked like every other building we'd passed. "I lived there, and your mother was a block back that way." He jerked his thumb over his shoulder.

"Where?"

"Right behind us."

I kneeled on the seat and looked out the back window, my heart in my throat. My mother? "I want to see," I said.

"It's just like all the other ones."

"It's still early." It was Maundy Thursday, and the people who went to Mass had either gone early or they would go late, after work. The only people walking around were women out doing their shopping. We were double parked, and just as my father was about to tell me no, the car right in front of us pulled out like it was issuing an invitation.

"Well, what am I supposed to say to that?" my father said, and took the space.

The day had turned overcast since we left Pennsylvania but it wasn't raining and we walked back down the street a block, my father limping slightly in the cold. "Right there. First floor."

The building looked like all the others, but to think that my mother had lived there made me feel like we had landed on the moon, it was that impossible. There were bars over the windows and I raised my hand to touch them.

"Those keep out the knuckleheads," my father said. "That's what your grandfather used to say. He put them on."

I looked at him. "My grandfather?"

"Your mother's father. He was a fireman. A lot of nights he slept at the station, so he put bars on the windows. I don't know if he needed them, though; not much happened back then."

My fingers curled around one of the bars. "Does he still live here?"

"Who?"

"My grandfather." I had never put those two words together before.

"Oh, heavens no." My father shook his head at the memory. "Old Jack's been dead forever. There was something wrong with his lungs. I don't know what. Too many fires."

"And my grandmother?" Again, the sentence astounded me.

I could tell by his face that this wasn't what he'd signed on for. He only wanted to drive through Brooklyn, show me the places he knew, the building where he had lived. "Pneumonia, not too long after Jack died."

I asked him if there were any others.

"You don't know this?"

I shook my head. He peeled my fingers off the window bar, not unkindly, and turned me back towards the car while he spoke. "Buddy and Tom died of the flu, and Loretta died having a baby. Doreen moved to Canada with some fellow she married, and James, James was my friend, he died in the war. Your mother was the baby of the family and she outlasted all of them, except maybe Doreen. I guess Doreen could still be up there in Canada."

I reached down deep to find something in myself I wasn't sure was there, the part of me that was like my sister. "Why did she leave?"

"The guy she married wanted to move," he said, not understanding. "He was from Canada or he got a job there. I can't remember which."

I stopped walking. I didn't even bother to shake my head, I just started again. It was the central question of my life and I had never asked before. "Why did my mother leave?"

My father sighed, sank his hands down in his pockets and raised his eyes to assess the position of the clouds, then he told me she was crazy. That was both the long and the short of it.

"Crazy how?"

"Crazy like taking off her coat and handing it to someone on the street who never asked her for a coat in the first place. Crazy like taking off *your* coat and giving it away too."

"But aren't we supposed to do that?" I mean, we didn't do it, but wasn't it the goal?

My father shook his head. "No. We're not. Listen, there's no sense wondering about your mother. Everybody's got a burden in life and this is yours. She's gone. You have to live with that."

After we were back in the car the conversation between us was done and we drove into Manhattan like two people who had never met. We made our way to Barnard and picked Maeve up right on time. She was waiting on the street in front of her dorm wearing her red winter coat, her black hair in a single heavy braid lying across her shoulder. Sandy was always telling Maeve she looked better when she braided her hair but at home she'd never do it.

I was overwhelmed by the need to talk to my sister alone but there was nothing to be done about it. If it had been up to me we would have said goodbye to our father on the spot and sent him home, but there was a plan for the three of us to have lunch. We went to an Italian restaurant Maeve knew not far from campus, where I was served a giant bowl of spaghetti with meat sauce, something Jocelyn never would have believed possible for lunch. My father asked Maeve about her classes and Maeve, basking in this rare light, told him everything. She was taking Calculus II and Economics, along with European History and a course on the Japanese novel. My father shook his head in disbelief over the novel part but offered no criticism. Maybe he was glad to see her, or maybe he was glad he wasn't standing on a street corner in Brooklyn talking to me, but for once in his life he gave his daughter his full attention. Maeve was in her second semester and he had no idea what her classes were, but I knew everything: *The Makioka Sisters* was her reward for having finished *The Tale of Genji*; her economics professor had written the textbook they used in class; she was finding Calculus II to be easier than Calculus I. I stuffed my mouth with spaghetti to keep myself from changing the subject.

When lunch was over, and it was over soon enough because my father had no patience for restaurants, we walked him back to the car. I didn't know if I was supposed to come home that night or the next day. We hadn't talked about it, and I hadn't brought anything with me, but there was no mention of my return. I was Maeve's again and that was that. He gave her a quick embrace and slipped some money in her coat pocket, then Maeve and I stood together and waved goodbye as he pulled away. A cold rain had blown in during lunch, and while it wasn't heavy, Maeve said we should take the subway to the Metropolitan and see the Egyptian exhibit because there was no point in getting wet. After the Empire State Building, the subway was the thing I'd been most excited to see, and now I hardly paid attention as we went down the stairs.

Maeve stopped and gave me a hard look just before we got to the turnstile. She might have thought I was going to throw up, which wouldn't have been a bad guess. "Did you eat too much?"

I shook my head. "We went to Brooklyn." There must have

been some better way to tell her this but the morning was more than I knew how to shape into words.

"Today?"

There was a black metal gate in front of us, and on the other side of the gate was the platform for the train. The train came up and the doors opened and the people got off and got on but Maeve and I just stood there. Other people rushed past, trying to get through the turnstile in time. "We left too early. I think he and Andrea must have had a fight because she was going to come with us, Andrea and the girls, and then Dad came down alone and he was in a huge hurry to leave." I had started to cry when there was nothing to cry about. I was long past the age anyway. Maeve took me to a wooden bench and we sat there together and she fished a Kleenex out of her purse and handed it to me. She had her hand on my knee.

Once I'd told her the whole of the story I could see there wasn't much to it, but I couldn't stop thinking that all of the people who had lived in that apartment were dead now, except for the sister who went to Canada and our mother, and they could easily be dead too.

Maeve was very close. She'd eaten a peppermint from a bowl by the door in the restaurant. We both had. Her eyes weren't blue like mine. They were much darker, almost navy. "Could you find the street again?"

"It's Fourteenth, but I couldn't tell you how to get there."

"But you remember the coffee shop and the shoe repair, so we could find it." Maeve went to the man in the booth who sold tokens and came back with a map. She found Fourteenth Avenue and then figured out the train, then she gave the map back and gave me a token.

Brooklyn is a big place, bigger than Manhattan, and a person wouldn't think that a twelve-year-old boy who had never been there before could possibly find his way back to a single apartment building he'd seen for five minutes, but I had Maeve with me. When we got off the train she asked directions to Bob's Cup and Saucer, and once we were there I knew how to find it: a turn at the corner, a turn at the light. I showed her the bars our grandfather had put on the windows as a defense against knuckleheads, and for a while we stood there, our backs against the bricks. She asked me to tell her the names of the uncles and the aunts. I could remember Loretta and Buddy and James but not the other two. She said I shouldn't worry about it. When the rain got harder we walked back to Bob's. The waitress laughed when we asked for a cruller. She said they were gone by eight o'clock every morning. That was fine with us, seeing as how we weren't hungry. Maeve had a cup of coffee and I had hot chocolate. We stayed until we were warm and halfway dry.

"I can't believe he showed you where she lived," Maeve said. "All the years I asked him about her, about her family, about where she had gone, he'd never tell me anything."

"Because he thought it would kill you." I didn't like being in the position of defending my father to my sister but that was the case. Our mother's leaving had made Maeve sick.

"That's ridiculous. People don't die from information. He just didn't want to talk to me. One time when I was in high school I told him I was going to India to try to find her and you know what he said?"

I shook my head, stunned by the horrible thought of Maeve in India, both of them gone.

"He told me I needed to think of her as dead, that she probably *was* dead by now."

And still, as terrible as it was, I understood. "He didn't want you to go."

"He said, 'There are almost 450 million people in India now. Good luck with that.'"

The waitress came back and held up her pot of coffee but Maeve declined.

I thought about the bars on the windows of the apartment. I thought of all the knuckleheads in the world. "Do you know why she left?"

Maeve finished what was in her cup. "All I know for sure was that she hated the house."

"The Dutch House?"

"Couldn't stand it."

"She didn't say that."

"Oh, she did. She made it known every day. The only room she'd ever sit in was the kitchen. Whenever Fluffy would ask her a question, she'd say, 'Do whatever you think best. It's your house.' She was always saying it was Fluffy's house. It drove Dad to distraction, I remember that. She told me once if it were up to her she'd give the place to the nuns, let them turn it into an orphanage or an old folks' home. Then she said the nuns and the orphans and the old folks would probably be too embarrassed to live there."

I tried to imagine such a thing. Hate the dining-room ceiling, sure, but the entire house? There was no better house. "Maybe you misunderstood her."

"She said it more than once."

"Then she was crazy," I said, but as soon as I said it I was sorry.

Maeve shook her head. "She wasn't crazy."

When we got back to Manhattan, Maeve took me to a men's store and bought me extra underwear, a new shirt, and a pair of pajamas, then she got me a toothbrush at the drugstore next door. That night we went to the Paris Theater and saw *Mon*

Oncle. Maeve said she was in love with Jacques Tati. I was nervous about seeing a movie with subtitles but it turned out that nobody really said anything. After it was finished, we stopped for ice cream then went back to Barnard. Boys of every stripe were expressly forbidden to go past the dorm lobby, but Maeve just explained the situation to the girl at the desk, another friend of hers, and took me upstairs. Leslie, her roommate, had gone home for Easter break and so I slept in her bed. The room was so small we could have easily reached across the empty space and touched fingers. I slept in Maeve's room all the time when I was young, and I had forgotten how nice it was to wake up in the middle of the night and hear the steadiness of her breathing.

I ended up staying in New York for all of Friday and most of Saturday, and if Maeve ever called the house to let anyone know our plans, I wasn't there to witness it. She said she'd been studying too much to do all the tourist things she'd meant to, and so we went to the Museum of Natural History and the zoo in Central Park. We went to the top of the Empire State Building in spite of the rain and all we could see were the deep wet clouds we were standing inside. She walked me around the Columbia University campus and told me that this was where I should go to college. We went to Good Friday service at the Church of Notre Dame and the beauty of the building held my attention through nearly half of that interminable exercise. Maeve finally had to excuse herself and go out to the vestibule on the side of the church to give herself some insulin. She told me later that people probably thought she was a junkie in a sweater set. Late on Holy Saturday she took me to Penn Station. She said Dad would want me home for Easter, and anyway, we both had to go back to school on Monday. She bought me a ticket, promising that she would call the house and tell

Sandy when to meet me, making me promise I would call her as soon as I got home. Maeve gave the porter a tip and asked him to seat me next to the safest-looking person on the train, but as it turned out there were only a handful of us going to Philadelphia in the late afternoon of Holy Saturday and I had a whole row to myself. Maeve had bought me the book about Julius Caesar I had begged her for in Brentano's but I wound up keeping it on my lap and looking out the window the entire time. The train was past Newark before I realized I'd forgotten to show her the apartment building where Dad had grown up, and that she had forgotten to ask.

I hadn't thought about Andrea at all while I was gone, but now I wondered if there had been some god-awful fight. Then I remembered what my father had told me, that the things we could do nothing about were best put out of our minds. I gave it a try and found that it was easier than I imagined. All I did was watch the world shoot past the train window: towns then houses then trees then cows then trees then houses then towns, over and over again.

Sandy picked me up at the train station as Maeve had promised, and I told her all about the trip in the car. Sandy wanted to know how Maeve was doing, and about her dorm room, which I told her was very small. She asked me if I thought she was getting enough to eat. "She looked so skinny at Christmas."

"Do you think?" I asked. She seemed just the same to me.

When we got back to the house they were all eating dinner, and my father said, "Look who's back."

There was a setting at my usual place.

"I'm going to get a rabbit for Easter," Bright said to me.

"No you're not," Norma said.

"Let's wait for tomorrow and see what happens," Andrea said, not looking at me. "Eat your dinner."

Jocelyn was there, and she gave me a wink as she brought me my plate. She'd come over to help since Sandy had to get me at the station.

"Are there rabbits in New York City?" Bright asked. The girls were funny the way they treated me like I was already grown, closer to my father and Andrea in age and station than I was to them.

"Loads of them," I said.

"Did you see them?"

In fact, I had seen rabbits in an Easter window display at Saks Fifth Avenue. I told her how they hopped around the ankles of mannequins in fancy dresses, and how Maeve and I had stood out on the street with crowds of other people and watched them for a good ten minutes.

"Did you get to see the play?" Norma asked, and then Andrea did look up. I could tell how crushed she'd be to think that Maeve and I had done something she wanted to do.

I nodded. "There was a lot of singing but it was better than I thought it would be."

"How in the world did you get tickets?" my father asked.

"A friend of Maeve's at school. Her father works in the theater." I didn't have much experience lying in those days but it came naturally to me. No one at that table would have checked my story, and even if they had, Maeve would have backed me without a thought.

There were no more questions after that, so I kept the penguins at the Central Park Zoo and the dinosaur bones at the Museum of Natural History and Mon Oncle and the dorm room and all the rest of it to myself. I planned to tell my friend Matthew everything when we were in school on Monday. Matthew was half-crazed by the idea of seeing Manhattan. Andrea started up about tomorrow's Easter lunch and how busy she would be, even though Sandy had told me in the car that every bit of the cooking was done. I kept waiting for my father to catch my eye, to give me some small signal that things had changed between us, but it didn't come. He never asked me about my time with Maeve or the play I hadn't seen, and we never talked about Brooklyn again.

*   *   *

"DON'T YOU THINK it's strange we never see her?" I asked Maeve. I was in my late twenties then. I thought it might have happened once or twice.

"Why would we see her?"

"Well, we park in front of her house. It seems like we would have overlapped at some point." We had once seen Norma and Bright walking across the yard in their swimsuits but that was it, and that was ages ago.

"This isn't a stakeout. It's not like we're here all the time. We drop by every couple of months for fifteen minutes."

"It's more than fifteen minutes," I said, and it might well have been more than every couple of months.

"Whatever. We've been lucky."

"Do you ever think about her?" I didn't think of Andrea often, but there were times when we were parked in front of the Dutch House that she might as well have been in the back seat of the car.

"Sometimes I wonder if she's dying," Maeve said. "I wonder when she'll die. That's about it."

I laughed, even though I was pretty sure she wasn't joking. "I was thinking more along the lines of—I wonder if she's happy, I wonder if she ever met anyone."

"No. I don't wonder about that."

"She couldn't be very old. She could have found someone."

"She'd never let anyone in that house."

"Listen," I said, "she was horrible to us in the end, I'll grant you that, but sometimes I wonder if she just didn't know any better. Maybe she was too young to deal with everything, or maybe it was grief. Or maybe things had happened in her own life that had nothing to do with us. I mean, what did we ever know about Andrea? The truth is I have plenty of memories of her being perfectly decent. I just choose to dwell on the ones in which she wasn't."

"Why do you feel the need to say anything good about her?" Maeve asked. "I don't see the point."

"The point is that it's true. At the time I didn't hate her, so why do I scrub out every memory of kindness, or even civility, in favor of the memories of someone being awful?" The point, I wanted to say, was that we shouldn't still be driving to the Dutch House, and the more we kept up with our hate, the more we were forever doomed to live out our lives in a parked car on VanHoebeek Street.

"Did you love her?"

I let out a sound that could only be described as exasperation. "No, I didn't love her. Those are my two choices? I love her or I hate her?"

"Well," my sister said, "you're telling me you didn't hate her, so I just want to know what the parameters are. I think it's a ridiculous conversation to be having in the first place, if you want my opinion. Say there's a kid who lives next door, a kid you have no particular friendship with but no problems with either. Then one day he walks into your house and kills your sister with a baseball bat."

"Maeve, for the love of God."

She held up her hand. "Hear me out. Does that present fact obliterate the past? Maybe not if you loved the kid. Maybe if you loved the kid you'd dig in and try to find out what had happened, see things from his perspective, wonder what his parents had done to him, wonder if there wasn't some chemical imbalance. You might even consider that your sister could have played a role in the outcome—did she torment this boy? Was she cruel to him? But you'd only wonder about that if you loved him. If you only *liked* the kid, if he was never anything more to you than an okay neighbor, I don't see the point in scratching around for good memories. He's gone to prison. You're never going to see the son-of-a-bitch again."

I was doing my residency in internal medicine at Einstein College of Medicine in the Bronx, and every two or three weeks I took the train to Philadelphia. There wasn't enough time to spend the night but I never let an entire month go by without visiting. Maeve was always saying she thought she'd see more of me when medical school was over but that wasn't the case. There was no extra time in those days and I didn't want to spend the little of it I had sitting in front of the goddamn house, but that's where we wound up: like swallows, like salmon, we were the helpless captives of our migratory patterns. We pretended that what we had lost was the house, not our mother, not our father. We pretended that what we had lost had been taken from us by the person who still lived inside. There had already been a few cold nights and the leaves on the linden trees were starting to yellow.

"Okay," I said, "I'll drop it."

Maeve turned away from me and looked at the trees. "Thank you."

So alone I tried to remember the good in her: Andrea laughing with Norma and Bright; Andrea coming in to check on me once in the middle of the night after I had my wisdom teeth out, her standing in the door of my room, asking if I was okay;

a handful of moments early on when I saw her bring a lightness to our father, his briefly resting his hand against the small of her back. They were minuscule things, and in truth it made me tired to think of them, so I let my mind go back to the hospital, checking off the patients I would need to see tonight, preparing what I would say to them. I was back on call at seven.

CHAPTER 6

Maeve came home after she graduated, but there was never any talk of her moving back into the house. She'd scarcely been in residence since her exile to the third floor. Instead, she got herself a little apartment in Jenkintown, which was considerably cheaper than Elkins Park and not far from Immaculate Conception where we went to church. She took a job with a new company that shipped frozen vegetables. Her stated plan was to take a year or two off before going back to get her masters in economics or a law degree, but I knew she was hanging around to keep an eye on me for my last years of high school, give me something regular I could count on.

Otterson's Frozen Vegetables didn't know what hit them. After two months of working in the billing department, Maeve came up with a new invoice system and a new way of tracking inventory. Pretty soon she was preparing both the company's taxes and Mr. Otterson's personal taxes. The work was ridiculously easy for her, and she said that's what she wanted: a break. Maeve's friends from Barnard were taking breaks as well, spending a year in Paris or getting married or doing an unpaid internship at the Museum of Modern Art while their fathers footed the bill for their Manhattan apartments. Maeve always had her own definition of rest.

There was something like peace in those days. I was playing varsity basketball as a sophomore, or I should say I was sitting on the varsity bench, but I was happy to be there, earning my place in the future. I had plenty of friends and so plenty of places I could go after school, including Maeve's apartment. I wasn't trying to avoid being home, but like every other fifteen-year-old boy I knew, I found fewer reasons to be there. Andrea and the girls seemed to exist in their own parallel universe of ballet classes and shopping trips. Their orbit had drifted so far from mine that I almost never thought about them. Sometimes I would hear Norma and Bright in Maeve's room when I was studying. They would be laughing or fighting over a hairbrush or chasing each other up and down the stairs, but they were nothing more than sound. They never had friends over, just like Maeve and I never had friends over, or maybe they didn't have friends. I thought of them as a single unit: Norma-and-Bright, like an advertising agency consisting of two small girls. When I got tired of hearing them I turned on my radio and closed the door.

My father had spun away as well, making my own absence a convenience for everyone. He said it was because the suburbs were booming and he had an eye towards doubling his business, and while that was true, it also seemed pretty clear he had married the wrong woman. If we all kept to our own corners it was easier for everyone. Not just easier, happier, and the house gave us plenty of space in which to carry on our individual lives. Sandy served an early dinner to Andrea and the girls in the dining room and Jocelyn saved me a plate. When I came home from basketball practice I ate, regardless of the pizza I'd already had with friends. Sometimes I would ride my bike in the dark to take sandwiches to my father at his office, and I would eat again with him. He would unroll the huge white sheaves of architectural renderings and show me what the future held. Every commercial building going up from Jenkintown to Glenside had the name CONROY on a big wooden sign at the front of the construction site. Three Saturdays a month he would send me wherever I was needed—to carry lumber and hammer nails and sweep out the newly built rooms. The foundations were poured, the houses framed. I learned to walk on rafters while the regular workers, the guys who did not go home to their own mansions in Elkins Park, heckled me from below. "Better not fall there, Danny boy!" they'd call out, but once I'd learned to leap from board to board like they did, once I was talking about the electrical and the plumbing, they left me alone. I was cutting crown molding in the miter box by then. More than school or the basketball court, more than the Dutch House, I was at home on a building site. Whenever I could I'd work after school, not for the money—my father considered very few of my hours to be billable—but because I loved the smell and the noise. I loved being part of a building being made. On the first Saturday of the month, my father and I still made the rounds to collect the rents, but now we talked about scheduling the cement truck for one project while making someone else wait. There were never enough trucks, enough men, enough hours in the day for all we meant to accomplish. We talked about how far behind one project was and how another was due to come in right on time.

"The day you get your driver's license may well be the happiest day of my life," my father said.

"Are you sick of driving? You could teach me."

He shook his head, his elbow pointing out the open window. "It's a waste of time, that's all, both of us going out. Once you're sixteen you can collect the rent yourself."

That's the way it goes, I thought, admiring my own maturity. I would rather have kept the one Saturday a month with the two of us together in the car but I would take his trust instead. That was what it meant to grow up.

As it turned out, I got neither. He died when I was still fifteen.

I'm sorry to say I thought my father was old when he died. He was fifty-three. He was climbing the five flights of stairs in a nearly completed office building to check on some window flashing and caulk on the top floor that the contractor told him was leaking. The day was boiling hot, the tenth of September. The building was still a month away from having the electricity turned on, which meant no elevator and no air conditioning. There were lights rigged up in the stairwell that ran off a generator that only made it hotter. Mr. Brennan, who was the project manager, said it must have been a hundred degrees. My father complained about being out of shape when they passed the second floor, and after that he said nothing. He was never fast on account of his knee but on this day it took him twice as long. He was sweating through his suit jacket. Six steps short of his destination, he sat down without a word, threw up, and then fell straight forward, his head hitting the concrete stair, his long body following in a tumble. Mr. Brennan couldn't catch him, but he stretched him out on the landing as best he could and ran down the stairs and across the street to a pharmacy where he told the girl at the register to call an ambulance, then he rounded up four of the men working at the site and together they carried my father down the turns of the stairs. Mr. Brennan said he had never seen a man go as white, and Mr. Brennan had been in the war.

Mr. Brennan rode along in the ambulance, and when they got to the hospital, he called Mrs. Kennedy at my father's office. Mrs. Kennedy called Maeve. Some kid came into my geometry class and handed a folded note to the teacher, who read it to himself and then told me to get my things and go to the principal's office. No one comes into the middle of geometry and tells you to get your things because you're going to be a starter at the next basketball game. When I went down the hall I had only one thought and it was for Maeve. I was so sick with fear it was all I could do to make myself walk. She had run out of insulin or the insulin wasn't any good. Too much, not enough, either way it had killed her. Until that minute I never realized the extent to which I carried this fear with me everywhere, every minute of my life. I was the tallest boy in my class, and muscled up from basketball and construction. The principal's office was a glass-fronted room that opened onto the lobby and when I saw Maeve standing at the desk with her back to me, her unmistakable hair in a braid trailing down her back, I made a sound, something high and sharp that seemed to have come up from my knees. She turned around, everybody turned around, but I didn't care. I had asked God for one thing and God had given it to me—my sister wasn't dead. Maeve was crying when she put her arms around me and I didn't even ask her. Later she would say she assumed I knew because of the look on my face, but I had no idea. I didn't know until we got in the car and she said we were going to the hospital and that our father was dead.

We made a terrible mistake but even now it's hard for me to say exactly whose mistake it was. Mr. Brennan's? Mrs. Kennedy's? Maeve's? My own? Mrs. Kennedy made it to the hospital before us and was waiting with Mr. Brennan when we arrived. Mr. Brennan told us what had happened. He told us that he didn't know CPR. Hardly anyone knew CPR in those days. His wife was a nurse and she had told him he should take the class but he hadn't done it. There was such pain on his face that Maeve hugged him and Mr. Brennan leaned against her shoulder and cried.

They had kept our father in a small room off to the side of the emergency room so that we wouldn't have to go to the morgue. He was in a regular hospital bed, his tie and jacket gone, his blue shirt unbuttoned at the neck and stained with blood. His mouth was open in a way that made it clear to me his mouth could not be closed. His bare white feet were sticking out from the bottom of the sheet. I couldn't imagine where his shoes and socks had gone. I hadn't seen my father's feet in years, since whatever summer it was we had last gone to the lake. There was a terrible, bloodless cut on his forehead that had been crudely taped together. I didn't touch him, but Maeve leaned over and kissed his forehead just beside the bandage, then kissed it again, her long braid falling across his neck. She didn't seem to mind his open mouth but it was horrifying to me. She was so tender with him, and I found myself thinking that when he woke up I would tell him how good she was, how much she loved him. Or maybe I would tell him when I woke up. One of us was sleeping and I didn't know which one of us it was.

The nurse gave us too much time alone with him, and then the doctor came into the room and explained the nature of the death. He told us that the heart attack had happened very fast and that there was nothing that could have been done to save him. "Chances are he was dead before he fell. Even if it had happened right here in the hospital," he said, "chances are it wouldn't have been any different." This was before I knew that doctors could lie as a means of comfort. Without an autopsy, he was telling us nothing more than a likely story, but we clung to it without question. Maeve was given papers to sign and in return received his suit jacket and tie in a bag, along with a manila envelope containing his wallet, watch and wedding ring.

We were very young, and our father had died. To this day I don't think we were responsible. We came in the kitchen door and Sandy and Jocelyn were there and we told them what had happened. The second they started to cry I knew what we had done. Sandy had her arms around me and I twisted to get away from her. I had to find Andrea. It had to be me finding Andrea, she could not find us there, but as soon as I'd had the thought she walked into the kitchen, into the mess of the four of us and our collective, exclusive grief. She had heard the howling. Jocelyn turned and put her arms around her employer, something I would guarantee she'd not done before or since. "Oh, Mrs. Smith," was what she said.

The look of terror that came over Andrea then—that look has stayed with me all these years. Long after I could no longer see my father on his hospital bed, I could still see the fear on Andrea's face. She took a step back from us.

"Where are my girls?" she whispered.

Maeve shook her head the smallest bit, because of course by then she realized it too. "They're fine," she said, her voice barely coming out of her mouth. "It's Dad. We've lost Dad."

There was the plastic bag of his clothes on the kitchen table, the evidence against us. Later we would tell ourselves that we were sure Mrs. Kennedy had called her, but nothing had happened to make us think that. The truth was we had come this far and had never given Andrea a thought. Our cruelty became the story: not our father's death but how we had excluded her from it.

Had we done a better job would the outcome have been the same? Had Mr. Brennan called Andrea and not Mrs. Kennedy (but Mr. Brennan had never met Andrea, and had worked with Mrs. Kennedy for twenty years), had Mrs. Kennedy called Andrea and not Maeve (but Andrea was rude to Mrs. Kennedy on the phone every time she called our father at work, never saying one thing more than "Let me speak to my husband." Mrs. Kennedy would never have called Andrea. She told me as much at the funeral). Had Maeve left Otterson's and rushed to the Dutch House to tell Andrea instead of coming to the school to get me, or if we had left the school together and gone to pick her up, the three of us going to the hospital, where would we be now?

"Right here," Maeve would say. "We didn't make her who she is."

But I was never sure.

Andrea's hurt was her prize blue ribbon, and in return what I felt in those blinded days just after my father's death was not the grief for who I had lost but the shame over what I had done. Norma and Bright were solemn every minute they could remember to be, but they were still too young. The sadness was impossible for them to hold onto. Andrea kept them out of school the day after he died but on the next day they begged to go back. Home was so sad. I went back to school too, not wanting to be in the house with her. She bought twin plots in the Protestant cemetery and made clear her plans to bury him there beside the empty space where she planned to go to herself someday. That was when Maeve called Father Brewer. Andrea and the priest disappeared into the library for twenty-five minutes, the doors closed, and when they came out again my father's rights were restored. Andrea had agreed to have our father buried in the Catholic cemetery. She held that against us as well.

"He'll be all alone now," she said when she passed me in the hall. No preamble. "Just the way you want it. Well, good for you. I'll be damned if I'm going to spend eternity with a bunch of Catholics."

The day after they were married, Maeve and my father and

I were going off to Mass. Andrea was sitting alone in the dining room, and in an attempt to be friendly I asked my new stepmother if she and the girls wanted to come with us.

"You wouldn't catch me dead in that place," she said, and went on eating her soft-cooked eggs as if she had reminded me to take an umbrella.

"If she hates the Catholics so much you have to wonder why she married one," Maeve said as we were climbing into the car.

And my father laughed, a big-hearted laugh of the kind we rarely heard from him. "She wanted the Catholic's house," he said.

Contrary to what Maeve assumed, I thought about our mother very little when I was young. I didn't know her, and I found it hard to pine for a person or a time I couldn't remember. The family she left me with—a cook, a housekeeper, a doting sister and distant father—functioned to my advantage. Even when I looked at the few pictures of her that were squirreled away, the tall thin woman with a sharp jaw and dark hair was too much like Maeve to make me think there was something I had missed. But on the day of our father's funeral, my mother was all I could think of, and I longed for her comfort with an ache I could never have imagined.

The house was overburdened with flowers. Andrea didn't think we'd get enough, and so she ordered dozens of arrangements. If she'd been clever, she would have thought to forge some cards. Andrea had never understood our father's place in the community; the flowers poured in from everywhere, from the people at church and the men who worked construction, the people in his office and at the bank. There were flowers from cops and restaurateurs and teachers, people my father had done quiet favors for over the years. The flowers came from the tenants who paid their full rent every month, as well as the ones he had carried in lean times. For the most part they were people I knew, but there were also flowers sent from people who were well before my time, people who had moved away or bought houses of their own. Some of their names I recognized from the ledger. The flowers made a continuous blanket across every table and over the piano. They balanced on rented pedestals and stood on wire easels. The house was a garden of impossible pairings and sudden explosions of height. There was no place to put down a glass. Andrea insisted that the arrangements that had been sent to Immaculate Conception for the funeral be gathered up and driven over to the house while we were at the graveside watching strong men lower his casket into the ground with straps. When we came home there were bouquets lining the front steps, and the doors of the house were opened wide. Andrea had put it in the obituary: *a reception to follow at the house*, forgetting that there were people like her who would come to gawk even on a day like this. Sandy and Jocelyn were in the kitchen making finger sandwiches that were being passed around by hired women in black dresses and white aprons. Sandy and Jocelyn were hurt because they hadn't been excused from work to attend the service, and they were hurt that they weren't deemed good enough to be in the front rooms filling glasses. "I guess it takes someone prettier than me to pour a glass of wine," Sandy said. Maeve went back to the kitchen to be with them, spreading cream cheese on slices of soft white bread, a dish towel tied around the waist of her best navy dress, while I stayed in the front to look after Andrea and the girls. I usually had little patience for the way Norma and Bright followed me, but on this day I kept them close. If my father was no longer there to tell me what kind of man I should be, I still knew what he would have expected. The girls ran their fingers along the petals, dipping their faces too deeply into the clustered roses to breathe them in. They said they were trying to decide which bouquet was their favorite because their mother had told them they could each take one vase up to their bedroom, Maeve's room.

"Which one do you want?" Norma asked. She was wearing a black cotton dress with smocking across the front. She was twelve and Bright was ten. "I bet she'd let you have one."

In the spirit of the game, I chose a small vase with some strange orange flowers that looked like they must have grown on the ocean floor. I had no idea what they were, but I gave them credit for being orange on a day of so much terrible whiteness.

It seems funny to remember how worried I was about Andrea then. She'd been crying for four days. She'd cried through every minute of the funeral. In that short span of time since my father's death she'd grown even smaller, her blue eyes swollen with tears. Again and again the people my father worked with came and held her hand, paying their respects in quiet voices. Neighbors who had never been invited to the house were everywhere. I recognized them, and they spoke to me warmly while trying to take in as much of their environment as discretion allowed. I met a quiet Swede who bowed his head when giving his condolences. He asked to be remembered to my sister. It turned out to be Mr. Otterson. When I told him to wait, that I would find Maeve and bring her back, he gave me a definitive no. "You mustn't disturb her," he said, as if she might have been up on the third floor crying instead of in the kitchen putting the sandwiches on trays. Father Brewer stayed on the porch, trapped against the house by two women from the altar society. When I saw Maeve taking him a glass of tea, I told her Mr. Otterson was there to see her. I'd only been talking to him a minute before but when we set out to look we couldn't find him anywhere.

There was no place I could go in the crowd without being petted or hugged. The entire day was like a dream, in just the way they tell you it's like a dream. How had my family shifted away from me? I had done so well with just one parent but now I could see that one parent was no insurance against the future. Maeve would go to graduate school soon enough, and I would live with Andrea and the girls, with Sandy and Jocelyn? I'd knock around in the house with only women? That wasn't right, that wasn't what my father would have wanted. He and I, I said to myself, but the sentence went no further. That was exactly what I meant to say about my past life, *he and I.*

The fragrance of the competing flowers was beginning to overtake the crowded room and I started to wonder if Father Brewer was staying outside in order to breathe. From a distance I saw Coach Martin come into the foyer with the entire varsity basketball team, every last one of them. They had been at the funeral but I didn't think they'd come to the reception. They'd never been to my house before. I took a glass of wine off the tray of a woman in a maid's uniform and when she didn't so much as look at me, I went in the bathroom and drank it.

The Dutch House was impossible. I had never had that thought before. When Maeve told me that our mother had hated it, I couldn't even understand what she was saying. The walls of the powder room were bas-relief, swallows carved into walnut, swallows shooting through flowered stalks towards a crescent moon. The panels had been carved in Italy in the early 1920s and shipped over in crates to be installed in the downstairs powder room of the VanHoebeeks' house. How many years of someone's life had gone into carving those walls in some other country? I reached up and traced a swallow with one finger. Is this what our mother had meant? I could feel the entire house sitting on top of me like a shell I would have to drag around for the rest of my life. It didn't go like that, of course, but on the day of his funeral I thought I was seeing the future.

As for the future, the first shots were quickly fired. Maeve came back to the house the next day and told Andrea she would quit her job at Otterson's and go to work at Conroy. It didn't need to be said that Andrea had never taken any interest in the business, and that she might not even fully understand what it was our father did. At her best she probably wasn't competent to run the company, and in her present grief she was far from her best.

"I can make sure all the scheduled projects are completed," Maeve said. "I can take care of payroll and taxes. It would just be for now, just until we decide what we're going to do with the company." We were all sitting in the drawing room, Bright with her head in Maeve's lap and Maeve running her fingers through the tangle of Bright's yellow hair, Norma on the sofa beside her.

"No," Andrea said.

At first Maeve thought maybe Andrea doubted she was capable, or doubted it would be what was best for the company or, God knows, best for Maeve. "I can do it," she said. "I used to work in the office in the summers before college. I know the books. I know the people who work there. It isn't so different from what I do at Otterson's now."

We waited. Even Bright looked up for the explanation that would follow, but nothing came.

"Do you have another plan?" Maeve asked finally.

Andrea nodded slowly. "Norma, go tell Sandy to bring me a cup of coffee."

Norma, anxious to get away from the tension and the boring conversation, leapt to her feet and vanished.

"Don't run!" Andrea called behind her.

"I'm not talking about taking over," Maeve said, as if maybe she'd been seen as overreaching. "It's just for now."

"Your mother would have made you cut that hair," Andrea said.

"What?"

"I must have said it to your father a hundred times: make her cut that hair. But he wouldn't do it. He didn't care. I always wanted to tell you myself, for your own good—it's appalling—but he wouldn't let me. He always said it was your hair."

Bright blinked up at my sister.

The comment was so strange that it was easy to push it away, put it down to grief, to shock, whatever. Andrea couldn't really have cared about Maeve's hair. The flowers from the funeral were everywhere. I kept thinking what a catastrophe it was going to be when they all died. I wondered if our conversation should have started with something smaller—an offer to empty the vases when the time came, to write the thank-you notes. "I can pick up the rent on Saturday," I said, hoping to bring us back to the land of the reasonable. "Maeve can drive me. I know the route."

"That won't be necessary."

This I didn't understand at all. "I've always collected the rent."

"Your father always collected the rent," Andrea said. "You rode in the car."

A silence came over the room that none of us knew how to get out from under. I felt the VanHoebeeks' eyes drilling into my skull. I always did.

"What we're trying to say is that we want to be helpful," Maeve said.

"I know you do," Andrea said, and then tilted her head sideways and smiled at her daughter in my sister's lap. "You know she does." She looked up at us again. "I don't know how it can take so long to bring a cup of coffee. You know they have a pot of it in the kitchen. Maybe they think it's their coffee." Andrea tapped her open hands on her thighs in a gesture of impatience, then stood. "Looks as if I'll have to get it myself. You know what they say, don't you? 'If you want something done right.'"

We waited for quite a while after she left, Maeve and Bright and I, and then we heard footsteps upstairs. She had gone up the kitchen stairs with her coffee. The interview was over.

In the two brief weeks after his death, I grieved both the loss of my father and what I saw as the postponement of my place in the world. Had there been the option, I would have quit high school at fifteen and run the Conroy business with Maeve. The business was what I wanted, what I expected, and what my father had planned for me. If it had come before I was ready then I would just have to get ready faster. I didn't believe I knew how to do everything, not by a long shot, but I knew every single person who could help me. Those people liked me. They'd been watching me work for years.

The rest of my problem was a marriage of sadness and discomfort that could not be picked apart. Andrea avoided me while the girls stayed close. Either Norma or Bright came into my room almost every night to wake me up to tell me their dreams. Or they didn't wake me up but I'd find one of them asleep on the couch in my room in the morning. The loss of my father was their loss too, I guess, though I could barely remember him ever speaking a word to either of them.

Then one afternoon I came home from school, said hello to Sandy and Jocelyn, and made myself a ham sandwich in the kitchen. Twenty minutes later Maeve flew in the back door. She looked like she had run all the way from Otterson's to the Dutch

House her face was so flushed. I was reading something, I can't remember what.

"What's wrong? Why aren't you working?" Most days Maeve didn't get off until six.

"Are you all right?"

I looked down as if checking to see if there was blood on my shirt. "Why wouldn't I be all right?"

"Andrea called. She told me to come and get you. She said I had to come right away."

"Come and get me for what?"

She ran her sleeve over her forehead, then put her keys on top of her purse. I don't know where Sandy and Jocelyn had gone but at that moment Maeve and I were alone in the kitchen.

"She scared the shit out of me. I thought—"

"I'm fine."

"Let me find out," she said. I got up to follow her, seeing as how I was the one who was supposed to be going someplace.

We went to the foyer and looked around. I hadn't seen the girls since I came home but that wasn't unusual. They were forever practicing for one thing or another. Maeve called Andrea's name.

"I'm in the drawing room," she said. "You don't need to shout."

She was in front of the fireplace, standing there beneath the two massive VanHoebeeks, just where we first found her all those years before.

"I came from work," Maeve said.

"You need to take Danny." Andrea was looking only at her.

"Take him where?"

"To your house, to a friend's house." She shook her head. "That's up to you."

"Is something going on?" Maeve was the one speaking but we were both asking the question.

"Is something going on?" Andrea repeated. "Well, let's see, your father died. We can start there." Andrea looked very nice. Her hair was put up. She was wearing a red-and-white checked dress I didn't remember, red lipstick. I wondered if she was on her way to a party, a luncheon. I didn't realize she had gotten dressed up for us.

"Andrea?" Maeve said.

"He isn't my son," she said, and right there her voice broke. "You can't expect me to raise him. He isn't my responsibility. Your father never told me I was going to have to raise his son."

"No one's asking you—" I started, but she held up her hand.

"This is my house," she said. "I deserve to feel safe in my house. You've been awful to me, both of you. You've never liked me. You've never supported me. I guess when your father was alive it was my obligation to accept that—"

"This is your house?" Maeve said.

"When your father died, that's when you showed yourself. Both of you. He left this house to me. He wanted me to have it. He wanted me to be happy here, me and the girls. I need you to take him—go upstairs and get his things and leave. This isn't easy for me."

"How is this your house?" Maeve asked.

I could see the two of us almost as if we were reflected in her eyes, how ridiculously tall we were by comparison, how young and strong, basketball, construction work. I had passed Maeve in height long ago, just like she had promised I would. I was still wearing my clothes from practice, a T-shirt and warm-up pants.

"You can talk to the lawyer," Andrea said. "But we've been

over everything, every inch. He has all the papers. Talk to him as long as you want but for now you need to leave."

"Where are the girls?" Maeve said.

"My daughters are none of your business." Her face was burnished with the energy it took to hate us, the energy it took to convince herself that every wrong thing that had happened in her life was our fault.

I still didn't fully grasp what was happening at that point, which was ridiculous because Andrea could not have been more clear. Maeve, on the other hand, understood exactly, and she drew herself up like Saint Joan to meet the fire. "They'll hate you," she said, her voice matter-of-fact. "You'll come up with some lie for them to swallow with dinner tonight but it won't hold. They're smart girls. They know we wouldn't just leave them. Once they start to look, they'll find out what you've done. Not from us, but they'll hear about it. Everyone will know. Your daughters will hate you even more than we do. They'll hate you after we've forgotten who you are."

There I was, still thinking I might be able to work something out, that maybe in the future Andrea and I would find a way to talk and she would see I wasn't her enemy, but Maeve closed that door and nailed it shut. She wasn't writing Andrea's future—Andrea was doing that herself—but what Maeve said, the way she said it, it sounded like a curse.

Maeve and I went up to my room and filled my single suitcase with clothes, then she went down to the kitchen to get some lawn and leaf bags and came back with Sandy and Jocelyn. Both of them were crying.

"Hey," I said, "hey, don't do that. We'll figure this out." I didn't mean that I would somehow smooth out this present moment, but that Maeve and I would be revealed as the rightful heirs to the Dutch House and overthrow the interloper. I was the Count of Monte Cristo. I had every intention of coming home.

"It's a nightmare," Jocelyn said, shaking her head. "Your poor father."

Sandy was emptying my dresser into a leaf bag drawer by drawer when Andrea came and stood in the doorway to watch what we were taking. "You need to be gone before the girls get home."

Jocelyn ran her wrist beneath her eyes. "I need to finish dinner."

"Don't finish dinner," she said. "All of you go, the four of you. You've always been in this together. I don't need spies left behind."

"Oh, for god's sake," Maeve said, raising her voice for the first time in all of this. "You can't fire them. What in the world did they ever do to you?"

"You're a set." Andrea smiled like she'd said something funny. She hadn't intended to fire Sandy and Jocelyn. It clearly hadn't occurred to her until just that minute, but once she'd said it, it felt right. "You can't break up the set."

"Andrea," I said. I took a step towards her, I don't know why. I wanted to stop her somehow, restore her to herself. She was never my favorite person but she wasn't as bad as this.

She took a step back.

"I'll tell you what we did to her," Jocelyn said, as if Andrea wasn't there. "We knew your mother, that's what. Your mother hired us, first Sandy, then me. Sandy told your mother that she had a sister who needed a job, and Elna said, bring your sister over tomorrow. That's who your mother was, everyone was welcome. People came to this house all day long and she gave them food and she gave them work. She loved us and we loved her and this one knows it." She gave her head a small back-wards hitch to acknowledge the woman behind her.

Andrea's eyes were round with disbelief. "That woman left her children! She left her husband and she left her children. I won't stand here and listen to you—"

"There was never a kinder woman than your mother," Joce-lyn went on as if no one else was speaking. She scooped up my sweaters and dropped them into the open bag. "And a true beauty, right from her heart. Every person who met her saw it, and everybody loved her. She was a servant, do you know what I mean?" She was looking right at me. "Just like Jesus tells us. All of this was hers and she never gave it a thought. All she wanted to know was what she could do for you, how she could help."

Sandy and Jocelyn never talked about our mother. Never. They had saved this bomb to detonate on exactly this occasion. Andrea put her hand on the doorframe to steady herself. "Finish up," she said in a voice without volume. "I'll be downstairs."

Jocelyn looked at the woman she had once worked for. "Every single day you were in this house we said to each other, 'What could Mr. Conroy have been thinking?'"

"Jocelyn," her sister said, just that one word as a warning.

But Jocelyn shook her head. "She heard me."

Andrea's mouth opened slightly but there were no words. She was losing herself, we could see it. She took her blows and left us to our work.

What was I thinking on that day, in that hour? Not about the room I'd slept in pretty much every night of my life. Maeve said my crib had been in the corner where the couch was now, that Fluffy slept in the room with me at first so our mother could rest. I wasn't thinking about the light that filled the room or the oak tree that brushed up against my window when it stormed. My oak tree. My window. I was thinking about getting the hell out of there and away from Andrea as quickly as possible.

We went down the wide staircase, the four of us each with a trash bag, and loaded Maeve's car. The house was magnificent as we were walking away from it: three stories of towering windows looking down over the front lawn. The pale-yellow stucco, nearly white, was the exact color of the late afternoon clouds. The wide veranda where Andrea, wearing her champagne-colored suit, had thrown the wedding bouquet over her shoulder was the very place people stood in line to pay their respects to my father's widow four years later. I picked up my bike and shoved it in the back of the car on top of the bags, only because I'd left it lying in the grass and all but tripped over it. Andrea was always telling my father to tell me to pick up my bike. She would tell him that when both of us were there in the room together, "Cyril, can't you teach Danny to take better care of what you've given him?"

We kissed Sandy and Jocelyn goodbye. We made promises that once things were sorted out we'd all be back together, none of us understanding that we were out of the Dutch House for good. When we got in the car Maeve's hands were shaking. She turned her purse over on the front seat and pulled open the bright yellow box where she kept her supplies. She needed to test her blood sugar. "We have to get out of here," she said. She was starting to sweat.

I got out of the car and walked around to the other side. This was all that mattered: Maeve. Sandy and Jocelyn had already gone off in Sandy's car. There was nobody watching us. I told Maeve to move over. She was fixing a syringe. She didn't tell me that I didn't know how to drive. She knew I could at least get us to Jenkintown.

The idiocy of what we took and what we left cannot be overstated. We packed up clothes and shoes I would outgrow in six months, and left behind the blanket at the foot of my bed my mother had pieced together out of her dresses. We took the books from my desk and left the pressed-glass butter dish in the kitchen that was, as far as we knew, the only thing that had made its way from that apartment in Brooklyn with our mother. I didn't pick up a single thing of my father's, though later I could think of a hundred things I wished I had: the watch that he always wore had been in the envelope with his wallet and ring. It had been in my hands the whole way home from the hospital and I had given it to Andrea.

Most of Maeve's things had been sorted through and boxed up when Norma took her room, and many of those boxes had been taken to her apartment after college, as Andrea had said that Maeve was an adult now and should be a steward of her own possessions (a direct quote). Still, Maeve's good winter coat was in the cedar closet because the summer before she'd had a problem with moths, and there were some other things— yearbooks, a couple boxes of novels she'd already read, some dolls she was saving for the daughter she was sure she would have one day, all in the attic under the eaves and behind the tiny door in the back of the third-floor bedroom closet. Did Andrea even know about that space? Maeve had shown it to the girls the night of the house tour, but would they remember or ever think to look in there again? Or would those boxes just belong to the house now, sealed into the wall like a time cap- sule from her youth? Maeve claimed not to care. She had all the photo albums. She had taken those with her to college. The only photo that was lost was a framed one of my father taken when he was a boy, holding a rabbit in his lap. That had some- how stayed behind in Norma's room. Later, when we had fully realized what had happened, Maeve would be angry over the loss of my stupid scouting certificates framed on the wall, some basketball trophies, the quilt, the butter dish, the picture.

But the thing I couldn't stop thinking about was the portrait of Maeve hanging there in the drawing room without us. How had we had forgotten her? Maeve at ten in a red coat, her eyes bright and direct, her black hair loose. The painting was as good as any of the paintings of the VanHoebeeks, but it was of Maeve, so what would Andrea do with it? Stash her in the damp basement? Throw her away? Even as my sister was right in front of me I felt like I had somehow left her behind, back in the house alone where she wouldn't be safe.

Maeve was feeling better but I told her to go upstairs and sit down while I lugged what I had up the three flights of stairs to her apartment. There was only one bedroom and she told me to take it. I told her no.

"You're going to take the bed," she said, "because you're too long for the couch and I'm not. I sleep on the couch all the time."

I looked around her little apartment. I'd been there plenty of times but you see a place differently when you know you're going to be living there. It was small and plain and suddenly I felt bad for her, thinking it wasn't right that she should be in this place when I was living on VanHoebeek Street, forgetting for a minute that I wasn't living there anymore. "Why do you sleep on the couch?"

"I fall asleep watching television," she said, then she sat down on that couch and closed her eyes. I was afraid she was going to cry but she didn't. Maeve wasn't a crier. She pushed her thick black hair away from her face and looked at me. "I'm glad you're here."

I nodded. For a second I wondered what I would have done if Maeve hadn't been there—gone home with Sandy or Jocelyn? Called Mr. Martin the basketball coach to see if he would have me? I would never have to know.

That night in my sister's bed I stared at the ceiling and felt the true loss of our father. Not his money or his house, but the man I sat next to in the car. He had protected me from the world so completely that I had no idea what the world was capable of. I had never thought about him as a child. I had never asked him about the war. I had only seen him as my father, and as my father I had judged him. There was nothing to do about that now but add it to the catalog of my mistakes.

CHAPTER 7

L AWYER GOOCH—THAT WAS what we always called him—was
our father's contemporary and his friend, and it was as a
friend he agreed to see Maeve the next day on her lunch hour.
She did not agree to let me miss school to come with her. "I'm
just going to get the lay of the land," she said over cereal the
next morning at her little kitchen table. "I have a feeling there
will be many more opportunities for us to go together."

Maeve dropped me off at school on her way to work. Everyone knew that my father had died and they all made a point of
being nice to me. For the teachers and the coach that meant
taking me aside to tell me they were there to listen, and that I
could have whatever time I needed on work that was due. For
my friends—Robert, who was a slightly better basketball player
than I was, and T.J., who was considerably worse, and Matthew,
who liked nothing more than to come to the construction sites
with me—it meant something else entirely: their discomfort at
my circumstances manifested itself as awkwardness, a con-
certed effort not to laugh at anything funny in my presence, the
temporary suspension of the grief we gave one another. No
grief for grief, something like that. It would never have occurred to me to pretend my father wasn't dead, but I didn't
want anyone to know about the Dutch House. That loss was

too private, shameful in a way I couldn't understand. I still believed Maeve and Lawyer Gooch would get it all straightened out and we would be back before anyone had to know I'd been thrown out.

But did "back in the house" mean being there without Andrea and the girls? What would happen to them exactly? My imagination had yet to work out that part of the equation.

I had a late practice, so Maeve was already home from work when I got to the apartment. She said she was planning to make scrambled eggs and toast for dinner. Neither of us knew how to cook.

I dropped my book bag in the living room. "Well?"

"It's so much worse than anything I imagined." There was a lightness in her tone that made me think she was joking. "Do you want a beer?"

I nodded. The invitation hadn't been extended before. "I'd take a beer."

"Get two." She leaned over to light her cigarette off the stove's gas flame.

"I wish you wouldn't do that." What I meant to say was, *You are my sister, my only relation. Do not put your face in the fucking fire.*

She straightened up and exhaled a long plume of smoke across the kitchen. "I've got it down now. I burned off my eyelashes at a party in the Village a couple of years ago. You only have to do that once."

"Terrific." I took out two bottles of beer, found the opener, and handed one to her.

She took a swig, then cleared her throat to begin. "So, to the best of my understanding, what we own in the world is pretty much what you see around you."

"Which is nothing."

"Exactly."

I hadn't considered the possibility of nothing before and a flush of adrenaline shot through me, preparing me for fight or flight. "How?"

"Lawyer Gooch, and he was lovely, by the way, could not have been nicer, Lawyer Gooch said the general rule of thumb is shirtsleeves to shirtsleeves in three generations, but we made it in two, or I guess technically we made it in one."

"Which means what?"

"It means that traditionally the first generation makes the money, the second generation spends the money, and the third generation has to go to work again. But in our case, our father made a fortune and then he blew it. He completed the entire cycle in his own lifetime. He was poor, then rich, and now we're poor."

"Dad didn't have money?"

She shook her head, glad to explain. "He had tons of money, just not tons of acumen. His young wife told him she believed that marriage was a partnership. Remember those words, Danny: *Marriage is a partnership.* She had him put her name on everything."

"He put her name on all the buildings?" That didn't seem possible. There were a lot of buildings, and he bought them and sold them all the time.

She shook her head and took another drink. "That would be for amateurs. Conroy Real Estate and Construction is a corporation, which means that everything in the company is gathered together under one roof. When he sold a building, the cash stayed in the corporation, and then he used it to buy another building. Andrea had him put her name on the company, which means she has joint ownership with right of survivorship."

"That's legal?"

"All assets are passed by operation of the law to his wife because of joint titling. Are you following this? I know it took me a minute."

"I'm following." I wasn't sure that was true.

"Smart boy. The same goes for the house. The house and all its contents."

"And Lawyer Gooch did this?" I knew Lawyer Gooch. He came to my basketball games sometimes and sat in the bleachers with our father. Two of his sons had gone to Bishop Mc-Devitt.

"Oh, no." She shook her head. She liked Lawyer Gooch. "Andrea came with her own lawyer. Someone in Philadelphia. Big firm. Lawyer Gooch said he talked to Dad about it many times, and you know what Dad said? He said, 'Andrea's a good mother. She'll look after the children.' Like, he married her because he thought she was good with children."

"What about the will?" Maybe Maeve was right about the second generation because even I knew enough to ask about a will.

She shook her head. "No will."

I sat down in a kitchen chair and took a long drink. I looked up at my sister. "Why aren't we screaming?"

"We're still in shock."

"There has to be a way out of this."

Maeve nodded. "I think so, too. I know I'm going to try. But Lawyer Gooch told me not to get my hopes up. Dad knew what he was doing. He was competent. She didn't make him sign the papers."

"Of course she made him!"

"I mean she didn't hold a gun to his head. Think about it: Mommy leaves him, then this slinky chinchilla comes along and tells him she's never going to leave him. She wants to be part of everything he does, what's mine is yours. She'll look after all of it and he'll never have to worry."

"Well, that much is true. He doesn't have to worry."

"The wife of four years gets it all. She even owns my car. Lawyer Gooch told me that. She owns my car but she told him I could keep it. I'm definitely going to sell it before she changes her mind. I think I'm going to get a Volkswagen. What do you think?"

"Why not?"

Maeve nodded. "You're smart," she said, "and I'm pretty smart, and I used to think Dad was smart, but the three of us together couldn't hold a candle to Andrea Smith Conroy. Lawyer Gooch wants you and me to come in together. He said there are still a few things left to go over. He said he'd keep working on our behalf, free of charge."

"It would have been better if he'd worked on our behalf while Dad was still alive."

"Apparently he tried. He said Dad didn't think he was old enough for a will." Maeve thought about this for a minute. "I bet Andrea has a will."

I drained my beer while Maeve leaned against the stove and smoked. We were delinquents in our own small way. "Two dead husbands," I said, though Andrea must have been, what then? Thirty-four? Thirty-five? Ancient by the standards of a teen-aged boy. "Did you ever wonder what happened to Mr. Smith?" I asked.

"Never once."

I shook my head. "Me neither. That's strange, isn't it? That we never thought about Mr. Smith, how he died?"

"What makes you think he's dead? I always thought he put

her out on the curb with the kids, and Dad must have driven by at just the wrong moment, offered them a ride."

"I feel bad for Norma and Bright over there by themselves."

"May they rot in hell." Maeve stubbed her cigarette out on a saucer. "All three of them."

"You don't mean that," I said. "Not the girls."

My sister reared back with such ferocity that for a split second I thought she meant to hit me. "She stole from us. Do you not understand that? They're sleeping in our beds and eating off our plates and we will never, never get any of it back."

I nodded. What I wanted to say, what I did not say, was that I'd been thinking the same thing about our father. We would never get him back.

Maeve and I set up housekeeping together. We found a second-hand dresser at the Goodwill and stuck it in the corner of the bedroom so I could put my clothes away. I still didn't like taking the bedroom, but every night, Maeve went to the couch with her stack of blankets. I wanted to ask her about finding a bigger place, but seeing as how it was all on her—our food and our shelter—I thought better of it.

When everything was all set up, we called Sandy and Jocelyn to come and see what we'd accomplished. Maeve brought home a white box of cookies from the bakery. She arranged the cookies on a plate and threw out the box, as if we were going to fool them. I straightened up the cushions on the couch, she put away the glasses that were in the drainboard. When the bell finally rang we threw open the door and the four of us exploded with joy. What a reunion! You would have thought it had been years since we'd seen one another.

It had been two weeks.

"Look at you," Sandy said, reaching up to put her hands on my shoulders. I thought her hair was grayer. There were tears in her eyes.

Sandy and Jocelyn hugged us and kissed us in a way they never had at home. Jocelyn was wearing dungarees and Sandy had on a cotton skirt with cheap tennis shoes. They were regular people now, not the people who worked for us. Still, they handed over one big jar of minestrone soup (Maeve's favorite) and another of beef stew (mine).

"You can't feed us!" Maeve said.

"I've always fed you," Jocelyn said.

Sandy took a skeptical glance around the living room. "I could come by every now and then, help you keep things up."

Maeve laughed. "How could I not keep this clean?"

"You have a job," Sandy said, looking down and running the toe of her shoe across the floor. "You don't need to worry about keeping house on top of everything else. Anyway, how long could the whole thing take me, an hour?"

"I can do it," I said, and the three of them looked at me like I was suggesting I make my own clothes. "Maeve won't let me get a job."

"Stick to basketball," Sandy said.

"And making decent grades," Jocelyn said.

Maeve nodded. "Let's just wait for a little bit, see how we do."

"We're doing fine, really," I said.

Sandy disappeared into the bedroom and came back five seconds later, looking at me. "Where do you sleep?"

"Does he know how to take care of you?" Jocelyn asked my sister.

Maeve waved her hand. "I'm fine."

"Maeve," Jocelyn said. It's a funny thing to say but she was being stern. Sandy and Jocelyn were never stern with Maeve.

"I take care of everything."

Jocelyn turned to me. "I have found your sister passed out cold on more than one occasion. Sometimes she forgets to eat or she doesn't take enough of her insulin. Sometimes it's nothing she's done wrong but her sugar goes off all the same. You've got to keep an eye on her, especially when things are stressful. She'll tell you stress has nothing to do with it, but it does."

"Stop," Maeve said.

"She has sugar tablets. You make her show you where she keeps them, make sure she has extras in her purse. If she's in trouble you have to give her a sugar tablet and call an ambulance."

I tried to take in the thought of Maeve on the floor. "I know that," I said, keeping my voice steady. I knew about the insulin but not the sugar. "She showed me."

Maeve sat back, smiling. "Straight from the horse's mouth."

Jocelyn looked at us for a minute, then shook her head. "You're appalling, both of you, but it doesn't matter. Now that he knows about it he'll make you show him. You'll bug her once we leave, won't you Danny?"

Even though I was sensitive to the fluctuation of Maeve's blood sugar, I realized I didn't know the details. I knew how to stand by and watch her take care of herself, but that was not the same thing as taking care of her. Jocelyn was right though, I would make Maeve explain everything to me once they were gone. "I will."

"You know I've been living in this apartment by myself all this time, don't you?" Maeve said. "It's not like Danny's been riding his bike over here at night to give me injections."

"Or you can call me," Jocelyn said, ignoring her completely. "I'll tell you everything you need to know."

Sandy had found a job keeping house in Elkins Park. "They're nice enough. Not as much money," she said, "and not as much work." Jocelyn had found a family to cook for in Jenkintown but she also had to help with the two children and was expected to walk the dog. Not as much money and considerably more work. The sisters laughed. Better to have been fired, was what they said. That made it a badge of honor. They wouldn't have stayed in that house a minute without me anyway.

"Once I get settled I'm going to try to talk my family into hiring Jocelyn. They need a cook. That way we could be together again," Sandy said.

Had I handled the situation better and not been critical—not just at the end but for all the years Andrea had been in our lives—Sandy and Jocelyn would still be sitting together at the blue kitchen table, shelling peas and listening to the radio.

Sandy was looking up at the ceiling, the windows, like she was measuring the place in her head. "Why didn't you move into one of your father's buildings?" she asked my sister.

"Oh, I don't know," Maeve said. She was still flustered about the insulin.

Jocelyn took the spot beside Sandy on the couch. Maeve had the chair and I sat on the floor. "I didn't think about it when you got this place but it doesn't make any sense," Sandy said. "You must have really had to work to find an apartment building in this town your father didn't own."

I'd wondered about it myself. The only reason I could come up with was that she had asked him for an apartment and he'd said no.

Maeve looked at us, the three of us, all the family she had. "I thought I would impress him."

"With this place?" Sandy leaned over and straightened a stack of my school books on the coffee table in front of her.

Maeve smiled again. "I made out a budget and this was what

I could afford. I thought he'd notice that I hadn't asked him for anything, that I'd saved up my spending money from my last year of school. I had first and last month's rent. I got the job. I bought the bed and then the next month I bought the couch and then I bought the chair at Goodwill. You know him, the way he liked to go on about the wonders of poverty, how making it all by yourself was the only way to learn anything. I thought I was showing him I wasn't like the rich girls I knew from school. I wasn't waiting around for him to buy me a horse."

Sandy laughed. "I never thought anyone was going to buy me a horse."

"Well, that's just fine." Jocelyn smiled. "I know he was proud of you, the way you did all this yourself."

"He didn't notice," Maeve said.

Sandy shook her head. "Of course he did."

But Maeve was right. He'd never seen what she had meant to show him. He had no notion of her self-reliance. The only thing my father ever saw in my sister was her posture.

Maeve made coffee and she and Jocelyn smoked while Sandy and I watched them. We ate the cookies and dredged up every awful memory of Andrea we had. We traded them between us like baseball cards, exclaiming over every piece of information one of us didn't already know. We talked about how late she slept and every unflattering dress she'd worn and how she would spend an hour on the phone with her mother but would never invite her mother to the house. She wasted food and left the lights on all night and gave no evidence of having ever read a book. She'd sit by the pool for hours just staring at her fingernails and then expect Jocelyn to bring her lunch on a tray. She didn't listen to our father. She gave away Maeve's bedroom. She threw me out. We dug a pit and roasted her.

"Can anyone explain to me why he married her in the first place?" Maeve asked.

"Sure." Jocelyn didn't need to give it a thought. "Andrea loved the house. Your father thought that house was the most beautiful thing in the world and he found himself a woman who agreed."

Maeve threw her hands up. "Everyone agreed! It's not like it would have been so hard to find a decent woman who liked the house."

Jocelyn shrugged. "Well, your mother hated it and Andrea loved it. He thought he'd solved the problem. But I got to her, didn't I? Saying all that about your mother."

Sandy covered her face with her hands and laughed. "I thought she was going to drop dead right on the spot."

I looked at Sandy and then Jocelyn. Now they were both laughing. "You didn't mean it?"

"What?" Sandy said, wiping at her eyes.

"About our mother being, I don't know, like a saint?"

The tension in the room shifted and then we were all very aware of how we were sitting and what we were doing with our hands. "Your mother," Jocelyn said, and then she stopped and looked at her sister.

"Of course we loved your mother," Sandy said.

"We all loved her," Maeve said.

"She was gone a lot," Jocelyn said, trying to pick her words.

"She was working." Maeve was tense but in a different way from Sandy and Jocelyn.

I had no idea what any of them were talking about, nor did I know that our mother had ever had a job. "What did she do?"

Jocelyn shook her head. "What didn't she do?"

"She worked for the poor," Maeve said to me.

"In Elkins Park?" There were no poor people in Elkins Park, or none that I'd ever seen.

"She worked for the poor everywhere," Sandy said, though I could tell she was trying her best to explain the situation kindly. "She could always find people who needed something."

"She went out looking for poor people?" I asked.

"Dawn to dusk," Jocelyn said.

Maeve stubbed out her cigarette. "Okay, stop this. You make it sound like she was never there."

Jocelyn shrugged and Sandy reached down for the thumb-print cookie with the round spot of apricot jam.

"Well," Maeve said, "we were always happy when she came home."

Sandy smiled and nodded. "Always," she said.

Early Sunday morning Maeve came into the bedroom and opened the blinds. "Get up, get dressed. We're going to church."

I pulled a pillow over my head, hoping to find my way back into the dream I was falling out of, a dream I already couldn't remember. "No."

Maeve leaned over and pulled off the pillow. "I mean it. Up, up."

I looked at her from one slitted eye. She was wearing a skirt, and her hair, still wet from the shower, was braided. "I'm sleeping."

"I've been very nice. I let you sleep through the eight o'clock service. We're going to make the ten-thirty."

I dug my face into the pillow. I was waking up and I did not want to wake up. "There's no one watching. No one can make us go to church anymore."

"I can make us go."

I shook my head. "Make yourself go. I'm going back to sleep."

She dropped down hard on the edge of the bed, making me bounce a little. "We go to church. That's what we do."

I turned over on my back and opened my eyes grudgingly. "You're not following."

"Up, up."

"I don't want anyone hugging me or telling me how sorry they are. I want to go back to sleep."

"They'll hug you this Sunday and next Sunday they'll just wave like nothing ever happened."

"I'm not going next Sunday either."

"Why are you being like this? You never complained about going to church before."

"Who would I have complained to? Dad?" I looked at her. "You win all the fights. You know that, right? When you have kids of your own you can make them go to church every morning and say the rosary before school. But I don't have to go, you don't have to go. We don't have parents. We can go out for pancakes."

She shrugged. "Get your own pancakes," she said. "I'm going."

"You don't need to do this for me." I raised up on my elbows. I couldn't believe she was carrying her point so far. "I don't need a good example."

"I'm not doing this for you. Jesus, Danny. I like going to Mass, I like believing in God. Community, kindness, I buy into the whole thing. What in the hell have you been doing in church all these years?"

"Memorizing basketball stats mostly."

"Then go back to sleep."

"Are you telling me you went to church when you were in

college? You got up all those Sunday mornings in New York when no one was watching?"

"Of course I went to church. Don't you remember when you came to see me? We went to Good Friday service together."

"I thought you were just making me go." That was the truth, too. Even at the time I assumed she'd promised our father that she'd get me to church for Good Friday if he let me stay.

She started to say something else then let it go. She patted my ankle beneath the bedspread. "Get some rest," she said, and then she left.

It would have been hard to say exactly why we went to church, but everyone did. My father saw his colleagues and his tenants there. Maeve and I saw our teachers and our friends. Maybe my father went to pray for the souls of his dead Irish parents, or maybe church was the last vestige of respect he paid our mother. To hear people talk, she had loved not only the church and the parish community but every last priest and nun. Maeve said our mother had felt most at home in the church when the sisters stood and sang. From what little I knew of her, I was sure she wouldn't have married my father if he hadn't been willing to go to church, and without her he continued to drag us to the altar, preserving the form in the absence of content. Maybe it was because he had never considered it could have been otherwise, or maybe because his daughter listened to the homily leaning forward, the missalette in her hands, while his son considered the Sixers' chances in the playoffs and he contemplated a building that was for sale at the edge of Cheltenham township, though for all I knew my father listened to the priest and heard the voice of God. We never talked about it. In my memory, it was always Maeve who was racing around on Sunday morning, making sure we were ready: dressed, fed, in the car in plenty of time. After she had gone to college, it would have been so easy for my father and me to put the whole enterprise to bed. But then there was Andrea to consider. She despised Catholicism, thought it was a cult of lunatics who worshiped idols and claimed to eat flesh. My father could go to the office before first light Monday through Friday and find excuses to stay out through dinner. He could eat up Saturdays in the car collecting rent or visiting various construction projects. But Sunday was a tricky day to occupy. Church was all he had to work with if he wanted to get away from his young wife. My father talked to Father Brewer about my becoming an altar boy, then signed me up without consultation. The altar boys had to be at church a half hour early to help prepare the sacraments and assist Father Brewer with his vestments. And while I was slated for eight o'clock Mass, there were plenty of times I worked the ten-thirty as well. Someone was always calling in sick or going on vacation or simply refusing to get out of bed, luxuries I had never been afforded. Since I was an altar boy, my father thought it was important for me to attend Sunday school as well, to be a good example he said, even though Sunday school was for public school kids who weren't already getting some brand of religious indoctrination five days a week. But there was no place in the conversation to tell my father he was being ridiculous. After Mass, he sat in the car with his cigarettes and newspaper and waited for me, and when all the work was done, every last prayer recited and chalice washed, he would take me to lunch. We had never gone out to lunch when Maeve was at home. Thus our single hour of Mass stretched to cover half of Sunday, protecting us from family obligations and giving us at least some time together between the lighting of the candles and the blowing out. For this I will always be grateful, though not grateful enough to get out of bed.

But on Monday morning Coach Martin called me into his

office and reiterated his sorrow for my circumstances. Then he said I needed to be at Mass to pray for my father. "All the varsity players at Bishop McDevitt go to Mass," he told me. "Every single one of them."

I would be included in that number for a little while longer.

A week later the lawyer's office called to set up our appointment. He could meet with us at three o'clock, once school was out, though it still meant I would miss practice and Maeve would have to take half a personal day from work. The three of us sat around a table in a small conference room, and there he told us that the one thing our father had put in place for us was an educational trust.

"For both of us?" I asked. My sister was sitting in the chair beside me wearing the same navy dress she'd worn to the funeral. I was wearing a tie.

"The trust is for you, and for Andrea's daughters."

"Norma and Bright?" Maeve almost went across the table. "She gets everything and we have to pay for their education?"

"You don't pay for anything. The trust pays for it."

"But not for Maeve?" I asked. That was the travesty, the part he didn't bother to mention.

"Since Maeve's already finished college, your father felt her education was complete," Lawyer Gooch said.

Aside from that single lunch in the Italian restaurant in New York, our father had never talked to Maeve about her education, nor had he listened when she talked about it. He thought if she went to graduate school she'd only get married halfway through and quit what she'd started.

"The trust will pay for college?" Maeve asked. The way she said it made me realize it was one more thing she'd been worried about, how she was going to send me to college.

"The trust pays for education," Lawyer Gooch said, enunciating the word *education* very clearly.

Maeve leaned forward. "All education?" They may as well have been alone in the room.

"All of it."

"For all three of them."

"Yes, but Danny of course will go first, being the oldest. I think there's very little chance it's going to run out. Norma and Bernice should be able to get through school just fine."

Bright, I wanted to say and did not say. No one called her Bernice.

"And what happens to the money that's left, if there's any left?"

"Any money still in the trust when all three children have completed their education will be divided equally among the four of you."

He might as well have said that half the money went back in Andrea's handbag.

"And you administer the trust?" Maeve asked.

"Andrea's lawyer set it up. She told your father she wanted to ensure the children's education and from there—" He tipped his head from side to side.

"'As long as we're in the lawyer's office, why not go ahead and put my name on everything you own?'" Maeve was giving it her best guess.

"More or less."

"Then Danny needs to think about graduate school," Maeve said.

Lawyer Gooch tapped his pen thoughtfully against a yellow legal pad. "That's a long way off, but yes, were Danny interested in graduate education, the cost would be covered. The trust stipulates that he maintain a minimum grade point average of 3.0 and that the education be contiguous. Your father felt strongly that school was not to be a vacation."

"My father never had to worry about Danny's grades."

I would have liked to have said something for myself on this point but I didn't think either of them would have listened. My father cared nothing about my grades, though maybe he would have if there had been a problem. He didn't care about my free throw as long as I sank it. What he cared about was how fast and straight I could hammer a nail, and that I understood the timing involved in pouring cement. We cared about the same things.

"Did you know I went to Choate?" the lawyer asked, as if his high school years were suddenly relevant to the conversation.

Maeve sat with this for a minute, and then told him no, she hadn't known that. Her voice was surprisingly soft, as if the thought of Lawyer Gooch being shipped off to boarding school made her sad. "Was it very expensive?"

"Almost as much as college."

She nodded and looked at her hands.

"I could make some phone calls. They don't usually accept students in the middle of the year but given the circumstances I imagine they'd want to take a look at a basketball player with excellent grades."

The two of them decided I would start Choate in January.

"Do you know what kind of kids go to boarding school?" I said to Maeve in the car after we left the office. My tone was full of accusation when in fact I'd never known anyone who'd gone to boarding school. I'd only known kids whose parents had threatened to send them after they'd been caught smoking weed or failing Algebra II. When Andrea complained to my father that I didn't put my dirty clothes in the hamper, that I seemed to think Sandy was there to pick my clothes off the floor and wash them and fold them and take them back to my room, he would say, "Well, I guess we're going to have to send him to boarding school then." That's what boarding school was—a threat, or a joke about a threat.

Maeve had other ideas. "Smart rich kids go to boarding school, and then they go to Columbia."

I slumped down in my seat and felt very sorry for myself. I didn't need to lose my school and my friends and my sister on top of everything else. "Why don't you cut to the chase and send me to an orphanage?"

"You don't qualify," she said.

"I don't have parents." It wasn't a topic we discussed.

"You have me," she said. "Disqualified."

*   *   *

"WHAT ARE YOU doing now?" Maeve asked. "I know I should know this but I can never remember. I think they move you around too much."

"Pulmonology."

"The study of trains?"

I smiled. It was spring again. In fact, it was Easter, and I was back in Elkins Park for two whole nights. The cherry trees that lined the Buchsbaums' side of the street were pink and trembling, exhausted by the burden of so many petals. They turned the light pink and gold. This was the cherry trees' day, their very hour, and I, who never saw anything outside of the hospital, was there to witness it. "The trains are almost finished. Orthopedics starts next week."

"Strong as a mule and twice as smart." Maeve dangled her arm out the window of her parked car, her fingers reenacting the memory of bygone cigarettes.

"What?"

"Haven't you heard that? I guess it isn't a joke orthopedists make. Dad used to say it all the time."

"Dad had something against orthopedists?"

"No, Dad had something against cauliflower. He hated orthopedists."

"Why?"

"They put his knee on backwards. You remember that."

"Someone put his knee on backwards?" I shook my head. "That must have been before my time."

Maeve thought about it for a minute. I could see her scrolling through the years in her mind. "Maybe so. He meant it to be funny but I have to say when I was a kid I thought it was true. His knee really *did* bend the wrong way. He used to go to orthopedists all the time, trying to get it to bend the other way I guess. When I think of it now it's kind of horrifying."

There would never be an end to all the things I wished I'd asked my father. After so many years I thought less about his unwillingness to disclose and more about how stupid I'd been not to try harder. "Even if the surgeon put the knee on backwards, which, of course, isn't possible, we should probably be grateful he didn't amputate the leg. That happens all the time in war, you know. It takes a lot more time to save something than it does to cut it off."

Maeve made a face. "It wasn't the *Civil* War," she said, as if amputation had been abandoned after Appomattox. "I don't think they even did surgery on his knee. He said in France the doctors were in such a hurry that they didn't always pay attention. Things got turned around. Really, it's kind of touching that he could even make a joke about it."

"He must have had surgery when it happened. If you get shot in the knee then somebody is going to have to operate."

Maeve looked at me like I had just opened the car door and

taken the seat beside her, a complete stranger. "He wasn't shot."

"Of course he was."

"He broke his shoulder in a parachute jump and he tore something in his knee, or he jammed the knee. He landed on his left leg and then he fell over and broke his left shoulder."

There was the Dutch House right behind her, the backdrop to everything. I wondered if we had grown up in the same house. "How have I always thought he was shot in the war?"

"I have no idea."

"But he was in a hospital in France?"

"For his shoulder. The problem was no one paid attention to his knee when it happened. I guess the shoulder really was a mess. Then the knee hyperextended over time. He wore a brace for years and then the leg got stiff. They called it artho—" She stopped mid-syllable.

"Arthrofibrosis."

"Exactly."

I remembered the brace as being the source of the pain: heavy and ill-fitting. He complained about the brace, not the knee. "What about his shoulder?"

She shrugged. "I guess it turned out okay. I don't know, he never mentioned his shoulder."

All through medical school, and for at least a decade after, I had dreams in which I was in grand rounds, presenting a patient I had never examined, which was how I felt that Easter morning. *Cyril Conroy is an American paratrooper, thirty-three years of age. He was not shot . . .*

"I'll tell you something," Maeve said. "When he had his heart attack, I always thought it was the stairs. I couldn't imagine him trying to make it to the sixth floor of anything. He must have been mighty pissed off at someone to walk up a stairwell in that kind of heat to look at window sealing. As far as I know he only went to the third floor of the Dutch House twice in his life: the day he brought Mommy and me to see the place for the first time, and the day I came home for Thanksgiving and Andrea announced my exile. Remember that? He carried my bag upstairs. And then when we got up there he had to lie down on the bed. His leg was killing him. I put my suitcase under his foot to elevate it. I should have been screaming mad about Andrea but all I could think was that I was never going to get him down the stairs again. We were going to have to live in the two little bedrooms off the ballroom, me and Dad. It's sort of a sweet thought, really. I wish we had. He said, 'It's a nice-looking house but it's too damn tall.' I told him he should sell it then and buy a ranch house. I told him that would solve every problem he had, and we both laughed. That really was something," she said, looking out the windows at the Buchsbaums' cherry trees, "getting Dad to laugh about anything in those days."

* * *

THERE ARE A few times in life when you leap up and the past that you'd been standing on falls away behind you, and the future you mean to land on is not yet in place, and for a moment you're suspended, knowing nothing and no one, not even yourself. It was an almost unbearably vivid present I found myself in that winter when Maeve drove me to Connecticut in the Oldsmobile. She kept meaning to get rid of it but we had so little from the past. The sky was a piercing blue and the sun doubled back on the snow and all but blinded us. In spite of everything we'd lost, we'd been happy together that fall we spent in her little apartment. Andrea had sold the company lock, stock, and barrel. Every last building our father had owned was gone. I couldn't even imagine how much money it must have come to. I wanted to tell Maeve that wringing some spare change out of Norma and Bright's future, when I probably wasn't even capable of staying in school long enough to do that, wasn't reason enough for us to be separated. I'd go to college, of course I'd go to college, but for now I still wanted to play basketball with my friends and sit with her at the kitchen table over eggs and toast and talk about our days. But the world was in motion and it felt like there was nothing we could do to stop it. Maeve had made up her mind that I was going to Choate. She had also made up her mind that I would go to medical school. When she added in a sub-specialty it was the longest and most expensive education she could piece together.

"Does it even matter to you that I don't want to be a doctor?" I asked. "Does what I want to do with my life factor into this?"

"Well, what do you want to do?"

I wanted to work with my father, to buy and sell buildings. I wanted to build them from scratch, but that was gone. "I don't know. Maybe I'll play basketball." I sounded petulant even to myself. Maeve would have loved to have had my problems, to explore the limits of how extensively and expensively she could be educated.

"Play all you want when you get off work at the hospital," she said, and followed the signs to Connecticut.

Part
Two

CHAPTER 8

THE SNOW WAS coming down heavy and wet in New York on the Wednesday before Thanksgiving. Penn Station looked like a feedlot and we, the anxious travelers, were the cows standing in pools of melting slush, bundled up and pressed together in the overheated terminal. We couldn't take off our coats and hats and scarves because our arms were full of suitcases and bags and books we didn't want to put on the disgusting floor. We stared at the departures board, awaiting instruction. The sooner we could get to the train, the better our chances of claiming a seat that was forward facing and not too close to the toilet. A kid with a backpack full of bricks kept turning to say something to his girlfriend, and every time he did he clocked me with the full weight of his possessions.

I wanted to be back in my dorm room at Columbia.

I wanted to be on the train.

I wanted to be out of my coat.

I wanted to learn the layout of the periodic table.

Maeve could have saved me from all of this had she troubled herself to come to New York. Now that she had overseen the delivery of who knew how many tons of frozen vegetables to grocery stores for the holiday, Otterson's was closed until Monday. My roommate was having Thanksgiving with his parents in Greenwich, so Maeve could have slept in his bed and we could have eaten Chinese and maybe seen a play. But Maeve would come to New York City only if circumstances demanded it—say, when my appendix ruptured the first semester of my freshman year of college. I rode to Columbia-Presbyterian with the hall proctor in an ambulance. When I woke up from surgery, Maeve was there asleep, her chair pulled next to the bed, her head on the mattress beside my arm. The dark mess of her hair spread out across me like a second blanket. I had no memory of calling her, but maybe someone else had. She was my emergency contact after all, my next of kin. I was still floating in and out of the anesthesia, watching her dream, thinking, *Maeve came to New York. Maeve hates coming to New York.* It had something to do with how much she had loved Barnard and all the potential she had seen in herself then. New York represented her shame about things that were in no way her fault, or at least that's what I was thinking. I closed my eyes and when I opened them again she was sitting up in that same chair, holding my hand.

"There you are," she said, and smiled at me. "How are you feeling?"

It would be years before I understood the very real danger of what had happened to me. At the time I saw the surgery as something between a nuisance and an embarrassment. I started to make a joke but she was looking at me with such tenderness I stopped myself. "I'm okay," I said. My mouth was sticky and dry.

"Listen," she said, her voice quiet. "It's me first, then you. Do you understand?"

I gave her a loopy smile but she shook her head.

"Me first."

The spinners started clicking a jumble of letters and numbers and when they stopped, the sign read HARRISBURG: 4:05, TRACK 15, ON TIME. Basketball had taught me how to move through a crowd. Most of the poor cows came to Penn Station just once a year and were easily confused. In the collective shuffling, very few turned in the right direction. By the time they'd puzzled out which way they were supposed to go, I was already on the train.

On the plus side, the trip would give me more than an hour to study, time that was necessary to my continuing redemption in Organic Chemistry. My professor, the aptly named Dr. Able, had called me to his office in early October to tell me I was on track to fail. It was 1968 and Columbia was burning. The students rioted, marched, occupied. We were a microcosm of a country at war, and every day we held up the mirror to show the country what we saw. The idea that anyone took note of a junior failing chemistry was preposterous, but there I was. I had already missed several classes and he had a stack of my quizzes in front of him so I don't suppose it took an act of clairvoyance to figure out I was in trouble. Dr. Able's third-floor office was crammed with books and a smallish blackboard that featured an incomprehensible synthesis I was afraid he would ask me to explain.

"You're listed as pre-med," he began, looking at his notes. "Is that right?"

I told him that was right. "It's still early in the semester. I'll get things back on track."

He tapped his pencil on the pile of my disappointing work. "They take chemistry seriously in medical school. If you don't pass, they don't let you in. That's why it's best we talk now. If we wait any longer you won't catch up."

I nodded, feeling an aching twist in my lower intestines. One of the reasons I'd always worked hard in school and gotten good grades was an effort to preclude this exact conversation.

Dr. Able said he'd been teaching chemistry long enough to have seen plenty of boys like me, and that my problem wasn't a lack of ability, but the apparent failure to put in the necessary time. He was right, of course, I'd been distracted since the beginning of the semester, but he was also wrong, because I didn't think he'd seen plenty of boys like me. He was a thin man with a badly cut thatch of thick brown hair. I couldn't have guessed how old he was, only that in his tie and jacket he resided in what I thought of as the other side.

"Chemistry is a beautiful system," Dr. Able said. "Every block builds on the previous block. If you don't understand chapter 1, there's no point in going on to chapter 2. Chapter 1 provides the keys to chapter 2, and chapters 1 and 2 together provide the keys to chapter 3. We're on chapter 4 now. It isn't possible to suddenly start working hard on chapter 4 and catch up to the rest of the class. You have no keys."

I said it had felt that way.

Dr. Able told me to go back to the beginning of the textbook and read the first chapter, answer every question at the end of that chapter, throw them out, wake up the next morning, and answer them again. Only when I had answered all of the questions correctly on both tries could I proceed to the next chapter.

I wanted to ask him if he knew there were students sleeping on the floor of the president's office. What I said instead was, "I still have to keep up in my other classes," making it sound like we were in negotiation for how much of my valuable time he was entitled to. The class had never been asked to answer all the chapter questions, much less to answer them twice.

He gave me a long, flat look. "Then this might not be your year for chemistry."

I could not fail Organic Chemistry, could not fail anything. The draft was looming, and without academic deferment I'd be sleeping in a ditch in Khe Sanh. Still, what my sister would have done to me had I lost my academic standing would have far exceeded anything the government was capable of meting out. This wasn't a joke. This was falling asleep at the wheel while driving through a blizzard on the New Jersey Turnpike at midnight. Dr. Able had shaken me just in time to see headlights barreling straight towards my windshield, and now I had a split second to jerk the car back into my own lane. The distance between me and annihilation was the width of a snowflake.

I took an aisle seat on the train. There was nothing I needed to see between Manhattan and Philadelphia. Under normal circumstances, I would have put my bag on the seat beside me and tried to make myself look over large, but this was Thanksgiving week and no one was getting away with two seats. Instead, I opened my text book and hoped to project exactly what I was: a serious student of chemistry who could not be drawn into a conversation about the weather or Thanksgiving or the war. The Harrisburg contingent of the Penn Station cows had been pressed through a turnstile and shaped into a single-file line that came down the platform and into the car, each of them whacking their bags into every seat they passed. I kept my eyes on my book until a woman tapped her freezing fingers against the side of my neck. Not my shoulder, like anyone would have done, my neck.

"Young man," she said, and then looked down at the suitcase by her feet. She was somebody's grandmother who wondered how she had found herself in a world in which men allowed women to wrestle their own bags onto trains in the name of equality. The cows behind her kept pushing, unable to understand the temporary blockage. They were too afraid the train might leave without them. I got up and hoisted her luggage—a sad suitcase of brown plaid wool cinched at the middle with a belt because the zipper could not be trusted—onto the overhead rack. With this single act of civility, I advertised my services as a porter, and women up and down the length of the car began to call. Several had Macy's and Wanamaker's bags full of wrapped Christmas presents in addition to their suitcases, and I wondered what it would be like to think so far in advance. Bag after bag, I worked to cram items onto the metal bars above the seats where they could not possibly fit. The universe might have been expanding but the luggage rack was not.

"Gentle," one woman said to me, raising her hands to pantomime how she would have done it were she a foot taller.

When finally I looked in both directions and decided there was nothing more that could be done, I turned against the tide and pushed my way back to my seat. There I found a girl with loopy blond curls sitting at the window, reading my chemistry book.

"I saved your place," she said as the train lurched forward.

I didn't know if she meant in the book or on the train, and I didn't ask because neither had required saving. I was on chapter 9, chemistry having presented me with the keys at last. I sat down on my coat because I'd missed the chance to put it overhead.

"I took chemistry in high school," the blonde said, turning the page. "Other girls took typing but an A in chemistry is worth more than an A in typing."

"Worth more how?" Chemistry had a better chance to serve

the greater good, but certainly many more people would need to know how to type.

"Your grade point average."

Her face was a confluence of circles: round eyes, rounded cheeks, round mouth, a small rounded nose. I had no intention of talking to her but I also didn't know what choice I had as long as she was holding my book. When I asked her if she'd gotten an A in the class she kept reading. She'd stumbled onto a point of interest and in response to my question gave an absentminded nod. She found the chemistry more compelling than the fact that she had once gotten an A in chemistry, and that, I will admit, was winning. I waited all of two minutes before telling her I was going to need the book back.

"Sure," she said, and handed it over, one finger marking the second section of chapter 9. "It's funny to see it again, sort of like running into somebody you used to spend a lot of time with."

"I spend a lot of time with chemistry."

"It doesn't change," she said.

I looked at the page while she rifled through her bag, pulling out a slim volume of poetry by Adrienne Rich called *Necessities of Life*. I wondered if she was reading it for a class or if she was just one of those girls who read poetry on trains. I didn't ask, and so we sat in companionable silence all the way to Newark. When the train stopped and the doors opened, she took a stick of Juicy Fruit from the pack in her pocket and stuck it into her book, then she looked at me again with unbearable seriousness.

"We should talk," she said.

My girlfriend Susan had said *We should talk* at the end of our freshman year before telling me we were breaking up. "We should?"

"Unless you want to take down the luggage for all the women

getting off in Newark and then put up the luggage for all the women getting on."

She was right, of course. There were women glowering in my direction and then looking pointedly up at their bags. There were other able-bodied men on the train, but they were used to me.

"So you're going home," my seatmate said, leaning forward, smiling. She had put something on her lips to make them shiny. From a distance a person would have thought we were engaged in meaningful conversation, or that we were engaged. I was close enough to smell the vestiges of her shampoo.

"For Thanksgiving," I said.

"Nice." She nodded slightly, holding my gaze in a lock so that I could plainly see the slight droop in her left eyelid, a defect that would have passed unnoticed had it not been for an episode of intense staring. "Harrisburg?"

"Philadelphia," I said, and because we were for that moment very close, I added my suburb. "Elkins Park." I forgot for a minute that I didn't live in Elkins Park anymore. I lived in Jenkintown, inasmuch as I lived anywhere. Maeve lived in Jenkintown.

At the mention of Elkins Park a light of familiarity sparked in her eyes. "Rydal." She touched the blue wool scarf that covered her sternum. Elkins Park was one town over from Rydal, which meant that we were practically neighbors. A woman leaned over us to say something but my seatmate waved her away.

"Buzzy Carter," I said, because his was the name to drop when speaking of Rydal. Buzzy and I had been in Scouts together and later played on opposing church league basketball teams. He was born popular, and by the time we got to high school he had good grades, good teeth, and a knack for racking up forty points a game, not including assists. He was playing at Penn now on a full ride.

"He was a year ahead of me," she said with a look on her face that girls got when thinking of Buzz. "He took my cousin to junior prom though I never knew why. You were at Cheltenham?"

"Bishop McDevitt," I said, not wanting to get into anything complicated, "but the last two years I went to boarding school."

She smiled. "Your parents couldn't stand you?"

I liked this girl. She had good timing. "Yeah," I said. "Something like that."

When the train left the station again, we resumed our commitment to be strangers, she with her poetry book, me with my chemistry. In our peaceful coexistence, we very nearly forgot about the other altogether.

When the train pulled into 30th Street Station, the woman with the plaid suitcase, the one who'd started it all, shot straight to my side and dragged me down the aisle to get her bag. It really was stuck up there, jammed between all the other bags. Even if she'd stood on the armrest she couldn't have reached it. Then another woman needed help, and another and another, and soon I started worrying that the doors were going to close and I'd have to ride the train to Paoli and double back. I saw the blond head of my seatmate going towards the door. Maybe she'd waited as long as felt prudent, or maybe she hadn't waited at all. I told myself it didn't matter. I tugged down one last bag for a woman who seriously seemed to think I was supposed to carry it to the platform for her, then I shook myself loose, grabbed my coat and suitcase, my textbook, and slipped off the train just ahead of the closing doors.

My sister was never hard to find. For one thing, I could pretty much count on her being taller than everyone else, and for another she was always on time. If I was coming in on a train, Maeve would be front and center in the waiting crowd. She was there on this particular Wednesday before Thanksgiving across the terminal, wearing jeans and a red wool sweater of mine I thought I'd lost. She waved to me and I lifted my hand to wave back but my seatmate grabbed my wrist.

"Goodbye!" she said, all blond and smiling. "Good luck with the chemistry." She hoisted her bag up on her shoulder. I guess she'd put it down to wait for me.

"Thanks." I had some strange inclination to hide her or to shoo her away, but there was my sister, striding towards us. Maeve wrapped me in her arms, lifted me an inch or so off the ground, and shook me. The first time she'd done that was the first Easter I'd come home from Choate, and she'd kept up the tradition just to prove she could.

"Did you meet someone on the train?" Maeve said, looking at me instead of her.

I turned to the girl. She was a perfectly average size, though everyone looked small when they stood between me and my sister. I remembered then that I hadn't asked her name.

"Celeste," the girl said, and held out her hand, so we all shook hands. "Maeve," said Maeve, and I said, "Danny," and then we all wished one another a happy Thanksgiving, said goodbye, and walked away.

"You cut off your hair!" I said once we were out of earshot.

Maeve reached up and touched her neck just below the place where her dark hair ended in an abrupt bob. "Do you like it? I thought it made me look more like an adult."

I laughed. "I would have thought you'd be sick of always looking like the adult."

She linked her arm through mine and dipped her head sideways to touch my shoulder. Her hair fell forward and covered

her face for an instant, so she tossed her head back. *Like a girl,*
I thought, and then remembered Maeve was a girl.

"These will be the best four days of the year," she said. "The
best four days until you come home for Christmas."

"Maybe for Christmas you'll come see me. I came to see you
for Easter when you were in college."

"I don't like the train," Maeve said, as if that were the end
of that.

"You could drive."

"To Manhattan?" She stared at me to underscore the stu-
pidity of the suggestion. "It's so much easier to take the train."

"The train was a nightmare," I said.

"Was the girl a nightmare?"

"No, the girl was fine. She was a big help, actually."

"Did you like her?" We were nearly to the door that led out
to the parking lot. Maeve had insisted on driving in to get me.

"I liked her as well as you like the person you sit next to on
the train."

"Where's she from?"

"Why do you care where she's from?"

"Because she's still standing there waiting and no one's come
to meet her. If you like her then we could offer her a ride."

I stopped and looked over my shoulder. She wasn't watching
us. She was looking in the other direction. "Now you have eyes
in the back of your head?" I had always thought it was possible.
Celeste, who had seemed so competent on the train, looked
decidedly lost in the station. She had saved me from a lot of
luggage handling. "She's from Rydal."

"We could spare the extra ten minutes to drive to Rydal."

My sister was more aware of her surroundings than I was.
She was also a nicer person. She waited with my bags and sent
me back to ask Celeste if she needed a ride. After taking a few

more minutes to scan the station for some member of her family—it had never been made clear which one of them was supposed to pick her up—she asked me again if she wasn't going to be a huge imposition. I said she was no trouble at all. The three of us walked to the parking lot together while Celeste continued to apologize. Then she crawled into the back of my sister's Volkswagen and we drove her home.

* * *

"YOU WERE THE one who said we should give her a ride," Maeve said. "My memory on this is perfectly clear. We were going to the Gooches' for Thanksgiving and I needed to get home and make the pie, then *you* said you'd met this girl on the train and promised that I'd drive her home."

"Utter bullshit. You've never made a pie in your life."

"I needed to go the bakery and pick up the pie I'd ordered."

I shook my head. "I always took the 4:05 train. The bakery would have been closed by the time I came in."

"Would you *stop*? All I'm saying is that I'm not responsible for Celeste."

We were in her car and we were laughing. The Volkswagen had been gone for years, replaced by a Volvo station wagon with seat heaters. That car chewed through snow.

But on this particular day it was only cold, not snowing. The lights in the Dutch House were already lit against the dark. This was part of a new tradition that came years later: after Celeste and I had dated and broken up and come back together again, after we had married and after May and Kevin were born, after I had become a doctor and stopped being a doctor, after we had all tried for years to have Thanksgiving together in a civilized manner and then had given up. Every year Celeste and the kids and I drove to Rydal from the city on

the Wednesday before Thanksgiving. I left the three of them at
her parents' house and went to have dinner with my sister. On
Thanksgiving Day, Maeve served lunch to the homeless with a
group from church and I went back to eat with Celeste's enormous and ever-expanding family. Later in the evening, the
kids and I would go back to see Maeve in Jenkintown. We'd
bring refrigerator dishes heaped with leftovers and slices of pie
Celeste's mother had made. We ate the food cold while we
played penny-ante poker at the dining-room table. My daughter, whose dramatic nature was evident in earliest childhood,
liked to say it was worse than having divorced parents—all the
back and forth. I told her she had no idea what she was talking
about.

"I wonder if Norma and Bright still come home for Thanksgiving," Maeve said. "I wonder if they married people Andrea
hates."

"Oh, they must have," I said, and for an instant I could see
how it all would have played out. I felt sorry for those men I
would never meet. "Pity the poor bastards brought to the Dutch
House."

Maeve shook her head. "It's hard to imagine who would've
been good enough for those girls."

I gave my sister a pointed look, thinking she would get the
joke, but she didn't.

"What?"

"That's what Celeste always says about you," I said.

"What does Celeste always say about me?"

"That you think no one would have been good enough
for me."

"I've never said no one was good enough for you. I've said
you could have found someone better than her."

"Ah," I said, and held up my hand. "Easy." My wife made

disparaging remarks about my sister and my sister made disparaging remarks about my wife, and I listened to both of them because it was impossible not to. For years I worked to break them of their habits, to defend the honor of one to the other, and I had given up. Still, there were limits to how far they could go and they both knew it.

Maeve looked back out the window to the house. "Celeste has beautiful children," Maeve said.

"Thank you."

"They look nothing like her."

Oh, would that we had always lived in a world in which every man, woman and child came equipped with a device for audio recording, still photography, and short films. I would have loved to have evidence more irrefutable than my own memory, since neither my sister nor my wife would back me on this: it was Maeve who had picked out Celeste, and it was Maeve that Celeste first loved. I was there on that snowy car ride between 30th Street Station and Celeste's parents' house in Rydal in 1968, and Maeve was warm enough to clear the ice off the roads. Celeste was in the back seat, wedged between our suitcases, her knees pulled up because there was no room in the back of the little Beetle. Maeve's eyes kept drifting to the rearview mirror as she piled on the questions: Where was she in school?

Celeste was a sophomore at Thomas More College. "I tell myself it's Fordham."

"That's where I would have gone. I had wanted to study with the Jesuits."

"Where did you go to school?" Celeste asked.

Maeve sighed. "Barnard. They came through with a scholarship so that was that."

As far as I knew nothing in this story was true. Maeve certainly hadn't been a scholarship student.

"What are you studying?" Maeve asked her.

"I'm an English major," Celeste said. "I'm taking Twentieth Century American Poetry this semester."

"Poetry was my favorite class!" Maeve's eyebrows raised in amazement. "I don't keep up the way I should. That's the real drag about graduating. There's never as much time to read when there's no one there to make you do it."

"When did you ever take a poetry class?" I asked my sister.

"Home is so sad," Maeve said. "It stays as it was left, shaped to the comfort of the last to go as if to win them back. Instead, bereft of anyone to please, it withers so, having no heart to put aside the theft."

Once she was certain Maeve had stopped, Celeste picked up the line in a softer voice. "And turn again to what it started as, a joyous shot at how things ought to be, long fallen wide. You can see how it was: look at the pictures and the cutlery. The music in the piano stool. That vase."

"*Larkin*," the two cried out together. They could have been married on the spot, Maeve and Celeste. Such was their love at that moment.

I looked at Maeve in astonishment. "How did you *know* that?"

"I didn't clear my curriculum with him." Maeve laughed, tilting her head in my direction, and so Celeste laughed too.

"What was your major?" Celeste asked. When I turned around to look at her now she was utterly mysterious to me. They both were.

"Accounting." Maeve downshifted with a smack of her open palm as we gently slid down a snowy hill. Over the river and through the woods. "Very dull, very practical. I needed to make a living."

"Oh, sure," Celeste nodded.

But Maeve hadn't majored in accounting. There was no such thing as an accounting major at Barnard. She'd majored in math. And she was first in her class. Accounting was what she did, not what she'd studied. Accounting was what she could do in her sleep.

"There's that cute little Episcopal church." Maeve slowed down on Homestead Road. "I went to a wedding there once. When I was growing up the nuns about had a fit if they heard we'd even set foot in a Protestant church."

Celeste nodded, having no idea she'd been asked a question. Thomas More was a Jesuit school but that didn't necessarily mean the girl in the back of the car was a Catholic. "We go to St. Hilary."

She was Catholic.

The house, when we pulled up in front of it, proved to be considerably less grand than the Dutch House and considerably grander than the third floor walk-up where Maeve still lived in those days. Celeste's house was a respectable Colonial clapboard painted yellow with white trim, two leafless maples shivering in the front yard, one of them sporting a rope swing; the kind of house about which one could make careless assumptions about a happy childhood, though in Celeste's case those assumptions proved true.

"You've been so nice," Celeste started, but Maeve cut her off. "We'll take you in."

"But you don't—"

"We've made it this far," Maeve said, putting the car in park. "The least we can do is see you to the door."

I had to get out anyway. I folded my seat forward and leaned back in to help Celeste out, then I took her bag. Her father was still at his dental practice filling cavities, staying late because the office would be closed on Thanksgiving and the day after.

People came home for the holidays with toothaches they'd been putting off. Her two younger brothers were watching television with friends and shouted to Celeste but didn't trouble themselves to leave their program. There was a much warmer greeting from a black Lab named Lumpy. "His name was Larry when he was a puppy but he's gotten sort of lumpy," Celeste said.

Celeste's mother was friendly and harried, cooking a sit-down dinner for twenty-two relatives who would descend the next day at noon. Small wonder she'd forgotten to pick up her third child at the train station. (There were five Norcross children in total.) After introductions had been made, Maeve got Celeste to write her phone number on a scrap of paper, saying that she drove into the city every now and then and could give her a ride, could even promise her the front seat next time. Celeste was grateful and her mother was grateful, stirring a pot of cranberries on the stove.

"You two should stay for dinner. I owe you such a favor!" Celeste's mother said to us, and then she realized her mistake. "What am I saying? You're just home yourself. Columbia! Your parents must be dying to see you."

Maeve thanked her for the invitation and accepted a small hug from Celeste, who shook my hand. My sister and I went down the snowy front walk. It seemed that every light in every house was on, up and down the block, on both sides of the street. Everyone in Rydal had come home for Thanksgiving.

"Since when did you ever take a poetry class?" I asked once we had climbed back in the car.

"Since I saw her shove a book of poetry in her bag." Maeve cranked up the car's useless heater. "So what?"

Maeve never tried to impress anyone, not even Lawyer Gooch, whom I believed she was secretly in love with. "Why would you care if Celeste of Rydal thinks you read poetry?"

"Because sooner or later you'll find someone, and I'd rather you found a Catholic from Rydal than a Buddhist from, I don't know, *Morocco.*"

"Are you serious? You're trying to find me a girlfriend?"

"I'm trying to protect my own interests, that's all. Don't give it too much thought."

I didn't.

CHAPTER 9

IF YOU LIVED in Jenkintown in 1968 or went to school at Choate, chances were good you'd cross paths with most of the people there eventually, even if just to nod and say hello, but New York City was a wild card. Every hour was made up of a series of chances, and choosing to walk down one street instead of another had the potential to change everything: whom you met, what you saw or were spared from seeing. In the early days of our relationship, Celeste loved nothing better than to recount our origin story to friends, to strangers, and sometimes to me when we were alone. She'd meant to be on the 1:30 train from Penn Station that day but her roommate wanted to take the subway together as far as Grand Central. The roommate that then proceeded to dawdle with her packing for so long Celeste missed the train.

"I could have gone on some other train," she said, putting her head on my chest. "Or I could have taken the 4:05 and wound up in a different car. Or I could have been in the right car but picked another seat. We could have missed each other."

"Maybe on that day," I would say, running the tips of my fingers along her fascinating curls. "But I would have found you eventually." I said this because I knew it was what Celeste wanted to hear, this warm girl in my arms who smelled like

Ivory soap, but I believed it too, if not romantically then at least statistically: two kids from Jenkintown and Rydal going to college in New York City were likely to bump into one another somewhere along the way.

"The only reason I picked that seat was because I saw the chemistry book. You weren't even sitting there."

"That's right," I said.

Celeste smiled. "I always did like chemistry."

Celeste was plenty happy in those days, though in retrospect she was the ultimate victim of bad timing, thinking that because she was good in chemistry she should marry a doctor instead of becoming a doctor herself. Had she come along a few years later she might have missed that trap altogether.

The chemistry book was its own piece of chance. Had I paid attention from the beginning of the semester the way I should have, Dr. Able would have had no reason to put the fear of God into me about failing, and I wouldn't have turned *Organic Chemistry Today* into an extension of my arm. Who knew a chemistry book could act as bait for pretty girls?

Had I not been close to failing, I wouldn't have been reading chemistry on the train. Had I not been reading chemistry on the train, I wouldn't have met Celeste, and my life as I have known it would never have been set in motion.

But to tell this story only in terms of book and train, kinetics and girl, was to miss the reason I had very nearly failed chemistry to begin with.

Maeve scotched any hopes I'd had of trying out for Columbia's basketball team. She said I'd be distracted from my classwork, wreck my GPA, and lose my chance to liquidate the trust before Norma and Bright could get to it. It wasn't much of a team anyway. The upshot was I played ball whenever I could find a game, and on a sunny Saturday morning in the beginning of my junior year, I fell in with five guys from Columbia heading over to Mount Morris Park. I had the ball. As a group we were skinny, long-haired, bearded, bespectacled, and in one case, barefoot. Ari, who left his dorm room without shoes, told us he had heard there were always guys looking for a game over at Mount Morris. His authority impressed us, though in retrospect I'm pretty sure he had no idea what he was talking about. Harlem was a bloody mess, and while Mayor Lindsay was willing to walk the streets, Columbia students tended to stay on their own side of the gate. It had been different in 1959 when Maeve went to Barnard. Girls and their dates still got dressed up to go to the Apollo for amateur night, but by 1968 pretty much every representation of hope in the country had been put up against a wall and shot. Boys at Columbia went to class and boys in Harlem went to war, a reality not suspended for a friendly Saturday pick-up game.

Walking to the park, the six of us began to get the message. We kept our eyes open, and so saw the open eyes of everyone we passed—the kids lying out across the stoops and the men clustered on the corner and the women leaning out of open windows—everyone watching. The women and girls walking by suggested that we should go home and fuck ourselves. The trash bags piled up along the curbs split open and spilled into the streets. A man in a white sleeveless undershirt with a pick the size of a dinner plate tucked into the back of his afro leaned into the open window of a car and turned the radio up. A brownstone with its windows boarded over and its front door missing had a notice pasted to the brick: *Tax foreclosure. For sale by public auction.* I could see my father writing down the time and the date of the auction in the small spiral notebook he kept in his breast pocket.

"You see a sign like that," he said to me once when I was a

boy and we were standing in front of an apartment building in North Philadelphia, "it might as well say *Come and get it*."

I told him I didn't understand.

"The owners gave up, the bank gave up. The only people who haven't given up work for the Bureau of Internal Revenue because they never give up. All you have to do to own the building is pay the taxes."

"Conroy!" a kid from my chemistry class named Wallace called back to me. "Hustle up." They were already down the block and now I was a white guy alone, holding a basketball.

"Conroy! Move your ass!" said one of the three boys sitting on the steps of the next building, and then another one yelled, "Conroy! Make me a sandwich!"

That was it, the moment of my spiritual awakening on 120th Street.

I pointed to the building with the auction notice. "Who lives there?" I asked the kid who thought I'd come to fix his lunch.

"How the fuck do I know?" he said in ten-year-old parlance.

"He's a cop," the second boy said.

"Cops don't have balls," the third boy said, and this sent all three of them into rolling hysterics.

My team had been waiting and now, moving a little faster, they circled back. "Time to go, man," Ari said.

"He's a cop," the boy said again, then held out his finger like a gun. "All of you, cops."

I threw a chest pass to the kid in the red T-shirt and he threw it straight back—one, two.

"Throw it here," the next one said.

"Take these guys to the park," I said to the boys. "I'm going to be one minute." None of them seemed to think that this was a good idea, not my teammates and not the boys on the stoop, but I was already turning back to the liquor store on the corner to see if I could borrow a pen. Everything I needed to know could be written on the palm of my hand.

On my way to look for a pick-up game at Mount Morris I became the sole beneficiary to an inheritance greater than my father's business or his house. My entire life snapped into sudden Technicolor clarity: I needed a building, specifically the one on 120th near Lenox, in order to be who I was meant to be. I would put the windows in and replace the door myself. I would patch the dry wall and sand the floors and someday I would collect the rent on Saturdays. Maeve believed that medical school was my destiny and Celeste believed that she was my destiny and both of them were wrong. On Monday I called Lawyer Gooch and explained my situation: my father had made provisions for my education, yes, but wouldn't it be so much more in keeping with his wishes to use that money instead to buy a building and launch myself in the career he'd intended me to have? Looking past the violence and filth, the pockets of impenetrable wealth, Manhattan was an island, after all, and this part of the island was next to an ever-expanding university. Couldn't he petition the trust on my behalf? Lawyer Gooch listened patiently before explaining that wishes and logic were not applicable to trusts. My father had made arrangements for my education, not my career in real estate. Two weeks later I attended the public auction of the building that was meant to change my life. It sold for $1,800. I had no plans to recover.

But as usual, it turned out I was wrong. There were a lot of buildings in the neighborhood I now haunted, and it wasn't impossible to find another one that was burned out, full of squatters, and scheduled for auction. I spent so much time in Harlem I felt suspicious even to myself. A white person was someone who either had something to buy or to sell, or he had plans to disrupt the commerce of others. I was included in this, even though I meant to buy something bigger than a bag of weed, and I meant to stay. While most Columbia students had never been to Harlem, I could have given tours. I did labor intensive searches at the library and the records office to find the property taxes and price comps in a ten-block radius. I made appointments to see buildings that were for sale and tracked foreclosures in the paper. The only thing I neglected was chemistry, until I began to neglect Latin, physiology and European history as well.

My father had taught me how to check the joists beneath a porch for rot, how to talk an angry tenant down and how to ground an outlet, but I had never seen him buy anything bigger than a sandwich. I realized I had two narratives for his life: the one in which he lived in Brooklyn and was poor, and the one in which he owned and ran a substantial construction and real estate company and was rich. What I lacked was the bridge. I didn't know how he'd gotten from one side to the other.

"Real estate," Maeve said.

I'd called her at home on a Saturday, a sack of quarters I should have been saving on the metal shelf in front of the dorm pay phone. "I know it was real estate, but what was the deal? What did he buy? Who would have given him a loan if he was really as poor as he always said he was?"

The line was quiet for a minute. "What are you doing?"

"I'm trying to understand what happened in our life. I'm trying to do the thing you're always doing, I'm decoding the past."

"On a Saturday morning," she asked. "Long distance?"

Maeve was exactly the person I should have talked to, because she was my sister and because she had a knack for money. If anyone could have helped me solve the problem it was her, but Maeve wasn't going to listen to anything that might sidetrack me from her dream of medical school. And even if I could have told her, what would I have said? I'd found another building in Harlem up for auction? A rooming house with a single bathroom on every floor? "I'm just trying to figure out what happened," I said, and that much was true. I had spent countless hours in my father's company and never asked him a thing. The operator came on and said I needed to put in another seventy-five cents for the next three minutes, and when I declined to do so the line went dead.

Dr. Able alone had seen me slip away, and it was Dr. Able who called me into his office to bring me back to the righteous path of chemistry. He sent me to the department secretary to schedule appointments so that I could meet with him once a week during office hours. He said I had no absences left, and from then on would be expected to be present in class regardless of my health. While the rest of the students would be assigned four or five questions from the end of every chapter, I was to answer all of the questions and come in to have my answers checked. I was never sure if I'd been singled out for punishment or benevolence, but either way I didn't think I deserved it.

"Bring your parents by," he said to me a few days before parents' visiting weekend. "I'll tell them how well you're doing, relieve their troubled minds."

I was standing at the door of Dr. Able's office and took an extra beat to decide whether to tell him the truth or just say thank you and leave it at that. I liked my persecutor, but my story was complicated and tended to engender a kind of sympathy in other people I'd never been able to tolerate.

"What?" he said, waiting for my answer. "No parents?"

He meant it as I joke and so I laughed. "No parents," I said.

"Well, I'll be in the office on Saturday as part of the festivities if you and your legal guardian want to come by."

"We might do that," I said, and thanked him as I left.

I put it together easily enough, and years later, Maurice Able, whom everyone called Morey, confirmed my suspicion: he went to the registrar's office to look at my file. He never asked about my parents again, but he started to suggest we hold our weekly meetings over lunch at the Hungarian Pastry Shop. He invited me to the dinners he and his wife hosted for the graduate students in chemistry. He checked to see how I was doing in my other classes and alerted those teachers to my situation. Morey Able took pity on me and became my advisor, thinking it had been my parentless state that had put me in academic peril, when in fact it was my father. Halfway through college, I had come to see I was a great deal like my father.

Archimedes' Principle states that any body completely or partially submerged in a fluid at rest is acted upon by an upward force, the magnitude of which is equal to the weight of the fluid displaced by the body. Or to put it another way, you can hold a beach ball under water but the second you stop it's going to shoot straight back up. And so throughout my interminable academic career I suppressed my nature. I did everything that was required of me while keeping a furtive list of the buildings I passed that were for sale: asking price, selling price, weeks on the market. I lurked at the periphery of foreclosure auctions, a habit I found hard to break. Like Celeste, I got an A in Organic Chemistry. I then went on to biochemistry second semester and followed that with a year of physics with a lab my senior year. Dr. Able, who had met me when I was drowning, never took his eye off me again. With the exception of that one half-semester, I was a good student, but even after I had recovered my standing, he always had it in his mind I could do better. He taught me how to learn and then relearn, to study until the answer to every question was coded in my fingerprints. I had told him I wanted to be a doctor and he believed me. When the time came to apply, he not only wrote me a letter of recommendation, he walked my application twenty blocks uptown and handed it to the director of admissions at the medical school at Columbia himself.

The fact that I had never wanted to be a doctor was nothing more than a footnote to a story that interested no one. You wouldn't think a person could succeed in something as difficult as medicine without wanting to do it, but it turned out I was part of a long and noble tradition of self-subjugation. I would guess at least half the students in my class would rather have been anywhere else. We were fulfilling the expectations that had been set for us: the sons of doctors were expected to become doctors so as to honor the tradition; the sons of immigrants were expected to become doctors in order to make a better life for their families; the sons who had been driven to work the hardest and be the smartest were expected to become doctors because back in the day medicine was still where the smart kids went. Women had yet to be allowed to enroll at Columbia as undergraduates but there were a handful of them in my medical school class. Who knows, maybe they were the ones who actually wanted to be there. No one expected their daughters to become doctors in 1970, the daughters still had to fight for it. P&S, as the College of Physicians & Surgeons was known, had a thriving theater troupe made up of medical student actors, and to watch the shows the P&S Club put on—the dreary soon-to-be radiologists and urologists in half an inch of eyeliner bursting into gleeful song—was to see what they might have done with their lives had their lives belonged only to them.

The first day of orientation took place in a lecture hall with stadium seating. Various faculty laid out impossible cases and told us that by the end of the year we would be able, if not to solve these cases, then to at least discuss them knowledgeably. The head of cardiac surgery took the stage to extol the wonders of the cardiac surgery program, and the boys who had told their mothers they were going to be heart surgeons whistled and hollered and clapped, each one thinking that this was going to be him one day: the lord of it all. Then a neurologist came out and other members of the audience cheered. One by one every organ had its moment in the sun: Kidneys! Lungs! Oh, how they beamed! We were the smartest bunch of idiots around.

When I was in medical school I had a telephone in my apartment. We all did. Even in our first year they wanted us to know we could be called to the hospital at any hour. My phone was ringing when I came in the door during my second week of school.

"I have the *most* fantastic news," Maeve said. Long-distance rates went down at six o'clock and then again at ten. The clock read five past ten.

"All ears."

"I had lunch with Lawyer Gooch today, strictly social, he thinks he's supposed to be my father now. Halfway through the meal he mentions that Andrea had contacted him."

There was a time when this news might have perked me up but I was too tired to care. If I started my homework immediately I might be asleep by two in the morning. "And?"

"She called him to say she thought that sending you to medical school was excessive. She said she'd been given to believe that the trust was for college only."

"Who gave her to believe that?"

"No one. She's making it up. She said she hadn't complained about Choate because you'd just lost your father, but at this point she feels we're bilking the trust."

"We are bilking the trust." I sat down in the single kitchen chair and leaned against the little table. The phone was in the kitchen, what I called the kitchen closet. I tracked the path of a cockroach as it wandered down the front of the yellow metal cabinet and slipped beneath the door.

"He told me she'd looked up the cost of Columbia and that it was the single most expensive medical school in the country. Did you even know that? Number one. She said it's her proof that this is all a plot against her, and that you could go to U-Penn for half of what Columbia costs and leave some money for the girls. She told him she simply wasn't going to pay for Columbia anymore."

"But she doesn't pay for it. The trust pays for it."

"She perceives herself to be the trust."

I rubbed my eyes and nodded to no one. "Well, what does Lawyer Gooch say? Does she have any case?"

"None!" Maeve's gleeful voice was loud in my ear. "He said you can stay in school for the rest of your life."

"That's not going to happen."

"You never know. There are lots of fascinating things to pursue. You could live the life of the mind."

I thought of the endless maze that was the Columbia-Presbyterian Medical Center, our professors in their white coats sailing down the hallways like gods in their heaven. "I don't want to be a doctor. You know that, right?"

Maeve didn't miss a beat. "You don't have to *be* a doctor, you only have to study to be one. Once you're finished you can play a doctor on television for all I care. You can be anything you want, as long as it requires a great deal of schooling."

"Go help the poor," I said. Maeve taught an evening class on how to make a budget through Catholic Charities and on Tuesday nights she stayed up late to grade their notebooks and correct their math. "I need to study."

"I wish you could be happy about this," she said. "But the truth is it doesn't matter. I'm happy enough for both of us."

Happiness had been suspended for the foreseeable future. I was taking Human Histology, Embryology, and Gross Anatomy. The lessons of chemistry that Dr. Able had drilled into me held fast: I answered every question at the end of every chapter and in the morning I woke up and answered them again. We were put in groups of four, given a cadaver, a saw, and a scalpel, and told to go to work. The only other dead person I'd seen until that point was my father, and I found it far too easy to picture a group of white coats perched like vultures around his bed, waiting to open him up. Disassemble, reassemble. Our cadaver was older than my father, a smaller, brown-skinned man. His mouth was open in the same horrible way, as if it were the universal last act to try and fail to gasp a final breath. I would have thought that in order to cut a man apart and label him I would have needed at the very least some degree of curiosity, but that wasn't the case. I did it because it was the assignment. Some of my classmates vomited in the lab that first day, others made it to the hall or even the bathroom, but the carnage of our work didn't hit me until I was outside again, the sweet-sick smell of formaldehyde still painted in my nose. I threw up on the sidewalk in Washington Heights along with the junkies and the drunks.

I had seen Celeste from time to time during my junior and senior years of college. I had seen other women, too. Dating was an activity that required thoughtfulness and planning and time, and in medical school I had none of those luxuries. Going out with Celeste felt the least like dating. She asked almost nothing of me and she gave the most in return. She was agreeable and cheerful, pretty without being distracting. When I went to Philadelphia on the train she came with me. Maeve and

I would drive her to Rydal but Celeste never insisted that I spend time with her family. Maeve and Celeste were still affectionate with each other in those days. Maeve was happy because Columbia Medical was expensive, had top rankings and offered me no financial aid. Celeste was happy because it was farther north than Columbia's main campus and therefore easier for her to get to from Thomas More, where she was still an undergraduate English major. My tiny apartment was two blocks from the medical school, and Celeste would come down from the Bronx after her last class on Friday afternoon and stay with me until it was time for her to work her shift at the front desk in the dean's office Monday morning. When I was an undergraduate, we worked around my roommate's schedule, but in medical school we fell into a kind of three-day-a-week marriage, which, in retrospect, was probably as much marriage as we were capable of. We lived under the rules that had been established when we met on the train: I had to study and she had to let me. But we also lived in the America of 1969: the war was grinding on, protestors filled the streets, students still commandeered administrative offices, and we had as much guilt-free, diaphragm-protected sex as time allowed. I will forever associate the study of human anatomy not with my cadaver but with Celeste's young body lying naked on my bed. She let me run my hands across every muscle and bone, naming them as I went along. The parts of her I couldn't see I felt for, and, in doing so, learned how best to bind her to me. The little fun I had in those days I had with Celeste—the splurge of Szechuan noodles in white paper cartons eaten on the roof of the hospital late at night, the time she got free passes to see *Midnight Cowboy* from her French professor who had meant for her to go with him. Everything went so well for us until she turned her attention to her impending graduation. She wanted to start making plans for the future. That was when she told me we'd have to get married.

"I can't get married after my first year of medical school," I said, not mentioning the fact that I didn't want to get married. "Things are going to get harder, not easier."

"But my parents won't let us live together, and they won't pay for me to get my own place and wait here while you finish school. They can't afford something like that."

"So you'll get a job, right? That's what people do after college."

But as soon as I said it I understood that *I* was supposed to be Celeste's job. The poetry courses and the senior thesis on Trollope were all well and good but I was what she'd been studying. She meant to keep the tiny apartment clean and make dinner and eventually have a baby. Women had read about their liberation in books but not many of them had seen what it looked like in action. Celeste had no idea what she was supposed to do with a life that was entirely her own.

"You're breaking up with me," she said.

"I'm not breaking up with you." What I wanted was what I had: three nights a week. And to be perfectly honest, I would have been happier with two. I didn't understand why she had to sleep over on Sundays and then get up so early Monday morning to catch the train back to school.

Celeste sat down on the bed and stared out the window into the dirty air shaft and the brick wall beyond. She was sitting with her spine rounded, her pretty blond curls tangled over her slumped shoulders, and I wanted to tell her sit up straight. Everything would have gone so much better for her had she been able to sit up straight.

"If we aren't going forward then you're breaking up with me."

"I'm not breaking up with you," I said again, but I didn't sit down on the bed beside her and I didn't hold her hand.

Her impossibly round blue eyes were brimming over with tears. "Why won't you help me?" she asked, her voice so small I could barely hear her.

* * *

"HELP HER?" MAEVE said. "She isn't talking about you changing a flat. She wants you to marry her."

I had taken the train home for the weekend. I needed to talk to my sister. I needed to think things through without Celeste in my bed, which, despite her continued insistence that I was breaking up with her, was still where she was sleeping Friday through Sunday. I had come home to sort out my life.

Maeve said she had an emergency pack of cigarettes in the glove box and we decided that this was a good time to relapse. The leaves and flowers of early spring were already crowding out our view of the Dutch House. Wrens patrolled the sidewalk, looking for twigs. "You can't marry her a year into medical school. That's insane. She has no business asking you for that. And even when you're finished with school, once you're in your residency, things are only going to get worse. You're not going to have any time until you've finished."

As it stood now, medical school made my undergraduate education look like one long game of badminton. I wasn't so sure how I was supposed to hold it all together once things got worse. And things would always get worse. "When I've finished training I'm not going to have any time," I said. "I'll be starting a practice, I'll be working. Or I won't be starting a practice because I have no intention of being a doctor, so then I'll have to go out and find a job and *that* won't be the right time. I can say that for the rest of my life, can't I? This isn't the right time." Though Dr. Able had told me it wasn't like that. He said the first year was the hardest, then the second, then the third. He said it was all about learning a new system of learning, and that the farther along I went, the more fluid I would become. I hadn't told Dr. Able about Celeste.

Maeve peeled the cellophane off the pack. Once she lit her cigarette I could tell she hadn't really quit. She looked too natural, too relaxed. "Then the question isn't about timing," she said. "You deserve to get married and the timing will always be bad."

"Diabetics shouldn't smoke." I was far enough along in school to know that much. In fact, that was knowledge that had nothing to do with medical school.

"Diabetics shouldn't do anything."

"Have you tested your sugar?"

"Jesus, you're going to start asking me questions about my blood sugar? Stick to the topic. What are you going to do about Celeste?"

"I could marry her over the summer." I had meant it to sound snappish because she'd snapped at me, but as soon as I said it I had a surprising glimpse of the practicality. Why not? A clean apartment, good food, loads of sex, a happy Celeste, a level of adulthood I hadn't yet imagined. I repeated the words just to feel them leave my mouth. It sounded worldly somehow. *I could marry her over the summer.* All the various scenarios I'd played out in my mind up until now involved disappointing Celeste—she'd be hurt and I'd feel guilty, and then, after it was over, I would miss the naked girl in my bed. But I'd never considered the possibility of saying yes, of simply seeing this as one inconvenient time in a long string of inconvenient times ahead. Maybe marrying now wouldn't be worse. Maybe it would be better.

Maeve nodded as if this was what she'd expected me to say. "Do you remember when Dad and Andrea got married?"

"Of course." She wasn't listening to me.

"It's strange, but my memory always conflates their wedding and the funeral."

"No, I do that, too. I think it has to do with the flowers."

"Do you think he loved her?"

"Andrea?" I said, as if we could have been talking about someone else. "Not at all."

Maeve nodded again and blew a long stream of smoke out the window. "I think he was tired of being alone, that's what I think. I think there was this big hole in his life and Andrea was always there, telling him she was the person who could fill it up, and eventually he decided to believe her."

"Or he got tired of listening to her."

"You think he married her just to shut her up?"

I shrugged. "He married her to end the conversation about whether or not they should get married." As soon as I said it, I understood what we were talking about.

"So you love Celeste and you want to spend your life with her." She wasn't asking me a question. She was just making sure, finishing things off.

I wouldn't get married in the summer. The idea slipped off as quickly and completely as it had arrived, and the feeling I was left with was everything I had imagined: sadness, elation, loss. "No, not like that."

We sat with the final decision for a while. "You're sure?"

I nodded my head, lit a second cigarette. "Why don't we ever talk about your love life? It would be a huge relief for me."

"It would be for me, too," Maeve said, "but I don't have one."

I looked at her square on. "I don't believe you."

And my sister, who could outstare an owl, turned her face away. "Well, you should."

*   *   *

AFTER I CAME back from Jenkintown, Celeste decided everything was Maeve's fault. "She tells you to break up with me three weeks before finals? Who does something like that?"

We were in my apartment. I had told her not to come down, that I would take the train up to her and we could talk there, but she said that was ridiculous. "We're not going to talk in front of my roommate," she said.

"Maeve didn't tell me to break up with you. She didn't tell me anything. All she did was listen."

"She told you not to marry me."

"She did not."

"Who talks to their sister about these things anyway? Do you think when my brother was trying to decide whether or not to go to dental school he came out to the Bronx so we could hash it out together? People don't *do* that. It isn't natural."

"Maybe he wouldn't talk to you." I felt a quick gust of annoyance and I let it turn to anger, anger being infinitely preferable to guilt. "And maybe that's because he knew you wouldn't listen to him. Or maybe he would have talked it over with your parents because you *have* parents. I've got Maeve, okay? That's it."

Celeste felt her advantage tipping away and she changed her tack like a little sailboat on a windy pond. "Oh, Danny." She put her hand on my arm.

"Just leave it alone," I said, as if I was the one who was about to be hurt. "It's not going to work. It doesn't have to be anyone's fault. It's bad timing, that's all."

And for that small conciliatory sentence pulled from the air she went to bed with me one more time. Afterwards she said she wanted to spend the night, that she would leave first thing in the morning, but I said no. Without any more discussion we packed up what was hers and sat together on the train back up to the Bronx, each of us with a bag in our lap.

Chapter 10

I DID ESPECIALLY WELL in my surgical rotation. I was as consci-
entious as anyone else in my class but twice as fast, which
just goes to show that basketball had served me well. Fast was
how hospitals made their money, so while accuracy was very
much appreciated, speed got you noticed. Just before graduation, the attending pressed me to take another three years for a
subspecialty in thoracic surgery after my residency. I had spent
the last two hours assisting in a right lower lobectomy and he
admired the deftness of my knots. We were sitting in a tiny
room with a set of bunk beds and a desk, a place we were
meant to sleep for twenty minutes between cases. I kept thinking I could still smell blood and I got up for the second time to
wash my face in the small sink in the corner while the attending
droned on about my bankable talent. I wasn't in much of a
mood, and as I dried myself with paper towels I told him I
might have talent but I had no plans to use it.

"So what are you doing here?" He was smiling, anticipating
the punch line of what he was sure was the setup to my joke.

I shook my head. "It's the rotation. This one's not for me."
There was no point in explaining. His parents had probably
come from Bangladesh so that one day their son could be a
surgeon in New York. His entire family had doubtlessly been

crushed beneath a load of debt and didn't need to hear about the effort it took to liquidate an education trust.

"Listen," he said, pulling off his scrub top and throwing it in the bin. "Surgeons are the kings. If you can be a king there's no point being a jack, am I right?"

I could see every bone in his rib cage. "I'm a jack," I said.

He laughed even though I'd failed to make the joke. "There are two kinds of people who come out of this place: surgeons and the ones who didn't make it as surgeons. Nobody else. You're going to be a surgeon."

I told him I'd think about it just to shut him up. My twenty minutes were down to fourteen minutes and I needed every one of them. I was exhausted beyond anything I could remember. I wanted to tell him I wasn't going to do a residency, or an internship for that matter. Medical school would finish and I would crack the code on real estate and sail out of this place without so much as a backwards glance.

Except I didn't. I tried and failed and tried again and failed again. Buildings lingered on the market for years and then sold for a fraction of their worth. I saw buildings in foreclosure go for as little as $1,200, and even when they were burned-out shells covered in graffiti, even when every pane of glass had taken a brick, I thought I was the one to save them. Not the people, mind you, the ones who might have lived in those buildings. I had no grand ideas that I was the one to save the men and women who lined the hallways of the ER, waiting for a minute of my time. I wanted the buildings. But then I would have to settle up the back taxes, buy the doors, fix the windows, pay the insurance. I would have to dispatch the squatters and the rats. I didn't know how to do any of that.

Despite every promise I had ever made to myself, I went into the internship program at Albert Einstein in the Bronx. Not only was there no tuition for internships ("Okay," Maeve said, "I didn't know that"), they paid me. At this point, the trust was obligated only to cover my rent and give me a small amount for expenses, which I banked. I was no longer bilking Andrea in any meaningful way, not that I ever had. I was no longer avenging my sister. I was, in fact, finishing my training in medicine. I got along with the people I worked with, impressed the faculty, helped my patients, and every day reinforced the lessons I had learned in chemistry: you don't have to like your work to be good at it. I stayed at Albert Einstein for my residency, and while I still made the rare trip to the law school at Columbia where I stood in the back of the hall to take in a lecture on real estate law, those trips were few and far between. I followed the real estate market the way other men followed baseball: I memorized statistics and never played the game.

Dr. Able still kept an eye on me, or maybe, as he would have said, we had become friends. He invited me for coffee every three or four months and kept at me until we locked down a date. He would talk about his students, I would complain about my workload. We talked about departmental politics, or, when we were in the company of our better selves, science. I didn't talk to him about real estate, nor did I ask him if chemistry had been the thing he'd wanted to do with his life. It wouldn't have occurred to me. The waitress brought our coffee.

"We're going to London this summer," he said. "We've rented a flat in Knightsbridge. Two whole weeks. Our daughter is working there, Nell. You know Nell."

"I know Nell."

Dr. Able rarely mentioned his family, either in deference to my own situation or because that wasn't the nature of our relationship, but on this particular spring day he was too happy to keep his personal life to himself. "She's doing art restoration.

She went over there three years ago for a postdoc that turned into a full-time job. I don't think she's ever coming back."

There was no point in mentioning that Nell Able and I had exchanged a champagne-soaked kiss one New Year's Eve in his apartment years before. She had come into her parents' bedroom while I was digging through a pile of black coats on the bed, looking for the black coat that belonged to Celeste. The room was dark, a million miles down the hallway from the music and raucous laughter. Nell Able. We had tipped into the pile of coats for a couple of minutes before righting ourselves.

"We haven't been to see her a single time since she left," her father went on. "We always make her come home to us. But Alice finally secured the major gift for the Health Sciences Building campaign. Five years she's been chasing that money down. Alice told them she'd quit if they didn't give her the time off."

Alice Able, who had so kindly set a place for me at her table all these years, worked in the development office at the Columbia Medical School. I wondered if I had ever known any more about her job than that. I wondered if Dr. Able had been telling me this for years: his wife's job was to raise money for a new Health Sciences building. I wondered if Alice had told me this herself and I had just failed to register it. I used to run into her every now and then, walking across campus. She would ask me about my classes. Did I volley back a question in order to fulfill the tenets of polite conversation, or did I merely answer and wait for her to ask me something else?

"They do some kind of x-ray of the paintings now," Dr. Able was saying, "to find out if there's another painting underneath. Pentimento without all the guesswork."

"Where?" I asked. I could sense what was coming before I could fully comprehend it—my future, this moment.

"The Tate," Dr. Able said. "Nell's at the Tate."

I took a sip of coffee, counted to ten. "Where will they build the new Health Sciences building?"

He waved his hand as if to indicate up there, north. "I have no idea. You'd think that would be the first order of business, but until they get that major gift they don't make any commitments. I imagine it has to be somewhere near the Armory. Do you know about the Armory? What a disaster that's going to be."

I nodded my head, and when the waitress brought the check, I caught it. Dr. Able fought me, and for the first time since I had known him, I won.

I stopped by the Columbia bookstore to get some maps of the Medical Center campus and Washington Heights before heading back to the Bronx. The undergraduates I passed could have been boys of fourteen, shaggy-haired and barefoot on their way to the beach. I sat on the steps of the Butler Library in front of South Field and unfolded my purchases. Like Dr. Able, it seemed to me the area near the Track and Field Armory was inevitable, even if the medical school had yet to come to this conclusion. The Armory was about to be converted into an 1,800-bed homeless shelter, which would doubtlessly lower the price on surrounding parking lots. They weren't hard to find. By the end of the week I had two under contract with a six-month due diligence period. After all those years of banging on a locked door, I found the door wide open. The seller was a man long convinced he had no options. He had fired his broker and wore a collared shirt and tie to our meeting, hoping to take care of things himself. He was tired enough to take the deal I offered. I told him I was a doctor and doctors had no safe place to park. I made him laugh when I said that was why none of us had cars. He liked me enough to feel sorry to be sticking me with two parking lots that had been for sale for three years. He thought I was cutting my own throat when I asked for a specific performance clause in the contract: he would surrender the right to change his mind and I would surrender the right to change mine. We were locked in this together. The seller was promised he would walk out of the deal with money in hand in six months. The buyer promised to find that money and claim the parking lots. In retrospect, it looked perfectly obvious, but at the time I might as well have been standing with my back to a craps table, throwing dice over my shoulder. I was buying two parking lots next to a massive homeless shelter. I was betting money I didn't have on the assumption that I would own the land underneath a building that had yet to be placed. I was banking that the decision about the placement of the building would be made before I had to get a loan I'd never qualify for.

Five months later I sold the parking lots to the College of Physicians and Surgeons, and with the considerable proceeds I paid off the seller, got a loan from the Housing Fund, and put a deposit on my first building on West 116th. Most of the eighteen units were occupied, the storefront on the ground floor was split between a laundry and a Chinese takeout—both businesses in good health. According to the comps, the building was undervalued by twelve percent. I was finally pursuing opportunity beyond my resources. I was not a doctor. I was, at last, myself. I would have dropped out of the residency program on the day I signed the escrow papers, but Maeve said no.

"You could still get a doctorate in chemistry," she said on the phone. "You liked chemistry."

I didn't like chemistry, I just wound up being good at it. We'd had this conversation before.

"Then think about business school. That would come in handy now, or law school. You'd be unstoppable with a law degree."

The answer was no. I had my career, or at least the start of one. It was as close to insurrection as I ever came.

"Well," she said, "There's no point in quitting now. Finish what you started."

Maeve agreed to keep my books and handle the tax exchange codes while I went back to Albert Einstein with less than six months on the clock. I didn't regret it. Those final months were the only part of my medical training I ever enjoyed, knowing that I was just about to walk out the door. I bought two brownstones in foreclosure, one for $1,900 and another for $2,300. They were disasters. They were mine.

Three weeks later I went to Immaculate Conception back in Jenkintown to attend the funeral of Mr. Martin, my high school basketball coach. Non–small cell lung cancer at the age of fifty, having never smoked a day in his life. Mr. Martin had been good to me in those storm-tossed days after my father's death, and I remembered his wife, who'd sat in the bleachers for all of the games and cheered the team on, a mother to us all. There was a reception afterwards in the church basement and when I saw a girl in a black dress with her blond hair neatly pinned, I walked over and touched her shoulder. As soon as Celeste turned around I remembered every single thing I'd ever liked about her. There were no recriminations, no distance. I leaned down to kiss her cheek and she squeezed my hand, the way she might have done had it always been our intention to meet there in the basement after the funeral. Celeste had been a friend of the Martins' daughter, a detail I'd either forgotten or had never known.

I'd learned a lot about Celeste in the years she'd been gone: I came to see her willingness to not be a distraction as something that took effort. I didn't even know to be grateful for it until I was with other women who wanted to read me articles from the paper in the morning while I was studying, or read me their horoscope, or my horoscope, or explain their feelings to me while crying over the fact that I had never explained my feelings to them. Celeste, on the other hand, would sink into her giant British novel and stay there. She didn't slam the plates trying to get my attention, or walk on her toes to show how thoughtful she was about not making any noise. She would peel a peach and cut it up in a dish, or make me a sandwich and leave it on the table without comment the way Sandy and Jocelyn used to do. Celeste had been so adept at making me her job that I hadn't seen her doing it. It wasn't until after she left that I realized she'd stayed those Sunday nights because Sunday was when she washed the sheets and did the rest of the laundry, made the bed, then got back in it.

She and I picked up where we'd left off, or picked up in that better place where we'd been a couple of months before the ending. She was living back at her parents' house in Rydal. She taught reading at the public grade school. She said she missed the city. Pretty soon she was taking the train on Friday nights and going home on Sunday, the way I had always wanted her to. She worked on her lesson plans while I made rounds at the hospital. If her parents questioned the morality of the arrangement, they never said a word. Celeste was closing the deal, and they were going to let her do it her own way.

In all the years I'd known her, going back to that first train ride and the chemistry book, I'd never told Celeste anything about my plans. She knew I didn't have parents without having been told the details of what that meant. She didn't know about Andrea or the trust, or that we had ever lived in the Dutch House. She didn't know that I had bought two parking lots and sold them to buy a building, or that I would never practice medicine. I hadn't even made a conscious decision to exclude her from this information, only that I didn't make a habit of talking about my life. The residency program was almost over and the rest of my classmates had finished their interviews, accepted their offers, and put deposits on moving vans. Celeste, who prided herself on not asking too many questions, was left to wonder where I was going and whether or not she would be coming with me. I could see her pressing herself down, remembering what had happened the last time she'd presented an ultimatum. I knew that the uncertainty was terrifying for her and still, I made love to her and ate the dinners she'd prepared and put off talking to her for as long as I could, because it was easier.

In the end, of course, I told her everything. There was no such thing as jumping into a lake partway. One explanation led to another and soon we were falling back through time: my mother, my father, my sister, the house and Andrea and the girls and the trust. She took it all in, and as the stories of the past unfolded she had nothing but sympathy for me. Celeste wasn't wondering why I had taken so long to tell her about my life, she took the fact that I was telling her now as proof of my love. I put my hand on her thigh and she crossed her other leg over it, securing me to her. The only part that was incomprehensible to her was the least interesting detail in the entire saga: I wasn't going to be a doctor.

"But how could you go through all that training if you aren't going to use it?" We were sitting on a bench looking out across the Hudson River. We were both wearing T-shirts in late April. "All that education. All the money."

"That was the point," I said.

"You didn't want to go to medical school. Fine. You got there in your own way. But you're a doctor now. You have to at least give it a try."

I shook my head. There was a tugboat not too far from us

pushing an enormous barge and I took a moment to revel in the physics. "I'm not going to be a doctor."

"You haven't even done it yet. You can't quit doing something you haven't started."

I was still watching the river. "That's what residency is. You're practicing medicine."

"Then what are you going to do with your life?"

Everything in me wanted to turn the question back on her, but I didn't. "Real estate and development. I own three buildings."

"You're a doctor and you're going to sell real estate?"

There was no place for Celeste to cast her vote in the matter of my future. "It's a little bit more than that." I could hear the peaceful condescension in my voice. She refused to grasp the simplest part of what I was saying.

"It's such a waste," she said, her eyes bright with anger. "I don't know how you can live with it, really. You took someone's spot in the program, do you ever think about that? Someone who wanted to be a doctor."

"Trust me, whoever that person was, he didn't want to be a doctor either. I did that guy a favor."

The problem wasn't mine, after all, it was hers. Celeste had her heart set on marrying a doctor.

*　*　*

MAEVE AND I had been playing tennis over at the high school when she broke up the game after a single crack of lightning. I had an aluminum racquet and she said she wasn't about to watch me get electrocuted during a serve, so we got in the car and drove to the Dutch House, just to check on things before dark. The summer was essentially over and soon it would be time for me to go back for my second year at Choate. We were both miserable about it, each in our own way.

"I remember the very first time I saw this house," Maeve said, straight out of nowhere. The felted sky hung over us, waiting to split apart.

"You do not. You were just a baby then."

She cranked down the window of the Volkswagen. "I was almost six. You remember things from when you were six. I'll tell you what, you would've remembered coming here."

She was right, of course. I had remembered my life very clearly ever since Fluffy cracked me open with the spoon. "So what happened?"

"Dad borrowed some guy's car and he drove us up from Philadelphia. It must have been a Saturday, either that or he'd taken off from work." Maeve stopped and looked through the linden trees, trying to put herself back there. In the summer you really couldn't see anything, the leaves were so thick. "Coming up the driveway, the house was shocking. That's the only word for it. I mean, it's second nature to you, you were born here. You probably grew up thinking everyone lived in a house like this."

I shook my head. "I thought everyone who went to Choate lived in a house like this."

Maeve laughed. Even though she'd forced me into boarding school, she was happy whenever I maligned it. "Dad had already bought the place and Mommy didn't know a goddamn thing about it."

"*What?*"

"I'm serious. He bought it for her as a surprise."

"Where did he get the money?" Even when I was in high school that was my first question.

Maeve shook her head. "All I know is that we were living on the base and he said we were going to go for a ride in his friend's car. Pack a lunch! Everybody in! I mean, that was pretty crazy all by itself. It's not like we'd ever borrowed someone's car before."

The family was the three of them. I was nowhere in the picture.

Maeve had one tan arm stretched along the top of the seat behind my head. She'd gotten me a job at Otterson's for the summer, counting out the plastic bags of corn and taping them into boxes. On the weekends we played tennis at the high school. We kept the racquets and a can of tennis balls in the car, and sometimes she'd show up at lunch to whisk me off for a game. Right in the middle of the work day and no one said a word to us about it, like she owned the place. "Dad was practically gleeful on the drive. He kept pulling over to the side of the road to show me the cows, show me the sheep. I asked him where they all slept at night, and he said there were barns, great big barns just on the other side of that hill, and that every cow had her own room. Mommy looked at him and they broke up laughing. The whole thing was very jolly."

I thought of the countless miles my father and I had logged in together over the years. He was not a man to pull the car over and look at a cow. "Hard to picture."

"Like I said, it was a long time ago."

"Okay, so then you got here."

She nodded, digging through her purse. "Dad pulled all the way up to the front and the three of us got out of the car and stood there, gaping. Mommy asked him if it was a museum and he shook his head, then she asked him if it was a library, and I said, 'It's a house.'"

"Did it look the same?"

"Pretty much. The yard was in rough shape. I remember the grass was really high. Dad asked Mommy what she thought about the house and Mommy said, 'It's something, all right.' Then he looked right at her with this huge smile and he said, 'It's *your* house. I bought it for you.'"

"Seriously?"

The air inside the car was heavy and hot. Even with the windows down our legs stuck to the seats. "Not. One. Clue."

What was that supposed to be? Romantic? I was a teenage boy, and the idea of buying your wife a mansion as a surprise had all the bells and whistles of love as I imagined it, but I also knew my sister, and I knew she wasn't telling me a love story. "So?"

Maeve lit her cigarette with a match. The lighter in the Volkswagen never worked. "She didn't get it, though really, how could she? The war had just ended, we were living at the naval base in some tiny little cracker box that had two rooms. He might as well have taken her to the Taj Mahal and said, Okay, now we live here, just the three of us. Somebody could look you straight in the face and tell you that and you aren't going to understand them."

"Did you go inside?"

"Sure we went inside. He had the keys in his pocket. He *owned* it. He took her hand and we went up the front stairs. When you think about it, *this* is really the entrance to the house"—she held out her open palm to the landscape—"the street, the trees, the driveway. That's what keeps people out. But then you get up to the house and the front is glass so right away the whole thing is laid out for you. Not only have we never seen a house like that, we've never seen the kinds of things that belong in a house like that. Poor Mommy." Maeve shook her head at the thought. "She was terrified, like he was going to shove her into a room full of tigers. She kept saying, 'Cyril, this is someone's house. We can't go in there.'"

This was how it had gone for the Conroys: one generation got shoved in the door and the next generation got shoved out. "What about you?"

She thought about it. "I was a kid, so I was interested. I was upset for Mommy because she was so clearly petrified, but I also understood that this was our house and we were going to live here. Five-year-olds have no comprehension of real estate, it's all about fairy tales, and in the fairy tale you get the castle. I felt bad for Dad if you want to know the truth. Nothing he was trying to do was going right. I might've even felt worse for him than I did for her." She filled her lungs with soft gray smoke and then sent it out to the soft gray sky. "There's a staggering admission for you. Remember how hot the front hall would get in the afternoon, even when it wasn't really hot outside?"

"Sure."

"It was like that. We started to walk around, not very far at first because Mommy didn't want to get too far from the door. I remember the ship in the grandfather clock was just sitting in the waves because no one had wound it. I remember the marble floor and the chandelier. Dad was trying to be the tour guide, 'Look at this mirror! Look at the staircase!' Like maybe she couldn't see the staircase. He'd bought the most beautiful house in Pennsylvania and his wife was looking at him like he'd shot her. We wound up going through every single room. Can you imagine it? Mommy kept saying, 'Who are these people? Why did they leave everything?' We went down the back hall with all those porcelain birds on their own little shelves. Oh my god, I loved those birds so much. I wanted to stick one in my pocket. Dad said the house had been built by the VanHoebeeks in the early 1920s and all of them were dead. Then we went into the drawing room and there they were, the giant VanHoebeeks staring at us like we were thieves."

"All of them are dead," I said on my father's behalf, "and I bought their house from the bank and we get to keep all their stuff." Was everything still there? Were the clothes hanging in the closets? I didn't even know my mother but I was feeling sick for her when I thought about it that way.

"It took a while for Dad to get up the stairs. We went through all the bedrooms. Everything was there: their beds and their pillows and the towels in their bathrooms. I remember there was a silver hairbrush on the dresser in the master bedroom that had hair in it. When we got to my room, Dad said, 'Maeve, I thought that you might like it here.' What kind of a kid wouldn't like that room? Do you remember that night we showed it to Norma and Bright?"

"I do, as a matter of fact."

"Well, I'll tell you, that was exactly what I was like. I went straight to the window seat and Dad pulled the drapes shut. Shangri-la. I lost my mind, and then Mommy lost her mind because she was still thinking that this whole thing was going to be resolved and I was going to be crushed to not have my own princess suite. She said, 'Maeve, get out of there. That doesn't belong to you.' But it did. I knew it did."

"You knew it at the time?" I'd never been in the position of getting my head around what I'd been given. I only understood what I'd lost.

She gave me a tired smile and ran her hand once over the back of my head. My hair was short, shaved at the neck. That's the way things were at Choate, even in the mid-sixties. "I understood parts of it, but no, to tell you the truth, I didn't really understand the whole thing until Norma and Bright did their reenactment of my childhood. I think that's why I felt sorry for them, because in some way I was just feeling sorry for myself."

"That was the night for it. I was certainly feeling sorry for myself."

Maeve let that go. For once it was her story and not mine. "After the bedroom fiasco we went up to the third floor. Dad wanted to show us everything. He knew the tour was getting worse but he couldn't stop himself. The third floor just about did him in. He wore a brace on his knee back then that didn't fit right and he had to straight-leg it up the stairs. The stairs were hell for him. He was okay to do one set but not two. He hadn't gone to the third floor when he bought the place, and when we finally got up there it turned out part of the ceiling in the ballroom had fallen in. It looked like a bomb had gone off, big chunks of plaster smashed all over the floor. Raccoons had eaten their way into the house, the ones with the fleas. They had ripped apart the mattress from the little bedroom to make their nest, ripped into the pillows and the spread, and there was fluff and feathers everywhere. There was this horrible, feral smell, like a wild animal and the shit of that animal and the dead cousin of that animal all at the same time." She made a face at the memory. "If he was looking to make a good first impression he would *not* have taken us to the third floor."

I was still at a point in my life when the house was the hero of every story, our lost and beloved country. There was a neat little boxwood hedge that had been trained to grow up and over the mailbox, and I wanted to get out of the car and go across the street and run my hand over it like I used to do whenever Sandy sent me out to get the mail, like it was my house even then. "Please tell me you left after that."

"Oh, darling, no, we were just getting started." She turned her back on the house so that she was facing me. She was wearing the T-shirt I'd brought her home from Choate and an old pair of shorts, and she pulled her long, tan legs into the seat. "Dad's leg was killing him but he went out to the car and got the sack lunch, then he got plates from the kitchen and filled glasses with water from the tap and set us up in the dining room while Mommy sat on one of those awful French chairs in the foyer, shaking. He put the sandwiches on the plates and called us in. To the dining room! I mean, if he'd ever even looked at her to see what was going on he would have let us eat in the kitchen or in the car or someplace that didn't have a blue and gold ceiling. The dining room was intolerable in the very best of times. He led her to the table like she was blind. She kept picking up her sandwich and putting it down while Dad went on chirping about acreage and when the place was built and how the VanHoebeeks had made their money in cigarettes during the last war." She took a final drag off her cigarette and stubbed it into the ashtray in the car. "Thank you, VanHoebeeks."

There was a clap of thunder and all at once the rain came, an explosion of enormous drops that swept the windshield clean. Neither of us moved to roll up our window. "But you didn't sleep there." I said it as if I knew because I could not bear it to be otherwise.

She shook her head. The rain made such a pounding on the roof that she had to raise her voice a little. Our backs were getting soaked. "No. He took us around outside for a minute but the grounds were a mess. The pool was full of leaves. I wanted to take off my shoes and socks and put my feet in the water anyway but Mommy said no. I thought she was holding my hand because she was afraid I was going to run away, but she was holding on to me because, you know, she needed to hold on. Then Dad clapped his hands together and said we should probably be heading home. He had borrowed the car from the banker

for the day and he had to give it back. Can you imagine? He
buys this house but he doesn't own a car? We went back inside
and he picks up all the sandwiches and wraps them and puts
them back in the bag. None of us had really eaten anything so
of course we were going to take the sandwiches home and have
them for dinner. He wasn't going to waste the sandwiches.
Mommy started to pick up the plates, and Dad, I remember
this most of all, he touched her wrist and he said, 'Leave those.
The girl will get them.'"

"No."

"And Mommy said, 'What girl?' Like on top of everything
else she now has a slave."

"Fluffy."

"God's truth," Maeve said. "Our father was a man who had
never met his own wife."

CHAPTER 11

IT FELL TO Sandy to call and tell me Maeve was in the hospital. "She had plans to get in and get out without you knowing, but that's ridiculous. They say they're probably going to have to keep her in two nights."

Asking Sandy what the problem was, I could hear the doctor in my voice, that studied calm designed to soothe all fear, *Tell me what's been going on.* What I wanted to do was run out the door, to run all the way to Penn Station.

"She's got this awful-looking red streak going up her arm. I saw it on her hand, and when I asked her what it was she told me to mind my own business, so I called Jocelyn and Jocelyn straightened her out. She came right over and took Maeve to the doctor. She said if Maeve didn't get in the car she was calling an ambulance. Jocelyn's always been a better bully than me. She could make your sister do things I never could. I couldn't even get Maeve to brush her hair."

"What did the doctor say?"

"He said she had to go to the hospital right that minute, that's what he said. He didn't even let her go home to pack a bag. That's why she had to call me, so I'd go get her things. She made me swear I wouldn't tell, but I don't care. Does she think I'm not going to tell you she's in the hospital?"

"Did she say how long she's had the red streak?"

Sandy sighed. "She said she'd been wearing sleeves so she wouldn't think about it."

It was the middle of the week so Celeste was at her parents' house in Rydal. I called her from a pay phone when I got to Penn Station and told her what time my train was getting in. She picked me up in Philadelphia and drove me to the hospital, dropping me off in the circular driveway out front. Celeste was irritated with Maeve for not pushing me to set up a practice in internal medicine, as though I would have done it if Maeve told me to. She still thought it was Maeve's fault that I'd broken up with her years before and ruined her college graduation. Celeste blamed Maeve for everything she was afraid to blame me for. For her part, Maeve had never forgiven Celeste for insisting I marry her in my first year of medical school. Maeve also believed that Celeste had contrived her appearance at Mr. Martin's funeral, knowing full well she'd run into me there. I disagreed with that, not that it mattered. What mattered was that Celeste didn't want to see Maeve and Maeve didn't want to see Celeste, and I just wanted to get out of the car and find my sister.

"Let me know if you need a ride home," Celeste said, and she kissed me before she drove away.

It was the twenty-first of June, the longest day of the year. Eight o'clock at night and still the sun came slanting in through every window on the hospital's west side. The woman at the information desk had given me Maeve's room number and sent me off to do my best. The fact that I had spent the last seven years of my life in various hospitals in New York in no way qualified me to find my sister's room in a hospital in Pennsylvania. There was no logic to the way any hospital was laid out—they grew like cancers, with new wings metastasizing unexpectedly at the end of long tunneled halls. It took me some time to find the general medical floor, and then to find my sister in that undif-ferentiated sea. The door to her room was ajar, and I tapped twice before walking in. She had a double room but the divider curtain was pulled back, revealing a second bed that was neatly made and waiting. A fair-haired man in a suit sat in the chair beside Maeve's bed.

"Oh, Jesus," Maeve said when she saw me. "She swore to me on her sister's head that she wouldn't call you."

"She lied," I said.

The man in the suit stood up. It took me just a second and then I placed him.

"Danny." Mr. Otterson held out his hand.

I shook his hand and leaned over to kiss Maeve's forehead. Her face was flushed and slightly damp, her skin hot. "I'm fine," she said. "I could not be more fine."

"They're giving her antibiotics." Mr. Otterson pointed to the silver pole from which an ever-collapsing bag of fluid was hung, then he looked at Maeve. "She needs to rest."

"I'm resting. What could be more restful than this?"

She looked so awkward in the bed, like she was trying out for the role of the patient in a play but underneath the blankets she would have on her own clothes and shoes.

"I should be going," Mr. Otterson said.

I thought that Maeve would try to stop him but she didn't. "I'll be back by Friday."

"Monday. You think we can't even make it a week without you."

"You can't," she said, and in return he gave her a smile of great tenderness.

Mr. Otterson patted her good hand then nodded to me and left. We had met many times over the years, and I'd worked in his factory in the summers when I was home from Choate, but I never had a sense of him as being anything other than shy. I could never understand how such a man had grown such a business. Otterson's frozen vegetables now shipped to every state east of the Mississippi. Maeve told me that with no small amount of pride.

"If you'd called me first I could have told you not to come," she said.

"And if you'd called me first I could have told you what time I'd be here." I picked up the metal chart that hung from a hook at the foot of her bed. Her blood pressure was ninety over sixty. They were giving her Cefazolin every six hours. "Are you going to tell me what happened?"

"If you're not going to pursue medicine professionally then I can't see how you're allowed to pursue it personally."

I walked around the bed and picked up the hand with the IV. An angry red streak of cellulitis started at a cut on the top of her hand, then twisted up and around to the inside of her arm, then disappeared into her armpit. Someone had outlined it with a black marker so as to track the infection's progress. Her arm was hot, slightly swollen. "When did this start?"

"I have something to tell you if you'd put down my god-damn arm. I was going to wait until the weekend but you're here now."

I asked her again when it had started. Maybe medical school had done me some good after all. It certainly taught me how to persist with a question that no one saw the point in answering. "How did you hurt your hand?"

"I have no idea."

I moved my fingers up to her wrist.

"Get away from my pulse," she said.

"Did anyone explain to you how these things go? You get

blood poisoning, you become septic, your organs shut down."
Maeve worked at clothing drives, food drives, stocking the closets and pantries of the poor on weekends. She was always getting cut, some rogue staple or nail catching her skin. She was
bruised by the boxes she loaded into the trunks of waiting cars.

"Would you stop being so negative? I'm lying in a hospital
bed, aren't I? They're pumping me full of antibiotics. I'm not
exactly sure what else I'm supposed to be doing."

"You're supposed to get yourself to the doctor before the
infection that started in your hand gets to your heart. It looks
like someone ran a paintbrush up your arm. Did you not notice?"

"Do you want to hear my news or not?"

The anger I felt when she was lying there was unseemly. She
had a fever. She could have been in some pain, though I was the
last person she would have admitted that to. I told myself to
stop it or she'd never tell me anything. I went back to the other
side of the bed and sat in the chair, still warm from Mr. Otterson. I started again. "I'm sorry you're sick."

She looked at me for a moment, trying to gauge my sincerity.
"Thank you."

I folded my hands in my lap to keep from plucking at her.
"Tell me your news."

"I saw Fluffy," she said.

I was twenty-nine years old that day in the hospital. Maeve
was thirty-six. The last time we'd seen Fluffy I'd been four.
"Where?"

"Where do you think?"

"You've got to be kidding me."

"It really would have been better if I could have told you this
in the car. I had it all planned."

We saved our most important conversations for the car, but

considering the circumstances we'd have to make do with the hospital room, the green tile floor and the low acoustical ceiling, the intermittent alert over the public address system that someone was coding. "When?"

"Sunday." The top half of her bed was tilted slightly up. She stayed on her back but had turned her head to face me. "I'd just gotten out of church and I thought I'd swing by the Dutch House for a minute on my way home."

"You live two blocks from the church."

"Don't interrupt. Not five minutes later another car pulls up behind me and a woman gets out and crosses the street. It's Fluffy."

"How in God's name did you know it was Fluffy?"

"I just did. She's got to be past fifty now, and she's cut off all that hair. It's still red though, or maybe she dyes it. It's still fluffy. I remember her so clearly."

So did I. "You got out of the car—"

"I watched her first. She was standing at the end of the driveway and I could tell she was thinking it over, like maybe she was going to walk up and knock on the door. She grew up there, you know, just like us."

"Nothing like us."

Maeve nodded into her pillow. "I crossed the street. I hadn't set foot on that side of the street since the day we left and it made me feel a little sick if you want to know the truth. I kept thinking Andrea was going to come running down the driveway with a frying pan."

"What did you say?"

"Just her name. I said *Fiona*, and she turned around. Oh, Danny, if you could have seen the look on her face."

"She knew who you were?"

Maeve nodded again, her eyes feverish. "She said I looked

like Mommy did when she was young. She said she would have known me anywhere."

A young nurse in a white cap came in and when she saw us there she stopped. I was leaning so far over my chin was practically on Maeve's shoulder.

"Is this a bad time?" the nurse asked.

"Such a bad time," Maeve said. The nurse said something else but we didn't pay any attention. She closed the door behind her and Maeve started again. "Fluffy said she'd just been passing through and she wondered if we still lived in the house."

"And you said No, I just stalk the place."

"I told her we had left in '63 after Dad died. I shouldn't have said it that way but I wasn't thinking. As soon as it was out of my mouth, poor Fluffy turned red, her eyes filled up. I think she was hoping she was going to find him there. I think she'd come to see him."

"So then what?"

"Well, she was crying, and I didn't want to be standing out there on the wrong side of the street so I asked her to come and sit in my car so we could talk."

I shook my head. "You and Fluffy parking in front of the Dutch House."

"In a manner of speaking. Danny, it was the most amazing thing. When she got in the car, we were as close as you and I are now, and the way I felt—I was so incredibly *happy*, like my heart was going to break open. She was wearing this old blue cardigan and it was almost like I remembered it. I could have leaned over and kissed her. I've always had it in my mind that I hated Fluffy, that she had hit you and she had slept with Dad, but it turns out I don't hate her at all. It's like I'm incapable of hating anyone or anything in my life that came before Andrea, and those were the Fluffy days. She still has that pretty face, even now. I don't know if you remember her face but it was soft, very Irish. All of her freckles are gone now but she still has those big green eyes."

I said I remembered her eyes.

"I did a lot of talking at first. I told her about Dad getting married and Dad dying and Andrea throwing you out, and you know what she says?"

"What?"

"She says, 'What a cunt.'"

"Fluffy!"

Maeve laughed until her cheeks darkened and she started to cough. "I'll tell you what, she cut right to it," she said, and I handed her a tissue. "She wanted to know all about you. She was impressed that you were a doctor. She kept saying how wild you were, that she couldn't imagine you holding still long enough to read a book much less study medicine."

"She's trying to cover her tracks. I wasn't that wild."

"Yes you were."

"Where has she been all this time?"

"She used to live in Manhattan. She said she had no idea what to do that day Dad threw her out. She said she just stood there at the end of the driveway bawling and finally Sandy walked out and told her she'd call her husband to come and get her. Sandy and her husband took her in."

"Good old Sandy."

"She said they brainstormed for a few days and finally decided to go to Immaculate Conception and talk to the priest. Old Father Crutcher helped Fluffy find a job as a nanny with some rich people in Manhattan."

"The Catholic Church helps a woman who was fired for hitting a kid to get a job looking after kids. That's beautiful."

"Seriously, you have *got* to stop interrupting me. You're

throwing the story off. She gets a good job as a nanny, and while the children were still young she marries the doorman in the building where she works. She said they kept it a secret until she got pregnant, so she wouldn't lose her job. She said the first baby they had was a girl and that girl is at Rutgers now. She was on her way to see her and she decided to swing by the old house."

"No one takes geography anymore. The Dutch House isn't on her way to Rutgers from the city."

"She lives in the Bronx now," Maeve said, ignoring me, "she and her husband. They had three children in all, the girl and then two boys."

It took everything in me not to point out that the Dutch House was not on the way to Rutgers from the Bronx either.

"Fluffy said she checked on the place every now and then, that she couldn't help it. It had been her job before we ever moved there. It had been her job to keep an eye on things after Mrs. VanHoebeek died. She said she'd been afraid to go and knock because she didn't know what Dad would say when he saw her, but that she'd always hoped she'd run into one of us there."

I shook my head. Why did I miss the VanHoebeeks after all these years?

"She asked me if I still had diabetes, and I told her of course, and then she got upset all over again. I remember Fluffy as being very tough when we were children but who knows? Maybe she wasn't."

"She was."

"She wants to see you."

"Me?"

"You don't live that far from her."

"Why does she want to see me?"

Maeve gave me a look as if to say that surely I was smart enough to get this one myself, but I had no idea. "She wants to make amends."

"Tell her no amends are in order."

"Listen to me. This is important, and it's not like you're busy." Maeve didn't count the work I was doing on the building as a job. In this way she and Celeste were in agreement.

"I don't need to reconnect with someone I haven't seen since I was four years old." I'll admit, the story held a certain lurid fascination when it was about Maeve seeing Fluffy, but I had no interest in pursuing a relationship myself.

"Well, I gave her your number. I told her you'd meet her at the Hungarian Pastry Shop. That's not going to be any trouble for you."

"It's not a matter of trouble, I just don't want to do it."

My sister yawned extravagantly and pushed her face deeper into the pillow. "I'm tired now."

"You're not getting out of this."

When she looked up at me, her blue eyes rimmed in red, I remembered where we were and why we were there. The overwhelming need to sleep had hit her suddenly, and she closed her eyes as if she had no choice in the matter.

I stayed in the chair and watched her. I wondered if I needed to be closer to home. Now that my residency was finished, I didn't have to live in New York. I owned three buildings but knew for a fact that perfectly good real estate empires had been made outside of the city.

When the doctor came in later to check on Maeve I stood up and shook his hand.

"Dr. Lamb," he said. He wasn't much older than me. He might have even been my age.

"Dr. Conroy," I said. "I'm Maeve's brother."

Maeve didn't stir when he lifted her arm to run his fingers down the track that disappeared into the sleeve of her gown. At first I thought she must be faking it, that she wanted to avoid the questions, but then I realized she really was asleep. I didn't know how long Otterson had been there before me. I'd kept her up too long.

"She should have gotten here two days ago," Dr. Lamb said, looking at me.

I shook my head. "I was the last to know."

"Well, don't let her snow you." He spoke as if we were alone in the room. "This is serious business." He rested her arm at her side and pulled the sheet up to cover it again. Then he made his mark on the chart and left us there.

CHAPTER 12

THE COMPLETION OF my brief medical career had filled me with an unexpected lightness. After I finished my residency, I went through a period in which I was able to see the good in everything, especially the much-maligned north end of Manhattan. For the first time in my adult life I could waste an hour talking to a guy in the hardware store about sealant. I could make a mistake fixing something, a toilet say, without mortal repercussions. I sanded the floors and painted the walls in one of the empty apartments in my building, and when I was finished, I moved in. By the standards of all the dorm rooms and efficiencies I'd lived in since my extravagant youth, the apartment was generous in size—sunny and noisy and my own. Owning the place where I lived, or having the bank own it in my name, plugged up a hole that had been whistling in me for years. Celeste made the curtains in Rydal on her mother's Singer and brought them in on the train. She got a job at an elementary school near Columbia and started teaching reading and what they called Language Arts while I went to work on the other units in the building and then the brownstones. I had no reason to think she'd made peace with my decision, but she had the sense to stop asking me about it. We had stepped into the river that takes you forward. The building, the apartment, her job, our relationship, all came together with irrefutable logic. Celeste loved to tell a softened version of our story, how we had gone separate ways after she graduated from college, victims of timing and circumstance, and then how we had found each other again, at a funeral of all places. "It was meant to be," she would say, leaning into me.

So Fluffy was not on my mind. She was not on my mind until the phone rang months after Maeve got out of the hospital, and the voice on the other end said, "Is that Danny?" and I knew, the same way Maeve had known when she saw Fluffy there on VanHoebeek Street. I knew that she had taken so long to call because she was trying to work up her courage, and I knew that we would have coffee at the Hungarian Pastry Shop whether I wanted to or not. Any energy I expended trying to fight it would be energy lost.

There was never a time that the Pastry Shop wasn't crowded. Fluffy had come early and waited to get a seat in the window. When she saw me coming down the sidewalk, she tapped on the glass and waved. She was standing up when I got to the table. I had wondered if I'd recognize her based on Maeve's description. I had never considered that she might recognize me based on the four-year-old I had been.

"Could I hug you?" she asked. "Would that be all right?"

I put my arms around her because I couldn't imagine how to say no. In my memory, Fluffy was a giant who grew taller over time, when in fact she was a small woman, soft at the edges. She was wearing slacks and the blue cardigan Maeve had mentioned, or maybe she had more than one blue cardigan. She pressed the side of her face against my sternum for just an instant then let me go.

"Whew!" she said, and fanned her face with her hand, her green eyes damp. She sat back down at the table in front of her coffee and Danish. "It's a lot. You were my baby, you know. I feel this way whenever I see any of the kids I took care of but you were my very first baby. Back then I didn't know you weren't supposed to give your whole heart to a baby that isn't yours. It's suicide, but I was just a kid myself, and your mother was gone and your sister was sick and your father." She skipped his descriptive clause. "I had a lot of reasons to be attached." She stopped just long enough to drink down half a glass of ice water, then touched the paper napkin to her lips. "It's hot in here, right? Or maybe it's me. I'm nervous." She pinched the rounded collar of her blouse away from her neck and fanned it back and forth. "I'm nervous but I'm also *that age*. I can say that to you, right? You're a doctor, even though you look like you should still be in high school. Are you really a doctor?"

"I am." There was no point getting into that one.

"Well, that's good. I'm glad. Your parents would have been proud of that. And can I say something else? I'm sitting here looking at you, and your face is perfectly fine. I don't know what I was expecting but there isn't a mark on you."

I considered pointing out the small scar by my eyebrow but thought better of it. A waitress I knew named Lizzy who wore her black curls pulled onto the top of her head with a rubber band came to the table and put a coffee and a poppy-seed muffin down in front of me. "Fresh," she said, and walked away.

Fluffy watched her retreat with wonder. "They know you here?"

"I live close by."

"And you're handsome," she said. "A woman's going to remember a handsome man like you. Maeve says you've got a girl though, and she doesn't think much of her, in case you didn't know. That's not my business. I'm just glad I didn't wreck your face. The last time I laid eyes on you, you were covered in blood and screaming, then Jocelyn runs in to take you to the hospital. I thought for sure I'd killed you, all that blood, but you turned out fine."

"I'm fine."

She pressed her lips into an approximation of a smile. "Sandy told me you were fine but I didn't believe her. What else was she going to say? I carried it around with me for years and years. I felt so awful. I didn't stay in touch with any of them, you know. Once I moved to the city that was it—no looking back. Sometimes you've got to put the past in the past."

"Sure."

"Which brings me to your father." She took down the rest of her water. "Maeve told me he died. I'm sorry about that. You know you look an awful lot like him, right? My kids are mutts, all three of them. They don't look like me or my husband, either one. Bobby's Italian, DiCamillo. Fiona DiCamillo is a mutt name if ever there was one. Bobby never knew about me and your father." She stopped there, a sudden flush of panic rising up her neck. This was a woman whose biology betrayed her at every turn. Emotions stormed across her face with a flag. "Maeve told you that, didn't she? About your father and me?"

"She did."

Fluffy exhaled, shook her head. "My god, I thought I just put my foot in it. Bobby doesn't need to know about that. You probably don't need to know about it either but there you go. I was just a kid then, and I was stupid. I thought your father was going to marry me. I slept right there on the second floor in the room next to you and your sister, and I thought it was only a matter of me moving across the hall. Well, hah!"

The waitresses at the Hungarian Pastry Shop had to turn sideways to get between the tables, holding their coffee pots high. Everyone was jostled and the light poured in across the

Formica tables and the silverware and the thick white china cups and I saw none of it. I was back in the kitchen of the Dutch House, and Fluffy was there.

"That morning," she said, and nodded to make sure I understood which morning we were talking about, "your father and I had a fight and I wasn't thinking clearly. I'm not saying it wasn't my fault, but I'm saying I wasn't myself."

"A fight about what?" I let my eyes wander over to the pastry case, the pies and cakes all twice as tall as pies and cakes were meant to be.

"About our not getting married. He'd never come right out and said he was going to marry me but what year was it then, 1950, '51? It never crossed my mind that we weren't getting married. I was right there in his bed, if you'll forgive me for saying so, and he got up to get dressed and I was feeling so happy about things that I said I thought we should start making plans. And he said, 'Making plans for what?'"

"Oh," I said, feeling the discomfort of familiarity.

Fluffy raised her eyebrows, making her green eyes appear all the larger. "If it was just that he wasn't going to marry me, well, that would have been bad enough, but the reason—" She stopped and took a bite of her Danish with a fork. Then, bite by bite, she proceeded to eat the entire thing. That was it. Fluffy, who had not stopped talking since I walked in the door, shut down like a mechanical horse in need of another nickel. I waited well past the point of prudence for her to pick her story up again.

"Are you going to tell me?"

She nodded, her tremendous energy having deserted her. "I have a lot to tell you," she said.

"All ears."

She gave me a stern look, the look of a governess to a

smart-mouthed child. "Your father said he couldn't marry me because he was still married to your mother."

That was something I never considered. "They were still married?"

"I was willing to be immoral, I think I've established that. I was sleeping with a man I wasn't married to—okay, fine, my mistake, I'll live with it. But I thought your father was *divorced*. I never would have gone to bed with a married man. You believe that, don't you?"

I told her I did, absolutely. What I didn't tell her was that a man who wants to sleep with the pretty young nanny across the hall never has any intention of marrying her. What better lie than to tell her he's still married? My father wasn't much more of a Catholic than I was, but he was too Catholic to be a bigamist, and Andrea was too smart to marry a bigamist, and Lawyer Gooch was too thorough to have overlooked such a detail.

"I *never* would have done *any*thing against your mother. I liked your father fine, I did. He was handsome and sad and all those nonsense things girls think are so important at that age, but Elna Conroy was my heart. I never saw myself filling her shoes, no one could have done that, but I meant to take care of you and your sister and your father the way she would have wanted. She was so worried about you before she left. She loved the three of you so much."

Before there was a chance to formulate all the questions there were to be asked, I felt a strong hand on my shoulder. "Danny! You got a day off." Dr. Able was beaming. "I should be seeing more of you now that your residency has finished, not less. I've been hearing rumors."

Fluffy and I were sitting at a four-top. There were two empty places set with silverware and napkins that I hoped he had the sense to overlook. "Dr. Able," I said. "This is my friend, Fiona."

"Morey." Dr. Able leaned across the table to shake her hand. "Fluffy."

Morey Able smiled and nodded. "Well, I can see you two are busy. Danny, you won't make me have to track you down, will you?"

"I won't. Say hello to Mrs. Able for me."

"Mrs. Able knows who owned those parking lots," he said and laughed. "You may not get an invitation to Thanksgiving this year."

"Good," Fluffy said to him. "Then Danny can come and have Thanksgiving with us."

When he walked away from the table, Fluffy seemed to understand that our time at the Hungarian Pastry Shop was not infinite. She decided to get to the point. "You know your mother's here," she said. "I've seen her."

Lizzy sailed past, tipping her coffee pot in my direction. I shook my head while Fluffy held up her cup for more. "What?" It was a cold wind coming in the door. *She's dead* I wanted to say, *Surely she's dead by now.*

"I couldn't tell your sister. I couldn't make her diabetes worse."

"Knowing where your mother is doesn't make diabetes worse," I said, trying to apply logic to a conversation where no logic existed.

Fluffy shook her head. "It certainly can. You don't remember how sick she was. You were too young. Your mother would come and go and come and go, and when she finally left for good, Maeve nearly died. That's just a fact. After that, your father told her she could never come home again. He wrote her a letter when Maeve was in the hospital. I know that. He told her she'd all but killed the two of you."

"The two of us?"

"Well," she said, "not you. He only threw you in to make her feel worse. If you ask me, he was trying to get her to come back. He just went about it wrong."

Had anyone asked me an hour before this meeting how I felt about my mother I would have sworn I had no feelings on the subject, which made it difficult to understand the enormity of my rage. I held up my hand to stop Fluffy from talking for a second, just to give my brain the chance to catch up, and she raised her hand and touched her palm lightly to mine as if we were measuring the length of our fingers. Maybe because he was sitting with a student two tables away, a boy around the age I must have been when we first met, I saw myself standing in the door of Morey Able's office.

No parents? he asked.

"Where is she now?" I was suddenly struck by the possibility that my mother was going to walk in the Hungarian Pastry Shop and pull up a chair, that this entire reunion was a setup for some horrific surprise.

"I don't know where she is *now*. I saw her more than a year ago, maybe two. I'm bad with time. I'm sure it was in the Bowery though. I looked out the window of a bus and there she was, Elna Conroy, just standing there like she was waiting for me. It about stopped my heart."

I exhaled, my own heart starting again. "You mean you saw someone who looked like my mother when you were on a bus?" The idea of seeing anyone you knew out the window of a bus seemed far-fetched, but I never took the bus, and when I did, I don't suppose I looked out the window.

Fluffy rolled her eyes. "Jesus, I'm not an idiot, Danny. I got *off* the bus. I went back and found her."

"And it was her?" Elna Conroy, who had run off to India in the night, leaving her husband and two sleeping children, was in the Bowery?

"She was just the same, I swear it. Her hair's gone gray and she wears it in a braid now, the way Maeve used to. They both have that ridiculous hair."

"Did she remember you?"

"I haven't changed that much," Fluffy said.

I was the one who had changed.

Fluffy dumped her coffee into her water glass and let the ice melt. "The first thing she asked about was you and Maeve, and since I didn't know there was nothing I could tell her. I didn't even know where you lived. The shame of it all came back on me like the whole thing had happened yesterday. I'll never get over it. To think I'd been fired, to think *why* I'd been fired, and that I hadn't stayed to look after you the way I'd promised her I would." Her grief hung between us.

"We were her children. It seems like she should have stayed and looked after us herself."

"She's a wonderful woman, Danny. She had a terrible time of it."

"A terrible time of it living in the Dutch House?"

Fluffy looked down at her empty plate. This wasn't her fault. Even if she'd hit me, even if she'd been thrown out because of it. There was very little forgiveness in my heart and what I had I gave to Fluffy.

"There's no way for you to understand," she said. "She couldn't live like that. She's doing her penance down there serving soup. She's trying to make up for what she's done."

"Who is she making it up to? To me, to Maeve?"

Fluffy considered this. "To God, I guess. There's no other reason she'd have been in the Bowery."

I, who had bought property in Harlem and Washington Heights, would not have touched the Bowery with a stick. "When did she leave India?"

Fluffy tore open two sugar packets, added them to her iced coffee and stirred. I wanted to tell her the whole thing would have gone better if she'd put the sugar in the coffee while the coffee was still hot. In fact, I wanted to tell her it would have been infinitely preferable to get together in order to discuss how sugar dissolves. "A long time ago. She said it had been years and years. She said the people had been very kind to her. Can you imagine? She would have been happy to stay there but she had to go where she was needed."

"Which wasn't Elkins Park."

"She gave up everything, that's what you have to understand. She gave up you and your sister and your father and that house so she could help the poor. She's lived in India and God only knows how many other horrible places. She was down there on the Bowery. The whole place stinks, you know. It's foul down there, the trash and the people, and your mother's serving soup to the junkies and drunks. If that's not being sorry, I don't know what is."

I shook my head. "That's being delusional, not sorry."

"I wish I could have talked to her more," Fluffy said, her feelings clearly hurt. "But I was going to be late for my job. I'm a baby nurse now. I get in and get out before I get too attached. And to tell you the truth, the bums were crawling all over the place and I didn't feel so comfortable standing there on the street. Just as soon as I had that thought, she told me she was going to walk me to the bus stop. She put my arm in hers like we were two old friends. She told me she'd be working down there for a while, and that I could come back and serve if I wanted to, or just come back and visit. I kept thinking I'd go see her again on my day off, but Bobby wasn't having it. He said I had no business making lunch for a bunch of guys on the needle."

I sat back in my chair, trying to take it in. I was glad that Maeve didn't come to the city. I didn't want her looking out a bus window and seeing our mother on the street. "Do you know where she is now?"

She shook her head. "I should have tried to find you sooner so I could have told you. It wouldn't have been hard. I feel bad about that."

I motioned to Lizzy for the check. "If my mother had wanted to see us she would have found us herself. Like you said, it wouldn't have been hard."

Fluffy was twisting the paper napkin in her fingers. "Believe me, I know what a bad time everyone went through. I was there. But your mother has a higher calling than we do, that's all."

I put my money on the table. "Then I hope she enjoys it."

When I looked at my watch, I realized I was already late. I'd scheduled a meeting with a contractor as a means of ensuring my time with Fluffy would be limited. She walked with me two blocks before it became clear she was going in the wrong direction. She took my hand. "We'll do this again, won't we?" she said. "Maeve has my number. I'd like to see you both. I want you to meet my kids. They're great kids, like you and your sister."

Maeve was right. Not only was it remarkable to see Fluffy again, but I felt a complete absence of anger towards her. She had been in an impossible situation. No one would say that what had happened had been her fault. "Would you leave them?"

"Who?"

"Your great kids," I said. "Would you walk away and leave them now and never let them know that you were still alive? Would you have left them before they were old enough to remember you? Left them for Bobby to raise on his own?"

I could see the blow travel through her and she took a step away from me. "No," she said.

"Then you're the good person," I said, "not my mother."

"Oh, Danny," she said, and her voice caught in her throat. She hugged me goodbye. When she walked away, she turned back to look at me so many times she appeared to be going up the sidewalk in a loose series of concentric circles.

The fact of the matter was I had seen my mother, too, though I hadn't known it at the time. As I walked to 116th street after leaving Fluffy, I had no doubt that it had happened. It had been in the emergency room at Albert Einstein around midnight, maybe two years before, maybe three. All the chairs in the waiting room were full. Parents held half-grown children in their laps, paced with children in their arms. People were propped up against the walls, bleeding and moaning, vomiting into their laps, a standard Saturday night in the Gun and Knife Club. I had just scoped a young woman with a crushed airway (a steering wheel? a boyfriend?), and once I got the endoscope down past her nasal passages, both of her vocal cords were collapsed. Blood and spit were bubbling in every direction and it took forever to get an endotracheal tube in place. When I finished the procedure, I went to the waiting room to look for whoever had brought her in. As I called the name on the chart, a woman behind me tapped my shoulder saying, *Doctor.* Everyone did that, the sick and those advocating for the sick, they chanted and begged, *doctor, nurse, doctor, nurse.* The emergency room at Albert Einstein was a cyclone of human need and the trick was to keep focused on the thing you'd come to do, ignoring the rest. But when I turned around the woman looked at me with such—what? Surprise? Fear? I remember raising my hand to my face to see if there was blood on it. That had happened before. She was tall and dismally thin, and in my mind I assigned her to the ash heap of late-stage lung cancer or tuberculosis. None of this distinguished her in that particular crowd. The only reason she'd stuck with me at all was because she called me Cyril.

I would have asked her how she knew my father, but then a man was there saying it was his girlfriend I had just scoped. I was taking him into the hallway, wondering if he in fact had strangled her. I'd been in the waiting room for less than a minute, and by the time I had the chance to wonder about the woman with the gray braid who'd called me by my father's name, she was long gone, and I was no longer interested. I didn't wonder if she'd been a tenant in one of the Conroy buildings or if she was someone he had known in Brooklyn. I certainly never thought about my mother. Like everyone else who worked in an ER, I pressed ahead with what was in front of me and made it through the night.

To grow up with a mother who had run off to India, never to be heard from again, that was one thing—there was closure in that, its own kind of death. But to find out she was fifteen stops away on the Number One train to Canal and had failed to be in touch was barbaric. Whatever romantic notions I might have harbored, whatever excuses or allowances my heart had ever made on her behalf, blew out like a match.

The contractor was waiting for me in the lobby when I got back and we talked about the window frames that were pulling

away from the brick in the front of the building. He was still
there taking measurements an hour later when Celeste came
home from school. She was so buoyant, so bright, her yellow
hair tangled from the wind that had kicked up. She was telling
me about the children in her class, and how they had all cut out
leaves from construction paper and printed their names on the
leaves so she could make a tree on her classroom door, and as
I listened, less to what she was saying and more to the pleasing
sound of her voice, I knew that Celeste would always be there.
She had proven her commitment to me time and again. If men
were fated to marry their mothers, well, here was my chance to
buck the trend.

"Ah!" she said, dropping her book bags on the floor and
reaching up to kiss me. "I'm talking too much! I'm like the kids.
I get all wound up. Tell me about the grown-up world. Tell me
about your day."

But I didn't tell her anything, not about the Pastry Shop or
Fluffy or my mother. I told her instead that I'd been thinking,
and I thought it was time we got married.

CHAPTER 13

I WISHED MY PART of the work hadn't all fallen to Maeve, who drove to Rydal to have lunch with Celeste and her mother and talk about napkin colors and the merits of having hard liquor at the reception vs only serving beer and wine with champagne for the toast.

"Frozen vegetables," Maeve said to me later. "I wanted to tell her that would be my contribution. I'll flood their backyard with little green peas, which would spare me having to sit through another conversation about whether the lawn will still be green enough in July."

"I'm sorry," I said. "You shouldn't have to deal with that."

Maeve rolled her eyes. "Well it isn't like you're going to do it. Either I get involved or we have no representation at the wedding."

"I'm planning on representing us at the wedding."

"You don't understand. I'm not even married and I understand."

Celeste said it was hard for Maeve to watch me get married before she did. Celeste said that, at thirty-seven, there was pretty much no chance of Maeve finding someone, and so the wedding plans were no doubt filling her with something less than joy. But that wasn't it. In the first place, Maeve would never begrudge me any happiness, and in the second place, I had never once heard her mention even a passing interest in marriage. Maeve didn't care about the wedding. Her issue was with the bride.

I tried to explain to my sister that I had dated plenty of women and Celeste really was the best choice. I hadn't rushed into anything, either. We'd been going together off and on since college.

"You're picking the woman you like the best from a group of women you don't like," Maeve said. "Your control group is fundamentally flawed."

But I had picked the woman who had committed herself to smoothing my path and supporting my life. The problem was that Maeve thought she was taking care of that herself.

As for Maeve's love life or lack thereof, I knew nothing. But I will say this: I'd watched her test her blood sugar and inject herself with insulin all my life, but she didn't do it around other people, not unless it was a full-on emergency. When I was in medical school, and then later in my residency, I tried to talk to her about her management, but she would have no part of it. "I have an endocrinologist," she'd say.

"And I have no interest in being your endocrinologist. I'm just saying as your brother that I'm interested in your health."

"Very kind. Now cut it out."

Maeve and I had endless reasons to be suspicious of marriage—the history of our youth would be enough to make anyone bet against it—but if I'd had to guess, I wouldn't have put the blame on Andrea or either of our parents. If I'd had to guess, where Maeve was concerned, I would have said she could never have allowed anyone else in the room when she stabbed a needle into her stomach.

"Tell me again what my not being married has to do with you marrying Celeste."

"Nothing. I just want to make sure you're okay."

"Trust me," she said. "I don't want to marry Celeste. She's all yours."

Had it not been for Maeve, every aspect of the wedding, all the costs and decisions, would have fallen to the Norcross family. Maeve believed we Conroys should not begin the alliance of families in such a state of inequality. After all, when you added in uncles and aunts and all the various degrees of cousins both by marriage and blood, there were more Norcrosses than there were stars in the sky, and there were only the two of us Conroys. I understood that someone from our side needed to show up, and since our side consisted of Maeve and me, it fell to Maeve. I was meeting with electricians in those days and learning the surprisingly difficult skill of repairing drywall. I was too busy to participate in the details, and so I sent my sister, who lived a scant fifteen minutes from Celeste's parents, as my emissary.

In this spirit of division of labor, Maeve volunteered to write our engagement announcement for the paper. *Mary Celeste Norcross, daughter of William and Julie Norcross, will marry Daniel James Conroy, son of Elna Conroy and the late Cyril Conroy, on Saturday, the 23rd of July.*

But Celeste didn't like the word "late." She thought it was a downer in light of the happy occasion.

"And your mother?" Maeve said to me over the phone, doing an uncanny imitation of Celeste's voice. "Do you seriously want your mother's name in the engagement announcement?"

"Ah," I said.

"I told her you do in fact have a mother. A missing mother and a dead father. That's what we've got. Then she asked if we could just leave them out altogether, seeing as how they're not here? It's not as if we'd be hurting their feelings."

"Well?" It didn't strike me as an outrageous proposal.

"We'd be hurting *my* feelings," Maeve said. "You're not a mushroom who popped up after a rain. You have parents."

Julie Norcross, my ever-rational future mother-in-law, broke the tie in Maeve's favor. "That's the way it's done," she said to her daughter. The proposed compromise, to which Maeve finally capitulated after much grousing, was that our parents' names would not appear on the wedding invitation.

And through all of this, I never told my sister that our mother was out there, circling. I put it off not because I thought it would harm Maeve's health, but because we were better off without her. That was what Fluffy's news had made me realize. After so many years of chaos and exile, our lives had finally settled. Now that it was no longer my job to draw down the trust, we rarely spoke of Andrea at all. We didn't think about her. I wasn't practicing medicine. I owned three buildings. I was getting married. Maeve, for whatever reasons of her own, continued on at Otterson's without complaint. She seemed happier than I had ever known her to be, even if she didn't want me to marry Celeste. After years of living in response to the past, we had somehow become miraculously unstuck, moving forward in time just like everyone else. To tell Maeve our mother was out there, to tell her I wasn't sure if our parents had ever divorced, meant reigniting the fire I'd spent my life stamping out. Why should we go looking for her? She'd never come looking for us.

I don't mean that Maeve didn't deserve to know, or that I would never tell her. I just didn't think this was the time.

Celeste and I were married on a sweltering day in late July at St. Hilary's in Rydal. A fall wedding would have been more comfortable, but Celeste said she wanted to have everything settled and done before school started in September. Maeve said Celeste didn't want to give me time to back out. The Norcrosses rented a tent for the reception, and Celeste and Maeve put aside their considerable differences for the occasion. Morey Able stood up as my best man. He found my defection from science to be hilarious. "I wasted half of my professional career on you," he said, his arm around my shoulder like any proud father. Years later, I would buy a building on Riverside Drive, a pre-war jewel box with an Art Deco lobby and green glass inlays on the elevator doors. I gave the Ables half of the top floor and a key to the roof for what they would have paid for an efficiency. They would stay there for the rest of their lives.

Celeste flung her diaphragm into the Atlantic on our honeymoon. In the early morning hours we watched it catch a gentle wave and bob away from the coast of Maine.

"That's a little disgusting," I said.

"People will think it's a jellyfish." She snapped shut the empty pink case and dropped it in her purse. We had tried to get in the water the day before but even in late July we found it impossible to go past our knees, so we went back to the hotel and Celeste put her swimsuit on so that I could take it off again. She thought we had very nearly waited too long as it was. At twenty-nine, she wasn't going to put nature off another cycle. Our daughter was born nine months later. Over protests, I named the baby for my sister, and as a compromise we called her May.

Everything about May was easy. I told Celeste we could throw a tarp over the bed and I could deliver her myself if she felt like staying home, but she didn't. We took a taxi to Columbia-Presbyterian in the middle of the night, and six hours later our daughter was delivered by one of my former classmates. Celeste's mother came up for a week and Maeve came for a day. Maeve and Julie Norcross had grown fond of each other through the wedding preparations, and Maeve had found that things between her and Celeste were better when Celeste's mother was around. She planned her brief visits accordingly. Celeste quit her teaching job at the Columbia school and five months later she was pregnant again. She was good at having babies, she liked to say. She was going to play to her strength.

But babies are largely a matter of luck, and there was no guarantee that what was easy once would be easy twice. Twenty-five weeks into the second pregnancy, Celeste started to have contractions and was sent to bed to stay. She was told her cervix was lazy, unable to hold the baby in place against the tireless pull of gravity. She took it to be a personal indictment.

"No one said it was lazy last year," she said.

They would have kept her in the hospital if it hadn't been for the fact that I was considered to be enough of a doctor to administer the medications and watch her blood pressure. What I couldn't manage, along with work and Celeste, was taking care of May.

"We're going to need to hire someone," I said. Celeste had made it clear she didn't want her mother moving to New York, and the idea of having Maeve come in to help wasn't up for discussion.

"I just wish there was someone we knew," Celeste said. She was frustrated and scared and angry at herself for not being able to take care of things the way she always had. "I don't want a stranger taking care of May."

"I could try Fluffy," I said, though the suggestion was half-hearted. To call in Fluffy, like some other things, seemed to be taking a big step backwards. I was holding May on one hip and she squirmed and reached her chubby hands for her mother.

"What's fluffy?"

"*Who's* Fluffy.*"

"What are you talking about?"

"I never told you about Fluffy?"

Celeste sighed and straightened her blanket. "I guess not. No one forgets a Fluffy."

In the earliest days of our relationship Celeste had asked about the small scar beside my eye and I'd told her I'd caught a backhand playing doubles at Choate. I wasn't about to tell the pretty girl in my bed that my Irish nanny had hit me with a spoon. If I'd never even mentioned Fluffy then Celeste didn't know about my father's affair, either. It would have been difficult to put forward a candidate who'd slept with the employer and hit the child, but in truth I'd forgiven her for all of it. Like Maeve said, there was no holding a grudge against anyone from that time in our lives. "She was our nanny. She lives in the Bronx now," I said.

"I thought Sandy and Jocelyn were your nannies."

"Sandy was the housekeeper, Jocelyn was the cook, Fluffy was the nanny."

Celeste closed her eyes and nodded peaceably. "I have trouble keeping the household staff straight."

"Should I call her?" May, who had an uncanny ability to concentrate her weight, had turned into a fifty-pound sack of potatoes in my arms. I put her down beside her mother.

"Why not try? You turned out nice enough." Celeste reached for our daughter, whom she could lie beside but not pick up. "At least it's a place to start."

And so it came to pass that, nearly thirty years after we had last lived under the same roof, Fluffy came to 116th Street to care for our daughter. Celeste could not have been more pleased with the arrangement.

"The fleas were everywhere!" I heard Fluffy saying to my

wife the day after we'd hired her. I'd just come in the front door
and I stood in the tiny entry hall to listen. I wasn't eavesdrop-
ping, the apartment was too small for that. They knew perfectly well I was there. "The first time I went over to meet the
Conroys they were standing there scratching. I was dying to
make a good impression, you know. I'd been the caretaker for
the house when it was empty and I was hoping they'd keep me
on, so I put on my best dress and went over to introduce myself,
and there they were with their pile of boxes. I could see the fleas
on Maeve's little legs. They went after her like a sugar loaf."

"Wait," Celeste said, "didn't you live in the house?"

"I lived in the garage. There was an apartment on the top
where my parents had lived when they worked for the VanHoebeeks. Of course I stayed in the house when I was taking care
of the old lady, I never left her alone. But after she died, well,
the whole business made me sad, so I went back to the garage.
I'd grown up there. I had been one of the house girls, then I was
the only servant in the entire place, then I was the nursemaid,
then I was the caretaker, then I was the Conroys' nanny, first
for Maeve, then Danny."

Then you were the mistress, I thought, putting down the
mail.

"I was good at all my jobs, except being the caretaker. I was
awful at that."

"But it's completely different work," Celeste said. "Taking
care of people or taking care of an empty house."

"I was afraid of the house. I kept thinking the VanHoebeeks
were still in there, that they were ghosts. I just couldn't imagine
the place without them, even if they were dead. I could barely
make myself dart in there once a week and look around at the
height of the day, so I didn't know the raccoons had eaten their
way into the ballroom with all those fleas. They must have just

hatched because there were no fleas when the banker came and there were no fleas when the Conroys came to see the house, but by the time they moved in the fleas were everywhere, you could see them hopping around in the rugs, on the walls. I wouldn't have blamed them if they'd put me out on the spot."

"The fleas weren't your fault," Celeste said.

"But they were, if you think about it. I was asleep at my post. What do you think? Should I put this girl down and make you some lunch?"

"Danny?" Celeste called. "Do you want lunch?"

I came into the bedroom. Celeste was stretched out in our bed and Fluffy was sitting in a chair with May asleep in her arms.

Celeste looked up at me and smiled. "Fluffy's been telling me about the fleas."

"His mother kept me on," Fluffy said, smiling like it was something I had done myself. "She wasn't much older than I was but I acted like she was my mother. I was so lonely! And she was so kind. As miserable as Elna was, she always made me feel like she was happy I was there."

"She was miserable because of the fleas?"

"Because of the *house*. Poor Elna hated the house."

"I could stand some lunch," I said.

"Why 'poor Elna?'" Celeste asked. Ever since I'd told her the story of my life, my wife had held my mother in particularly low regard. She believed there could be no reason to leave two children.

Fluffy looked down at my daughter asleep on her chest. "She was too good to live in a place like that."

Celeste looked up at me, confused. "I thought you said it was a nice place."

"I'll go get sandwiches," I said, turning away. I wanted to

tell Fluffy to stop it, but why? She was telling these stories to Celeste, the only person in the world who wanted to hear them. Fluffy told Celeste the stories of the Dutch House like Scheherazade trying to win another night, and Celeste, whose mind was finally off her troubles, wouldn't have let her go for anything in the world.

Kevin came early, and spent his first six weeks of life in an incubator box, staring at us through the clear plastic wall with his frog eyes while Fluffy stayed home with May. "Everything's fine," Fluffy would say to me, kissing my daughter on the head, a series of rapid-fire pecks. "We're all where we need to be." Maeve came up on the train while Celeste was in the hospital, as much to spend days with Fluffy as with her namesake. Maeve and Fluffy had an insatiable appetite for the past when they were together. They went through the Dutch House room by room. "Do you remember that stove?" one of them would say. "How you had to light the burners with a match? I always thought I was going to blow us all to kingdom come, it took so long for the fire to catch." "Do you remember those pink silk sheets in the bedroom on the third floor? I've never seen sheets like that again in my life. I bet they're still perfect. No one ever slept in that bed." "Do you remember when the two of us went swimming in the pool, and Jocelyn said it wasn't good to have to see the nanny splashing around like a seal in the middle of a workday?" Then they would laugh and laugh until May laughed with them.

I had bought Celeste a brownstone just north of the Museum of Natural History right after May was born and worked on it myself on the weekends—a big four-story, beyond our means, the kind of house we could stay in for the rest of our lives. The neighborhood was imperfect but it was better than the one we were in. The winds of gentrification were starting to shift towards the Upper West Side and I wanted to get ahead of them. To make a new life we would have to travel all of twenty-five blocks. I would pay Sandy and Jocelyn to come up on the weekend and, along with Fluffy, get our things boxed and un-boxed.

"We're moving *now*?" Celeste said while we sat in the waiting room of the NICU. Visiting hours started at nine.

"There's never a good time to move," I said. "This way Kevin can come home to his new house."

The new house had four bedrooms, though we kept Kevin and May together in one when they were small. "Less running around to do," Fluffy said. "There are too many damn stairs in this place." Celeste agreed, and had me squeeze a single bed into the crowded nursery. She'd had an emergency caesarean in the end, and she said she'd just as soon not have to go too far when one of the children cried.

One night, after getting Celeste a sweater from our bedroom on the top floor, then turning over a load of laundry on the ground floor, then changing May's diapers and getting her another outfit on the third floor and taking the soiled clothes back down to the wash, Fluffy fell onto the couch next to Celeste, her cheeks flaming, chest heaving.

"Are you okay?" Celeste asked, Kevin in her arms. May took a few uneven steps in the direction of the fireplace where I had just laid a fire.

"*May*," I said.

Fluffy pulled in a deep breath then held out her hands, at which point May turned around and toddled straight to her.

"Too many damn stairs," Celeste said.

Fluffy nodded, and in another minute she found her breath. "It makes me think of poor old Mrs. VanHoebeek when she was dying. I hated all those stairs."

"Did she fall?" I asked, because I did not know one single thing about the VanHoebeeks other than they'd manufactured cigarettes and were dead.

"Well, she didn't fall down the stairs, if that's what you mean. She fell in the garden, out cutting peonies. She fell over in the nice soft grass and broke her hip."

"When?"

"When?" Fluffy repeated, temporarily stumped by the question. "We were well into the war, I know that. All the boys were dead by then. Mr. VanHoebeek was dead. Me and the Missus were alone in the house."

Fluffy had tried to call Celeste *Missus* when she first came to work for us but Celeste would have none of it.

"How did the boys die?" Celeste pulled the blanket up around Kevin's neck. Even with the fire going the room was cold. I needed to work on the windows.

"Are you counting all of them? Linus had leukemia. He went young, couldn't have been twelve. The older boys, Pieter and Maarten, they both died in France. They said if the US wouldn't take them they'd go back to Holland to fight. We got the word that one of them was gone and it wasn't a month later we had news about the other. They were beautiful men, like princes from a picture book. I could never decide which one I was more in love with."

"And Mr. VanHoebeek?" I sat down in the big chair near the fireplace. The clock ticked out the minutes of the night. I hadn't meant to stay with them and yet I stayed. The living room wrapped around us in the flickering light. I could hear the cars racing up and down Broadway a block away. I could hear the rain.

"Emphysema. That's why I never did smoke. Old Mr. Van-

Hoebeek smoked enough for every member of the family. It's a terrible death," Fluffy said, looking at me.

Celeste pulled her feet up beneath her. "So Mrs. VanHoebeek?" She wanted a story. May babbled for a minute in Fluffy's lap and then settled as if to listen.

"I called the ambulance and they came and picked her up out of the garden and carted her off. I drove over behind them in the last car we had. My father had been the chauffeur, you know, so I knew how to drive. I asked them at the hospital if I could sleep in the old lady's room, keep an eye on her, and the nurse told me no. She said they were going to have to put a pin in her hip and that she'd need to rest. My parents had found a job together in Virginia, all the other servants had been let go through the Depression. I was the only one left in the house back then. I was more than twenty and I'd never spent the night alone in my life." Fluffy shook her head at the thought. "I was petrified. I kept thinking I could hear people talking. Then at some point after it got dark I realized that I was the one who was there to keep the Missus safe, not the other way around. Did I think this tiny old woman had been protecting me?"

May yawned and flopped her head onto the shelf of Fluffy's breasts, looking up at her one last time to confirm that she was really there before letting her eyes drift closed.

"Did she die in the hospital?" I asked. I didn't think the outcome for pinning hips would have been very good in the forties.

"Oh, no. She came through fine. I went to see her every day, and at the end of two weeks the ambulance men brought her back. This was what my story was about in the first place, why I hated the stairs. They carried her up the stairs on a stretcher and laid her out in her bed and I got her pillows all fixed. She was so happy to be home. She thanked the men, said she was sorry to be so heavy, when the fact was she weighed about as much as a hen. She slept in the big front bedroom where your parents slept. After the men had gone I asked her if she wanted tea and she said yes so I ran downstairs to fix it, and from there on out it never stopped. There was one thing and one thing and one more thing. I was up and down those stairs every five minutes, and that was fine, I was young, but after about a week or so I realized what a mistake I'd made. I should have set her up downstairs, right there in the foyer where she would have had the view. Downstairs she could have looked at the grass and the trees and the birds, everything that was still hers. Where she was upstairs, all she had to look at was the fireplace. She couldn't see anything out the window from where she was but the sky. She never complained but it made me so sad for her. I knew she wasn't going to get better. There wasn't any reason for her to. She was such a sweet old bird. Every time I needed to go to the store or get her medicine, I'd have to give her an extra pill and knock her out, otherwise she'd get confused if I wasn't right there and she'd try to get out of bed by herself. She couldn't remember that her hip was broken, that was the problem. She was always trying to get up. I'd tell her to hold still and then I'd fly down the stairs to get what she needed and come right back up and half the time she'd be crawling out, one foot touching the floor, so then I started pulling her over to the middle of the bed and making a wall of pillows around her like you'd do with a baby, then I'd go down the stairs twice as fast. I could have run a marathon but I don't think they had marathons back then." She looked down at May and swept her hand over the baby's fine black hair. "There wasn't a soft spot on me."

There were times, early on, when Celeste would have something to say about Maeve, but Fluffy wouldn't hear it. "I love my children," she'd say, "and Maeve was my first. I saved her life, you know. When she came down with diabetes, I was the one who took her to the hospital. Imagine little May growing up and someone wanting me to listen to bad things about her." She gave May a few bounces on her hip and made her laugh. "Isn't. Gonna. Happen," she said to the baby.

Celeste quickly fell in line. The central adult relationship in her life was with Fluffy now, and she lived in terror of the day when the children would be deemed old enough for her to manage on her own. Not only was it necessary to have an extra set of hands for two children so close in age, but Fluffy knew what to do for an earache, a rash, boredom. She knew better than I did when a call to the pediatrician was in order. Fluffy was a genius as far as babies were concerned, but she had a keen sense for mothers as well. She took care of Celeste as much as she did of Kevin and May, praising her for every good decision, telling her when to rest, teaching her how to make stew. And when it rained or was dark or was simply too cold to go out, there was the endless trove of VanHoebeek stories to open again. Celeste had fallen in love with those too.

"The garage was way over to the side of the house, but if I stood on the toilet seat and opened the window I could see the guests coming in for the parties. Nothing exists like the parties they had back then, nothing in the world. All the windows would be open and the guests would walk in through the windows from the terrace. When the weather was cold they danced upstairs in the ballroom, but when it was nice outside there were workmen who would come out during the day and put down a dance floor made out of pieces of polished wood that all snapped together. That way the guests could dance on the lawn. There was a little orchestra, and everyone was laughing and laughing. My mother used to say the silkiest sound on earth was a rich woman's laugh. She would work in the kitchen all day to get things ready, then she served until two or three in the morning, then she cleaned it all up. There were plenty of people there to help but it was my mother's kitchen. My father would take all the cars away and bring them back for the guests when they were ready to leave. I'd be fast asleep on the couch when they came in, no matter how hard I'd tried to stay awake, I was a just a tiny thing, and my mother would wake me up and give me a glass of flat champagne, whatever little bit was left in the bottle. She'd wake me up and say, 'Fiona, look what I brought you!' And I'd drink it up and go right back to sleep. I couldn't have been more than five. That champagne was the most wonderful thing in the world."

"How do you think my father got the money to buy the house?" I asked Fluffy late one night in an almost sacred moment of silence, both of the children asleep in their cribs, Celeste asleep on the little bed in the nursery where she had lain down just for a minute and then was lost. Fluffy and I were standing side by side, she washing the dishes while I dried.

"It was the boy in the hospital when your father was in France."

I turned to her, a dinner plate in my hands. "You know this?" I wasn't even sure what had made me ask her but I had never considered that she might know the answer.

Fluffy nodded. "He fell out of the plane and broke his shoulder. I guess he was in that hospital forever, and there were lots of people coming and going all the time. For a few days there was a boy on the cot next to his who'd been shot in the chest. I try not to think too much about that. The boy wasn't awake very often but when he was he talked to your father. This boy said if he had money he'd buy up land in Horsham. No doubt about it, he said, and so your father asked him why. I imagine it must have been nice to have someone to talk to. The boy told him that what with the war and all he wasn't at liberty to say, but that Cyril should remember those two words: Horsham, Pennsylvania. Your father remembered."

I took another plate from her soapy fingers, then a glass. The kitchen was at the back of the house and there was a window over the sink. Fluffy always said there was no greater luxury for a woman than to have a window over the sink. "My father told you this?"

"Your father? Lord, no. Your father wouldn't have told me the time if I'd asked him. Your mother told me. We were thick as thieves, your mother and I. You have to remember, when they showed up at the Dutch House that first day she believed they were poor people. She made him tell her how he got the money. She *made* him. She was sure he'd done something illegal. Nobody had money like that back then."

I thought of myself as an undergraduate, finding that first building in foreclosure, wondering how my father had struck it rich. "What happened?"

"Well, the poor boy died, of course, leaving your father plenty of time to think about him. He stayed in that cot for another three months before there was a spot on a transport ship to send him home. After that he was put on a desk job at the shipyard in Philadelphia. He had never been to Philadelphia a day in his life. After he and your mother were settled he got out a map and what does he see but Horsham, not an hour away. He decided to go out there, I guess to be respectful to the boy. I have no idea how your father got there but the place was nothing but farmland. He made some inquiries, just to see if anything was for sale, and he found a man who had ten acres he'd part with, dirt cheap. That's where the expression came from, you know. Cheap dirt was dirt cheap."

"But where did he get the money to buy the land?" Things

can be cheap but if you didn't have money it hardly mattered. I knew that from experience.

"He'd saved up from the TVA. He worked on the dams for three years before the war. They paid him next to nothing, but your father was a man who hadn't parted with his first nickel. Now mind you, your mother didn't know about any of this, and they were married then. She didn't know about the savings or the boy or Horsham, none of it. Six months later the Navy was calling him up, saying that's just where they meant to build a base."

"I'll be damned."

Fluffy nodded, her cheeks red, her hands red in the water. "And it would have been a good story if that was all there was to it, but he took the money from the sale and put it down on a big industrial building on the river, and when he sold that he started buying up tracts of land, and all that time your mother was soaking pinto beans for supper and he was working for the Navy ordering supplies and they were living on the base with your sister. Then one day he says, 'Hey, Elna, I borrowed a car. I've got a big surprise to show you.' It really was a wonder she didn't kill him."

As we stood there shoulder to shoulder, the dishes done and the most frustrating mystery of my life resolved, I remembered that this was the woman who had hit me once when I was a child. She had slept with my father and wanted to marry him. I thought of what a better life it would have been had Fluffy gotten her way.

Chapter 14

I SOLD THE BUILDING we'd lived in when we were first married for a good price, and I sold those first two brownstones, and with the profit I bought a mixed-use building on Broadway six blocks from where we lived. It had thirty rental units and an Italian restaurant downstairs. I could have been in that building every waking hour, every day of the year, and still not made all the necessary repairs: uncontrollable steam heat, illegal garbage disposals, one tenant whose daughter flushed an orange down the toilet to see if it would go, another who left her door open so her cat could shit in the hall, and the terrier two doors down who would always find the shit and gobble it up and vomit on the hall floor. With every crisis I learned how to fix something else, and I learned how to soothe the people whose problems were not mine to solve.

I made money. I hired a super and started a management company. The surest way to know if a building was worth buying was to manage it first, or to manage a building on a block where another building went up for sale. Pretty much everything in New York was for sale in those days if you knew who to ask. I knew the councilmen, the cops. I went in and out of basements. Maeve kept my books and did the taxes for the corporation, as well as our personal taxes. It drove Celeste to distraction.

"Your sister has no right to have her nose in every corner of our lives," she said.

"Sure she does, if I'm the one asking her to do it."

Celeste had a habit of overthinking things now that she was home with the kids by herself. Fluffy was a baby nurse again, working for friends of ours ten blocks south who had adopted twins. She had stayed with us years past her original promise, and she still came over once a week to see us, to make us soup, to waltz Kevin around the kitchen in her arms. Celeste alone did the laundry now, and arranged for playdates at the park and read *The Carrot Seed* a million times in a voice of animated engagement: " 'A little boy planted a carrot seed. His mother said, "I'm afraid it won't come up." ' " She gave her best effort to everything but still, her big, wandering brain was underutilized, and would often turn itself against my sister.

"You can't have someone in your family do the books. You need to find a professional."

"Maeve *is* a professional. What do you think she does at Otterson's?" Both of the kids were sleeping, and even though a fire truck could come wailing down Broadway and not disturb their dreams, the sound of their parents arguing could pull them straight up from a coma.

"Jesus, Danny, she ships vegetables. We have a real business. There's money at stake."

As for my business, Celeste had no idea what was at stake. She knew nothing about the strength of our holdings or the size of our debt. She didn't ask. Had she understood the outrageous financial risk I'd put us in, she wouldn't have slept another night. All she could be sure of was that she didn't want Maeve close, even though in many ways Maeve, with her understanding of tax codes and mortgages, was the one who steered the ship. "Okay, first, Otterson's is a real business." Maeve had told me the profits, though she probably shouldn't have.

Celeste held up her hands. "Please don't lecture me about lima beans."

"Second, look at me, I'm serious. Second, Maeve is completely ethical, which is more than you could say about some accountants who deal with New York real estate. She has nothing but our best interest at heart."

"*Your* best interest," she said in a flat whisper. "She could care less about mine."

"It's in your best interest for our business to succeed."

"Why don't you just invite her to live with us? Wouldn't she like that? She could sleep in our bedroom. We have no secrets."

"Your father cleans our teeth."

Celeste shook her head. "Not the same."

"Your teeth, my teeth, the kids' teeth. And you know what? I like it. I'm grateful to your father. He does a good job so I go to Rydal for a filling. I trust him."

"I guess that proves what we've both long suspected."

"Which is what?"

"You're a better person than I am." Then Celeste left the bedroom to go and make sure the children hadn't heard the things we'd said.

Everything Celeste didn't like about me was Maeve's fault, because being mad at your husband's sister was infinitely easier than being mad at your husband. She might have packed her original disappointments away in a box, but she carried the box with her wherever she went. It would never be completely forgotten that I hadn't married her when she graduated from Thomas More, and had been the cause of her return to Rydal, a failure. Nor was it lost on her that the deeper I got into real estate, the happier I became. Celeste had misjudged me. She had planned on giving me the freedom to realize the error of my ways, but medicine never crossed my mind unless I was having lunch with Morey Able, or ran into one of my classmates who applied pressure to gunshot wounds in some emergency room for a living. When May was old enough to ask for a Monopoly set for Christmas, I sat beside the tree and we played. I couldn't imagine my father playing a board game but this one was genius: the houses and hotels, the deeds and the rent, the windfalls and taxes. Monopoly was the world. May always chose the Scottie dog. Kevin wasn't quite old enough to stick with the game in those days but he ran the sports car along the edge of the board and made pyramids out of the tiny green houses. Every time I rolled the dice and moved the little iron forward, I thought how lucky I was: city, job, family, house. I wasn't spending my days in a box-like room telling somebody's father he had pancreatic cancer, telling somebody's mother I felt a lump in her breast, telling the parents we had done everything we knew how to do.

Which didn't mean my being a doctor never came up. There were plenty of times as the children grew that what I'd learned all those years before was hauled into service. For example, the time we drove the station wagon to Brighton Beach with the Gilbert family, friends we'd made through the kids because that's how people make friends at a certain time in life, and Andy, the Gilbert boy, put a nail through his foot. The nail was in a board, the board was half-buried in the sand, I didn't see it happen. The boys were coming out of the water, chasing each other. I was down the beach with Andy's father, a wiry public defender named Chuck, and the two girls, one of them his and one of them mine. The girls were standing in the low waves with their buckets looking for bits of sea glass when, over the sound of the ocean and the wind and all the other kids horsing around and yelling, we heard Andy Gilbert's scream. Celeste and the boy's mother were much closer in, lying on their towels talking, keeping an eye out for the boys while they swam. We all ran towards Andy at once: fathers, mothers, sisters. He must have been around nine, he was Kevin's friend and Kevin was nine that summer. The boy's mother, a beautiful woman with straight brown hair and a red two-piece (I'm sorry to say I remember that fact while forgetting her name) was reaching down for her son's foot without any idea of what she was going to do about it, when Celeste put a hand on her shoulder and said, "No, let Danny."

The woman, the other mother, looked at my wife and then at me, no doubt wondering what I knew about taking nails out of people's feet. We had just reached them when our son Kevin said to his screaming, crucified friend, "It's okay, my dad's sort of a doctor."

And in that second when the Gilberts were still stunned by confusion and fear, I put a foot on either side of Andy's foot to hold the board in place, got the tips of my fingers between the soft meat of his instep and the board, and lifted up very fast. He screamed, of course he screamed, but there wasn't too much blood so at least he hadn't sliced an artery. I picked him up, howling and shivering in the heat, slick from the ocean, and started walking to the car in the blinding afternoon sun while the rest of the group scrambled to gather up our day at the beach. Chuck Gilbert came behind me, picking up the board to keep some other child from making the same mistake. Or maybe it was the lawyer's impulse towards the collection of evidence, as my impulse had been the removal of the nail.

That night at the dinner table, May could not stop telling us the story of our day. I had thought we should drive back into the city and go to the hospital there, but the Gilberts were worried about getting stuck in traffic, and so we wound up in an emergency room in Brooklyn, all of us sitting there, tired and gritty with sand. The ER doctor gave Andy a tetanus shot and cleaned his foot, x-rayed and wrapped it. In our hasty departure from Brighton Beach, Mrs. Gilbert had left her cover-up behind, and so had to sit in the waiting room, then talk to the doctor, in her red swimsuit top with a towel wrapped around her waist. May told us all of this as if she were bringing back news from a foreign land. I doubt the Gilberts, whom we had dropped off at their apartment on the East Side, would have appreciated her relentless reenactment. Having started her story in the middle (sea glass; scream) she doubled back to the beginning upon reaching the end. She then told us about our ride out to the beach, what each of us had had for lunch and how the boys had gone right in to swim even though they weren't supposed to so soon after eating. She told us how she and Pip, who was Andy's sister and May's friend, had gone with me and Mr. Gilbert. "Pip had just found a shell," May said darkly, "when we heard the first scream."

"Enough," her mother said finally. "We were there." Celeste was handing around a plate of cold chicken. She'd gotten too much sun and her pale skin had burned to a dark red, her shoulders and chest, her face. I could practically feel the heat coming off her. All of us were tired.

"You didn't ask Andy if you could touch his foot," May said to me, undeterred. "You didn't even ask his parents. Don't you have to ask first?"

I smiled at her, my beautiful black-haired girl. "Nope."

"Did they teach you how to do that in medical school?" Kevin asked. Neither of the children had sunburns. Celeste had been careful with them and not herself.

"Sure," I said, aware for the first time how glad I was that it hadn't been my son's foot pinned to the sand. "One semester there's a class on pulling boys' feet off of nails at beaches, and the next semester you learn how to save people who've choked on fish bones."

What medical school had taught me was how to be decisive: identify the problem, weigh the options, and act—all at the same time. But then, real estate had taught me the same thing. I would have pulled Andy Gilbert's foot off the nail without a single day of anatomy.

"You shouldn't make light of it," my wife said. "You knew what to do."

May and Kevin stopped. Kevin held an ear of corn in one hand. May put down her fork. We were waiting for her to say it. We looked at Celeste and waited. She shook her head, her curls made somehow lighter after a single afternoon in the sun. "Well, it's true."

"You're a *doctor*," May said, leaning forward and leveling her eyes at me. "You should *be* a doctor." May could do all of us but she'd made her impersonation of Celeste into high art.

It didn't matter that we were living a very good life, a life my friends from medical school would never know unless they sold off pages from their prescription pads, Celeste would have preferred to introduce me as a doctor. *My husband, Dr. Conroy.* In fact she used to do it despite my requests she knock it off. My title was the source of most of the arguments we had that weren't about my sister.

But that night in bed Celeste stretched out on top of me, her head against my shoulder, every argument worn out of her by the day. "Do my spine," she said.

She hadn't taken her shower yet and she still smelled like the ocean, like the wind coming over Brighton Beach. I reached my fingers beneath her hair and felt the base of her skull. "Atlas, axis, first cervical vertebra." I pressed each one like a piano key, touch and then release, counting all seven. "Thoracic. You've got to do a better job with the sunscreen."

"Hush. Don't ruin it."

"Thoracic." I counted out the twelve, and then I got to the lumbar. I rubbed deep circles in her lower back until she made soft, cowlike sounds.

"Do you remember?" she asked.

"Of course I remember." I loved the weight of her spread across me, the terrible heat coming off her skin.

"All those years I helped you study."

"All those years you kept me from studying." I kissed the top of her head.

"You were a great doctor," she whispered.

"I was no such thing," I said, but she raised her face to mine all the same.

Years and years after medical school was behind me, when some buildings I had bought and sold had turned enough of a profit to pay off our house and shore up our savings, I became fixated on the impossible notion of fairness. So much time and money had been wasted on my education, while nothing had come to Maeve. There was already a trust in place for May and Kevin, so why shouldn't Maeve go to law school, business school? It wasn't too late for that. She had always been the smart one, after all, and whatever she decided to study she could be a huge help to me.

"I'm already a huge help to you," she said. "I don't need a law degree for that."

"Get a degree in mathematics then. I'm the last person to

tell you to study something you're not interested in. I just don't want to see you give your entire life to Otterson's."

She was quiet for a minute. She was trying to decide whether or not she wanted to get into it. "Why does my job bother you so much?"

"Because it's beneath you." Everything in me leapt to tell her what she already knew. "Because it's the job you got the summer you came home from college and you're forty-eight and you're still doing it. You were always pushing me to make more of myself. Why not let me return the favor?"

The madder Maeve got, the more thoughtful she became. In this way she reminded me of our father—every word she spoke came individually wrapped. "If this is my punishment for sending you to medical school, fine, I accept that. I wasn't pushing you to make more of yourself anyway. I think you know that. But if you're saying you're interested in my livelihood then let me tell you: I like what I do. I like the people I work with. I like this company I've helped to grow. I've got job flexibility, health insurance that includes vision and dental, and enough paid vacation saved up that I could go around the world, but I don't want to go around the world because I *like* my job."

I don't know why I wasn't ready to let it go. "You might like something else, too. You haven't tried."

"Otterson needs me. Can you get that? He knows a lot about trucking and refrigeration and a little about vegetables and absolutely nothing about money. Every day I get to believe that I'm indispensable, so leave me alone."

The full-time job she had at Otterson's, Maeve did in half the time. At this point, Otterson didn't care where she did her work or how much time she spent on it, she always got it done. He gave her the title of Chief Financial Officer, though I couldn't imagine the company needed a CFO. She did the books for my business on the side, and never gave it anything less than her full attention. Maeve's eye was on the sparrow: if a lightbulb burned out in the lobby of a building I owned, she wanted a record of its replacement. Once a week I mailed her a folder of receipts, bills, rent checks. She made note of everything in a ledger that was not unlike the one our father kept. We banked in Jenkintown, and Maeve's name was on all the accounts. She wrote the checks. She kept up with New York state tax laws, city taxes, rebates, and incentives. She wrote firm and impartial letters to tenants who were past due. Once a month I included a check for her salary and once a month she failed to cash it.

"I pay you or I pay someone else," I said. "And for someone else this would be an actual job."

"You'd have to really hunt for someone who could turn this into a job." The work she did for me she did over dinner at her kitchen table. "On Thursdays," she said.

Maeve had long lived in a rented red brick bungalow two blocks from Immaculate Conception that had two bedrooms and a deep front porch. The kitchen was sunny, outdated, and looked over a wide rectangular yard where she planted dahlias and hollyhocks along the back fence. There was nothing wrong with the house really, other than it was too small: tiny closets, one bathroom.

"I don't care how rich you are, you can only use one bathroom at a time," Maeve said.

"Well, I'm here sometimes." Though it was the case I very rarely slept over anymore. Maeve would have been the first to point this out.

"How many years did we share a bathroom?"

I offered to buy her a house in lieu of a salary but she refused that as well. She said no one was ever going to tell her where she could and could not live again, not even me. "It's taken me five years to get a decent crop of raspberries," she said.

So I went to her landlord and bought the house she lived in. In my history of buying and selling property it was doubtlessly the worst deal I ever made. Once it had been established that I wanted something that wasn't for sale, the owner was free to set an obscene price, and he did. It didn't matter. I dropped the deed in the weekly folder of bills and receipts and mailed it to her. Maeve, who was rarely excited and never surprised, was both.

"I've been walking around this place all afternoon," she said when she got me on the phone. "A house looks different when you own it. I never knew that before. It looks better. No one's ever going to get me out of here now. I'm going to be like old Mrs. VanHoebeek. I'm going out feet first."

* * *

I WAS HEADING back to the city and on a lark we stopped by the Dutch House for just a minute. This way we could miss the worst part of the late afternoon traffic on our way to the train. Behind the linden trees, two men on giant riding mowers were driving straight lines back and forth across the wide lawn, and we rolled down our windows to let in the smell of cut grass.

We were both in our forties then, me near the beginning and Maeve near the end. My trips to Jenkintown had long become routine: I took the train down in the morning on the first Friday of every month and came back the same night, using my commute to get in order the paperwork I was taking to Maeve. As much as the company was expanding, I could have easily gone every week to sift through bills and contracts with my sister, and I definitely should have gone twice a month, but every departure meant a struggle with Celeste. She said that this was the time to be with our children. "Kevin and May still like us," Celeste would say. "That's not always going to be the case." She wasn't wrong, but still, I couldn't stop going home, and I didn't want to. The compromise I made was heavily tilted in Celeste's favor, even if Celeste never saw it that way.

Maeve and I had so much work to do when we were together that months would go by when the Dutch House scarcely crossed our minds. The fact that we were parked there now was really just an act of nostalgia, not for the people we'd been when we lived in the house, but for the people we'd been when we parked on VanHoebeek Street for hours, smoking cigarettes.

"Do you ever wish you could get back in the house?" Maeve asked.

The mowing made me think of plows and mules. "Would I go in if the house were on the market? Probably. Would I go up and ring the doorbell? No."

Maeve's hair was going gray and it made her look older than she was. "No, what I'm talking about is more like a dream: would you go in by yourself if you could? Just to look around and see what had happened to the place?"

Sandy and Jocelyn in the kitchen laughing while I sat at the blue table doing homework, my father with his coffee and cigarette in the morning in the dining room, a folded newspaper in his hand, Andrea tapping across the marble floor of the foyer, Norma and Bright laughing as they ran up the stairs, Maeve a schoolgirl, her black hair like a blanket down her back. I shook my head. "No. No way. What about you?"

Maeve tilted her head back against the headrest. "Not for anything. I think it would kill me if you want to know the truth."

"Well, I'm glad you won't be invited back then." The light

painted every blade of grass, turning the lawn into stripes the width of a lawnmower—dark green, light green, dark green.

Maeve turned her head towards the view. "I wonder when we changed."

We had changed at whatever point the old homestead had become the car: the Oldsmobile, the Volkswagen, the two Volvos. Our memories were stored on VanHoebeek Street, but they weren't in the Dutch House anymore. If someone had asked me to tell them very specifically where I was from, I would have to say I was from that strip of asphalt in front of what had been the Buchsbaums' house, which had then become the Schultzes' house, and was now the house of people whose names I didn't know. I was irritated by the landscapers' truck, the lengthy metal trailer cutting into our spot. I wouldn't have bought a house on that street, but if the street itself was for sale, it would have been mine. I said none of that. All I said in answer to her question was that I didn't know.

"You really should have gone into psychiatry," she said. "It would have been so helpful. Fluffy says the same thing, you know. She says she wouldn't go back either. She says for years she had dreams where she was walking from room to room in the Dutch House and we were there: her parents and Sandy and Jocelyn and all the VanHoebeeks, and everyone was having a fabulous time—one of those big, Gatsbyesque parties they used to have when she was a kid. She said for so long all she wanted was to get back in the house, and now she doesn't think she could go in there if the door were open."

Fluffy had long been repatriated back into the fold. Sandy and Jocelyn and Fluffy and my sister were all together again: the staff of the Dutch House and their duchess, going out for quarterly lunches and taking apart the past with a flea comb.

Maeve believed in the veracity of Fluffy's memories over Sandy's or Jocelyn's, or even her own, because Fluffy had walked away with her facts. Sandy and Jocelyn talked endlessly to each other, gnawing on the bones of our collective history along with my sister, but not Fluffy. After my father sent her to the end of the driveway with her suitcase, who could she have talked to? Her new employers? Her boyfriend? Even when she worked in our house, she told the stories Celeste liked to hear, the ones about the VanHoebeeks, the parties and the clothes. Celeste's attention wandered once the Conroy family took possession of the property, I think because Maeve was too firmly at the center of those chapters, but that was all for the better. Fluffy's stories had stayed fresh because she had kept them to herself. Fluffy still knew what she knew.

"Fluffy told me Mommy had wanted to be a nun," Maeve said. "Don't you think *that* would have come up at some point? She was already a novice when Dad came and pulled her out of the convent to marry her. Fluffy said they'd grown up in the same neighborhood. He was friends with her brother James. I told her we knew that, that we'd been out to Brooklyn when we were kids and found the apartment buildings where they lived. Fluffy said that Dad had gone to visit her before she took her vows and that was that. All those times she used to go away before she left for good? She was going back to the convent. The nuns loved her. I mean, everybody loved her but the nuns loved her especially. They were always calling Dad and telling him to let her stay a few more days. 'She just needs some rest.' That's what they'd say."

"That must have gone over well."

The two lawnmowers were coming down the driveway and then out into the street. A man motioned to Maeve to back up so they could pull onto the trailer. "I have to say, I don't even care about it now," she said. "But if I'd known that when I was growing up, I swear I would have joined the convent just to irritate him."

I smiled at the sudden picture in my mind of Maeve, tall and stern in her navy-blue habit. I wondered if our mother was still out there, working in a soup kitchen somewhere, and if that was the part of her that had wanted to be a nun. I should have told Maeve that story years ago, when it happened, but I never had. The problem was compounded by the realization that I had waited too long. "I'm sure that would have gotten his attention."

"Yeah." Maeve started the car and put it in reverse. "That probably would have been the thing to do."

* * *

"JESUS," CELESTE SAID later when I was trying to tell her the story. "It's like you're Hansel and Gretel. You just keep walking through the dark woods holding hands no matter how old you get. Do you ever get tired of reminiscing?"

I would go through long periods of my life in which I took a private vow to tell my wife nothing about my sister, to comment only on the weather in Jenkintown or the train ride home and leave it at that. But that strategy enraged Celeste, who said I was shutting her out. So then I would reverse myself, deciding she was right. Married couples told each other what was going on. No good came of secrets. In those periods I answered her honestly when she asked me how my trip to Jenkintown was or what was going on with my sister.

It never made any difference what I said. My answers, however benign, ignited her. "She's nearly fifty years old! Is she really still thinking she's going to get her mother back, she's going to get her house back?"

"That's not what I said. I said she told me our mother had wanted to join the convent when she was young. I thought it was an interesting story. Period."

Celeste wasn't listening. Where Maeve was concerned she didn't listen. "At what point do you say to her, Okay, it was an awful childhood, it's a terrible thing to be rich and then not be rich, but now everybody has to grow up?"

I refrained from pointing out the things Celeste already knew: that her own parents were alive and well, still in the Norcross foursquare in Rydal, still nursing the pain of having lost a succession of noble Labrador retrievers over the course of their long marriage, one of whom, years before, had darted out the front gate and was hit by a car in the springtime of her youth. They were good people, Celeste's people, and good things had happened to them. I wouldn't have wished it any other way.

What I didn't appreciate was that Celeste took such issue with Maeve not coming into the city, when Maeve coming to be with us was the last thing she wanted. "She's too busy with her important job in frozen vegetables to come here for the day? She expects you to drop everything—your business, your family—and run to her when she calls?"

"I'm not going out there to cut her lawn. She does all this work that she doesn't charge us for. Going out there seems like the least I could do."

"Every single time?"

What was never said but was perfectly clear was that Maeve had no husband, no children, and so her time was less valuable. "You should be careful what you wish for," I said. "I can't imagine you'd be happier if Maeve came here once a month."

And while I was sure we were careening towards a full-on argument, this sentence stopped Celeste cold. She put her face in her hands and then she started to laugh. "My god, my god," she said. "You're right. Go to Jenkintown. I don't know what I'm saying."

Maeve didn't have to give me a reason why she hated New York: traffic, garbage, crowding, incessant noise, the omnipresent visible poverty, she could have her pick. When I finally asked her, after many years of wondering, she looked at me like she couldn't believe I didn't know.

"What?"

"Celeste," she said.

"You gave up the entire city of New York to avoid Celeste?"

"What other reason would there be?"

Whatever injustices Maeve and Celeste had committed against each other years before had become abstractions. Their dislike for each other was a habit now. I could never help but think that had they met on their own, two women who had nothing to do with me, they would have liked each other very much; certainly they had at first. They were smart and funny and fiercely loyal, my sister and my wife. They claimed to love me above all others, while never acknowledging the toll it took on me to watch them pick each other apart. I blamed them both. They could have avoided it now. The grudge could be set aside if they made the choice. But they didn't. They clung to their bitterness, both of them.

Even if Maeve didn't come to the city as a rule, she recognized that rules came with exceptions. She was there for May's and Kevin's First Communions, and every now and then she turned up for a birthday. She was happiest when the children came to see the Norcrosses. Maeve was always invited to dinner. She would take Kevin home with her for the night and then to work with her in the morning. Kevin, who had no use for vegetables on his dinner plate, found them irresistible in frozen form. He couldn't get enough of the factory. He loved the order and precision of giant steel machines as applied to little carrots, he loved the chill that permeated the place, the people wearing sweaters in July. He said it was because Mr. Otterson's family was Swedish. "Cold-weather people," he said. He saw Mr. Otterson as the Willy Wonka of produce. Once he was satisfied by a day of watching peas being sealed into plastic bags, Maeve would return him to his grandparents, where he would immediately call his mother and tell her he wanted to work in vegetables.

A day spent with May bore no resemblance to a day spent with Kevin. May wanted to go through photo albums with her aunt page by page, resting her finger beneath every chin and asking questions. "Aunt Maeve," she'd say, "were you really so young?" May loved nothing more than to park in front of the Dutch House with her aunt, as if the pull to the past was an inherited condition. May insisted that she, too, had lived there when she was very young, too young to remember. She layered Fluffy's stories about parties and dancing onto her own memories of childhood. Sometimes she said she had lived above the garage with Fluffy and together they drank the flat champagne, and other times she was a distant VanHoebeek relative, asleep in a glorious bedroom with the window seat she'd heard so much about. She swore she remembered.

One night, Maeve called me after my daughter was asleep in her guest room. "When I told her the house had a swimming pool she was indignant. It's so hot here. It must have been a hundred today, and May said, 'I have every right to swim in that pool.'"

"What did you tell her?"

Maeve laughed. "I told her the truth, poor little egg. I told her she has no rights at all."

CHAPTER 15

MAY WAS VERY serious about her dancing in those days. She had secured a spot in the School of American Ballet when she was eight. We were told she had a high instep and good turnout. Every morning she stood with one hand on the kitchen counter and pointed her toes to sweep a series of elegant half circles, her hair pinned up in a high bun. Years later, she told us she saw ballet as her most direct route to the stage, and she was right. At eleven she landed a role in the army of mice in the New York City Ballet production of *The Nutcracker*. While another girl might have wanted to wear a tulle skirt and dance with the snowflakes, May was thrilled with her oversized furred head and long, whiplike tail.

"Miss Elise said that smaller companies reuse the children in different parts," May told us when she was cast. "But New York has too much talent. If you're a mouse, you're a mouse. That's all you're going to get."

"No small parts," her mother said. "Only small mice."

May stayed in character through the long autumn of rehearsals, keeping her hands curled beneath her chin as she scurried around the house, nibbling at carrots with her front teeth in a way that irritated her brother to no end. She insisted that her aunt come to see her on the New York stage (May's phrasing), and her aunt agreed that this was exactly the sort of occasion for which rules were broken.

Maeve made plans to bring Celeste's parents into the city for the first Sunday matinee. She would pick them up in Rydal then drive to the train station so they could all come in together. One of Celeste's brothers lived in New Rochelle, and her sister was in the city, so they came with their families as well. We made a strong showing in the audience, considering there would be no way of knowing which mouse was ours. When the theater darkened and the audience ceased its collective rustling, the curtain rose to Tchaikovsky's overture. Beautiful children dressed as children never are came racing out to the Christmas tree, and the lights came up on a set that might as well have been the Dutch House. It was a kind of architectural mirage, if such a thing were possible, a visual misunderstanding that I knew wasn't true but was still, for a moment, wildly convincing. Maeve was a half-dozen seats away from me in the long row of the Norcross and Conroy families, so there was no leaning over to ask if she saw it too: the two giant portraits of people who were not the VanHoebeeks, each slightly turned in the direction of the other above an elaborate mantel. There was the long green settee. Had ours been green? The table, the chairs, the second sofa, the massive burled secretary with the glass front full of beautiful leather-bound books that all turned out to be written in Dutch. I remembered the first time I'd taken the key out of the desk as a boy and stood on a chair to open those glass doors, the amazement of taking down book after book and seeing my familiar alphabet arranged into a senseless configuration. The set of the ballet was like that. I knew the chandelier suspended above the stage, there was no mistaking it. How many countless hours had I spent on my back staring into that chandelier, the light and the crystal combining as I doubled down on my childhood attempts at self-hypnosis? I had read about it at the library. Of course the grouping of furniture had been flattened out, pushed back into an unnatural line in order to make room for the dancers, but were I able to go onstage and rearrange it, I could have recreated my past. In truth, it wasn't just *The Nutcracker.* Any configuration of luxury seen from a distance felt like a window on my youth. That's how far away youth was. Celeste was on my left, Kevin on my right, their faces warmed by stage light. The party guests were dancing and the children held hands and formed a ring around them. After they had all danced off into the wings and stage-night fell, the mice made their entrance behind the evil Mouse King. They rolled around on the floor, kicking their little feet furiously in the air. I covered Celeste's hand with my hand. So many mice! So many children dancing. The soldiers of the Nutcracker came, the war was fought, dead mice were dragged away by the living to make room for more dancers.

There was a certain amount of storyline in the first act but the second act was nothing but dancing: Spanish dancers, Arab dancers, Chinese dancers, Russian dancers, endless dancing flowers. Too much dancing wasn't a valid complaint to make about a ballet, but without the mice to look forward to, without the furniture to consider, I struggled to find meaning. Kevin poked my arm and I leaned over to him. I could smell the butterscotch Lifesaver in his mouth. "How can it be so long?" he whispered.

I looked at him helplessly and mouthed the words *No idea.* Celeste and I had made a few halfhearted attempts to get the kids to church when they were young, and then we gave up and left them in bed. In the city of constant stimulation, we had failed to give them the opportunity to develop strong inner lives for those occasions when they would find themselves sitting through the second act of *The Nutcracker*.

When at last the ballet was over and the Sugar Plum Fairy and the Nutcracker and Clara and Uncle Drosselmeyer and the snowflakes each had their fair share of thunderous applause (no curtain call for mice!), the audience collected their coats and stood to make their way to the aisles, all except Maeve. She stayed in her seat, eyes straight ahead. I noticed my mother-in-law had her hand on Maeve's shoulder, then she was leaning over to say something. There was a tremendous bustle of activity around us. Our family, standing without moving forward, was blocking the path. The grandmothers and mothers who had filled the row beside us, turned their charges around to exit in the opposite direction.

"Danny?" my mother-in-law called.

We were a significant group, the few Conroys and many Norcrosses—spouses, children, parents, siblings. I made my way past all of them. The sweat was beading on Maeve's nose and chin. Her hair was soaked through, as if she had slipped out for a swim while the rest of us watched the ballet. Maeve's purse was on the floor and I found the same old yellow plastic box inside, now held together by a rubber band, and took two glucose tablets out of the little plastic bag she kept.

"Home," she said in a quiet voice, still looking straight ahead though her eyelids were drooping.

I pushed a glucose tab between her teeth and then another. I told her to chew.

"What should I do?" my father-in-law asked. Maeve had picked them up and brought them in on the train because none of us liked the idea of Bill Norcross driving into the city. "Does she need an ambulance?"

"No," Maeve said, still not turning her head.

"She'll be okay," I said to Bill, like this was our routine. A very old calm settled on me.

"I need—" Maeve said, then closed her eyes.

"What?"

Then Celeste and Kevin were there with a glass of orange juice and a cloth napkin full of ice. I hadn't seen them leave and already they were back with what we needed. They had known. Standing in the row behind us, Celeste lifted the sopping wool of Maeve's hair and rested the ice pack against her neck. Kevin handed me the juice.

"How did you get this so fast?" The aisles were packed with little girls and their minders excitedly recounting each jeté.

"I ran," said my son, who had choked on his own excess of energy throughout the performance. "I said it was an emergency."

Kevin knew how to move around people—a benefit of growing up in the city. I held my handkerchief under Maeve's mouth. "Sip."

"You know this will make your sister insanely jealous that you were the one who got the juice," Celeste said to Kevin. "She would rather have been the hero than a mouse."

Kevin smiled, his stoicism in the face of boredom rewarded. "Is she going to be okay?"

"Okay," Maeve said quietly.

"You get everyone out to the lobby," Celeste told her father, who, like Kevin, was looking for work. "I'll be there in one minute."

Maeve pressed her eyes closed and then opened them wider. She was trying to chew the tablets and drink the juice with minimal success. Some of it was slipping from the side of her mouth. I gave the glass to Celeste and fished a test strip out of the yellow box. Maeve's hands were wet and cold when I stuck her finger.

"What do you think happened?" Celeste asked me.

Maeve nodded, swallowed. She was coming slowly into focus. "Dance so long."

Everyone was always in such a hurry to leave a theater. They hoped to be the first to get to the bathroom, to get a taxi, get to the restaurant before the reservation was cancelled. It had been scarcely ten minutes since the raucous ovation and the distribution of roses and already the giant New York State Theater was almost empty. The last of the little girls, the ones who had been sitting in the very front rows, came pirouetting up the aisle in their fur-collared coats. All those velvet seats had folded back in on themselves. One of the ushers stopped at our row, a woman in a white shirt and a buttoned green vest. "You folks need help?"

"She's okay," I said. "She just needs a minute."

"He's a doctor," Celeste said.

Maeve smiled, mouthed the word *doctor*.

The usher nodded. "If you need something, you let us know."

"We just need to sit here awhile."

"Take your time," the woman said.

"I'm sorry," Maeve said. I wiped down her face. The test strip reported her sugar at thirty-eight. It should have been ninety and I would have been happy with seventy.

"You should have told someone you weren't feeling well." Celeste moved the ice to the top of Maeve's head.

"Ah, that's good," Maeve said. "I didn't want to get up. I thought—" She inhaled deeply, closed her eyes.

I told her to take another sip of juice.

She swallowed, began again. "I'd be disruptive?" Maeve was wearing a blouse with a sweater over it, wool slacks, all of it wet.

Celeste had Maeve's hair gathered up in one hand, the ice pack in the other. "I'm going backstage to get May and we'll go on to dinner," she said to me. "When she's feeling better, bring her over to the house."

"Danny should go," Maeve said. She still hadn't tried to look at either of us.

"Danny isn't going to go," Celeste said. "There's a big crowd and no one will miss him. It's a detente, okay? You're sick. May's going to want to see you, so plan on coming back to the house." She handed me the shards of ice, the sopping napkin. The glucose was doing its job. I watched the life come creeping back into my sister's face.

"Tell May she was a good mouse," Maeve said.

"You'll tell her," Celeste said.

"I have to get your parents home." Maeve's voice, which had a tendency to boom in other circumstances, was so light I don't know how Celeste could have heard her. It floated up towards the high ceiling.

Celeste shook her head. "Just do what Danny tells you for a change. I have to go."

I leaned over and kissed Celeste. She was more than capable of rising to the occasion. She passed the ushers who were coming back down the aisles to pick up the scattered programs from the floor, sweeping the candy wrappers into their dustpans.

Maeve and I sat together in the theater seats. She let her head rest on my shoulder.

"She was very nice," Maeve said.

"Most of the time she is."

"Detente," Maeve said.

"You're feeling better."

"A little. But it's good to sit." She took my handkerchief and

blotted her face and neck. I took her hand and punched another hole in her fingertip to test her blood again.

"What is it?"

I peered at the strip. "Forty-two."

"We'll wait another minute." She closed her eyes.

I looked across the sea of empty seats, inhaled the mix of
perfumes hanging above us in the air. The mice and the snowflakes and the Christmas tree and the living room set, the audience who sat in the dark to watch—everything was gone now,
everyone was gone, and it was just the two of us.

It had been just a minor miscalculation. Maeve would be
fine.

I started to think I could put Maeve in my car and drive her
around to see my buildings. I could drive her to Harlem and
show her the very first brownstone I ever bought, then go to
Washington Heights and show her the Health Sciences building
that sat on top of the two parking lots I had owned for five
months. I could give her the entire tour. Maeve may have known
my business to the last dime but she'd never actually seen it. We
could wind up at Café Luxembourg when we were finished, eat
steak frites before going home. Kevin and May would be so
happy to have her in the house that maybe Maeve and Celeste
would see it was time to put it all to rest. If it was ever going to
happen then this would be the day, lost as we had been to *The
Nutcracker* and then the precipitous drop in blood sugar. Celeste had come to her aid, after all, and Maeve had been grateful. Even the oldest angers could be displaced. After a glass of
wine, if she felt up to a glass of wine, Maeve would climb the
stairs to May's room, push the stuffed animals off the second
bed so they could lie across from each other in the dark. May
would tell her what the world looked like from those two cut-
out eyeholes, and Maeve would tell her what she had seen from

the fourteenth row. Upstairs in our own bed, Celeste would tell me it was okay that my sister was here, or better than okay. She'd finally been able to see Maeve as the person I had always known.

"No," Maeve said. "Drive me home."

"Come on," I said. "It's a big night."

She picked at the neck of her sweater. "I can't wear these clothes for the rest of the night. I don't even know if I can stand them on the drive home."

"I'll get you some clothes. Do you remember when I came and stayed with you in college? Dad dropped me off without a toothbrush, without anything. You took me shopping."

"Oh, Danny, are you serious? I can't go shopping, and I can't spend the evening talking to the Norcrosses about ballet. I can barely keep my eyes open sitting here. My car's at the train station. I have a meeting at work in the morning. I want to eat something and fall asleep in my own bed." She turned to me in her seat. Soon enough we were going to wear out our welcome at the New York State Theater.

She was right, of course. I should have been thinking about how I was going to get her to the lobby, not how we would take a tour of the city and then stay up half the night. Fragility wasn't a word I could attach to my sister but everything in her countenance made it clear. She took hold of my hand. "I'll tell you what: you drive me home and spend the night. You haven't spent the night in how many years? In the morning we'll get up before the birds. I'll be fine then. You can drive me to the station to get my car and then drive straight back to the city before the traffic. You could be home by seven. There wouldn't be anything wrong with that, would there? Celeste has her family here."

There was plenty wrong with it, but I didn't know what else

we could have done. While everyone was off at May's dinner, before the mouse-shaped cake that Celeste had taken over to the restaurant had been served, Maeve and I took a taxi back to the house. I knew that May would be disappointed and Celeste would be furious, but I also knew how sick Maeve had been, how exhausted she was. I knew that she alone in all the world would have done the same for me. Maeve sat on a little bench we kept by the front door for pulling boots off and on in the winter, and I ran upstairs, packed a bag and left a note.

Maeve slept in the car most of the way home. It was early December and the days were short and cold. I drove to Jenkintown in the dark, thinking all the time about the dinner I was missing, about May dancing in the mouse head. I called as soon as we got to Maeve's house but no one answered. "Celeste, Celeste, Celeste," I said into the machine. I pictured her in the kitchen, looking at the phone and turning away. Maeve had gone straight in to take a bath. I made us eggs and toast and we ate at her little kitchen table. When we went to bed it wasn't even eight o'clock.

"At least we each have our own bedroom now," I said. "You don't have to sleep on the couch."

"I never minded sleeping on the couch," she said.

We said goodnight in the hallway. Maeve's second bedroom doubled as her office, and I looked at the bookshelf full of binders that said CONROY on the spine. I meant to pull one down for kicks, to take my mind off the disasters of the day, but then decided to close my eyes for just a minute and that was that.

When Maeve knocked on my door, she woke me from a dream in which I was trying to swim to Kevin. Every stroke I took towards him seemed to push him farther out, until I was struggling to see his head above the water's chop. I kept calling for him to swim back but he was too far away to hear me. I sat straight up, gasping, trying to make sense of where I was. Then I remembered. I had never been so happy to be awake.

Maeve opened the door a crack. "Too early?"

Now that it was morning, yesterday's plan seemed utterly sensible, necessary. Maeve in the kitchen was her own bright self, making coffee, telling me how fine she felt, like none of it had happened. ("I just needed a bath and a good night's sleep," she said.) I could see that I would be home early enough to make amends. We were outside in the dark again just past four o'clock, Maeve locking the back door of her little house. We were ahead of the schedule we had laid out for ourselves. Nothing would be lost.

"Let's go to the house," Maeve said once we were back in my car.

"Really?"

"We've never gone over there this time of day."

"We've never done anything this time of day."

"It's not like we're going to be late." She had so much energy. I had forgotten the way she was in the morning, like each new day came in on a wave she had managed to catch. The Dutch House wasn't far from where Maeve lived, and since it was in the general direction of where we were going, and since we had gotten out so early, I didn't see how there was any harm in it. The neighborhoods were dark, the street lights on. It wouldn't be light until after seven. I had left New York in the dark and I would get home before it was light again. That wasn't too bad.

The houses on VanHoebeek Street were never entirely dark. People left their porch lights on all night, as if they were always waiting for someone to come home. Gas lights flickered at the ends of driveways, a lamp in the front window of a living room stayed on through the night, but even with all these small bursts of illumination there was a stillness about the place that made it clear the inhabitants were all in their beds, even the dogs of Elkins Park were asleep. I pulled the car into our spot and turned off the engine. The moon in the west was bright enough to drown out any stars. It poured over everything equally: the leafless trees and the driveway, the wide lawn scattered with leaves and the wide stone stairs. Moonlight poured across the house and into the car where Maeve and I sat. When would I have seen this as a boy, up hours before dawn on the clear, cold winter night? I would have been like everyone else in the neighborhood, sound asleep in my bed.

"You'll tell May and Kevin I'm sorry," Maeve said.

We were in the car together, each of us deep in our separate thoughts. It took me a minute to realize she was talking about the ballet and the dinner after. "They won't be upset."

"I don't want to think I ruined it for her."

I couldn't focus myself on May when everything around me was shimmering frost and moonlight. Maybe I was still half asleep. "Do you ever come over here in the morning, early like this?"

Maeve shook her head. I don't think she was even looking at the house, how beautiful it was rising up out of the darkness. For the most part I had stopped seeing it a long time ago, but every now and then something would happen, something like this, and my eyes would open again and I would see it there— enormous, preposterous, spectacular. A brigade of nutcrackers could come pouring out of the dark hedges at any minute and be met by a battalion of mice. The lawn was sugared with ice. The stage at Lincoln Center hadn't been made to look like the Dutch House, it was that the Dutch House was the setting for a ridiculous fairy tale ballet. Was it possible our father had turned into the driveway that first time and been struck by the revelation that this was where he wanted to raise his family? Was that what it meant to be a poor man, newly rich?

"Look," Maeve said in a whisper.

The light in the master bedroom had come on. The master bedroom faced the front of the house, while Maeve's room, the better room with the smaller closet, looked over the back gardens. Several minutes later we saw the light in the upstairs hallway, and then the light on the stairs, like the first time Maeve had brought me back when I came home from Choate, but now the whole thing was happening in reverse. In the car, in the dark, we said nothing. Five minutes passed, ten minutes. Then a woman was walking down the driveway in a light-colored coat. While logic would suggest that it could have been a housekeeper or one of the girls, it was clear to both of us even from a distance that it was Andrea. Her hair, pulled back in a ponytail, was a brighter blond in the moonlight. She kept her arms around herself, holding her coat tightly closed, the edge of something pink trailing behind her. We could see some slippers that might have been boots. It looked for all the world like she was coming straight for us.

"She sees us." Maeve's voice was low and I put my hand on her wrist on the off chance she was planning to get out of the car.

When Andrea was still a good ten feet from the end of the driveway, she stopped and turned her face to the moon, moving one hand up to hold closed the collar of her coat. She hadn't stopped for a scarf. She hadn't expected the early morning dark to be so clear or the moon so full, and she stood there, taking it in. She was twenty years older than I was, or that's how I remembered it. I was forty-two, Maeve was forty-nine, soon to be fifty. Andrea took a few more steps towards us and Maeve slipped her fingers through mine. She was entirely too close, our stepmother, as close as a person on the other side of the street. I could see both how she had aged and how she was exactly herself: eyes, nose, chin. There was nothing extraordinary about her. She was a woman I had known in my childhood and now did not know at all, a woman who had, for several years, been married to our father. She leaned over, picked up the folded newspaper from the pea gravel, and, tucking it under one arm, turned away, walking into the frost-covered field of the front lawn.

"Where is she going?" Maeve whispered, because for all the world it looked like she was headed towards the hedge that bordered the property to the south. The moon hung on her pale coat, her pale hair, until she passed behind the line of trees and we couldn't see her anymore. We waited. Andrea didn't reappear at the front doors.

"Do you think she's gone around to the back? That doesn't make any sense. It's freezing." It hadn't occurred to me until now that I was never the one driving when we went to the Dutch House, and that from this vantage point the view was subtly changed.

"Go," Maeve said.

We stopped at a diner instead of going straight to the train station to pick up her car, and over eggs and toast, the same thing we'd eaten for dinner, broke down Andrea's trip to get the paper frame by frame. Had she seen something out there we couldn't see? Were those slippers or boots? Andrea had never gone to get the paper herself. She had never come downstairs in her nightgown, or maybe she had, when none of us were awake. Of course, she would be living in the house alone now. Norma and Bright, whom we always thought of as being so young, must be in their late thirties by now. How long had Andrea been there alone?

Finally, when we had exhausted every fact and supposition, Maeve put her coffee cup down in its saucer. "I'm done," she said.

The waitress came by and I told her we'd take the check.

Maeve shook her head. She put her hands on the table and looked at me straight, the way our father would tell her to do. "I'm done with Andrea. I'm making a pledge to you right here. I'm done with the house. I'm not going back there anymore."

"Okay," I said.

"When she started walking towards the car I thought I was having a heart attack. I felt an actual pain in my chest just seeing her again, and it's been how many years since she threw us out?"

"Twenty-seven."

"That's enough, isn't it? We don't need to do this. We can go someplace else. We can park at the arboretum and look at the trees."

Habit is a funny thing. You might think you understand it, but you can never exactly see what it looks like when you're doing it. I was thinking about Celeste and all the years she told me how insane it was that Maeve and I parked in front of the house we had lived in as children, and how I thought the problem was that she could never understand.

"You look disappointed," Maeve said.

"Do I?" I leaned back in the booth. "This isn't disappointment." We had made a fetish out of our misfortune, fallen in love with it. I was sickened to realize we'd kept it going for so long, not that we had decided to stop.

But I didn't need to say any of that because Maeve understood it all perfectly. "Just imagine if she'd come to get the paper sooner," she said. "Say, twenty years ago."

"We could have had our lives back."

I paid the check and we got in the car and drove to the parking lot at 30th Street Station. It had been only yesterday that Maeve had come to New York to see May dance. It could be said that by stopping at the Dutch House, and then going to the diner, we had wasted the advantage we'd gained by getting up so early. There wouldn't be much traffic for Maeve going back to Jenkintown, but I would hit the full force of rush hour driving into the city now. I would do my best to explain it all to Celeste. I'd tell her I was sorry I'd been gone, sorry I was late coming back, and then I would tell her what we had accomplished.

Maeve and I agreed, our days at the Dutch House were over.

Part

THREE

CHAPTER 16

"I F MAEVE GETS sick then you're the one who has to do the thinking," Jocelyn told me in the little apartment where Maeve and I lived after our father died. "Don't let yourself get upset. People who get upset only make more work." Funny what sticks. There wasn't a week that went by, and probably not even a day, when her instruction didn't come back to me. I equated my ability to be effective with my ability to stay calm, and time and again it proved to be the case. When Mr. Otterson called me from the hospital to tell me that Maeve had had a heart attack, I called Celeste and asked her to pack me a bag and bring up the car.

"Should I come with you?" she asked.

I appreciated that but told her no. "Call Jocelyn," I said, because Jocelyn was on my mind. My father was on my mind. He had been fifty-three, Maeve was fifty-two. I thought less about his dying and more about the deal I'd struck with God when I walked out of my high school geometry class that day at Bishop McDevitt: He would spare Maeve, and in return could take anything else. Anyone else.

The small waiting room for the coronary care unit was hidden past the restrooms and water fountains. Mr. Otterson was there, looking like he'd been sitting in that same gray chair for a week, his elbows resting on his knees, his hair thinning and gray. Sandy and Jocelyn were with him. They had heard the story about what had happened but they asked him to tell it again. Otterson had saved Maeve's life.

"We were meeting with an advertiser and Maeve stood up and said she needed to go home," Mr. Otterson began in his quiet voice. He was wearing gray suit pants and a white shirt. He'd taken off his jacket and tie. "No doubt she'd ignored whatever it was she was feeling for as long as possible. You know Maeve."

We all agreed.

They had left the meeting right away. He asked if her blood sugar was low and she told him no, this was something else, maybe the flu. "When I told her I was going to drive her home she didn't say a word about it," Mr. Otterson said. "That's how bad it was."

They were two blocks from her house when he turned the car around and drove her to the hospital in Abington. He said it was intuition as much as anything. She had put her head against the window of the car door. "She was melting," he said. "I can't explain it."

Had Mr. Otterson let her off at her house, walked her to the front door and told her to get some rest, that would have been that.

It was Maeve who told me the rest of the story when I saw her in recovery. She was still swimming up from the anesthesia and kept trying to laugh. She told me Mr. Otterson had raised his voice to the young woman at the desk in the emergency room. Otterson raising his voice was like another man pointing a gun. Maeve heard him say *diabetic*. She heard him say *coronary*, though she thought he was only throwing the word around so someone would come and help them. It had never occurred to her that it was her heart. Then finally she could feel it, the pressure creeping up into her jaw, the room swirling back, our father climbing the last flight of concrete stairs in the terrible heat.

"Stop making that face," she whispered. "I'm going back to sleep." They kept those rooms so bright, and I wanted to shade her eyes with my hand, but I held her hand instead, watching her heart monitor scaling slowly up and down until a nurse came and guided me away. I was calm through the night I spent in the waiting room, Mr. Otterson staying past midnight no matter how many times I told him he should go. I was calm the next afternoon when the cardiologist told me she'd had a malignant arrhythmia during the placement of the stent and they would need to keep her in the unit longer than had been expected. I went to Maeve's house to take a shower and a nap. I was calm, going back and forth from the waiting room to her house, receiving the visitors who were not allowed in to see her, waiting for the three times a day I could go and sit by her bed. I stayed calm until the fourth morning when I came into the waiting room and found another person there—an old woman, very thin, with short gray hair. I nodded at her and took my regular seat. I was just about to ask her if she was a friend of Maeve's because I was certain I knew her. Then I realized she was my mother.

Maeve's heart attack had lured her out from beneath the floorboards. She had not been there for graduations or our father's funeral. She had not been there when we were told to leave the house. She wasn't at my wedding or at the births of my children or at Thanksgiving or Easter or any of the countless Saturdays when there had been nothing but time and energy to talk everything through, but she was there now, at Abington Memorial Hospital, like the Angel of Death. I said nothing to her because one should never initiate a conversation with Death.

"Oh, Danny," she said. She was crying. She covered her eyes with her hand. Her wrist looked like ten pencils bundled together.

I knew what happened when people explored their anger in hospitals. The hospitals got rid of those people. It didn't matter if their anger was justified. Jocelyn had told me that people who got upset weren't helpful, and it was my job to take care of Maeve.

"You were the doctor," she said at last.

"That was me."

If Maeve was fifty-two that would make her what? Seventy-three? She looked a decade older.

"You remember?" she asked.

I gave a slow nod, wondering if I should acknowledge even this much. "You had a braid."

She ran her hand over her short hair. "I had lice. I'd had them before but this last time, I don't know, it bothered me."

I asked her what she wanted.

She dropped her eyes again. She could have been a ghost. "To see you," she said, not looking at me. "To tell you I'm sorry." She rubbed the sleeve of her sweater over her eyes. She was like any old woman in a hospital waiting room, only taller and thinner. She was wearing jeans and blue canvas tennis shoes. "I'm so sorry."

"Good," I said. "That's done."

"I came to see Maeve," she said, rolling the small gold band on her finger.

I made a mental note to kill Fluffy. "Maeve is very sick," I said, thinking I needed to get her out of there before Fluffy showed up to defend her, before Sandy and Jocelyn and Mr.

Otterson and all the rest of them arrived to cast their vote on whether she should stay or go. "Come back when she's better. She needs to focus on getting well now. You can wait, can't you? After all this time?"

My mother's head tipped down like a sunflower at the end of the day, down and down until her chin hovered just above the bony dip of her chest. The tears hung for a moment on her jaw and then fell. She told me she had already been in to see Maeve that morning.

It wasn't even seven o'clock. While I had eaten my eggs in Maeve's kitchen, our mother sat by Maeve's bed in the glass fishbowl of the coronary care unit, holding her hand and crying, laying the tremendous burden of her grief and shame directly on my sister's heart. She had gotten into the unit by the most direct means possible: she told the truth, or she told some of it. She went to the charge nurse and said her daughter Maeve Conroy had had a heart attack, and now she was here, the mother, just arrived. The mother looked like she was a minute away from coding herself, so when the nurse waived the rules and let my mother in for a visit that was both too long and not in keeping with the unit's schedule, she did so to benefit the mother, not the daughter. I know this because I spoke to the nurse myself. I spoke to her later, when I could speak again.

"She was happy," my mother said, her voice as quiet as a page turned. She looked at me with such tremendous need, and I didn't know if she was asking me to make this right, or telling me that she had returned to make this right.

I stood up quickly and left her in the waiting room, skipping the elevator in favor of the five flights of stairs. It was April and starting to rain. For the first time in my life I wondered if my father might have loved my sister, beyond the abstract and inattentive way I had always imagined he loved her. Was it possible that he believed Maeve to be in danger and so thought to keep her safe from our mother? I walked manically up and down the rows of cars. If someone were to look out the window of his hospital room and see me, he would say, *Look at that poor man. He doesn't remember where he parked.* I wanted to keep my sister safe from our mother, to keep her safe from anyone who could leave her so carelessly and then reappear at the worst time imaginable. I wanted to attest to my commitment, to reassure my sister that I was watching now and no harm would come again, but she was sleeping.

There is no story of the prodigal mother. The rich man didn't call for a banquet to celebrate the return of his erstwhile wife. The sons, having stuck it out for all those years at home, did not hang garlands on the doorways, kill the sheep, bring forth the wine. When she left them she killed them all, each in his own way, and now, decades later, they didn't want her back. They hurried down the road to lock the gate, the father and his sons together, the wind whipping at their coats. A friend had tipped them off. They knew she was coming and the gate must be locked.

A patient in the coronary care unit was allowed three fifteen-minute visits a day, one visitor at a time. My mother went to Maeve's bedside for the next two visits: the regular morning visit and the mid-afternoon. The nurse came into the waiting room and told us Maeve was asking for her mother. I was allowed in at seven that evening, and I understood that it was not a moment for petulance, confrontation or discussion. No wrongs would be righted, no injustices examined. I would go in and see my sister, that was all. Though I had been a doctor for only a short time, I knew the havoc the well could unleash upon the sick.

Maybe it was because a full twenty-four hours had passed

since I had last seen her, and maybe it was because our mother's arrival had thrilled her, but Maeve looked better than she had. She was sitting in the single chair beside her bed, her monitors all beeping in accordance with her improved heart function. "Look at you!" I said, and leaned down to kiss her.

Maeve gave me one of her rare Christmas-morning smiles, no guile, all teeth. She looked like she might pop straight up and throw her arms around me. "Can you believe it?"

And I didn't say, *What?* And I didn't say, *I know! You're doing so much better!* because I knew what she was talking about and this wasn't the time to be coy. I said, "It was a big surprise."

"She told me Fluffy found her and told her I was sick." Maeve's eyes were shining in the dim light. "She said she came right away."

And I didn't say, *Right away plus forty-two years.* "I know she's been worried about you. Everyone's been worried about you. I think that everyone you've ever known has come by."

"Danny, our *mother* is here. It doesn't matter about anyone else. Doesn't she look beautiful?"

I sat down on the unmade bed. "Beautiful," I said.

"You're not happy about this."

"I am. I'm happy for you."

"Jesus Christ."

"Maeve, I want you to be healthy. I want whatever's going to be best for you."

"You have got to learn to lie." Her hair had been brushed and I wondered if our mother had brushed it.

"I am lying," I said. "You can't believe how well I'm lying."

"I'm so happy. I've just had a heart attack and this has been the happiest day of my life."

I told her the truth, more or less, that her happiness was all I cared about.

"I'm just glad she came back for my heart attack and not my funeral."

"Why would you even say that?" For the first time since Mr. Otterson had called my office, I was in danger of giving way to my emotions.

"It's true," she said. "Let her sleep in the house. Make sure there's food. I don't want her in the waiting room all night."

I nodded. There was so much to hold back that I couldn't say another word.

"I love her," Maeve said. "Don't mess this up for me. Don't chase her off while I'm locked up in the aquarium."

Later that day I went back to Maeve's and packed up my things. It would be easier for me to stay in a hotel anyway. I asked Sandy to pick my mother up and take her to Maeve's. Sandy knew everything already, including how I felt, which was miraculous considering my inability to put my feelings into words. From what I could piece together, Sandy and Jocelyn and Fluffy had each dealt with the return of Elna Conroy in her own way.

"I know how hard this is," Sandy said to me, "because I know how hard it was. But I think if you'd known her back then you'd be happy to see her."

I just looked at her.

"Okay, maybe not, but we have to make this work for Maeve's sake." Meaning that I would make it work and she would help me. Sandy had always had a lighter touch than the other two.

My mother offered nothing to explain herself. When we were in the waiting room together she stayed near the window as if contemplating her exit. A high-pitched whine seemed to emanate from her misery, like fluorescent tubing just before it burns out, like tinnitus, something nearly imperceptible that almost drove me to insanity. Then, without a word, she would leave, as if even she could not stand herself another minute. When she returned hours later she was more relaxed. Sandy told me she went to the other floors and found people to walk with, patients or anxious family members waiting for news. She would loop around the various nurses' stations with strangers for hours.

"And they let her?" I asked. I would have thought there would be rules against it.

Sandy shrugged. "She tells them her daughter had a heart attack and that she's waiting, too. She isn't exactly a dangerous character, your mother."

It was a point on which I could not be convinced.

Sandy sighed. "I know. I think I'd still be mad at her too if she wasn't so old."

I believed that Sandy and my mother were pretty much the same age, at least in the same ballpark, but I also knew what she meant. My mother was like a pilgrim who had fallen into the ice for hundreds of years and then was thawed against her will. Everything about her indicated that she had meant to be dead by now.

Fluffy proved adept at avoiding me, and when I finally caught her alone at the elevator bank, she pretended she'd been looking for me. "I've always known you to be a decent man," she said, instructing me to be nicer.

"And I've known you to make some bad decisions, but you've really outdone yourself here."

Fluffy held her ground. "I did what was best for Maeve." An elevator door opened in front of us and when the people inside looked out we shook our heads.

"How is it that hearing from our mother was a bad idea for Maeve when she was just a diabetic, but now that she's a diabetic who's had a heart attack you think it's a good idea?"

"It's different," Fluffy said, her cheeks reddening.

"Explain it to me then because I don't understand." I tried to remember how deeply I trusted her, how she had taught Celeste and me to raise our children, how confidently we left the house with only Fluffy there to guard Kevin and May.

"I was afraid Maeve would die," Fluffy said, her eyes going watery. "I wanted her to see her mother before she died."

But of course Maeve didn't die. Every day she improved, overcame her setbacks. Every day she asked for no one but her mother.

I found it remarkable that our mother could work Maeve into her schedule. She had somehow secured the right to push the flower cart, to sit and visit with the people who had no mothers of their own to contend with. I didn't know whom she had talked into letting her do this, or how, since when we found ourselves together she was more or less mute. I thought she was too restless to sit in the waiting room, but it was probably closer to the truth to say she didn't want to sit with me. She couldn't look at me. When Fluffy arrived for a visit, or Sandy or Jocelyn or Mr. Otterson or the Norcrosses or good old Lawyer Gooch or any group of Maeve's friends from work or church or the neighborhood, there my mother would be, picking up the newspapers and magazines, seeing who wanted a bottle of water or an orange. She was forever peeling someone an orange. She had some special trick for it.

"So what was India like?" Jocelyn asked one afternoon, as if my mother had just returned from vacation. Jocelyn remained the most suspicious of our mother, or, I should say, the second-most suspicious.

I noticed the dark circles under my mother's eyes had diminished somewhat. She must have been the only person in human history to have been improved by a waiting room. Jocelyn and

I were there with Fluffy. Sandy was working. Sooner or later Elna was going to have to tell us something.

"India was a mistake," she said finally.

"But you wanted to help," Fluffy said. "You helped people."

"Why India?" I had meant to sit through the conversation in silence but on this point my curiosity got the better of me.

My mother picked at a piece of yarn that dangled from the cuff of her dark green sweater, the same sweater she wore every day. "I read an article in a magazine about Mother Teresa, how she asked the sisters to send her to Calcutta to help the destitutes. I can't even remember what magazine it was now. Something your father subscribed to."

That wasn't a connection I would have made, my mother sitting in the kitchen of the Dutch House, circa 1950, reading about Mother Teresa in *Newsweek* or *Life* while the other women on VanHoebeek street took leadership positions in the garden club and went to summer dances.

"She's a great lady, Mother Teresa," Fluffy said.

My mother nodded. "Of course she wasn't Mother Teresa then."

"You worked with Mother Teresa?" Jocelyn asked.

At this point anything seemed possible, including my mother in a white cotton sari holding the dying in her arms. There was such a plainness about her, as if she'd already shrugged off all human concerns. Or maybe I was reading too much into the bony contours of her face. The long, thin hands she kept folded in her lap made me think of kindling. The fingers of her right hand kept finding their way back to the ring she wore on her left.

"I meant to, but the ship went to Bombay. I don't think I even looked at a map before I left. I ended up on the wrong side of the country." She said it by way of acknowledging that everyone made mistakes. "They told me I'd have to take a train, and

I was going to, I was going to go to Calcutta, but once you've spent a couple of days in Bombay—" She finished the sentence there.

"What?" Fluffy prompted.

"There was plenty to do in Bombay," my mother said quietly.

"There's plenty to do in Brooklyn." I picked up the Styrofoam cup at my feet but the coffee was cold. Gone were the days I'd drink cold coffee in a hospital.

"Danny," Fluffy said, warning me of what I do not know.

"No, he's right," my mother said. "That's what I should have done. I could have served the poor of Philadelphia and come home at night but I didn't have the sense God gave a goose. That house—"

"The house?" Jocelyn said, as if she had no business blaming the Dutch House for her neglect.

"It took away all sense of proportion."

"It was huge," Fluffy said.

A television set that hung from a high corner near the ceiling of the waiting room was playing a show about tearing apart an old house. There was no remote, but on my first day there I stood on a chair and muted the sound. Four days later, the people on the television walked silently through empty rooms, pointing out the walls they were going to knock through.

"I could never understand why your father wanted it and he could never understand why I didn't."

"Why didn't you?" Surely there were worse hells than a beautiful house.

"We were *poor* people," my mother said. I hadn't known she was capable of inflection. "I had no business in a place like that, all those fireplaces and staircases, all those people waiting on me."

Fluffy let out a small snort. "That's ridiculous. We never waited on you. You made my breakfast every morning."

My mother shook her head. "I was so ashamed of myself."

"Not of Dad?" I would have thought my father was the obvious choice. After all, he had bought the house.

"Your father wasn't ashamed," she said, misunderstanding. "He was thrilled. Ten times a day he'd find something to show me. 'Elna, would you look at this banister?' 'Elna, come outside and see this garage.'"

"He loved the garage," Fluffy said.

"He never understood how anyone could have been miserable in that house."

"The VanHoebeeks were miserable," Fluffy said. "At least they were in the end."

"You went to India to get away from the *house*?" Of course it wasn't just the house or the husband. There were the two children sleeping on the second floor who went unmentioned.

My mother's pale eyes were clouded by cataracts and I wondered how much she could see. "What else could it have been?"

"I guess I just assumed it was Dad."

"I loved your father," she said. The words were right there. She didn't have to reach for them at all. *I loved your father.*

That was Fluffy's cue to stand. She stretched onto the balls of her feet, lifting her arms over her head. She said, as if responding to some unspoken request, that she would walk down the block and bring us back some decent coffee, at which point my mother stood as well, saying she was going to the third floor to look at the new babies, and I said I was going to the pay phone to call Celeste, and Jocelyn said if that was the case, then she'd be heading home. We had talked until we couldn't stand it another second, and then we stopped.

Of course it wasn't just my mother who was expected to provide the conversation on those long days. We were all looking to pass the time. Jocelyn had retired but Sandy kept working. She talked about her employer who wanted the carpet vacuumed in a single direction. Fluffy talked about the Dutch House before the Conroys had come, about taking care of Mrs. VanHoebeek after the money was gone, and how she took the train into New York with pieces of jewelry to sell. It seemed to me an astonishing act of bravery for a young woman at the time.

"You couldn't sell them in Philadelphia?" I asked her.

"Sure I could," she said, "but whoever I sold a ring to in Philadelphia would have just taken it into Manhattan and sold it again for double the price."

Fluffy sold a triple strand of pearls to cover the hospital bill when Mrs. VanHoebeek broke her hip, and when the old woman died, Fluffy sold a brooch for the funeral, a small gold bird with an emerald pinched in its beak.

"There were still things left," Fluffy said. "Nothing like what had been there to start, but the Missus and I paced ourselves. We didn't know how long she was going to last. Those bankers who sold the house? Absolute idiots. They asked me to make a list of everything of value so that they could have it appraised. I left most of it alone, but there were things I took." She held up her hand to show us a diamond ring in an old-fashioned setting, a little ruby on either side. For as long as I'd known Fluffy she'd worn that ring.

I suppose it was a stark confession, seeing as how the contents of the house had been purchased by my father in their entirety. After the ring had belonged to Mrs. VanHoebeek it would have belonged to him, along with everything else, and maybe he would have given it to my mother, who might have passed it on to Maeve when she was older, or given it to me to give to Celeste. But that idea was predicated on my father being the sort of man who would look through a jewelry box, which he was not, or my mother being the sort of person who would stick around. More likely, the ring would have sat where it was until Andrea arrived. Andrea would not have overlooked any jewelry the house had to offer.

Fluffy would have turned the ring over to either of us had we asked, but instead my mother leaned forward, peering at Fluffy's hand with her cloudy eyes. "So pretty," she said, and gave her hand a kiss. "Good for you."

* * *

THE FIRST TIME I made it back to Jenkintown after starting medical school must have been the Thanksgiving of 1970. The work had come down on me in an avalanche that first semester, just as Dr. Able predicted, and I scrambled to keep up. Add to that the fact that Celeste and I were putting the apartment to good use and I had neither the time nor the inclination to go home on the weekends. This was before there had been any talk of marriage, so Maeve and Celeste were still pals. Celeste and I had come to Philadelphia together on the train the night before Thanksgiving. Maeve picked us up and we dropped Celeste off at home, then the next day Maeve and I went back to have our dinner with the Norcrosses. The men and the boys played touch football in the yard—*in honor of the Kennedys,* we said—while the women and the girls peeled potatoes and made the gravy and did whatever last-minute things needed to be done. They sent Maeve out to set the table once they understood she really wasn't kidding about not being able to cook.

The dinner was a huge production, with kids stashed in the

den to eat off card tables like a collection of understudies who dreamed of one day breaking into the dining room. There were aunts and uncles and cousins, plus a large assortment of strays who had nowhere else to go, the category in which Maeve and I were included. Celeste's mother always did a spectacular job with the holidays, and after months in which dinner had meant grabbing something in the hospital cafeteria or picking rolls off of patient trays, I was especially grateful. At every table, hands were held and heads were bowed while Bill Norcross recited his tidy benediction, "For these and all His mercies may the Lord make us truly thankful." No sooner had we lifted our eyes than the bowls of green beans with pearl onions and the mountains of stuffing and mashed potatoes and sweet potatoes and platters of sliced turkey followed by boats of gravy began to make their clockwise march around the table.

"And what do you do?" the woman on my left asked me. She was one of Celeste's many aunts. I couldn't remember her name, though I knew we'd been introduced at the door.

"Danny's in medical school at Columbia," Mrs. Norcross said from across the table, on the off chance this was information I'd be unwilling to share myself.

"Medical school?" the aunt said, and then, remarkably, she looked at Celeste. "You didn't tell me he was in medical school."

The middle section of the long table fell silent and Celeste shrugged her pretty shoulders. "You didn't ask."

"What kind of medicine do you plan to practice?" one of the uncles asked. I had just that minute become interesting. I didn't know if he was the uncle who was matched to this particular aunt.

I envisioned all the empty buildings I'd seen up in Washington Heights, and for a minute I thought it would really be something to tell them the truth: I was planning on practicing real estate. From the end of the table I saw Maeve flash me a wild smile, confirming that she alone understood how insane this was. "I have no idea," I said.

"Do you have to cut people up?" Celeste's younger brother asked me. I had been told this was his first year in the dining room. He was the youngest person at the table.

"Teddy," his mother said in warning.

"*Au*topsies," Teddy said, bored out of his mind. "They have to do them, you know."

"We do," I said, "but they make us take an oath never to discuss it at dinner."

For that withholding, the room sent up a grateful round of laughter. From a distance, I heard someone ask Maeve if she was a doctor as well. "No," she said, holding up her fork speared with green beans. "I'm in vegetables."

When the dinner was over and we'd been piled up with left-overs for the weekend, Celeste kissed me goodbye. Maeve promised that we would pick her up Sunday morning on our way to the train. They trailed us out to the car, all those happy Norcrosses, telling us we should stay. There would be movies later on, popcorn, games of Hearts. Lumpy ran out of the house and into the yard, barking and barking at the piles of leaves until they shooed him back inside.

"This is our chance," Maeve whispered, and jumped into the driver's side. I went around and got in the car beside her while they stood there, the whole host of them waving and laughing as we pulled away.

The Norcrosses had their dinner early so it was barely dusk. We had just enough time to make it back to the Dutch House before the lights went on. We'd promised Jocelyn we'd come to her house later for pie, so this was just a brief interlude between dipping into other people's splendid meals. We were still young enough then to conjure up the exact feeling of how Thanksgivings had been when we were children, but it was a memory with no longing attached. Either it had been me and Maeve and our father eating in the dining room, and Sandy and Jocelyn trying their best not to look like they were rushing to get home to their own families, or it was the years with Andrea and the girls, in which Sandy and Jocelyn rushed openly. After that disastrous Thanksgiving when Maeve was banished to the third floor, she had stayed away from Elkins Park, and every year I looked at her empty place at the table and felt miserable, even though I never could understand how her being gone on Thanksgiving was any worse than it was on all the other nights of the year. Having spent this particular Thanksgiving with the Norcross family had made up for a lot, and we both left the dinner feeling restored, even if our exit had smacked of escape. Maybe it was possible, we thought, to rise above the pathetic holidays of our youth.

"You'll have to forgive me," Maeve said, rolling down her window to meet the frigid air, "but if I don't have a cigarette right this minute I'm going to die." She pulled one out then handed me the pack so I could decide for myself, then she handed me the lighter. Soon we were each blowing smoke out of our respective windows.

"As good as that dinner was, this cigarette might be better," I said.

"If you did an *au*topsy on me right now you would find I am nothing but dark meat and gravy, with maybe a tiny vein of mashed potatoes inside my right arm." Maeve was careful about her carbohydrates. She had forgone the Norcross pie in order to have a slice at Jocelyn's.

"I could present you at grand rounds," I said, and thought of Bill Norcross sawing into the carcass of the turkey.

Maeve shuddered slightly. "I can't believe they make you cut people up."

"I can't believe you make me go to medical school."

She laughed, and then pressed her fingers to her lips as if to quell her dinner's revolt. "Oh, stop complaining. Seriously, apart from dissecting other human beings, tell me one thing that's so terrible."

I tipped my head back, exhaling. Maeve always said I smoked every cigarette like I was on my way to my execution, and I was thinking this really should be my last one. I knew better, even though those were still the days when doctors kept a pack of Marlboros in the pocket of their lab coats. Especially orthopedists. You couldn't be an orthopedist without smoking. "The worst part is understanding you're going to die."

She looked at me, her black eyebrows raised. "You didn't understand that?"

I shook my head. "You *think* you understand it. You think that when you're ninety-six you'll lie down on the couch after a big Thanksgiving dinner and not wake up, but even then you're not really sure. Maybe there'll be some special dispensation for you. Everybody thinks that."

"I never for a minute thought I was going to die on the couch at ninety-six, or be ninety-six for that matter."

But I wasn't listening, I was talking. "You just don't realize how many ways there are to die, excluding gunshots and knife fights and falling out windows and all the other things that probably aren't going to happen."

"Tell me, Doc, what *is* going to happen?" She was trying not to laugh at me, but it was true: death was all I thought about in those days.

"Too many white blood cells, too few red blood cells, too much iron, a respiratory infection, sepsis. You can get a blockage in your bile duct. Your esophagus can rupture. And the cancers." I looked at her. "We could sit here all night talking about cancer. I'm just telling you, it's unsettling. There are thousands of ways your body can go off the rails for no reason whatsoever and chances are you won't know about any of it until it's too late."

"Which makes a person wonder why we need doctors in the first place."

"Exactly."

"Well," Maeve said, taking a long pull on her cigarette, "I already know how I'm going to die so I don't have to worry about that."

I looked at her profile lit up by the street lights clicking on, by the lights Andrea had turned on in the Dutch House. Everything about her was sharp and straight and beautiful, everything about her was life and health. "How are you going to die?" I don't know why I asked because I sure as hell didn't want to know.

Unlike the medical students in my class who sounded like they were idling over a catalog of disease when hypothesizing their deaths, Maeve spoke with authority. "Heart disease or stroke. That's how diabetics go. Probably heart disease when you factor Dad into the equation, which is fine by me. It's quicker, right? Bang."

Suddenly I was angry at her. She had no idea what she was talking about, and anyway, this was Thanksgiving, and we were supposed to be playing a game, not unlike the Norcrosses dealing out their hands of Hearts. "If you're so damned worried about a heart attack then why're we sitting here smoking?"

She blinked. "I'm not worried. I told you, I'm not the one who's going to die after dinner at ninety-six. That's you."

I threw my cigarette out the window.

"Jesus, Danny, open the door and pick that up." She gave my shoulder a smack with the back of her hand. "That's Mrs. Buchsbaum's yard."

CHAPTER 17

D O YOU REMEMBER when we lived in the little house, and Mrs. Henderson next door got a whole box of oranges from her son in California?" our mother would begin, sitting there beside the hospital bed in the private room Maeve had been moved to. "She gave us three."

Maeve was wearing the pink chenille bathrobe that May had picked out for her years before, and Mr. Otterson's tight bouquet of little pink roses was there beside her on the night stand. Her cheeks were pink. "We split two of the oranges three ways and you cut off all the zest and used the juice from the third orange to make a cake. When it came out of the oven you sent me over to get Mrs. Henderson so she could have cake with us."

"Those were pioneer days," our mother said.

They cataloged the contents of the little house with great affection: the nubby brown couch with maple feet, the soft yellow chair with a spattered coffee stain on one arm. There was the framed painting of a blacksmith's shop (where had it come from, they wondered; where had it gone?), the little table and chairs in the kitchen, the single white metal cupboard bolted to the wall above the sink: four plates, four bowls, four cups, four glasses.

"Why four?" I was looking at the monitor, thinking the cardiac output could still be better.

"We were waiting for you," my mother said.

My mother, under the safety of Maeve's wing, found it easier to speak.

"My bed was in the corner of the front room," Maeve said.

"And every night your father would unfold a screen beside the bed and he would say, 'I'm building Maeve's room.'"

When they lived in the little house they did their shopping at the PX on the base, and carried the groceries home in an ingenious sack my mother had made out of knotted string. They collected tin for the tin drive, watched the neighbors' baby, worked at the food pantry the church opened to the poor on Mondays and Fridays. It was Maeve and our mother, always the two of them. In the winter my mother pulled apart a sweater one of the women from church had given her and knitted it into a hat and scarf and mittens for my sister. In the summer, they weeded the garden that all of the families had planted together— tomatoes and eggplants, potatoes and corn, string beans and spinach. They put up jars of relish and made pickles and jam. They recounted every last one of their accomplishments while I sat in the corner with the newspaper.

"Do you remember the rabbit fence that trapped the rabbits in the garden?" my mother asked.

"I remember everything." Maeve had left her bed and was sitting up in a chair by the window, a folded blanket across her lap. "I remember at night we'd turn out the lights and bring a lamp into the bedroom closet, and push out the shoes so we could sit on the floor and read. Dad was on air raid patrol. You had to pull up your knees so you could fit and then I'd come in behind you and sit in your lap."

"This one could read when she was four years old," my mother said to me. "She was the smartest child I ever saw."

"You'd push a towel under the door so none of the light got

out," Maeve said. "It's funny, but somehow I had it in my mind that light was rationed, everything was rationed so we couldn't let the light we weren't using just pour out on the floor. We had to keep it all in the closet with us."

They remembered where the little house was on the base, on which corner, beneath what tree, but they couldn't remember exactly what it was our father did there. "Some kind of ordering, I think," my mother said. It didn't matter. They were sure about the small front stoop of poured concrete, two steps, red geraniums that had been rooted from a neighbor's plant blooming in terra cotta pots. The door opened straight into the front room, and the small bedroom where my parents slept was to the right and the kitchen was to the left with a bathroom in between.

"The house was the size of a postage stamp," Maeve said.

"Smaller than your house?" I asked, because Maeve lived in a doll's house as far as I was concerned.

The two of them looked at each other, my mother and my sister, and laughed.

I had a mother who left when I was a child. I didn't miss her. Maeve was there, with her red coat and her black hair, standing at the bottom of the stairs, the white marble floor with the little black squares, the snow coming down in glittering sheets in the windows behind her, the windows as wide as a movie screen, the ship in the waves of the grandfather clock rocking the minutes away. "Danny!" she would call up to me. "Breakfast. Move yourself." She wore her coat in the house on winter mornings because it was so cold, because she was so tall and thin and every ounce of her energy had been given over to growth rather than warmth. "You always look like you're leaving," my father would say when he passed her, as if even her coat annoyed him.

"*Danny!*" she shouted. "It's not coming up on a tray."

The bed where I slept was heaped with blankets, the very weight of which pinned me into place. There never was a winter morning in the Dutch House when my first thought was anything other than *What would it be like to spend the entire day in bed?* But my sister's voice from the bottom of the staircase pulled me up, along with the smell of coffee I was too young to drink. "Stunts your growth," Jocelyn would say. "Don't you want to be as tall as your sister?" I found my slippers on the floor, my wool bathrobe at the foot of the bed. I stumbled out onto the landing, freezing.

"There's the prince!" Maeve called, her face tilted up in the light. "Come on, we've got pancakes. Don't make me wait."

The joy of my childhood ended not when my mother left, but when Maeve left, the year Andrea and my father were married.

Where had our mother been all this time? I didn't care. She and Maeve sat in Maeve's bed together once Maeve was home, their four long legs stretched out side by side. I would hear sentences, words, as I moved through the house: India, orphanage, San Francisco, 1966. I had graduated from Choate in '66, started Columbia, while our mother chaperoned the children of a wealthy Indian family on a ship to San Francisco in exchange for a large donation to the orphanage where she worked. Or was that the leper colony? She never went back to India. She stayed in San Francisco. She went to Los Angeles and then Durango and then Mississippi. The poor, she discovered, were everywhere. I went out to the garage and found Maeve's lawn mower. I had to drive to the gas station to get a can of gas, and then I cut the grass. I felt such tremendous satisfaction in the job that when I finished I got out the weed-eater and edged the flower beds and the sidewalk. A building owner in Manhattan never cuts grass.

I gave up my hotel room and spent a single sleepless night on Maeve's couch once she was out of the hospital. I had wanted to be there in case her heart stopped but I couldn't stand it, not any part of it. The next morning I moved to Celeste's old bedroom at the Norcrosses'. Fluffy had gone home but my mother was always there. Maeve's friends left casseroles on her front porch, along with roasted chickens and bags of apples and zucchini bread, so much food that Sandy and Jocelyn had to take half of it home with them. Maeve and my mother ate like wrens—I watched them share a single scrambled egg. Maeve was happy and tired and utterly unlike herself. She didn't talk about her work at Otterson's, or what she needed to do for me, or any of the things that had been neglected in her absence. She sat on the couch and let our mother bring her toast. There was no distance between them, no recrimination. They were living together in their own paradise of memory.

"Leave them alone," Celeste said to me on the phone. "They've got it covered. People are beating down the door to be helpful, and anyway, what Maeve needs is rest. Isn't that what the doctors always say? She doesn't need more company."

I told her I didn't think of myself as company, but as soon as I said it I could see that's exactly what I was. They were waiting for me to go.

"Sooner or later you have to come back to New York. I have a list of good reasons."

"I'll be back soon enough," I told my wife. "I just want to make sure everything's okay."

"Is it okay?" Celeste asked. Celeste had never met my mother but her natural distrust exceeded even my own.

I was standing in Maeve's kitchen. My mother had affixed the doctor's order sheet to the refrigerator with a magnet. She kept the plastic medicine bottles in a neat row in front of the canisters and wrote down what time every pill was given. She was careful to limit the visitors and to nudge them towards the door when their time was up, except, of course, for Mr. Otterson, who was treated with deference. Mr. Otterson never outstayed his welcome, and if the weather was nice he would walk with Maeve down the street and back. Otherwise, my mother got Maeve to walk two circles around the backyard every couple of hours. They were in the living room now, talking about some novel they'd both read called *Housekeeping* which each of them claimed had been her favorite book.

"What?" Celeste asked, and then she said, "No. Wait a minute. It's your father. Here." She was talking to me again. "Say hello to your daughter."

"Hi, Daddy," May said. "If you don't come home soon I'm going to get a hypoallergenic dog. I'm thinking about a standard poodle. I'm going to call her Stella. I'd settle for a cat but Mom says there is no such thing as a hypoallergenic cat. She says Kevin is allergic to cats but how would she even know? He's never around cats."

"What are you talking about?"

"Wait a minute," May said in a low voice, and then I heard a door close. "Whenever I talk about getting a dog she leaves the room. It's like a magic trick. I'm coming to Jenkintown to see Aunt Maeve."

"Is your mother bringing you?"

May made the sound she used to cover all manner of adult idiocy. "I'm coming by myself. You're going to have to pick me up at the train."

"You're not coming on the train by yourself." We didn't let May ride the subway by herself. We let her ride buses and take taxis but not trains of any stripe.

"Listen, Aunt Maeve's had a heart attack," she said, breaking the news. "You know she's wondering why I haven't been to see her yet. And Mom told us about our Indian grandmother being home, and I want to meet her. It's a pretty big deal, finding a new grandmother at this stage of the game."

What stage of the game? "She's not Indian." I looked out of the kitchen at my pale Irish mother on the couch next to Maeve, then turned my back on them both. "She used to live in India but it was a long time ago."

"Either way I'm taking the train. You took the train alone from New York when you were twelve after you went to see Aunt Maeve for Easter, and I'm fourteen for god's sake."

"I hate it when you say god's sake. You sound like my father."

"Girls mature faster than boys, so when you think about it I'm technically more than two years older now than you were then."

Had I really told her that story? Of course May was older than I was then, probably by twenty years, but there was no way I was going to let her get on a train by herself. "It's a nice idea, but I'm coming home tomorrow after I take Maeve to the doctor."

"You *are* a doctor," she said, cracking herself up.

"Listen, May, be kind to your mother."

"I *am*," she said. "But she's driving me bananas. I'm going to write a book called *Six Million Reasons Not to Go to Pennsylvania*. Let me say hello to my grandmother."

My mother had not asked about my children. Not a word. Fluffy said that was because she had already told my mother all about them, so had Maeve—Kevin's grades in science, May's dancing. Fluffy said my mother was desperate to know, and that it was my own fault she didn't ask me because I went out of my way to layer frost onto every sentence that came out of my mouth. "She's asleep," I said.

"Why is she asleep? It's two o'clock. She's not the one who's sick."

"She's the one who's old," I said, turning again to look at my mother in the other room. She was laughing. With her short hair and weathered skin and freckled hands she could have been anyone's mother, but she was mine. "I'll tell her you called when she wakes up."

For as many places as our mother claimed to have been during her years of absence, there was no indication that she actually lived in any one of them. I wondered if she lived at Maeve's now because her suitcase was in Maeve's closet. I regaled Celeste with all of my suspicions once I was home again, breaking down the last two weeks play by play.

"Are you saying she's homeless?" Celeste asked. We were standing in the kitchen while she worked on dinner: salmon for the two of us and May, who didn't like fish but had read that fish made you smarter, and two hamburgers for Kevin, who could have cared less. The children had been happy to see me when I first came through the door the day before but since had discovered that I was the same person they'd always known.

"Homeless insofar as she doesn't have a home, not homeless like she's sleeping under a bridge." Though how would I know?

"Is there a chance your parents never got divorced? That's what Fluffy thinks. She thinks your mother may still own the house and not even know it."

I imagined Fluffy must have presented this as conjecture. She certainly wouldn't have told the whole story to Celeste. "They're divorced. My father paid a man from the American consulate to meet her ship in Bombay. He'd mailed the divorce papers and the man took my mother straight to the consulate and had her sign them in front of a notary. All very legal. The man with the divorce papers gave her a letter from my father as well, telling her to never come back. I think he took care of everything right on the spot." This was one of the countless stories that had been told near me rather than to me, with Maeve saying that surely had the letter been a testament of love and compassion our mother would have marched straight up the gangplank and sailed home again. My mother allowed as how that would have been the case.

"Then she isn't secretly rich."

I shook my head. "She is flamboyantly poor."

"And now the two of you are supposed to take care of her?" Celeste set to work on the little red potatoes in the sink, attacking each one with a scrub brush while I searched the refrigerator for an open bottle of wine.

"I'm not taking care of her."

"But you're taking care of Maeve, and Maeve will have to take care of her."

I thought about this. I located the wine. "Well, for the time being my mother's taking care of Maeve." The food, the pills, the laundry, the visitors.

"What's your part?"

I had been watching, that was my part. I had been inserting my uncomfortable presence into every situation. "I just want to make sure Maeve's okay."

"Because you're afraid she's going to have another heart attack or because you're afraid she's going to wind up liking your mother more than you?"

I had been about to pour us each a glass of wine but in light of the direction our conversation was going, I opted to pour one just for myself. "It's not a competition."

"Okay, that's great, if it's not a competition then leave them alone. You don't seem very interested in your mother and Maeve seems to have eyes for no one else."

I will mention here that Celeste had been remarkably thoughtful when Maeve was sick. She'd sent cards signed with love from the children every couple of days, and when Maeve went home there was an enormous bucket of peonies waiting on her front porch. There could not have been a peony left in all of Eastern Pennsylvania.

"You told Celeste I love peonies?" Maeve had asked me, looking at the card.

But the truth was I had no idea my sister loved peonies.

"Why are we arguing about this?" I asked Celeste. "I'm just glad to be home."

She dropped the last of the potatoes back in the colander and dried her hands. "For as long as I've known Maeve, she's wanted her mother back. You two park in front of the old homestead because it reminds her of her mother, you go through life like your wrists are bound together with wire because you were abandoned by your mother. And then your mother returns, and your sister, God love her, is finally happy, and you're bent on being miserable. It's like you don't want to be dislodged from your suffering. If you care so much about Maeve, and Maeve's happy, then why not just let her be happy? She can have a life with your mother, you can have a life with us."

"It's not a trade-off."

"But that's what you're afraid of, isn't it? That your mother won't be punished? That Maeve will be happier with her than she was with you?"

May shouted from upstairs. "Do you not realize I can hear every single word you're saying? There are vents in this house, people. If you want to fight, go to a restaurant."

"We're not fighting," I said, my voice loud. I was looking at my wife and for just a second I saw her, the round blue eyes and yellow hair. The woman I had known for more than half my life floated in front of me, and just as quickly she vanished.

"We're fighting," Celeste said, her eyes on me, her voice as loud as mine, "but we'll stop."

I could have spent the entire summer at home in New York, supervising the knocking-out of walls in various apartments, playing basketball with Kevin, helping May memorize soliloquies, and I don't think anyone would have noticed but Celeste, and Celeste would have been happy. But week after week I went back to Jenkintown, as if the only way I could believe that Maeve was really safe was to see it for myself. I would sleep at the ever-welcoming Norcross foursquare where the Labrador retriever was now a dog named Ramona. I drove in from the city because I needed a car to get back and forth to Maeve's, and because I needed to make endless trips to the hardware store. I was in constant search of another project, some way in which to justify my presence so that I didn't just sit in the living room and watch them. My desire to fix a light switch and paint cabinets and replace rotten windowsills was a metaphor that begged no scrutiny.

Week after week one or both of my children would announce that they wanted to come along for the ride. They seemed to like everything about the setup, the time with Celeste's parents, the time with Maeve, the summer days spent out of the city. They referred to my mother as the Person of Interest, as if she were a spy who had stumbled in from the cold. She was fascinating to them and they were fascinating to her. The desire Celeste and I shared to keep them away from my mother only made them race to the car, and that wasn't such a bad thing. Even at the time I recognized those trips as the great byproduct of circumstance. Kevin and I hashed out the merits of Danny Tartabull, trying to decide if he deserved to be the highest paid Yankee on the team, while May sang show tunes as the soundtrack to our conversations. We had taken her to see the revival of *Gypsy* two years before and she still wasn't over it. *"Have an eggroll, Mr. Goldstone. Have a napkin, have a chopstick, have a chair!"* she belted out in her enthusiastic alto. We made her sit in the back seat. She had dropped out of the School of American Ballet in order to have more time to focus on her singing.

"This is worse than ballet," Kevin said.

My mother had been working on her powers of speech. Even if there had been no real discussions between us, she was increasingly more comfortable in my presence. She had the children to thank for that as they had nothing against her. She and Kevin discussed the Dodgers vs Yankees world she had grown up in, while May spoke French with Maeve and Maeve French-braided May's hair. May had taken French since the sixth grade and thought that she should have been allowed to spend the summer in Paris. Instead of telling her that fourteen-year-old girls did not spend the summer alone in Paris, I said that, what with Maeve being sick, Paris would not be possible. And so she settled for the endless conjugation of verbs: *je chante, tu chantes, il chante, nous chantons, vous chantez, ils chantent.* I was working on replacing the flue in the chimney. I had spread newspapers over the carpet but it was a larger, dirtier job than I had predicted.

"I was in love with Frenchy Bordagaray," my mother said, thinking that a story about a baseball player named Frenchy would speak to the interests of both my daughter and my son. "My father got tickets for the two of us at Ebbets Field just before I went to the convent. I don't know where he found the money but the seats were right behind third base, right behind Frenchy. The whole time my father kept saying to me, 'Take a good look around, Elna. You don't see any nuns out here.'"

"You were a nun?" Kevin asked, unable to square what he knew about nuns with what he knew about grandmothers.

My mother shook her head. "I was more like a tourist. I didn't even stay two months."

"*Pourquoi es-tu parti?*" May asked.

"Why did you leave?" Maeve said.

My mother wore a permanent expression of surprise in those days, forever amazed by all we did not know. "Cyril came and got me. He'd gone to Tennessee to work for the TVA, he'd been gone for years, and when he was home again he saw my brother. He and James had always been friends. James told him where I was. James didn't like the idea of me being a nun. Cyril walked all the way to the convent from Brooklyn. When he finally got there, he told the sister at the door that he was my brother and he had some very bad news for me, tragic news, he said. She went to get me even though we weren't allowed to have any visitors then."

"What did he say?" For a moment Kevin had lost all interest in baseball.

"Cyril said, 'Elna, this is not for you.'"

We all looked at one another, my son and my sister and my daughter with her half-braided hair, until finally Maeve said, "That's it?"

"I know it doesn't sound like much now," my mother said, "but it changed everything. It's the reason the four of you are here, I'll tell you that. He said he'd wait for me outside and I went and got my little bag, told everyone goodbye. Young people were different in those days. We weren't as big on thinking things through. There was a war coming, everybody knew it. We walked from the convent, way up on the West Side, all the way through Manhattan. We stopped and had a cup of coffee and a sandwich just before going over the bridge, and by the time we were back in Brooklyn we'd worked the whole thing out. We were going to get married and have a family, and that's what we did."

"Did you love him?" May asked Maeve, and Maeve said, "*L'aimais-tu.*"

"*L'aimais-tu?*" May asked my mother, because some questions are best posed in French.

"Of course I did," she said, "or I did by the time we got back to Brooklyn."

Before we left that night, May brought out a bottle of iridescent pink polish from her purse and painted her grandmother's fingernails, and then her aunt's, and then her own, taking pains to concentrate on the application of each coat. When she was finished, my mother could not stop admiring the work. "They're like little shells," she said, and together they turned their hands back and forth in the light.

"You never painted your fingernails?" May asked.

My mother shook her head.

"Not even when you were rich?"

My mother took May's hand and put it on top of Maeve's and her own so as to see all those glistening shells together. "Not even then," she said.

Celeste was there, too, over the course of the summer. She would come to see her parents. She would drop Kevin off or pick May up, and in doing so met my mother many times, but even when they were in the room together Celeste figured out a way to avoid her. "I have to get back to my parents' house," she would say as soon as she walked in the door. "I promised my mother I'd help her with dinner."

"Of course!" my mother said, and Maeve went out to the yard to cut a bunch of purple hollyhocks for Celeste to take home, neither of them seeming to notice that Celeste was already backing towards the door. In the wake of the heart attack and our mother's return, the bright torch of anger Maeve had carried for my wife had been extinguished, forgotten. She would have been perfectly happy to have Celeste at the table, as she was perfectly happy to let her go. I was sitting on the kitchen floor, screwing a series of shallow wooden trays I'd made onto runners in the bottom of each cupboard so the pots and pans would be easier to pull out. Kevin sat beside me and handed me the screws as I needed them, and Celeste, who was forever in motion that summer, stopped for a minute and watched me, her hands full of flowers.

"I've always wanted those," she said, as if in wonder that I had even known such things existed.

I put down the power drill. "Really? Did I know that?"

She shook her head, looked at her watch, and told the children it was time to go.

So went the days. Maeve returned to Otterson's on her same irregular schedule. I would have said she worried less about her job but I don't think she'd ever worried about it. Kevin and May started back to school. The space between my trips to Jenkintown grew wider and then wider still. Our mother stayed. She threw away the dark-green sweater that had unraveled at the cuffs and Maeve bought her new clothes and a new bedspread and curtains for the guest room that they no longer referred to as the guest room. They drove into Philadelphia for the orchestra. They went to the Philadelphia Free Library for readings. My mother volunteered with a food pantry run by Catholic Charities, and within a couple of weeks she was meeting with the director. There was a larger need in the community, she said. She could come up with a plan to meet it.

Maeve and our mother were making chicken and dumplings together on a late autumn Friday. Our mother, as it turned out, was the one who knew how to cook. The kitchen was tight and warm and they moved around each other with efficiency. "You should stay," my mother said when I lifted the lid of the Dutch oven, dipping my face into the billowing steam.

I shook my head. "Kevin has a game. I should have been in the car twenty minutes ago."

Maeve wiped her floury hands on the dishtowel she had tied around her waist. "Come outside for a minute. I want to ask you about the gutter before you go."

She put on her red wool mackinaw at the door, what she always referred to as her barn coat, even though I doubted she had ever been in a barn. We trudged out into the cold late afternoon light, the red and gold leaves that I would be called upon to rake on my next visit piling around our feet. We stood at the corner of the house to see the place where the gutter was starting to pull away from the roof.

"So when is it over?" Maeve asked, looking up.

I thought she was talking about the roof and so looked up myself. "When is what over?"

"The petulance, the punishment." Maeve dug her hands into her coat pockets. "I know this has been hard for you but I'm kind of sick of thinking about it that way if you want to know the truth—that my heart attack was hard for you. That our mother coming back was hard for you."

I was surprised, and then just as quickly defensive. I had turned my life over to Maeve these past six months, and through considerable effort I'd kept my feelings about our mother to myself. If anything, I'd gotten nicer. "I'm worried about you, that's all. I want to make sure you're okay."

"Well, I'm fine."

It seemed impossible that we hadn't talked about this before, Maeve and I who talked about everything. But we were never alone anymore. Our chipper mother forever found the spot between us and settled in, reducing our conversation to soup recipes and nostalgic reminiscences of poverty. "You're fine with all of it?"

Maeve looked down the street. Since I hadn't realized we were coming outside to discuss the circumstances of our lives, I hadn't thought to put on my coat and now I was cold. "There is a finite amount of time," Maeve said. "Maybe I understand that better now. I've wanted my mother back since I was ten years old, and now she's here. I can use the time I've got to be furious, or I can feel like the luckiest person in the world."

"Those are the two choices?" I wished we could get in the car and drive over to the Dutch House, just sit by ourselves for a minute even though we didn't do that anymore.

Maeve looked back at the gutter and nodded. "Pretty much."

Other than Mr. Otterson's insight and Maeve's recovery, I couldn't imagine feeling lucky where any of this was concerned. Our mother's gain had been my decisive loss. "Does she even know what happened to us after she left? Have you told her about Andrea, about how she threw us out?"

"Jesus, of course she knows about Andrea. Do you think we've been playing cards all summer? I've told her everything that's happened, and I know what happened to her, too. It's amazing what you can find out about a person if you're interested. All these conversations were open to you, by the way. Don't think you've been excluded. Every time she opens her mouth you find a reason to leave the room."

"I'm not the one she's interested in."

Maeve shook her head. "Grow up."

It seemed like such a ridiculous thing to say to a forty-five-year-old that I started to laugh and then caught myself. It had been a long time since we'd had something to fight about. "Okay, if you know so much about her, tell me why she left. And don't say she didn't like the wallpaper."

"She wanted—" Maeve stopped, exhaled, her frozen breath making me think of smoke. "She wanted to help people."

"People other than her family."

"She made a mistake. Can't you understand that? She's covered up in shame. That's why she never got in touch with us, you know, when she came back from India. She was afraid we'd treat her pretty much the way you've treated her. It's her belief that your cruelty is what she deserves."

"I haven't been cruel, believe me, but it *is* what she deserves. Making a mistake is not giving the floorboards enough time to settle before you seal them. Abandoning your children to go help the poor of India means you're a narcissist who wants the adoration of strangers. I look at Kevin and May and I think, who would do that to them? What kind of person leaves their kids?" I felt like I'd been holding those words in my mouth since the moment I walked into the waiting room of the coronary care unit and saw our mother there.

"Men!" Maeve said, nearly shouting. "Men leave their children all the time and the world celebrates them for it. The Buddha left and Odysseus left and no one gave a shit about their sons. They set out on their noble journeys to do whatever the hell they wanted to do and thousands of years later we're still singing about it. Our mother left and she came back and we're *fine*. We didn't like it but we survived it. I don't care if you don't love her or if you don't like her, but you have to be decent to her, if for no other reason than I want you to. You owe me that."

Her cheeks were red, and while it was probably just the cold I couldn't help but worry about her heart. I said nothing.

"For the record, I'm sick of misery," she said, then she turned and went back inside, leaving me to stand in the swirl of leaves and think about what I owed her. By any calculation, it was everything.

And so I made the decision to change. It might seem like change was impossible, given my nature and my age, but I understood exactly what there was to lose. It was chemistry all over again. The point wasn't whether or not I liked it. The point was it had to be done.

Chapter 18

MAEVE AND MY mother had tickets to see the Pissarro show at the Philadelphia Museum of Art and said it would be easy to pick me up afterwards, so I took the train. I saw them as soon as I walked into the station, worrying over a couple of sparrows that had flown in through the open doors and gotten trapped inside. For once I saw my sister before she saw me. She was straight and strong, her head back, her finger pointing up towards the ceiling to show my mother where the birds had lighted. It had been just over a year since the heart attack—a year of good health, a whole year of the two of them together.

"You didn't pick up anybody on the train, did you?" Maeve asked when I came to them, an old joke that made me think of how she used to pick me up and shake me.

"A very uneventful ride." I kissed them both.

When we got to the parking lot, my mother told me she was driving. Once Maeve was fully recovered, she had launched our mother on a plan of self-improvement. In the past six months our mother had had cataract surgery on both of her eyes, three basal cell carcinomas removed (one from her left temple, one from the top of her left ear, one on her right nostril), and a significant amount of dentistry. Housekeeping, Maeve called it. I paid the bills. Maeve fought me at first but I told her if she wanted me to do better, she had to let me do better. I didn't mention any of this to Celeste.

"You have no idea what it's like to see again," our mother said. "That thing—" she pointed to a telephone pole. "Six months ago I would have told you that was a tree."

"It was a tree at some point," Maeve said, getting into the back seat of her own station wagon.

Our mother put on a giant pair of Jackie O sunglasses her ophthalmologist had given her as a gift. "Dr. Shivitz told me the reason my cataracts were so bad is because I never wore sunglasses. I've lived in a lot of sunny places."

Maeve opened her purse and began rooting around for her sunglasses while our mother left the parking lot, working her way through the maze of Philadelphia. I hadn't felt particularly confident about getting in the car with her, but once she found her place in the traffic she stayed up to speed. She and Maeve were still going on about Pissarro, his paintings of Normandy and Paris, the way he understood the people and the light. They spoke as if he were a friend they both admired.

"We should go to Paris," Maeve said to our mother. Maeve, who never wanted to go anywhere.

Our mother agreed. "Now's the time," she said.

I don't think I ever took the train to Philadelphia without thinking of chemistry, and how Morey Able told me that without a solid grasp of chapter 1, chapter 2 would be impossible. Maeve had done that work when our mother came back, gone all the way to the beginning until she was certain she understood what had happened. But for me, the discipline had been the exact opposite: when I could look at our mother only as the person she was now—the old lady driving the Volvo—I thought she was fine. She was energetic, helpful, she had a good laugh. She seemed like somebody's mother, and for the most part I

was able to block the fact that she was mine. Or, to put it another way, I thought of her as Maeve's mother. That worked for
all of us.

I paid little attention to their talk of Impressionism and kept
a close eye on the cars around us, noting their speed in relation
to our speed, calculating their distance. We were well out of the
city and there hadn't been so much as a near miss. I felt grateful
that my children showed no interest in learning to drive. One
of the many advantages of living in New York was that the
streets were full of taxis waiting to take them places. "You're a
good driver," I said to my mother finally.

"I've always driven," she said, turning her ridiculous sunglasses in my direction. "Even these past few years when I
couldn't see a thing. I drove in New York and Los Angeles for
heaven's sake. I drove in Bombay. I drove in Mexico City. I
really think that was the worst." She put on the turn indicator
and changed lanes without self-consciousness. "Your father
taught me to drive, you know."

"Now there's something we all have in common," Maeve
said.

He had given me a few lessons in the church parking lot
when I was fifteen. It had been one of the many means we had
of prolonging our Sundays out of the house. "He taught you to
drive in Brooklyn?"

"Oh, heavens, no. No one had a car in Brooklyn back then.
I learned to drive when we moved to the country. Your father
came home one night and said, 'Elna, I bought you a car. Come
on and I'll show you how it works.' He had me go up and down
the driveway a few times and then he told me to take it out on
the street. Two days later I had a driver's license. Nothing was
crowded back then. You didn't have to worry so much that you
were going to hit somebody."

Yet another thing I'd discovered about our mother: she liked to talk. "Still," I said, "two days is fast."

"That was the way your father did things."

"That was the way he did things," Maeve said.

"I was never as grateful for anything as I was that car. I didn't even feel bad about the money it cost. It was a Studebaker Champion. The good old Champion. Back then, all of this was farmland. Right over there"—she pointed to a long block of shop fronts and apartments—"that was a field of cows. I'd never lived in the country before and the quiet made me so nervous. You'd started school," she said to Maeve, "and all I did was sit there in that huge house all day waiting for you to come home. If it wasn't for Fluffy and Sandy I would have gone out of my mind, though they drove me out of my mind a little bit, too. Don't tell them I said that."

"Of course not," Maeve said, leaning forward so that her head was more or less between the two front seats.

"I loved them so much, but they wouldn't let me do *anything*. They were always running just in front of me so that they could wash something or pick something up. I hired Jocelyn because I was so afraid Sandy wouldn't stay without her sister, and then Jocelyn started doing all the cooking. The one thing I was good at was cooking and they wouldn't even let me make dinner. But once I got the Champion, things really did get better for a while. After I took you to school in the mornings, I'd drive into Philadelphia and see our friends on the base, or I'd drive to Immaculate Conception and make myself useful until school let out. That's when I got to be friends with the Mercy nuns. They were great fun. We started a clothing drive and the nuns and I would drive around picking up things people didn't need, then I would take the clothes home and get everything washed and mended and drive it all back to the church. There was a lot of clothing in the house when we first moved in, things that had been the VanHoebeeks'. A lot of it was hopeless but there were other things Sandy and I fixed up. We made all the coats work—cashmere, furs. You wouldn't have believed what we found."

I thought of Fluffy's diamond.

"I always wondered what happened to the clothes," Maeve said.

"Your father used to say I lived in that car," my mother said, undeterred from her original point. "He used to let me drive him around to collect the rent. You know he never liked to drive. I'd pack up the back seat with jars of stew. So many of those people had nothing. One day there was a family we called on, five little children in two rooms, the mother was crying. I said to her, 'You don't ever have to pay us rent! You should see the house we live in.' And that was that." My mother laughed. "He was so mad he never took me with him again. Then every week he'd come home and say people were asking where I was. He said they wanted their stew."

In my memory, my father loved to drive. Not that it mattered.

Our mother came to a stop sign, looked in one direction and then the other. "Look at this street, all full up. There used to be three houses on this street."

Two blocks later she turned left, and then turned left again. I had paid so much attention to how she was driving, I hadn't noticed where she was driving. We were in Elkins Park. She was heading towards VanHoebeek Street.

"Have you come back here since you've been home?" I asked, but really, I meant the question for Maeve. *Do you bring her here?* We had avoided the Dutch House for years and I could feel the strangeness of being in the neighborhood again, as if we'd been caught someplace we weren't supposed to be.

Our mother shook her head. "I don't know anyone over here anymore. Do you still know the neighbors?"

Maeve looked out the window. "I used to. Not anymore. Danny and I used to come over and park in front of the house sometimes." It sounded like a confession, but of what? Sometimes we sat in the car and we talked.

"You went back to the house?"

"We went back to the street," Maeve said. "We'd drive by. Why did we do that?" she asked me, the very soul of innocence. "Old times' sake?"

"Did you ever go see your stepmother?" our mother asked.

Had we been to see *Andrea*? Had we paid a social call? I had not been part of the conversations Maeve and my mother had about Andrea. I didn't want to be. Thinking about the past impeded my efforts to be decent in the present. I understood there was no way our mother could have foreseen Andrea's coming, but leaving your children meant leaving them to chance.

"Never once," Maeve said absently.

"But why, if you came over here, if you wanted to see the house?" Our mother slowed the car down and then pulled over. She was in the wrong place, still a block away from where the Buchsbaums had lived.

"We weren't—" I was looking for the word, but Maeve finished my sentence for me.

"Welcome."

"As adults?" Our mother took off her sunglasses. She looked at me and then my sister. The places the cancers had been cut away were puckered and red.

Maeve thought about it, shook her head. "No."

It was late spring, the prettiest time of year on VanHoebeek Street unless you counted the fall. I rolled down the window and the scent of petals and new leaves and grass swam into the car, making us dizzy. Was that what made us dizzy? I wondered if there was any chance Maeve still kept cigarettes in the glove compartment.

"We should go then," my mother said. "Pop in just to see it, say hello."

"We shouldn't," I said.

"Look at the three of us, undone by a house. It's insane. We'll go up the driveway, see who's there. It may be someone else by now."

"It's not," Maeve said.

"It will be good for us," our mother said, shifting the car into drive. Clearly, she saw this as a spiritual exercise. It meant nothing to her.

"Don't do this," Maeve said. There was no tension in her voice, no urgency, as if she understood that this was the way things were going to play out and nothing short of jumping from the car was going to stop it. We were moving forward, forward, forward.

When had our mother left? In the middle of the night? Did she walk outside with her suitcase in the dark? Did she tell our father goodbye? Did she go to our rooms to watch us sleeping?

She drove through the break in the linden trees. The driveway wasn't as long as I remembered but the house seemed exactly the same: sunlit, flower-decked, gleaming. I had known since my earliest days at Choate that the world was full of bigger houses, grander and more ridiculous houses, but none were so beautiful. There was the familiar crunch of pea gravel beneath the tires, and when she stopped the car in front of the stone steps I could imagine how elated my father must have felt, and how my sister must have wanted to run off in the grass, and how my mother, alone, had stared up at so much glass and wondered what this fantastical museum was doing in the countryside.

My mother exhaled. She took her dark glasses off the top of her head and left them in the console between the seats. "Let's go see."

Maeve kept her seatbelt on.

My mother turned around to look at her daughter. "Aren't you the one who always says the past is in the past and we need to let things go? This is going to be good for us."

Maeve turned her face away from the house.

"When I worked in the orphanage, people came back all the time. Some of them were as old as me. They'd come in and walk up and down the halls, look in the rooms. They'd talk to the children there. They said it helped them."

"This isn't an orphanage," Maeve said. "We weren't orphans."

My mother shook her head, then looked at me. "Are you coming?"

"Ah, no," I said.

"Go on," Maeve said.

I looked back but she wouldn't look at me. "We don't have to stay for this," I said to my sister.

"I mean it," she said. "Go with her. I'll wait."

And so I did, because the layers of loyalty that were being tested were too complicated to dissect, and because, I will admit this now, I was curious, like those aging Indian orphans were curious. I wanted to see the past. I got out of the car and stood in front of the Dutch House again, and my mother came and stood beside me. For that moment it was the two of us, me and Elna. I would never have believed it would happen.

As for what was coming, we were not made to wait. By the time we were at the foot of the steps, Andrea was on the other side of the glass door. She was wearing a blue tweed suit with gold buttons, lipstick, low-heeled shoes, like she was on her way to see Lawyer Gooch. When she saw us there she raised her hands and began slapping them hard against the glass, her mouth open in a rounded howl. I'd heard that sound in emergency rooms late at night: a knife pulled out, a child dead.

"That's Andrea," I told our mother, just to underscore what a spectacularly bad idea this had been. Our father's second wife was a tiny woman, either smaller than she once had been or smaller than I remembered, but she pounded the window like a warrior beats a drum. Along with the screaming and the slapping I could hear the sound of her rings, the distinctive crack of metal against glass. We were frozen, the two of us outside and Maeve in the car, waiting for the moment when the whole front of the house would shatter into a million knives and she would come for us like the fury of hell itself.

A heavyset Hispanic woman with a long single braid and the cheerful pastel scrubs of a pediatric nurse moved quickly into the frame and gathered Andrea into her arms, pulling her back. She saw the two of us there in front of the station wagon, tall and thin and similar. My mother, with her short brush of gray hair, deep wrinkles, and drilling gaze of preternatural calm, nodded as if to say, *Don't worry, we will not be advancing*, and so the woman opened the door. Clearly it had been her intention to ask who we were, but before she had the chance Andrea shot out like a cat. In a second she had crossed the terrace and came straight to me, at me, as if she meant to go through my chest. The force with which she hit punched the air from my lungs. She buried her face into my shirt, her small arms locking around my waist. She was wailing, her narrow back straining against her grief. In half a second Maeve was out of the car. She took hold of Andrea's shoulders and was trying to pull her off of me.

"Jesus," Maeve said. "Andrea, stop this."

But there was no stopping this. She had locked herself to me like a protester chained to a fence at a demonstration, and I could feel her heartbeat, her ragged breathing. I'd shaken Andrea's hand that first day she came to the house, and with the exception of brushing past her in the small kitchen or being forcibly crowded together for a Christmas photograph, we'd never touched again, not at the wedding and certainly not at the funeral. I looked down at the top of her head, her blond hair brushed back and caught in a clip at the nape of her neck. I could see the smallest line of white growing in where her hair was parted. I could smell the powder of her perfume.

My mother put her hand on Andrea's back. "Mrs. Conroy?" she said.

Maeve stayed very close to me. "What the *fuck*?"

The Hispanic woman, who clearly had a bad knee, came limping down the stairs towards us. "Missus," she said to Andrea. "Missus, you need to be inside."

"Can you get her off of him?" Maeve asked, her voice bright with rage, her hand on my shoulder. Only the two of us were there.

"You," Andrea said, and then gasped to find her breath. She was crying like the end of all the earth. "You, you."

"Missus," the woman said again when she reached us, her stiff knee making me think of our father. He went down the stairs like that. "Why are you crying? Your friends have come to say hello." She looked at me to confirm this but I had no idea what we were doing there.

"I'm Elna Conroy," my mother said finally. "These are my children, Danny and Maeve. Mrs. Conroy was their stepmother."

At this news, the woman broke into a wide smile. "Missus, look. Family! Your family has come to see you."

Andrea ground her forehead into the space beneath my sternum as if she could crawl inside of me.

"Missus," the woman said, petting Andrea's head. "Come inside now with your family. Come inside and sit."

Getting Andrea back in the house was no small feat. She had the will of a barnacle. I lifted her up one step and then another. She wasn't heavy but her clinging made her nearly impossible to maneuver. Her shoes slipped off her stocking feet and my mother bent down to retrieve them.

"I had this dream once," Maeve said to me, and I started to laugh.

"My mother wanted to visit," I told the woman over Andrea's head. She was a housekeeper, a nurse, a warden, I didn't know.

The woman rushed ahead of us into the house, as much as her knee allowed for it. "Doctor!" she shouted up the stairs.

"Don't," Andrea said into my shirt, and I knew exactly what she was saying, *Don't shout, don't run.*

I lifted her up the last step. I had to keep my arm around her back in order to do it. I had not been born with an imagination large enough to encompass this moment.

"She thinks your father's come back," my mother said, lifting her empty hand to shade her eyes from the reflection of the late afternoon sun. "She thinks you're Cyril." Then she walked into the foyer, past the round marble-topped table, the two French chairs, the mirror framed by the arms of a golden octopus, the grandfather clock where the ship rocked between two rows of painted metal waves.

In my dreams, the intervening years were never kind to the Dutch House. I was certain it would have become something shabby in my absence, the peeling and threadbare remains of grandeur, when in fact nothing of the sort had happened. The house looked the same as it did when we walked out thirty years before. I came into the drawing room with Andrea firmly affixed, the dark, wet smear of mascara and tears spreading across my shirt. Maybe a few pieces of furniture had been rearranged, reupholstered, replaced, who could remember? There were the silk drapes, the yellow silk chairs, the Dutch books still in the glass-fronted secretary reaching up and up towards the ceiling, forever unread. Even the silver cigarette boxes were there, polished and waiting on the end tables, just as they had been when the VanHoebeeks walked the earth. By folding Andrea onto the sofa with me I managed to sit. She pushed herself beneath my arm so as to nestle her small weight against my rib cage. She had stopped crying and was making quiet smacking noises instead. She was no one I had ever known.

Maeve and my mother floated into the room in silence, both of them looking at things they had never planned on seeing again: the tapestry ottoman, the Chinese lamp, the heavy tasseled ropes of twisted silk, blue and green, that held the draperies back. If I had ever seen the two of them in this room before it was in a time before memory. I was able to reach into my pocket and hand Andrea a handkerchief, remembering that it had been Andrea, not Maeve or Sandy, who had taught me to carry one. She wiped at her face and then pressed her ear to my chest to listen to my heart. My mother and sister went to the fireplace to stand beneath the VanHoebeeks.

"I hated them," my mother said quietly, still holding Andrea's shoes.

Maeve nodded, her eyes on those eyes that had followed us through our youth. "I loved them."

That was when Norma came running down the stairs saying, "Inez! I'm sorry, sorry. I was on the phone with the hospital. What happened?" She ran through the foyer. Norma was always running and her mother was always telling her to stop. What stopped her now? My mother and sister in front of the blue delft mantel? Me on the couch wearing her mother like a vine? Inez beamed. The family had come to visit.

I wouldn't have recognized her if I'd seen her on the street, and maybe I had seen her on the street, but in this room there was no question. Norma was considerably taller than her mother, infinitely sturdier. She wore small gold-rimmed glasses that spoke of a fondness for John Lennon or Teddy Roosevelt, her thick brown hair pulled back in an artless ponytail. It had been thirty years since we left but I knew her. She had woken me from a sound sleep on so many nights, wanting to tell me her dreams. "Norma, this is our mother, Elna Conroy," I said, and then I looked at my mother. "Norma was our sister-in-law."

"I was your stepsister," Norma said. She was staring at the room, the entire tableau of us, but her eyes kept going back to Maeve. "My god," she said. "I am so sorry."

"Norma got my room," Maeve said to our mother.

Norma blinked. She was wearing dark slacks, a pink blouse. No embellishment or frill, nothing to make herself noticeable, an outfit that said she was not her mother's daughter. "I didn't mean the room."

"The room with the window seat?" our mother asked, suddenly able to picture that place her daughter had slept all those years ago.

Maeve looked up at the ceiling, at the crown molding called egg-and-dart. "Actually, she got the whole house. I mean, her mother got the house."

That was when I saw Norma, eight again, the weight of that bedroom still crushing her. "I'm so sorry," she said again.

Did she sleep there all these years later? Did she live in this house and sleep in Maeve's bed?

Maeve looked right at her. "I'm kidding," she whispered.

Norma shook her head. "I missed you so much after you left."

"After your mother threw us out?" Maeve couldn't help herself, even if she didn't mean to say it to Norma. She had waited for such a long time.

"Then," Norma said, "and all the way up until a few minutes ago."

"How's your mother doing?" Elna asked her, as if we didn't know. Maybe she wanted to change the subject. The current that ran between Norma and Maeve was something our mother couldn't have understood. She hadn't been there.

A Kleenex box sat on the coffee table. There would never have been Kleenex in the drawing room had Andrea been in her right mind. Norma came closer in order to take a tissue. "It's primary progressive aphasia or it's plain old Alzheimer's. I'm not sure, and it doesn't really matter since there's nothing you can do about it either way." Norma's mother was, at least for that minute, the last thing on Norma's mind.

"Do you take care of her?" Maeve asked. I really thought she might spit on the carpet.

Norma held out her hand to the woman with the braid. "Inez does most of it. I only moved back a few months ago."

Inez smiled. It wasn't her mother.

Elna came and kneeled before Andrea, slipping her shoes back on her feet, then she sat on the couch so that my father's tiny widow was sandwiched between the two of us. "How wonderful that your daughter's come home," she said to my stepmother.

And Andrea, still smacking, looked at my mother for the first time, then she pointed to the painting that hung on the wall across from the VanHoebeeks. "My daughter," she said.

We turned to look, all of us, and there was the portrait of

my sister, hanging exactly where it always had been. Maeve was ten years old, her shining black hair down past the shoulders of her red coat, the wallpaper from the observatory behind her, graceful imaginary swallows flying past pink roses, Maeve's blue eyes dark and bright. Anyone looking at that painting would have wondered what had become of her. She was a magnificent child, and the whole world was laid out in front of her, covered in stars.

Maeve cut a wide path around the sofa where we were sitting and walked across the room to stand in front of the girl she had been. "I was sure she would have thrown that away," she said.

"She loves the painting," Norma said.

Andrea gave a deep nod and pointed at the painting. "My daughter."

"No," Maeve said.

"My daughter," Andrea said again, and then she turned and looked at the VanHoebeeks. "My parents."

Maeve stood there as if she were trying to get used to the idea. We were spellbound as we watched her put a firm hand on either side of the frame to lift the painting off the wall. The frame was wide and lacquered black, no doubt to match her hair, but the painting itself was only the size of a ten-year-old child from the waist up. She struggled for moment to free the wire from the nail and Norma reached up behind the canvas to help her. The painting came away from the wall.

"It's heavy," Norma said, and put out her hands to help.

"I've got it," Maeve said. There was a slightly darker rectangle left behind on the wallpaper, outlining the place where it had been.

"I'm going to give this to May," Maeve said to me. "It looks like May."

Andrea smoothed my handkerchief out across her lap. Then she started folding it again, each of the four corners in towards the middle.

Maeve stopped and looked at Norma. With her hands full, she leaned over and kissed her. "I should have come back for you," she said. "You and Bright."

Then she left the house.

I would have expected Andrea to panic when I got up to follow my sister, or to mark the painting's departure with some level of violence, but she was consumed by the pleasures of my handkerchief. When I stood she was unbalanced for a moment, then tilted over to rest against my mother like a plant in need of staking. My mother put an arm around her, and why not? Maeve was already gone.

I gave Norma a small embrace at the door. I had never known that Maeve thought about the girls again, but it made sense. Our childhood was a fire. There had been four children in the house and only two of them had gotten out.

"I'm going to stay a minute," my mother said to me. It was funny to see the two Mrs. Conroys sitting there together—though funny wasn't the word—the little one dressed like a doll, the tall one still reminiscent of Death.

"Take all the time you need," I said, and I meant it, all the time in the world. I would wait with my sister in the car.

I walked out the glass front doors and into the late afternoon of the beautiful day. It did not feel strange to see the world from this vantage point, nor did it make any difference. Maeve was in the driver's seat with the painting in the back. The windows were down and she was smoking. When I got into the car she handed me the pack.

"I swear to you, I don't smoke anymore," she said.

"Neither do I." I took the matches.

"Did that really happen?"

I pointed to the large stain on my shirt, the smear of lipstick and mascara.

Maeve shook her head. "Andrea lost her mind. What kind of justice is that?"

"I feel like we just went to the moon."

"And Norma!" Maeve looked at me. "Oh my god, poor Norma."

"At least you got the painting of Andrea's daughter. I wouldn't have had the presence of mind for that."

"I was sure she would have burned it."

"She loved the house. She loved everything in the house."

"Except."

"Well, she got rid of us. Then it was perfect."

"Everything was perfect!" she said. "Could you believe it? I don't know what I was expecting, but I didn't think it was going to look better after we left. I always imagined the house would die without us. I don't know, I thought it would crumple up. Do houses ever die of grief?"

"Only the decent ones."

Maeve laughed. "Then it was an indecent house. Did I ever tell you the story about the painter?"

I knew some of it, not all of it. I wanted to know all of it. "Tell me."

"His name was Simon," she said. "He lived in Chicago but he was from Scotland. He was very famous, or I thought he was famous. I was ten."

"It's a very good painting."

Maeve looked in the back seat. "It is. It's beautiful. Don't you think it looks like May?"

"It looks like you, and May looks like you."

She took a drag on her cigarette and tipped back her head

and closed her eyes. I could tell the way we felt was exactly the same, like we had nearly drowned and then been fished from the water at the last possible minute. We had lived without expecting to live. "Dad was a big one for surprises in those days. He hired Simon to come from Chicago to paint Mommy's portrait. Simon was going to stay for two weeks. The painting was supposed to be huge, the size of Mrs. VanHoebeek. He was going to come back and paint Dad later. That was the plan. Then when it was all done there would be two Conroys hanging over the fireplace."

"Where were the VanHoebeeks going?"

Maeve opened one eye and smiled at me. "I love you," she said. "That's exactly what I asked. The VanHoebeeks were going up to the ballroom to go dancing."

"Who told you all this?"

"Simon. Needless to say, Simon and I had a lot of time to talk."

"You're telling me our mother didn't want to spend two weeks standing in a ball gown to have her portrait painted?" Our mother, the little sister of the poor, the assemblage of bones and tennis shoes.

"Would not. Could not. And once she refused, Dad said he wouldn't have his portrait painted either."

"Because then he'd have to be over the fireplace with Mrs. VanHoebeek."

"Exactly. Of course the problem was the painter was already there, and half of the money had been paid up front. You were too little and squirmy to sit for a portrait, so I was hauled in at the last minute. Simon had to build a new stretcher in the garage and cut the canvas down."

"How long did you sit?"

"Not long enough. I was in love with him. I don't think you

can have another person look right at you for two weeks and not fall in love with them. Dad was so furious about the money and the fact that he had once again failed to please, and Mommy was furious or mortified or whatever she was in those days. They weren't talking to each other and neither of them would talk to Simon. If he walked in a room they just walked out. But Simon didn't mind. It didn't matter to him who he was painting as long as he was painting. All he cared about was light. I'd never thought about light until that summer. Just sitting in the light all day was a revelation. We wouldn't eat dinner until it was dark, and even then it would just be the two of us. Jocelyn left our food in the kitchen. One day Simon said to me, 'Do you have anything that's red?' and I told him my winter coat was red. He said, 'Go get your coat,' or 'Go geet yur coot.' I went to the cedar closet and pulled it out and put it on and he looked at me and said, 'Daughter, you should wear only red.' He called me daughter. I would have gone back to Chicago with him in a heartbeat if he'd taken me."

"I would have missed you too much."

She turned around and looked at the painting again. "That look on my face? That's me looking at Simon." She took a last pull on her cigarette and then tossed it out the window. "After he left everything really went to hell, or probably it went to hell those two weeks I was sitting in the observatory but I was too happy to notice it then. Mommy couldn't have stayed. I really do believe that. She would have gone crazy if she had to live in a mansion and have her portrait painted."

"She seems comfortable enough in there now." I looked over at the house but there was no one looking back at us through the windows. I threw out my cigarette and coughed, then we each lit another.

"Now there are people in the house she can feel sorry for.

When she lived there the only person she could feel sorry for was herself." She pulled the smoke in and then emptied her lungs of smoke. "That was untenable."

Maeve was right, of course, although the insight provided no comfort. When at last our mother came out of the house and got into the back seat with the painting, she was changed. Even before she spoke, there was an air of purpose I hadn't seen in her before. I knew things would be different now. Our mother was going back to work.

"Sweet people," she said. "Inez has been a saint. She's the first person Norma's been able to keep for more than a month. Norma's been out in Palo Alto since medical school. She'd been managing things from California but then she said it all fell apart. She had to move home to take care of her mother."

"We figured that much out." We each took the last draw off our final cigarettes and pitched them into the grass like darts, then Maeve headed down the driveway to VanHoebeek Street. We did not look back.

"Norma wanted to put her into care at first but Andrea won't leave the house."

"I could have gotten her out of the house," Maeve said.

"She's not comfortable out of the house, and she doesn't like people in the house either. The cleaners and repairmen, everything upsets her. It's been very hard for Norma."

"She's a doctor?" I asked. Someone in the family should have been.

"She's a pediatric oncologist. She told me it was all because of you. Apparently her mother felt very competitive when you went to medical school."

Poor Norma. It had never occurred to me that someone else had been forced into the race. "What about her sister? What about Bright?"

"She's a yoga instructor. She lives in Banff."

"The pediatric oncologist leaves Stanford to take care of her mother and the yoga instructor stays in Canada?" Maeve asked.

"I think that's right," our mother said. "All I know is that the younger girl doesn't come home."

"Go, Bright," Maeve said.

"Norma needs help, Norma and Inez. Norma's just started practicing at Philadelphia Children's Hospital."

I said that I felt certain there was still a great deal of money. The house hadn't changed. Andrea didn't go anywhere.

"Andrea knows more about money than J. D. Rockefeller," Maeve said. "Believe me, she's still got it."

"I don't think money's the problem. They just need to find someone they can trust, someone Andrea feels comfortable with."

Maeve hit the brakes so abruptly I was sure she was saving our lives, that there was a collision coming up in my blind spot. She and I had our seatbelts on but our mother and the painting were thrown forward into the seats in front of them with blunt force.

"Listen to me," Maeve said, whipping around, the cords of her neck straining to hold her head in place. "You're not going back there. You were curious. We went with you. It's done."

Our mother gave herself a shake to see if she was hurt. She touched her nose. There was blood on her fingers. "They need me," she said.

"*I* need you!" Maeve said, her voice raised. "I've always needed you. You are not going back to that house."

My mother took a tissue from her pocket and held it under her nose, then settled the painting back in its place. She put on her seatbelt using one hand. The Toyota behind us laid on the horn. "Let's talk about this at home." She had made her decision but had yet to find a way to make it palatable to her children.

Maeve had meant to drive me to the train station the next day but the traffic was so light, and she was so furious, she wound up taking me all the way to New York. "All this *bull*shit about service and forgiveness and peace. I'm not going to have her going back and forth between my house and Andrea."

"Are you going to tell her to leave?" I tried to keep any trace of eagerness from my voice, reminding myself that this was Maeve's mother, Maeve's joy.

She was stricken at the thought. "She'd just move in over there. You know they'd love that. She keeps saying that Andrea's comfortable with her and that's why she needs to help, as if I give a fuck about Andrea's comfort."

"Let me talk to her," I said. "I'll tell her it's not good for your health."

"I've already told her that. And by the way, it's *not* good for my health. The thought that she would go back there for her and not—" She stopped herself before she said it.

Somehow with everything that had happened we'd forgotten the painting in the back of the car. "Take it to May," Maeve said when she pulled up in front of my house.

"No," I said. "It's yours. Give it to May when she's grown and has her own house. You need to keep it awhile. Put it over your mantel and think of Simon."

Maeve shook her head. "I don't want anything that was in that house. I'm telling you, it will only make me crazier than I already am."

I looked at the girl in the portrait. They should have let her always be that girl. "Then you have to promise me you'll take it back later."

"I will," she said.

"Let's find a parking place and you can come in and give it to May." We were double-parked.

Maeve shook her head. "There's no such thing as a parking space. Please."

"Oh, come on. Don't be ridiculous. You're right here."

She shook her head. She almost looked like she was going to cry. "I'm tired." And then she said *please* again.

So I let her go. I went around to the back and pulled out the painting and my duffel bag. It had started to rain and so I didn't stand on the street and watch her drive off. I didn't wave. I found my keys and hustled to get the painting inside.

We talked plenty after that, about our mother's daily reports of Andrea and Norma and the house, and how it was turning Maeve into a complete wreck. She talked about Otterson's. I told her about a building I wanted to buy that would require me to sell another building I didn't want to sell. I told her May was ecstatic about the painting. "We put it in the living room, over the fireplace."

"Me in your living room every day?"

"It's gorgeous."

"Celeste doesn't mind?"

"It looks too much like May for Celeste to mind. Everybody thinks it's May except May. When anybody asks her she says, 'It's a portrait of me and my aunt.'"

Two weeks after our trip to the Dutch House, my mother called me just before daylight to tell me that Maeve was dead.

"Is she there?" I asked. I didn't believe her. I wanted Maeve to come to the phone and say it herself.

Celeste sat up in bed, looked at me. "What is it?"

"She's here," my mother said. "I'm with her."

"Have you called an ambulance?"

"I will. I wanted to call you first."

"Don't waste time calling me! Call an ambulance." My voice was splintering.

"Oh, Danny," my mother said, and then she started to cry.

CHAPTER 19

I REMEMBER VERY LITTLE about the time just after Maeve died, except for Mr. Otterson, who sat with the family at her funeral Mass and covered his face with his hands as he cried. His grief was a river as deep and as wide as my own. I knew that I should have gone to him later, I should have tried to comfort him, but there was no comfort in me.

Chapter 20

THE STORY OF my sister was the only one I was ever meant to tell, but there are still a few things to say. Three years later, when Celeste and I were working through the details of our divorce in the lawyer's office, she told me she didn't want the house. "I never liked it," she said.

"Our house?"

She shook her head. "It's not my taste. It's heavy and old. It's too dark. You don't have to think about that because you aren't home all day."

I'd wanted to surprise her. I took her through every room, letting her think it was something I was planning to buy as a rental. I told her I could cut it into two units. I could even make it four, though that, of course, would be real work. Celeste, infinitely game, went up and down the stairs with May strapped to her chest, looking at the bathrooms, checking the water pressure. I didn't ask her if she liked it then. I could have but I didn't. I handed her the deed instead. In my mind it had been one of the few truly romantic gestures I'd ever made. "It's our house," I said.

Everything in me wanted to excuse myself from the proceedings and go out to the hall and call my sister. That never stopped happening.

The irony, of course, was that I had been a better husband after Maeve died. In my grief I had turned to my family. For the first time I was fully with them, a citizen of New York, my wife and my children the anchors that held me to the world. But the joke I'd always half-believed turned out to be true: everything Celeste hated about me she blamed on my sister, and when my sister wasn't there to take the blame, she was forced to consider who she was married to.

Our mother stayed on in the Dutch House to take care of Andrea, and for years I didn't forgive her. Despite whatever residual bits of science still clung to me, I had come to believe the story our father told when we were children: Maeve got sick because our mother left, and if our mother ever came back, Maeve would die. Even the stupidest ideas have resonance once they've happened. I blamed myself for what I saw as my lack of vigilance. I thought of my sister every hour. I let our mother go.

But then one day, after we had been divorced long enough to be friendly again, Celeste asked me to drive a carload of things to her parents' house, and I said yes. Even the Norcrosses had slowed down, the last of the unruly Labradors replaced by a small, friendly spaniel named Inky. After I unloaded the car and we had our visit, I drove over to the Dutch House for old times' sake, thinking I would park across the street for just a minute. But whatever barrier had kept us from turning in the driveway all those years was gone now, and I went to the house and rang the bell.

Sandy answered.

We stood there in the foyer in the afternoon light. Again, I had expected deterioration to have come at last, and again I found the house to be exactly as I remembered. It irritated me to have to see the tenderness with which it had been maintained.

"I didn't come for a long time," Sandy said guiltily, holding onto my hand, her thick white hair still pinned in place with barrettes. "But I missed your mother. I kept thinking of Maeve, what she would have wanted me to do. No one's getting any younger."

"I'm glad you're here," I said.

"I just come by for lunch sometimes. Sometimes there's something I can do to help out. The truth is it's nice for me. I fill up Norma's bird feeders in the back. Norma loves the birds. She got that from your dad."

I looked up at the high ceiling, into the chandelier. "Lots of ghosts."

Sandy smiled. "The ghosts are what I come for. I think about Jocelyn when I'm here, the way we were then. We were all so young, you know. We were still our best selves."

Jocelyn had died two years before. She had the flu, and by the time anyone realized how serious things were, it was over. Celeste came with me to the funeral. The Norcrosses came. For the record, Jocelyn never had forgiven my mother, though she was nicer about it than I was. "She left us there to raise you but you couldn't be ours," she said to me once. "How am I supposed to forgive a thing like that?"

Sandy and I went to the kitchen and I sat at the little table while she made coffee. I asked about Andrea.

"A toothless beast," she said. "She doesn't know a thing. Norma really could move her out of here now and sell the place, but there's always this feeling that Andrea's going to die any minute, and what would be the point of seeing her through all these years just to shuttle her out at the end?"

"Unless it isn't the end."

Sandy sighed and took a small carton of milk from the refrigerator. The refrigerator was new. "Who knows? I think of my husband. Jamie was thirty-six when he got an infection in his heart. No one knew why. And then Maeve, who was stronger than all the rest of us put together. Even with the diabetes, Maeve should have lived to be a hundred."

I had never known what Sandy's husband died of, nor did I know his name. I didn't know what had killed Maeve for that matter, though there were a wealth of options. I thought of Celeste's brother Teddy at Thanksgiving all those years ago, asking me if I had to perform autopsies. I had performed plenty of them, and I would never let anyone subject my sister to that. "She should have outlived Andrea at the very least."

"But that's the way it goes," Sandy said.

I found it a comfort to be in that kitchen with her. The stove and the window and Sandy and the clock. There on the table between us was the pressed-glass butter dish that had belonged to my mother's mother in Brooklyn, a half-stick of butter inside. "Look at that," I said, and ran my finger along the edge.

"You shouldn't be so hard on your mother," Sandy said.

Wasn't that what I was always saying to May? "I don't think I am." We had overlapped very little in our lives, my mother and I. I couldn't imagine it was much of a loss for either of us.

"She's a saint," Sandy said.

I smiled at her. No one was kinder than Sandy. "She's not a saint. Taking care of someone who doesn't know you doesn't make you a saint."

Sandy nodded, took a sip of coffee. "I think it's hard for people like us to understand. To tell you the truth, it's unbearable sometimes, at least it is for me. I just want her to be one of us. But when you think about saints, I don't imagine any of them made their families happy."

"Probably not." I couldn't remember the saints themselves, much less their families.

Sandy put her small hand on top of my hand, squeezed. "Go upstairs and say hello."

And so I went up to my parents' room, wondering why a man with a bad knee would have bought a house with so many stairs. There on the landing was the little couch and the two chairs where Norma and Bright liked to sit with their dolls so they could see who was coming and going. I looked at the doors to my room, to Maeve's room. It wasn't hard. I had the idea that all of the hard things had already happened.

Andrea was in a hospital bed by the window, my mother sitting beside her, spooning in bites of pudding. My mother still wore her hair short. It was white now. I wondered what Andrea would have thought had she known that this was her husband's first wife feeding her, and that the first wife had often had lice.

"There he is!" my mother said, smiling at me as if I'd come through the door right on time. She leaned over to Andrea. "What did I tell you?"

Andrea opened her mouth and waited for the spoon.

"I was in the neighborhood," I said. Wasn't that more or less how she'd returned all those years later? I could see now how much she looked like Maeve, or how Maeve would have looked like her had she lasted. That was the face she would have grown into.

My mother held out her hand to me. "Come over here where she can see you."

I went to the bed and stood beside her. My mother put her arm around my waist. "Say something."

"Hi, Andrea," I said. No anger could survive this, at least no anger I'd ever had. Andrea was as small as a child. Thin strands of white hair spread out on the pink pillowcase, her face was bare, her mouth a dark, open hole. She looked up at me, blinked a few times, then smiled. She raised the little claw of her hand and I took it. For the first time I noticed that she and my mother wore the same wedding ring, a gold band no wider than a wire.

"She sees you!" my mother said. "Look at that."

Andrea was smiling, if such a thing could be called a smile. She was glad to see my father again. I leaned over and kissed them both on the forehead, one and then the other. It cost me nothing.

After Andrea was full of pudding, she curled in her arms and legs and went to sleep. My mother and I sat in the chairs in front of the empty fireplace.

"Where do you sleep?" I asked, and she pointed to the bed behind me, the one she had slept in with my father, the one where Mrs. VanHoebeek had lain with her broken hip, waiting to die.

"She gets confused in the night sometimes. She tries to get up. It helps to be in here with her." She shook her head. "I have to tell you, Danny, I wake up in here, and I can feel it—the room and the house—even before I open my eyes. Every morning I'm twenty-eight, just for a second, and Maeve is in her room across the hall, and you're a baby in the bassinet beside me, and when I turn over I expect to see your father there. It's a beautiful thing."

"You don't mind the house?"

She shrugged. "I gave up caring where I lived a long time ago, and anyway, I think it's good for me. It teaches me humility. *She* teaches me humility." She tipped her head backwards the way Maeve would do. "You have to serve those who need to be served, not just the ones who make you feel good about yourself. Andrea's my penance for all the mistakes."

"She doesn't look like she's going to last out the week."

"I know. We've been saying that for years. She keeps surprising us."

"How's Norma?"

My mother smiled. "Norma's golden. She works so hard, all those sick children, then she comes home to take care of her mother. She never complains. I don't think her mother made things easy for her when she was growing up."

"She certainly isn't making things easy for her now."

"Well," my mother said, looking at me with great kindness. "You know the way mothers are."

I realized how little time I'd spent in this room. I rarely came in when it was just my father's, and never came in, even once, during the years he'd shared it with Andrea. It was larger than Maeve's bedroom, and the fireplace with its huge delft mantel was a masterpiece, but still, Andrea was right—the room with the window seat was nicer. The way it faced the back gardens, the kinder light. "Here's a question," I said, because when had I ever asked her anything? When had we been alone together other than those few awkward encounters in hospital waiting rooms all those years ago?

"Anything," she said.

"Why didn't you take us with you?"

"To India?"

"To India, sure, or anywhere. If you thought this house was such a terrible place for you, did you wonder if it might have been a terrible place for us?"

She sat with it for awhile. Maybe she was trying to remember how she'd felt. It had all happened such a long time ago. "I thought it was a wonderful place for you," she said finally. "There are so many children in the world who have nothing at all, and you and your sister had everything—your father and Fluffy and Sandy and Jocelyn. You had this house. I loved you so much, but I knew you were going to be fine."

Maybe Sandy was right, and she was a saint, and saints were

universally despised by their families. I couldn't have said which life would have been better, the one we had with Andrea or the one in which we trailed after our mother through the streets of Bombay. Chances were it would have been six of one, half-dozen of the other.

"And anyway," she said as an afterthought, "your father never would have let you go."

Things changed again after that, change being the one constant. I found myself going back to Elkins Park. There was no one to tell me not to. The rage I had carried for my mother exhaled and died. There was no place for it anymore. What I was left with was never love but it was something—familiarity, maybe. We took a certain amount of comfort in each other. Sometimes May would come with me on those visits, even though she was so busy then. May was at NYU. She had her whole life mapped out. Kevin was at Dartmouth and so we saw less of him. He was a year behind her and twenty years behind her, as we all were. By going to Elkins Park, May could see all of her grandparents, and she was obsessed with the house. She went over the entire place like a forensic detective. She might as well have used a metal detector and a stethoscope. She started in the basement and worked up. I could never believe the things she found: Christmas ornaments and report cards and a shoe-box full of lipstick. She found the tiny door in the back of the third-floor closet that led into the eave space. I had forgotten about that. The boxes of Maeve's books were still there, half of them in French, her notebooks full of math equations, dolls I had never seen, the letters I had written to her when she was in college. May did an impromptu reading of one of them over dinner.

"Dear Maeve, Last night Andrea announced she didn't like the apple cake. The apple cake is everybody's favorite but now

Jocelyn isn't supposed to make it anymore. Jocelyn said it doesn't matter, and that she'd make me one at her house and smuggle it in in pieces." Somehow May knew exactly what I had sounded like at eleven. "Last Saturday we made thirty-seven stops for rent and collected $28.50 in quarters from the washing machines in the basements."

"Are you making this up?" I asked.

She waved the letter. "Swear to God, you really were that boring. It goes on for another page."

Norma laughed. The four of us were in the kitchen: me and Norma and May and my mother squeezed around the blue table. Suddenly I remembered my father always put the quarters he'd collected from the washers and dryers in a secret drawer in the dining room table, and whenever anyone needed a little money, we would go and help ourselves to a handful. "Come here a minute," I said, and the four of us went to the dreaded dining-room. I ran my hand beneath the table's lip until I found it. The drawer had warped and when I finally pried it open it was full of quarters. A treasure chest.

"I never knew about this!" Norma said. "Bright and I would have cleaned it out."

"He didn't do that when I lived here," my mother said.

May dragged the tips of her fingers through the coins. Maybe he hadn't left them there for everyone to take. Maybe they had just been for Maeve and me.

In the morning, I looked out the window and saw my daughter floating in the pool on a yellow raft, her black hair trailing behind her like strands of kelp, one long leg reaching out from time to time to push off from the wall. I went outside and asked her how she'd slept.

"I'm still sleeping," she said, and draped a wet arm across her eyes. "I love it here. I'm going to buy the house."

Andrea had finally died a few months before, and the conversations about what should be done with the Dutch House
were ongoing. Bright, who hadn't come home for the funeral,
told Norma that the house could burn to the ground for all she
cared. There was plenty of money. The way the neighborhood
was zoned, the land was sure to be redeveloped when they sold.
The house would most likely be torn down and sold for parts:
mantels, banisters, carved panels, the wreaths of golden leaves
on the dining-room ceiling were each worth a Picasso. To take
it all apart and then sell the land, or develop the land ourselves,
would double and maybe even triple what the place could be
had for.

"But then we'd have to kill the house," Norma had said, and
none of us knew if that was a good thing or a bad thing except May.

"It's not exactly a starter home," I told my daughter.

May reached up and pushed herself off from the diving board.
"I asked Norma to wait for me, just a couple of years. I have a
spiritual connection to the place." May had an agent now. She'd
done some commercials. She'd had small parts in two films,
one of which had gotten attention. May, as she would be the
first to tell you, was going places. "She said she'd hold onto it
for a while."

Neither Norma nor Bright had children. Norma said that
childhood wasn't something she could imagine inflicting on another person, especially not a person she loved. I imagined pediatric oncology only reinforced her position. "I'd just as soon
it went to May or Kevin," she said to me. "It's your house."

"Not my house," I said.

We found time to talk about all of it, Norma and I: childhood, our parents, the inheritance, medical school, the trust.
Norma had decided to return to Palo Alto. She got her job back

and gave notice to the people who had rented her house for years. She said she was starting to realize how much she missed her life. One night, after a couple glasses of wine, she suggested that maybe she could be my sister. "Not Maeve," she said, "never Maeve, but some other, lesser sister, like a half sister from a second marriage."

"I thought you were my half sister from a second marriage."

She shook her head. "I'm your stepsister."

My mother stayed on at the Dutch House. She said she was the caretaker of sorts, making sure no raccoons were setting up camp in the ballroom. She got Sandy to move over to stay with her. Sandy, who had bursitis in her hip, bemoaned all the stairs. My mother had started to travel again after Andrea died. She was never gone for very long but she said there was still plenty for her to do. That was around the time she started telling me stories about when she lived in India, or I started to listen. She said all she had wanted was to serve the poor, but the nuns who ran the orphanage were always dressing her up in clean saris and sending her off to parties to beg. "It was 1951. The British were gone, and Americans were considered very exotic then. I went to every party I was invited to. It turned out my special talent was asking rich people for money." And so she continued, relieving the rich of their burdens on behalf of the poor. She did that work for the rest of her life.

Fluffy had moved to Santa Barbara to live with her daughter but she came back for visits, and whenever she did, she wanted to sleep in her old room over the garage.

Norma had promised to hold onto the Dutch House until May fulfilled her destiny, which May did on her fourth film. She met the tidal wave of her success with a startling level of self-assurance. May had always told us this was the way it would happen, but we found ourselves stunned all the same.

She was still so young. There was nothing to do but brace ourselves.

On the advice of her agent, May had a high black metal fence
installed behind the linden trees, and there was now a gate at
the end of the driveway and a box you had to talk into if you
didn't know the code or the guard. I couldn't help but think
how much Andrea would have loved it.

May brought Maeve's painting back from New York and
returned it to the empty spot where it had hung before. She
didn't have much time to spend in Elkins Park, but when she
was there, she threw parties that were the stuff of legend, or
that's what she told me.

"Come on Friday," she said. "You and Mom and Kevin. I
want you to see this."

May had the tendency to seem like she was overselling, but
the truth was she always delivered. I was only sorry that Fluffy
and Norma weren't there. It was a June night and all the windows around the house were open again. The young people
who arrived in black sedans with tinted windows—people who
May assured me were achingly famous—climbed up the two
flights of stairs to dance in the ballroom and look out the windows at the stars. Celeste had come in early to help May's as-
sistants get everything ready. No one believed this blonde of
average height was May's mother.

"Tell them!" she said to me, and again and again I did. May's
genetics seemed to have ignored her mother's physical contribution completely, but she had Celeste's tenacity.

Kevin stationed himself at the door so as not to miss a thing.
I had hoped he would take over my business someday but he
started medical school instead. A lifetime spent listening to how
much better it was to be a doctor was not without influence.

Sandy and my mother stayed at the party for a while, but not

336 : ANN PATCHETT

very long. I drove them over to Maeve's old house in Jenkintown, where it was quiet. By the time I came back there were
too many cars in the driveway, so I parked on the street and let
myself in through the gate. The house was lit up like I had never
seen it before, every window on every floor spilled gold light,
the terrace was ringed with candles in glass cups, and the
music—I had told May to keep the music down—was a girl
with a dark, quiet voice singing over a little band. The sound
that she made was so clear and low and sad I imagined all of the
neighbors leaning forward to listen. I couldn't make out any of
the words, only the melody juxtaposed against the sound of
people screaming as they leapt into the pool. I was going to go
in and find Celeste, see if she wanted to drive back into the city
with me. We were too old for this, even if we weren't that old.
New York was the only chance we had of sleeping.

In the far corner of the yard where the linden trees met the
hedge, I saw someone sitting in an Adirondack chair, smoking.
The chair was well beyond the reach of the light from the house,
and all I could really be sure of in the shadows and darker
shadows was a person and a chair and the intermittent glow of
a tiny orange fire. I told myself it was my sister. Maeve had no
use for parties. She would have come outside. I stood there quietly, as if it were possible to scare her away. I gave myself this
small indulgence sometimes, the belief that, if only I paid attention, I would see her sitting in the darkness outside the Dutch
House. I wondered what she would have said if she could have
seen all this.

Fools, she would have said, blowing out a little puff of smoke.

The person in the chair then shook her head and stretched
her long legs out in front of her, pointing her bare toes. Still,
miraculously, the illusion held, and I looked up into the blanket
of stars to keep myself from seeing too clearly. Maeve threw

her cigarette in the grass and stood to meet me. For one more second it was her.

"Daddy?" May called.

"Tell me you're not smoking."

She came towards me from the darkness, wearing what looked to be a white slip covered in pearls. My daughter, my beautiful girl. She slipped her arm around my waist and for a minute dropped her head against my shoulder, her black hair falling across her face. "I'm not smoking," she said. "I just quit."

"Good girl," I said. We would talk about it in the morning.

We stood there in the grass, watching the young people fluttering in and out of the windows—moths to the light. "My god, I love this so much," May said.

"It's your house."

She smiled. Even in the darkness you could have seen it. "Good," she said. "Take me inside."

ANN PATCHETT is the author of eight novels, *The Patron Saint of Liars*, *Taft*, *The Magician's Assistant*, *Bel Canto*, *Run*, *State of Wonder*, *Commonwealth*, and *The Dutch House*. She was the editor of *Best American Short Stories, 2006*, and has written three books of nonfiction, *Truth & Beauty*, about her friendship with the writer, Lucy Grealy; *What now?*, an expansion of her graduation address at Sarah Lawrence College; and most recently, *This is the Story of a Happy Marriage*, a collection of essays.

In November 2011, she opened Parnassus Books in Nashville, Tennessee, with her partner Karen Hayes. She has since gone on to be a spokesperson for independent booksellers, talking about books and bookstores on *The Colbert Report*, NPR, *The Martha Stewart Show*, and CBS's *The Early Show*. Along with James Patterson, she was the honorary chair of World Book Night. In 2012 she was named by *Time* magazine as one of the 100 Most Influential People in the World.

Patchett lives in Nashville, Tennessee, with her husband, Karl VanDevender, and their dog, Sparky.

ANNPATCHETT.COM

ALSO BY ANN PATCHETT

TRUTH & BEAUTY
A Friendship

"Patchett's most resonant and impassioned love story yet. . . . A radically honest treatise on friendship."
—*Pittsburgh Post-Gazette*

A tender, intimate book about friendship and loyalty and being uplifted by the sheer effervescence of someone who knew how to live life to the fullest.

BEL CANTO
A Novel

"Blissfully romantic. . . . A terrific, spellcasting story."
—*San Francisco Chronicle*

A captivating story of strength and frailty, love and imprisonment, and an inspiring tale of transcendent romance.

RUN
A Novel

"Engaging, surprising, provocative and moving...a thoroughly intelligent book, an intimate domestic drama that nonetheless deals with big issues touching us all: religion, race, class, politics and, above all else, family."
—*Washington Post*

An engrossing story of one family on one fateful night in Boston where secrets are unlocked and new bonds are formed.

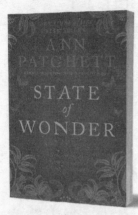

STATE OF WONDER
A Novel

"Expect miracles when you read Ann Patchett's fiction." —*New York Times Book Review*

A gripping adventure story and a profound look at the difficult choices we make in the name of discovery and love.

THIS IS THE STORY OF A HAPPY MARRIAGE

"A joyful celebration of life, love and the written word."
—*Kirkus Reviews*

Blending literature and memoir, Patchett examines her deepest commitments—to writing, family, friends, dogs, books, and her husband—creating a resonant portrait of a life.

COMMONWEALTH
A Novel

"Exquisite. . .impossible to put down."
—*New York Times*

Told with equal measures of humor and heartbreak, *Commonwealth* is a meditation on inspiration, interpretation, and the ownership of stories. It is a brilliant and tender tale of the far-reaching ties of love and responsibility that bind us together.